MICKY O'BRADY

Playing with #FIRE

Playing With #Fire
Copyright © 2020 Micky O'Brady
Cover Design: www.KimG-Design.com
Interior Format: Dorothy Dreyer

Published by Snowy Wings Publishing
PO Box 1035, Turner, OR 97392

ISBN eBook: 978-1-952667-13-8
ISBN Paperback: 978-1-952667-14-5

Table of Contents

CHAPTER ONE

#NotDeadYet

Life is a show. A *#PopularityContest.* A performance for an audience who can turn out to be the biggest supporters or the fiercest critics. Some people are lucky and get applause every turn along the way; others, not so much. They have to work hard for every tiny morsel of approval, for every slow clap, for every *like* clicked. And when they finally do get the acknowledgement they've been longing for, that doesn't mean it's guaranteed to stay.

It never is.

In fact, it can turn on you any second.

Trust me. I know.

#

Principal Gunn folds his hands in front of his considerable stomach and gives me one of his strict looks over the rim of his half-moon glasses. "Everly, just to clarify. There will be absolutely no posting or updating of your account while you're at school. Also, you will not hashtag or mention our school or any of the students even when off-campus. Is that clear?" He enunciates each word to perfection, as if he feared I had lost too many brain cells since he saw me last, before all of this happened. Before my fame—and my fall.

"Yes, sir. Crystal clear." I stare at the diploma hanging behind him—*Voted George McMillan High's Most Motivating Teacher 2002*. Huh. Wonder what happened since—because the Principal Gunn I know doesn't quite meet that definition.

He nods. "Good. The last thing I need is any of your two thousand followers finding out where you go to school and give us trouble." He huffs.

Ouch. *Two thousand* followers? Right. Try maybe *two hundred* thousand—or actually, make it *two hundred and fifty* thousand. Turns out a live streamed suicide attempt attracts followers. Who knew?

"Won't happen, sir." I'm as *#offline* as one can be. No phone. No internet at home. No Wi-Fi card in my laptop, just to be on the safe side. Nobody trusts a recovering addict, least of all my mom. Or Dad, for that matter. Not that I could fault them after Mom found me in a puddle of my own blood, but oh well.

The principal's expression softens. "Look, Everly, I know you've been through a lot in the last few months. It can't be easy to return to school, but I need you to understand that these kids out there"—he points to somewhere behind me—"are good kids. They've been your friends since you all started kindergarten, and you have their full support. They know what you've been through. They feel for you."

Heat rushes to my face. Of course they know what happened to me. For heaven's sake, I live streamed it. I'd be surprised if school gossip wasn't cranking it up and embellishing the story. Principal Gunn is right—they know. The part where he said they felt for me, though? Doubt it.

I'm the ugly duckling out of their midst who made it, at least for a while. The redhead who never quite was skinny enough to be considered pretty. Who was nobody, until she made it to internet fame with posts and campaigns, and then was known across the state and featured in a *Los Angeles Times* article as one of the up and coming Californian Influencers of the year. I'm also the one who didn't exist to them before said fame. Before she lost weight. Before she changed her style.

Funny how that goes. I was invisible forever, had my moment in the spotlight… and now? Maybe I don't want to know.

#

JamesDaMan
Saw @MatrixGirl come out of a nose job clinic. All #fake! #MatrixGirl #fakebeauty #fattygolucky

#

Gunn picks up a printout from an untidy pile of papers on his desk. "And to give you some reassurance, I've looked at some of the comments under those posts. I don't think any of them are from our students." He turns the paper around, showing one of the last posts from before… from before I broke.

\#

Moonsaulting_Spaceman
#MatrixGirl is a slut. Fucking around and spreading #herpes. Sign if you'd rather die than touch her!
#GoDieMatrixGirl @MatrixGirlSlut #STD

I'd recognize the golden-and-black monogram avatar anywhere: Moonsaulting_Spaceman. *That* post. My stomach cramps and bile rises up my throat.

That post... it hurt. A lot. Still does. Sweat breaks out, running down my neck in cold trails. *#PTSD*. Reading this brings the anticipated dread my therapist warned me about. Dad on the other hand said *none of this stuff* should bother me anymore, but look at that: it does. Clearly. I suck in one wheezy harsh breath that doesn't bring any oxygen to my brain.

\#

HunkMan:
What a bitch! IMO we'd all be better off without her! What a disgrace.
#MatrixGirlSucks #BeverlyBacon

\#

Josie_Posie:
I used to like her, but it's obvs she's not real, just a #poser and #faker. Want my money I supported her with back!
#MoneyBackBitch

#

_JD382:_
Wouldn't go near her with a ten-foot pole. Disgusting.
#GoKillYourselfMatrixGirl #BeverlyBacon #ByeFelicia

Principal Gunn glides a finger over the comments I know by heart, no matter how many there are. I know them all, each harsh word, each spiteful sentiment.

"JosiePosie, HunkMan... Who comes up with these names?" He shakes his head, sighs, and drops the paper back onto the pile. "But anyway, I'm very confident none of these were written by our students."

My jaw drops. "Really. And why would you think that?" Because while I can't prove it, I'm sure some of these comments came from here. They must. _#BeverlyBacon_ is a dead giveaway. Plus, many of my followers came from here in the beginning. Surprising, I know. Maybe just to keep tabs on me, maybe to hop on the bandwagon of success, who knows? But since my first campaign on Teen Voice was about this very school, it made sense, and it's probably fair to say I picked up some more of my fellow students along the way. Meaning, I'd be more than surprised if nobody from George McMillan High School posted anything negative about me, given our lovely history. And even if I'm wrong and that _BeverlyBacon_ hashtag popped up out of nowhere, I didn't see them defend me, either.

Gunn looks at me like I'm stupid. "Because this is not what our students do, Everly. It doesn't sound like them."

And that's that.

Life must be so easy when you're over forty. Or fifty, or... No clue how old he is.

"Anyway," he says, more than ready to put this all behind him. That makes two of us. "Do we have an agreement? Your mother said—"

"I know what my mother said. Sir," I tag on, then drop my gaze. I'm sure she had a long talk with Gunn when I insisted I was fit for school. When I refused to go to boarding school. When she let Dad set those *limits* for me for this school year.

The principal frowns. "Well, good. But as I discussed with your mother, no posting on TV."

"It's *Tee*Vee," I mumble.

"Excuse me?"

"*Tee*Vee, emphasis on the *T* for *Teen* Voice." Proves how out-of-date Gunn is. He's probably still on—correction: he's probably *not even* on Facebook. Awks.

He blinks twice. "Yes. Sure. *Tee*Vee. What's the difference?"

"The difference is that it's not just a social media platform. Sir. It's a political platform for young citizens to be heard and to make a difference in today's world." Quoted that one like on TeeVee's homepage.

Gunn stifles a yawn. "Yes. Of course. I see. Big difference. Anyway, circling back to no posting on whichever platform: do we have an agreement?"

#LostCause "Yes, sir."

"Wonderful. Then please, off you go. Class starts in five minutes and you have missed two months of the new school year already." He makes an impatient waving hand gesture as if I had voluntarily stayed home and dragged my feet for the last few months and not been under *close psychological observation*, as my mom would put it, because it sounds better than *suicide watch*.

"Thank you, sir." Let's face it. I'd still rather be here than what the alternative would be: inpatient psych—oh, sorry, we call it *boarding school*, I forgot. Thanks, Dad. Such a great suggestion coming from somebody who knows me so well—not.

"Anytime, Everly. Let me know if you need help with anything, okay?" He smiles, and to be honest, I think it's a sincere smile. He wants to help. Problem is, the *Most Motivating Teacher 2002* missed the train a while ago. But I shouldn't talk because right now that same train is passing me by without slowing down.

A massive lump forms in my throat.

First day back in school after a mobbing campaign and suicide attempt.

Piece of cake, really.

I take a deep breath and open the door to the hallway.

Well then, the show must go on.

#

To my complete and utter relief, Hazel waits around the corner from the principal's office. *#BFF* Her face lights up when she sees me, but I bet not as much as mine. She's the only person I really missed when I was in the hospital. And when I was on suicide watch. Not texting her, not video calling her... it's been *#DangHard*.

"Ever!" Her hug is so tight, she squishes all the air out of my lungs. "In one piece and alive, the way we like it!"

"Haze." A smile spreads over my face, the first today, that's for sure. I've truly missed this. The ease with her, my oldest friend.

She pulls away from me and tightens her dark-brown ponytail, so that the undercut on the left side of her head pops out better.

"How was Gunn?"

I shrug. "Meh, the usual. I'm not allowed to post, which is a no-brainer, but it seems to be the only thing that worries him. I don't know if he gets what happened." I drop my gaze to the floor. And it doesn't matter whether he gets it or not. *#DoneAndOver.*

Hazel sighs. "Probably not. But hey, you're back! Plus, we're in pretty much all classes together, and with your smarts, I doubt you're going to have any trouble catching up." She hooks her arm under mine, then hesitates. "Ready?"

Ready? I swallow hard. "How bad is it?"

"The rumors?"

I nod.

"Nothing out of the ordinary, but I think at this point, everybody has seen your stream. Sorry," she adds with a frown that makes the same dimple pop like when she laughs.

Forcing a smile, I swipe a strand of hair behind my ear. "Yeah, I figured so." I didn't really believe that I'd be spared the gossip. The only advantage I have is that I'm coming in way after school has started. At this point I'm hopefully old news. Or maybe, just maybe, the school might've stopped gossiping by now after what I did. You know, kind of out of respect?

"Although," Hazel adds, "some of them still think you did it as a publicity stunt."

"What?" My mouth pops open. "A publicity stunt?" WTF? So much for respect. Or compassion.

"Yeah, right? The two most common rumors are you didn't really try to kill yourself and it was all for show, and the other, quite contrary rumor is, that you really did it and only did it because you were hustling for more likes. So basically, no matter which scenario, it was all about likes."

Oh, sheesh. I close my eyes and force out a slow, deliberate breath. "Well, those likes wouldn't do me any good if I were dead. Would they now?"

"Nope. *Here rests Everly Aldaire. Two hundred and fifty thousand followers and counting.*" She sticks out her tongue at me and pokes her elbow into my side until I chuckle.

"Okay. Well, I guess I can handle idiot stuff like that better than…" I give her a nervous smile. She knows. Better than the name calling, the harassment, the judgment. Better than the pressure to perform and punishment when I didn't. Idiocy alone I can handle.

But wait, why exactly did I want to return to my old school?

Ah, because Dad's alternative was and still is a boarding school for troubled teens, that's why. Starting new… has a tempting ring to it, but without Hazel… Nope. Mom would like to see me in therapy more, but she isn't a hundred percent sold on the boarding school. Dad, since he is living the life on another continent, feels he has to tighten the reins. Hence, he favors said boarding school.

Hazel drops her voice and tightens her arm around mine. "I know the idiots are no problem for you. We're going to walk out there and go to class as if the last twelve months of TeeVee-fame and minor nervous breakdowns along the way didn't happen. Keep your head up high, Ever. They have nothing on you. But don't forget—you've got to let me in, or else I won't know when to help you."

I swallow against the ball of nerves stuck in my throat. "Let you in?"

"Talk to me. Not like over the summer and before. I like to hear stuff from you, not off TeeVee." A shadow crosses her face, gone as fast as it came. I know what she's referring to. I got sucked in deeper and deeper the last few months before *that* day, and Hazel noticed. She tried to talk to me, but… I've never been good with talking about feelings.

Ergo, she found out about my suicide attempt via pop-up alert.

Anyway.

Haze pats my arm with her free hand and maneuvers me down the admin corridor and away from the principal's office into the school's hallway maze filled with what looks like all seven hundred and thirty-five students enrolled in our small school that fits our equally small town like a glove.

Meaning, for us it's busy. Can be good, can be bad. Right now it's on the good side: The air is filled with chatter, noises, lockers being opened and slammed shut, and it feels like I'd never left.

That is, until we pass the first group of students. Freshmen. I think.

I'm not sure what I expected. Maybe the sea of students parting for us like it did for Moses. Maybe loud whispers and comments. Maybe. None of that happens, though.

But I do feel the stares.

See the heads turn.

Pick up on the slight drop in noise when I get closer.

And it makes me want to run in the opposite direction.

Hazel holds me like a bench vise. Proof that she knows me well, or that she has enough common sense to anticipate my response. "So, we have health first, followed by English, followed by chem. You should know all the teachers, and yay, we have Mr. Langen in health again this year." She pumps her fist, adding a *whoop whoop* sound, and I don't think I've loved Hazel enough until now. I mean, I love her. Best friends forever, but her chatting away is cutting down on the awkwardness for us walking the walk. It makes it bearable. More normal.

I chose well with my best friend, or actually, I should say she chose well by choosing me, not because I am so awesome—because I'm not, as already established—but because she is. Hazel and I go back to kindergarten, when our parents started us in the same judo dojo and we were the only girls at that time. After a few classes, they put me up for a practice fight with a bigger boy, and guess who yelled her lungs out supporting me? Hazel. And guess who did the same thing for her when it was her turn? Me. So yeah, *#InstantBesties*, and it's stayed like that ever since.

Still, the longer we walk and the closer we get to class, the more my hands get clammy. They all see me—the new me and every pound I've gained since it happened, no matter the oversized sweater.

"Haze?" I whisper under my breath. "I don't think I can do this. It's too soon—"

"Hell, yes you can do this." She pushes the words out through the corner of her mouth. "You ain't gonna give them more to talk about by running away. You're strong. You've got this."

Strong. Good one. All I want to do is hide, or in lieu of good hiding spots, take a razor and run it over my skin until it pops and bleeds. If I can't have that, I'd be okay pushing a finger down my throat until the few bites I took for breakfast reappeared. Old habits die hard, and either or would make me feel better—problem is, either or would also get me back in psych and then to boarding school, according to my dad.

If it didn't bring my anxiety to a whole new level, it'd be almost funny how they watch me. What do they expect me to do?

Whip out a knife and try to slice my radial arteries *again*? Lose it right in front of them until the men with the straightjackets come for me? Well, sorry, guys. I might be tempted to fall back into old patterns, but I worked too hard to give you the satisfaction of any of that.

I'll suffer silently on the inside, thank you very much.

And the good thing? Our school isn't that big. We reach Mr. Langen's classroom within two minutes, meaning I get to slide out of the public eye and into the more intimate setting of a classroom. *#NotMuchBetter*.

"Sit with me. I've been keeping the seat next to me free since the beginning of the school year." Hazel points to the second-to-last row.

I cock my head. "You did? But—"

She rolls her eyes and gives me a slight shove in the shoulder. "Yeah, doofus. I knew you were coming back when you were feeling better. And I'm not risking spending the whole year next to idiots like Soph or Nevaeh." She makes an exaggerated scrunched-up face, and that small gesture, dang it, it means a lot. Having somebody want me around, wait for me, and be nice… shouldn't be life-changing, but it surely is a teaching moment about how wrong my priorities were for the last year.

I suck in my lower lip. "Thanks, Haze."

"Anytime. Purely egoistic. I like having you in class." She winks and slides behind her desk, and so do I.

Feels so unreal. Me, sitting here. Without my phone. It was a different animal when I was in psych versus here. Here my fingers itch. I could have posted five times already, could have updated my followers, could have curated my feed—

But no.

Instead, I pull down my long sleeves and ball them up in my fist, then fold my hands in my lap like an old lady. Phones are not important. Posting is not important. Those faceless names are not important. What they think is not important.

If I keep repeating it long enough, I might actually start to believe it.

As the classroom fills, I keep a shy eye on everybody coming in. They all react differently. Some don't see me. Fine. Some smile and wave. Fine. Some see me and don't react. Also fine. Some see me, though, and it's like a little shock to their system. Like, eyes widening, averting their gaze, pretending they didn't notice me. And that makes me wonder about each person: Do you follow me? Did you see my stream when it happened? Did you write any of those comments that brought me to *that* moment?

On TeeVee, anybody can create a fake email address and set up a new account. Many people have several—heck, I have, well, *had,* two. One for family and private, and one for my quote-unquote business. Multiple accounts aren't a rarity; in fact, they are a cloak of invisibility for people, especially bullies. New identity, new comments, new victim: they get blocked, they just open up a new account.

If they get blocked.

Point in case, I never got Moonsaulting_Spaceman off TeeVee, or even off my list of followers.

Sabina takes out her phone and points it in my direction. *Shit.* Like my heart was jump-started, it doubles its speed, pumping adrenaline through my veins. Is she taking a picture? Posting? Which hashtags? How many likes will they get for my first day back? Dislikes? Can I—

She points out something on the screen to her desk neighbor, the phone lowered to chest level, neither of them looking at me.

Geez.

I blow out a slow puff of air. Not a picture of me. In fact, probably something completely unrelated to me, given the fact that they're both looking at the phone with a borderline worried expression.

Not about me.

My heart's still hammering away in my chest. I feel like I just ran a marathon, all shaky and stuff. Exhausted, from three seconds. Guess the doc was right. I didn't do my body any favors over the last year. Wonderful.

I sink lower into my seat, arms wrapped around my body. I'm always so cold these days. Still not used to that. That's a problem I didn't have before I lost all that weight.

One of my fellow students pops into the classroom, more a quick leaning-in than anything else, and whistles through his teeth. "Hey, freak! Catch!" He cocks his arm back and—

Out of reflex, my hands shoot up—only to drop right back down when I realize that wad of wet tissue paper wasn't aimed at me, but somebody behind me.

I hear it land with a wet smacking sound drowned out by laughter, and my heart skips a painful beat of relief: Wasn't aimed at me. I wasn't the freak. It wasn't—

"Use it in case you melt some more, will ya?" The idiot up front—blond, wide-shouldered football quarterback Arlo—palms his face and pulls his cheek down, like giving a one-handed parody of Edvard Munch's *The Scream*, and the class is eating it up, giggling half under their breath, half out loud.

What—

I turn to look over my right shoulder at the person who

became a victim instead of me. First, all I see is a grey baseball cap covering dark brown or black hair. I don't recognize that guy. Maybe he's new? Would explain the cap in school. Big no-no. The guy wipes the left side of his face with his sleeve. The lump of wet tissue lies on the desk in front of him, some water pooling and dripping down to the floor. He's wide-shouldered and muscular, his side profile showing a straight nose, wide chin, and high cheekbones. Not the type to usually be picked upon, which is weir—

He turns to the left and I suck in a sharp breath.

"Holy—" My entire body tenses. The right side of his face is... is... I don't know, *melted*, like Arlo said; it fits it quite well. Thick scars crisscross over his cheek from below his jaw line up to around his eye and into the hair on the right. In some places his skin is darker red, then pinker in others, and because of the scars, his right eye is droopy-looking.

His gaze shifts to me and I swear, the moment our eyes meet, it's like a fist to my stomach. I recognize that look—that vulnerable, hurt quality, that silent suffering. I recognize it because I see it every day when I look in the mirror, and it tugs on a heart string. Something flares up in his eyes, maybe a hint of panic, of fear, but it's gone too fast before he drops his gaze to the lump of wet paper on his desk.

And it makes me feel like shit.

Of all people, I should know what judgment, ridicule, and most importantly, mobbing feel like.

I work on a dry swallow, then turn to Hazel. "Who's that?" I nod my chin in the direction of the boy behind me.

"That?" She sighs. "Calan Adler. They call him freak. Nobody. Or nightmare."

Nightmare. "Why would they say that?"

She sighs and rolls her eyes as a means of reply.

Nightmare. "What's wrong with him?"

"Besides what's obvious? I don't know. He doesn't talk. Came here at the beginning of the school year and the vultures descended upon him. Doesn't help that he's not talking to anybody."

A lump works its way down my throat as I steal another glance at the boy behind me, his head lowered, the wet paper towel pushed to the edge of the table. No, the school didn't stop gossiping after what I did, after what happened to me. No, not at all.

They just found a *#New Target.*

CHAPTER TWO

#YouKiddingMe

Thirty minutes later, I'm soaked in cold sweat and ready to leave for home. Problem is, it's not even 9 A.M. Six more hours to go.

Crap.

For the last half hour, I've been giving it my best to ignore everything and concentrate on class. My favorite subject, my favorite teacher—but nothing is as it used to be. At the end of last school year, I sat here and made a couple of hundred bucks, sometimes even a thousand or more, per post on TeeVee, depending on whether it was a campaign or an incentivized share. Even the likes brought in some money. I was on top of my game, the center of attention. Today... not so much. Well, yes, still the center of attention, only differently so. *#Newsflash*: it doesn't feel as good.

And seriously, how stupid do my classmates think I am?

Hello? I'm right here! There is no magic wall of screens and wireless connections between us! I see your stares; I hear your whispers. I see you freakin' texting—or posting. Geez, I hope they're not posting. That thought alone gives me an anxiety boost of unknown proportions, complete with raspy breathing and even more cold sweat.

Deep breath.

I don't care if they post, no matter what it is.

Deep breath.

It's not important.

Deep breath.

It's not real life.

Deep—

But dang it, it *is*. It is my life, or at least it was.

I close my eyes and breathe some more for good measure, in through my nose, out through my mouth. And again. And again. And—

The bell rings. Like an invisible forcefield was lifted my classmates jump out of their seats and pack their stuff, storming out of the room in record time.

I blow out a slow, deliberate breath through pursed lips trying to calm my racing heart. First class of the day? Done. Only a million more to go.

Hazel taps my shoulder. "Come on, let's—"

Mr. Langen cuts in. "If you don't mind, Hazel, go ahead. I'd like to have a word with Everly." He lifts both palms up. "No worries, she's not in trouble. Yet," he adds with a wink.

Judging by the skeptical look Hazel shoots me I doubt she's hundo p on that, so I grab my bag and hold it out for her. "It's fine. Wait for me at the faucet?"

"Sure thing." She sighs, takes my backpack, and leaves me alone with Mr. Langen. Honestly, out of all of my teachers I don't mind being held back by him. Even though it may sound weird, I feel safe with Mr. Langen. Maybe because he's not one to strictly follow the rules, I mean, yeah, he does, but he's usually on our side. The students' side. Not the principal's, not the parents'. Ours. *#ScrewTheEstablishment*

He's so tuned in with us students, he explained to Mom how TeeVee worked when I started getting more active online. They spent the whole parent-teacher conference setting up an account for my mom. Still think it's a tad embarrassing she had Mr. Langen do that for her. They're about the same age, and if he knows how to do it, so should she! Or, just a suggestion, she could have asked me, but that never happened. *#SuitYourself*

Since that time though Mr. Langen is her favorite teacher of mine and the only one she sees for parent-teacher conferences. Can't really blame her for it though. I wouldn't want to sit across Mr. I-overlook-breakfast-leftovers-in-my-beard Quintero either. Or talk to Mr. I-think-I-ooze-sexappeal-but-really-it's-just-BO Dogra. *#ThankYouNoThankYou*

At least Mr. Langen is cool and easy on the eyes. And guess what, he knows how to use hair product. Not many teachers have picked up on the fact that stuff was invented already. For Langen with his wavy sand-blond hair styled into a bed-head it works. So does the professional, yet rebellious look, as Hazel calls it. Not quite clear why it's rebellious, but maybe because he's wearing dress pants and shirt, but rolls up the sleeves of said shirt, showing some serious biceps.

Anyway.

Mr. Langen gets up from behind his desk and sits on it, facing me, the legs of his black dress pants riding up on his ankles. "So. Looks like you didn't hear much of what I was teaching about today." He says it completely neutral, without accusation. That's Mr. Langen.

I frown. PTSD kept me in a soundproof cage this last hour. "Not really. Sorry."

"Don't worry about it. I didn't expect you coming back and falling right back into your routine."

Well, good. "That's actually kind of reassuring, because… it's… more difficult than I thought. Ignoring everybody, I mean." I swipe a strand of hair behind my ear. Every time somebody takes out a phone, I worry about what they're typing. Every. Single. Time.

"No kidding. And I can tell you it will get worse before it gets better."

My gaze shoots up to his. "Way to go making me feel better, Mr. Langen."

He grins. "Just keeping it real, Everly. Today is a test run. They don't know how to behave around you, and you don't know how to behave around them, either. Tomorrow they'll start testing the waters, and that's when we'll have to keep an eye on the usual suspects."

Huh. "Sounds surprisingly reasonable."

"For an old guy, you mean. I heard those unspoken words."

I shake my head. "Would never say or think that, Mr. Langen." For reals. If he's like Mom, he's what—in his early forties? Mid? Well, forty-something.

"Makes me feel better to hear that. But, change of topic, since I have you here. This year everybody got a project assigned, which is going to make up seventy percent of your health class grade for this semester."

I cringe. Seventy percent... for one single piece of work. "That's quite a big chunk for one project."

"Indeed it is, and for a reason. I've assigned everybody a new sport offered in the community to participate in. Requirements are that, well, it needs to be something they haven't practiced before, training needs to happen twice a week—three times for extra credit—and there will be an end-of-the-year performance in front of everybody to demonstrate what you have learned. And the district is even going to cover enrollment costs for students this semester. Quite the stroke of genius on my part and fun, right?" He wiggles his eyebrows at me.

Not quite sure which part of that I get hung up on more. No, on second thought, it's quite clear. "I'm not going to do a performance in front of everybody. No matter what it is." Can you imagine the hashtags, no matter what sport it is? Because I can: *#EarthQuake #BeverlyBacon #FatGirls #TalentFree,* to name a few.

Mr. Langen shrugs. "It's part of the grade. But we'll cross that bridge when we get there. For now, let's talk about which sport you want to choose."

Sounds to me like we're only ignoring my objection, not addressing it, but okay, I'll play the game.

A sport... That's going to be tough. My body is still mad at me for the last year of abuse, understandably so. Despite gaining some weight back, I'm what—fifteen pounds lighter than I officially should be at this point? Oh, and short of breath when I walk upstairs, meaning, sport doesn't sound ideal for me.

Hah! Instant *#GetOutOfJailFreeCard.* "Sorry, Mr. Langen, but I don't think I'm ready for it." I gesture down my body, and he gets the implication. After all, the teachers were *briefed on me*, and I'm sure Mom kept Mr. Langen more up to date than other teachers.

"We can adjust the goals, no problem. I'm expecting different of our athletes compared to somebody who was born with two left feet." He offers a wink with that. "You're somewhere in between right now. An athlete by birth, a tad off your game by circumstance. But I believe in you, Everly. This might actually help you."

Wait, I've heard that before. Enter my psychiatrist. *A healthy mind lives in a healthy body. Get out, be active, meet others, interact on a human level, not a screen level.*

#AnnoyingMuch, which is why I would love to not see her anymore.

A sigh leaves my throat. Nobody can say I wasn't open to reason. Let's cut to the chase. "Okay then: I'll start dance." I've never danced before, but it sounds like it might be a fun thing to learn. Might as well get something out of this project.

Mr. Langen shakes his head. "Taken."

"What do you mean, taken?"

"It means that I don't want twenty boys dribbling a soccer ball on their knees and twenty girls dancing to some pop song for end-of-the-year performance. I'm human, as hard to believe as it is, and having to watch that would break me. Every sport can be picked by two people max."

I grunt. "Okay then. No dance. Cheer."

"Taken."

"Tap?"

"Taken."

"Basketball." Getting *#desperate* here.

He gives me a look from under his lashes. "Whaddaya think? Taken."

Sheesh. Okay, gotta dig deeper. What else does our tiny town offer that's not taken yet? Oh, got it: "Golf." Because, who considers that a sport or interesti—

"Taken."

I deflate. "Well, then I don't know. Judo."

"Nuh-uh, Everly." He wiggles a finger in front of his face. "For one, it's taken, for another, I know you and Hazel have taken judo before. She told me you're a brown belt."

Traitor, that Hazel. "But I haven't practiced in, like, two years." Ever since I got too busy with TeeVee and other priorities took over. "Maybe I could go back—"

"And it's taken, like I said." He sighs and rubs two fingers across his forehead. "I know it's more difficult for you coming in late. You get second picks and the others already took the most popular sports." He drops his hand from his head onto his thigh and drums an annoying rhythm with his fingers onto it. "Would you like me to tell you what's still available? Because I have done my homework and checked our town and the surrounding ones for athletic opportunities within the realm of possibilities." He cocks his head at me, and I wave a dismissive hand through the air.

"Sure. What are my choices?" I'm sure they're thrilling.

"One, darts."

My eyes pop wide. "Darts."

"Yup."

I shake my head. "Nope." Neither am I remotely interested in it, nor is my mom going to let me participate in any sport using any kind of weapon, and I know she is going to consider those pointy ends of the darts as those. "What else?"

"Two, pro wrestling."

"You mean wrestling."

"No, I actually do mean pro wrestling. Wrestling, as in grappling, is taken."

I burst out laughing. "*Pro* wrestling? As in The Rock, John Cena, Hulk Hogan?"

Mr. Langen wiggles his eyebrows again, a wide smile on his face. "Exactly. You got it."

"Yeah, no. I'll pass." It's not a sport anyway. I mean, I'm sure you work up a sweat, but it's all fake—and I've been a fake for long enough. "What else is there?"

He gives me a slow shake of his head. "That's it, Everly. You guys are a big year; I have one slot in darts, one in pro wrestling."

"That's it?" I can't keep the horror from creeping into my voice. There's a reason why nobody picked those particular sports, and I bet it's because nobody wanted to expose themselves to that kind of ridicule. Men in tights beating each other up? Me in between, in tights—*ugh*—faking being thrown around by my hair, or whatever? I'm going to be the talk of the school—again. And not in a good way. I have absolutely no interest in that. "Could I do an alternate project?" *#PrettyPlease*

Mr. Langen grimaces. "You're the tenth person to ask me that question, and I didn't allow it for the other nine, either. Sorry, can't make an exception, Everly."

I let my head fall back and blow out a long puff of air. Aw, man. Just my luck. Crap. "And if my mom doesn't allow it?" Pro wrestling. I'm sure Mom would rather have me fail a class than sink to that level.

"We'll take it one step at a time." He picks up his bag from next to the desk and fumbles with the latches. "Let me give you some more information on it to help with the decision-making process. Here." He pulls out a business card and hands it to me.

"Ben Bullet's Pro Wrestling School?" I read off the card. Sounds ridiculous already.

"Correct. It's close to Vista Verde, so you'll have to take your Vespa there, sorry." He shrugs. "Maybe that's why people didn't want to pick it. Too much of a drive."

I really doubt that's it. "Uh, sure."

"But in any case, check it out, Everly. You don't have much choice otherwise. And hey, you might find wrestling hard to resist." He winks.

My mouth opens and snaps closed again. Here's to maturity and not blurting out the first thing that came to mind, something not quite PG-rated translating to *unlikely*. Might find wrestling hard to resist—puh-lease.

Engaging facial muscles to force a smile. "Okay, I'll check it out." But that's all I'll do, so I can say I did it and it won't work for me. There must be a way around it. Picking up wrestling is social suicide, and sorry, I have no wiggle room when it comes to social standing. Assigning me to wrestling is going to drop my ranking amongst peers right back into bullying territory. A shudder runs down my spine. That's a place I never want to revisit in my life.

So yeah: no wrestling for me.

#SocialSuicideSucks

#

"Can I see your backpack, please?" My mom holds out her hand the moment I enter our house.

"Yeah, sure." Because it's part of the deal—the deal to keep me alive. At least that's what Mom thinks is necessary to protect me from myself.

She takes my bag and zips open all pockets, a determined look on her face that says *not again on my watch*.

We used to be good, Mom and me. Great, actually. Dad abandoning us really brought us together, not just as mother and daughter, but also as friends, to a degree at least. Mom's always had my back with Dad, and I used to tell her everything that went on in my life. Until TeeVee, that is. TeeVee was different: It was mine. My playground. Personal.

To be fair, Mom tried. In the beginning, she got her own account—the one Mr. Langen started for her—and supervised my activity. Later though, when things started to take off for me and went well, when I was keeping my grades up and stayed responsible with my time spent online, she loosened her supervision, focused more on her tax consultant business, and let me do my thing. She trusted me.

But I guess the day I tried to kill myself I also killed that trust in me. At least since then there's a rift between us I don't know how to bridge.

And I don't think she knows, either.

Mom glances up at me. "How was the first day, sweetie?"

#Whaddayathink. "Good."

"What an extensive answer. Elaborate. Please." She fishes around in all pockets, for what, I'm not quite sure. Like, does she think I bought a new phone in school or got myself some pills or sharps to kill myself? One, even after I lost a few brain cells to attempted suicide, I wouldn't be stupid enough to leave that in my backpack. Two, if I wanted to kill myself, I'd find enough in this household. Easily. Mom's sleeping tablets she thinks I don't know about? Check one. Full bottle of Sapphire Vodka, extra large, brought by Grandma during her last visit in case she couldn't sleep? Check two. Steak knives still in their regular spot? Check three. That should be sufficient. But here's the kicker: I don't want to *#KillMyself.* Not right now. Maybe never again—or maybe I will at one point, if I really have to do pro wrestling. *J/k*

"Everly, come on." Mom zips the bag closed again. "Tell me. Hazel was in your classes. I know because I met her mom shopping yesterday and she told me that Hazel told her she kept you a seat. How was everything else?" She hands me my property back with a worried look on her face.

Here's the thing; yes, this annoys me. But I know Mom means well. She feels incredibly guilty for not picking up what was going on in my life and for almost losing me. Doesn't help that Dad is blaming her too, but Dad needs to shut up. You move out on us for a new family in Shanghai, you don't get to have a say in anything regarding this family. Unfortunately, the court ruled differently, so Mom and I have to live with his occasional interference—because let's be honest, it's nothing but that. Neither of us is a big fan of it.

But anyway; this, the whole routine she has come up with, is her way of overprotecting me and overcorrecting what went wrong. Can't say I like it but also can't truly blame her, so I give in. Building a bridge one answer at a time. "It was fine. Nobody said anything. Felt weird, though."

Mom's eyes soften. "I know, sweetie. It'll be better tomorrow, and each new day a bit more." She brushes a hand over my hair.

"Sure hope so." Because if I am to believe Mr. Langen, it's going to get worse before it'll get better. But speaking of. "I have a school project I need to talk to you about." One that you're hopefully going to protest and get me some good, old-fashioned replacement project for. Medical reasons. We can always claim medical reasons.

"Okay." She nods eagerly, and no kidding, I can feel the *#positivity* she's trying to radiate. Projects are good, projects mean forward movement, mean distraction from what was, mean redirection to a new life. Now, here comes the point where she's going to realize my health project is not what she would envision for me to work on.

"So, Mr. Langen has an assignment for us. Everybody takes one new sport for the semester, and most were taken, so I got assigned pro wrestling." I let that information simmer for a second. Three seconds to outrage… two…

"I know." She beams at me. "I think it's fantastic."

My jaw drops. "What the what? Why—First, how do you know? Second, why are you okay with it?"

"I, uh, ran into Mr. Langen down at Trader Joe's. We talked." Her cheeks take on a reddish hue as she shrugs, like it was no big deal at all and that my mom of all people didn't mind her daughter pro wrestling.

I groan. "Sheesh, Mom, whom else did you meet shopping?" Hazel's mom *and* Mr. Langen. When did he even have time to go shopping at this hour? Super.

She grins. "That's it, but I think it's a wonderful idea. Good workout. Good for athleticism. I'm all for it."

I can't believe she's saying that. "Mom, it's pro wrestling. You hated it when Dad turned it on." I would go so far and say there was a *#DirectCorrelation* between wrestling and their divorce. Or, oh wait, it could have been that new family he started himself during his business trips to Shanghai. *#Cheater*

Mom shrugs. "Maybe that's because I haven't given it a chance."

Oh, come on! "Well, I don't want to give it a chance, Mom! I really don't." I can hear the mockery already: *Everly Aldaire is taking pro wrestling, still as fake as before, that bitch. #MatrixGirlSucks #BeverlyBacon* And that's before we even get to that performance.

"Too bad, so sad, Everly. If this is your assigned task, you'll do it." Mom points to my feet, and I get the hint, leaning against the wall to take off my shoes. Doesn't mean I have to stop complaining. She can't ruin my life like this!

"Mom, it's all fake! If you want me to act, enroll me in freakin' acting classes! And it's not even a real sport! No real competition! It's like you mix theater and sports, and it's a joke!" Not a good one, though.

Mom blows me a kiss, happy that I put my shoes down neatly, then walks toward the kitchen. "I hear it's entertainment at its best. You're good at that, or else you wouldn't have made enough money via TeeVee to fund college *and* grad school."

"But—"

She stops and turns to me. "I know that's different, but I also know you need to be out there and reconnect with real life. And it doesn't get more real than wrestling."

I stare at her, incredulous. "Did you hear what you just said?"

She offers a shrug in return. "Well, I hear all kinds of people like wrestling."

That's not what I hear. One more try. "Mom, I really don't want to do it. The others are going to laugh—"

She shakes her head. "I doubt it, Everly. This is a sport picked and sanctioned by your teacher. Besides, I'd rather have a few of your classmates quote-unquote laugh at you than tens of thousands of people on TeeVee." Her lips press into a thin line as she continues her way to the kitchen.

Dang it. I let myself fall against the wall, then slide down and bang my head against it. Last effort. "I don't think I can physically do it, Mom." Not even lying.

"Mr. Langen said they'll build you up slowly. Nobody is expecting you to go from zero to a hundred on the first day."

Gah! I cover my face with my hands. Mr. Langen! If Mom doesn't take the bait about my weight, it doesn't look well for me.

"There's darts as an alternative," I call loud enough to hear for her in the kitchen.

Mom leans into the hallway. "Everly Aldaire, not going to happen."

I lift my head up. "But wrestling—"

"Is going to do you good."

Good? *Good?* "Good, Mom?" Really?

"Oh yes. You think you're eating enough? You're not. This will show you how badly you have treated your body. You're not fourteen and in good shape anymore, Everly, sorry to say so."

Good shape. Twenty pounds overweight, she means, but at least I wasn't *so boney.* "Ouch, Mom. If that's what you truly think, maybe I shouldn't do sports at all." Yes, please. Get me out of it.

"Not going to happen, Everly. Besides, Mr. Langen says he's going to keep an eye on you."

Ah, there we go. That would be the main reason why my mom is suddenly pro-pro wrestling. Of course. It's Mr. Langen. That man can do no wrong in my mom's eyes, and with that little promise, he guaranteed himself Mom's approval. He ticked all her boxes. Sneaky bastard.

Mom points at me. "Also, please remember that it was you who wanted to return to your old school. You said you were ready."

"I *am* ready!" More than ready! Uber ready! Nobody could stand isolation and therapy for any longer than I did, especially not given the alternative to returning to my old stomping grounds.

"And you know the requirement Dad gave you in order for that to happen?"

I close my eyes and bang my head against the wall once more, for good measure. "Yes, Mom. I remember. Full participation." Because he thought that would deter me from returning. Shows how much he knows me.

"Exactly. You do remember where Dad wanted to send you instead—and for once I'm kind of on his side—to make it a bit easier on you?"

Oh, how could I forget. And it wouldn't have been easier. Not for me, which is why I chose full participation over his option. "Yes," I push out through clenched teeth. "But I still don't think that boarding school would be easier."

"They have therapy."

"Hey! The shrink cleared me to go back to school!" Because as long as I'm *#offline*, she says my risk is low. I say being *#offline* increases the risk, but oh well. Difference in opinion.

"Therapy is still helpful, and speaking of, Dr. Shamus would love to see you more often in the next months—"

Dr. Shamus, really. All we do is talk, talk, talk—actually, all *she* does is talk. I don't. Not my style. And she'd love to see me more often than we discussed before discharging me? Because it's such joy? Yeah. So not going to happen! "Therapy isn't everything, Mom! Living my life is, like—" Oh, crap: *#ThinkBeforeYouTalk*! I cringe. "Sorry, I—"

"No, no, I get it." I catch only a glimpse of my mom's hurt features before she withdraws into the kitchen at lightning speed. "Living your life *is* important, Everly. I'm glad we agree on something." Her tone is icy, and I know it too well. Discussion time is over.

Bang, bang, bang.

I wish it hurt more. I wish I had a razor blade. I wish—

Sometimes I wish the last two years didn't happen. *#ToughLuckCarryOn.*

CHAPTER THREE

#Fire

Sometimes I surprise myself with my level of maturity. I could have fought harder. Could have enlisted the shrink to back me up. Pleaded… I dunno, *something*. But I didn't. Nope. Why? Because it was only a slim chance at best I'd get out of that stupid health assignment, and I do have some dignity left. Some. Meaning, it's Friday afternoon, and I have driven all the way out to Vista Verde after my second day of school.

If that doesn't show motivation, I don't know what does. *#Desperation*

Thing is, Ben Bullet's Pro Wrestling School is not only in Vista Verde, but it's close to Mar Vista at the very end of the very smallest town in our county. Good thing I filled up on gas, or my little Vespa would've died of starvation on the way over here. I dismount and take off my helmet. The gym—school, whatever you want to call it—looks a tad… I don't know. Not rundown.

Not new, either. More like industrial. This could have been some kind of factory at one point, and I think it actually was. Tires? Car parts? Something like that.

Now the high, one-story building has flickering floodlights to the left and right, and the way they illuminate the early evening dusk really makes for an inviting and romantic look. *#J/k.* On top of what I assume is the entrance—a roll-up garage door raised by about two feet—a round sign announces Ben Bullet's Pro Wrestling School. Light shines out from under the gate, and the sounds of sneakers on the ground plus people working out hits my ears.

Okay then, here we go.

In moments like that, I don't know how people deal without posting. *#FOMO* I mean, I'll live, but normally, I'd shoot out a quick update. Snap a pic of me half on my way to duck under the gate. *If you don't hear from me, please look for me, #schoolproject #creepy #prowrestling #MatrixGirlRocks*

Alas, not going to happen. Pity. Hazel would get a kick out of me tagging her with anything wrestling-related. I blame her brothers for that deviation in taste, although I have to admit the picture of Jungle Boy she put up in her room is easy on the eyes. But then, if she was so much into pro wrestling, she should have chosen *that* as her sport and not… whatever it is she picked. Huh. Don't even know.

Anyway.

I sigh and duck under the gate and into the school. The moment I straighten up and take in the scene before me, I cock an eyebrow.

"Whoa." Not what I expected. Yes, this must have been a huge factory hall or whatever at one point, but now it's almost empty besides the boxing—sorry, *wrestling*—ring in its center. The way it's illuminated against the rest of the room with dozens of lights hanging from the ceiling is almost beautiful in an artsy way. Its black surface and bright red ropes make it pop against the dark background. The twenty yards from where I am to the ring are dimmed in comparison to the hyper-illuminated ring, but it's bright enough for people to work on the heavy bags and other machinery strategically distributed through the front half of the school.

It's busy—almost every heavy bag or muscle-machine is in use, and so is the ring. Three people are, well, *wrestling* in there, two of them in regular sports outfits and one in a complete head-to-toe black-and-red wrestling outfit, including boots, a tight-fitting costume, and one of these face masks that cover everything besides eyes and mouth, kind of like a Spider-Man mask. Wow. Way to go overboard. Does he know we're still in tiny Vista Verde, California? Not the Staples Center, Los Angeles?

On the other hand—that guy knows how to move: He bearhugs one of the other men from behind and yanks him up and off balance, only to bridge himself back and slam the opponent onto his back. *Ow!* I cringe. They both land with a resounding *boom*, and while the guy who was thrown curls up in pain, wrestling-dude grabs his leg and pins him down. Person number three counts him out—and wrestling guy jumps up into a victory position, arms up, fingers showing a V, climbing up the ropes and beating his chest.

Ugh. Yeah, maybe be a tad over the top? And why exactly did I think taking up wrestling was a good idea? Right, newsflash: I didn't. It's my only choice. Or, maybe I haven't looked hard enough. *#CrochetingIsSpor—*

"Everly!" Person number three, the quote-unquote referee, ducks out from under the ropes and jumps off the ring. "You made it. On your second day. I'm impressed," he calls over.

My mouth drops open. No way. "Mr.... Mr. Langen?" Health and science teacher Mr. Langen works out here? My favorite teacher—here, in a wrestling school? In tights and a tank top? Do I see that right?

He waves and jogs over. "The one and only." He stops in front of me and wipes his sweaty forehead with his forearm. "Sorry, long workout. But glad you made it here."

"Yeah, but... but... I..." I blink twice. Mr. Langen and wrestling doesn't go together. My mind can't make sense of it. "You're... *wrestling?*" He's not exactly the type of person I would have associated with wrestling. For one, he's smart, educated. Two, he has a full set of teeth. Three, he didn't grow up or is currently living in Hillbilly County. Isn't using meth, or an alcoholic, as far as I know—

I cringe. Maybe it's time to check my prejudices at the door. Rolling gate. Whatever—I don't want to be judged, and I shouldn't judge others, either. Or their sport, for that matter.

Mr. Langen chuckles. "Yes, I'm wrestling. In fact, this is my school." He makes a circling movement with his hand.

"*Your* school?" Come again?

"Indeed. For the last ten years. Teacher salaries are not what they used to be, you know?" He winks at me, but I don't pick up on it.

Mr. Langen owns a wrestling school. Which means... "*You're* Ben Bullet?"

He nods. "My gimmick. Stage name. Ben Bullet—fast as lightning, deadly as steel." He bends his body into a very much un-teachery exaggerated dabbing position. "So, decided to give wrestling a chance?"

No, not really. "Well—" Wait a second. Something clicks into place in my mind. "You tricked me!"

"I did?" A mischievous sly grin appears on his face.

"When you said I might find wrestling difficult to resist—you meant because you're the owner and it'd look really bad if I blew you off!"

"That might have played a role, I admit." The grin spreads wider.

A faint groan escapes my lips. No wonder Mr. Langen said he would keep an eye on me—I bet Mom knew it's his gym. I bet. "Did you run into my mom on purpose?" At this point, I wouldn't put it past him.

"On purpose?" His voice goes up an octave too high at the end. "Uh, no. No. Of course not. That was a coincidence. Funny, how as a teacher you sometimes meet your students or their parents, right?" He works one hand through his damp hair, both his cheeks taking on a reddish hue. "Right?"

Awkward much? "Sure. Whatever. I was just—"

"No, yeah, right, anyway, it was convenient I saw her. I wanted to call her anyway to talk it through with her, but this way I got her okay for you faster." He rubs his hands together. "So that means you're in, Everly? Since you're kind of out of options?"

Yeah. *#OutOfOptions #thx*

Something cramps in my stomach. Maybe it's the fact that I haven't eaten since the morning, maybe it's the fear of what's most likely going to come once the others find out.

I close my eyes in surrender. "I have to, I guess." Great job, Mom and Mr. Langen. And worst part, I don't even have any internet to keep an eye on the comments on TeeVee. Maybe Hazel can moni—

"Wonderful, I was hoping so." Mr. Langen looks over his shoulder at the ring and waves. "Fire! Hey, Fire? Could you come over for a minute, please?"

"Sure!"

I turn to catch the last of the word spoken by the wrestler in the full costume—the wrestler who's standing on the top rope with his back to the ring and—

"Holy cow!" I suck in a sharp breath because that dude, he jumps off high, pulls off a backward flip in midair and lands belly-down on his opponent lying in the middle of the ring.

"One! Two! Three!" The referee, obviously not Langen this time, counts, and as soon as the bell rings, wrestling-dude gets up and helps his opponent back on his feet. They laugh and bro-hug, a couple of broken-off words making it over here, from *knew it* to *best one ever* to *you're back, man.* Some of the other guys manning the machines, heavy bags, or who're simply standing around, applaud. And wow, this is, like, a guys' club. I'm the only source of estrogen here tonight, the way it looks.

"Fire! Come on!" Mr. Langen waves over again. "Ain't nobody got all night!"

"Coming!" Wrestler-dude—Fire, apparently—ducks under the ropes and jumps off the ring, falling into a light jog on his way over, only to slow down almost comically when he sees me standing next to Mr. Langen, like, with a little stumble to his step, and this stumble, it rubs me the wrong way.

What? You're surprised a girl is here? At a wrestling school? Well, so am I, buddy, but that's no excuse for misogyny. I cross my arms in front of my chest and try to keep my glaring at him to a minimum. Confrontation is not my thing when it's *#RealLife*. Online, that's a different matter. One of my most popular campaigns on TeeVee was about a year ago, *Keep Misogyny out of the State Senate.* I got it supported and financed within forty-eight hours, which bought us a reporter's time for two months prior to the election and said reporter's expertise in calling out and reporting misogyny. Every article published that favored misogynistic details over political facts got called out in that newspaper. Roaring success, I might add. *#GenderWars*

That's the beauty about TeeVee and what I'm missing and going to miss the most: that I can actually change things and make my voice heard. TeeVee runs on money. Every post, every like, every dislike, every share or favorite, costs money. Generally speaking, you click, you pay. Only a few cents, depending on settings and tier—but it's for a reason. Most of it, at least. You click *like* on a post, that cent you're paying goes to the post's owner. Few people make lots of money with that, and it's not at the heart of TeeVee anyway: the campaigns are. Depending on the financial goal set for the post or campaign, most of that money goes to the cause. A certain percentage stays with the campaign owner, as an incentive to come up with something good, but even though that can add up too, the majority of the income is funneled into the pre-determined cause. And that can be anything, from hospital bills to the purchase of whatever, but most commonly, it's used for newspaper space, ad space, or even TV ad time. Okay, for the latter more than my meager-ish two hundred something thousand would be needed, but still. Starting a campaign, getting support—it makes us heard.

Without that, without TeeVee… I feel invisible all over again.

Anyway. This *Fire* guy stops next to Mr. Langen. "What's

up?" He's breathing a tad heavy and as soon as he stops, a wave of heat assaults me. *#WorkingOut*. It's not unpleasant, just unwanted. And what's up with that costume, I mean, he is the *#OnlyOne* wearing one in this gym. It clarifies, though, why Mr. Langen called him "Fire"—the costume gives it away. While it's kept mostly in black, red-orange flames lick up his legs, swirl around his body, and adorn most of his mask. And speaking of: I was right, that mask is covering his head completely, besides a narrow opening for the eyes and his mouth. Even there the costume includes stylized flames attached to the sides of his head. Fire, indeed. From what his outfit reveals, he's a good head taller than me and nicely built: wide shoulders, narrow hips, muscular body, nice, deep voice—all of which I would appreciate if I weren't so irritated by him.

Mr. Langen claps his shoulder. "Fire, this is Everly. Everly, this is Fire. He's from El Marino High in Mar Vista."

I know why Mr. Langen dropped that info. Translation, he's not from our school and hasn't heard about what's been going on with you.

The guy chews on his lower lip, and as cliché as it might be, I can all but feel the apprehension radiate off him. Way to go making the new girl feel welcome. "H-Hi," he says, then drops his gaze to the floor and back to Langen. "Anything else?"

Langen rolls his eyes. "Yes, Fire. Everly's school project for this year is wrestling, meaning, she is going to join us. She—"

"What?" Fire yelps, then slaps a hand across his mouth and tries to hide the outburst in a cough. Unsuccessfully so, I might add. What's his freakin' problem?

My health teacher slaps Fire across the head, only way too gentle in my opinion. "Yes, she is. Get over it. And since you're my best wrestler, it's going to fall to you to teach her."

"*Me?*" He sounds about as thrilled as I am.

"*Him?*" I don't need Mr. *#Misogynist* to be my instructor, especially with this reaction. "Mr. Langen, given my recent history, isn't it better if you taught—"

"Sorry, Everly. I get to teach once in a while here, but usually Fire and Eric over there run the training, and Eric just had a new baby—I mean, his wife did—but still, he won't have much time from now on. It's you and Fire."

Me and Fire.

I groan under my breath. *#JustPerfect*

"Don't worry." Mr. Langen raises both hands in a calming gesture. "Fire, you should have the time with Ronan out of the picture, am I correct?"

The Fire-guy stiffens. "I guess."

"Good. And Everly, we're talking twice a week and basic wrestling moves. I can't expect you to become fit or an expert in the few weeks until winter break. If you can show me two or three techniques, that's all I'm asking for."

Two or three techniques to pass this class and not be sent to *#BoardingSchool.*

Twice a week.

And nobody else from my school is here. Or wait… "Who else is doing wrestling?"

"Huh?" Mr. Langen cocks an eyebrow.

"I mean, you said two per sport. Here I am. Who's the other student?" Translation, whom do I have to watch out for? Who is going to be my possible downfall until they prove they can be trusted?

"Everly." Mr. Langen gestures from the left of the gym to the right and back. "Do you see anybody from your year training here?"

Aw, come on! I stomp my foot like a belligerent toddler. "Seriously? I'm the only one?" I mean, great, no observation, but man, talk about tough luck.

The most annoying health teacher of all times grins. "Well, we saved the best for last." He winks. "And I'm sure you're going to do fine."

I put my hands on my hips. "Fine. A few techniques, I show up twice a week, and you tell nobody at school which sport I'm doing." At least until that performance, if I can't find a way to wiggle myself out of it.

Langen slaps both hands over his heart. "Ouch, Everly. That's hurting my feelings."

I give him a pointed glance and he turns serious.

"Fine, don't worry about it. Nobody will know."

I blow out a sigh of relief.

#HeresToHope.

#

The next morning, I make it to Ben Bullet's Wrestling School by ten in the morning, after half a slice of toast with butter eaten under maternal supervision. *#Progress.* I'm playing this tactical: Today's Saturday, so maybe I'm lucky and Fire won't be here. I'll still count it as one of my two weekly required sessions, though, because it's not my problem if he isn't here. Maybe I'll be even luckier and they're closed. I will *still* count it.

Alas, no such luck. The gate is open to about my chest height, music blaring from the inside. *#Sigh.* Fingers crossed Fire isn't in and I can go to enjoy my *#freedom.*

Once I duck into the gym, all hope goes *poof,* though. Fire is definitely in, running from one side of the ring to the other, throwing his body into the ropes and using the recoil's momentum to propel himself forward.

#HamsterInAWheel

But anyway.

The only four or five other people up this early on a Saturday are working the machines or heavy bags in the front. No women, all guys, just like yesterday, and—

My eyes widen. One of them is Mr. Langen, working the heavy bag on the left. And while Fire is again—or maybe still, who knows—in his head-to-toe fire-wrestling outfit, Mr. Langen is wearing gym shorts.

And that's it.

He's barefoot and quite noticeably missing a shirt.

Uh…

Should students see their teacher topless? Yesterday's tank top was traumatizing enough.

By now the damage is done though—I can't unsee Mr. Langen without a shirt, and while it's awkward, I have to admit he's fit. For an older guy, at least. *#BuffOverForty*

"Everly." He greets me and waves, giving the heavy bag one more kick with his shin, then comes over to me. "Love the motivation of showing up on a Saturday."

See? "Figured I might as well get started." I push the lie out through my teeth. *Get it over with* is more like it.

"That's the spirit." He bites into the flap of the Velcro and pulls on it to unfasten his boxing gloves. "Fire is here more than anywhere else, including home, so you're most of the time in luck when it comes to finding him here."

Yay me. "Sounds great."

"You're ready? No need to change?"

Dread wraps around my heart. Please don't tell me I have to wear one of *those* outfits. I'm far too heavy for tights. Coming up with a quick smile I point down my body. "Athletic clothing, right?" So, my black sweatpants and saggy, long-sleeved shirt should do it.

He gives me a top-to-bottom eval, complete with a slight shadow crossing his face that freaks me out. What? I don't look fat in it, do I? I thought wearing black would hide—

"You got it. Perfect." He gives me a thumbs-up that does nothing to reassure me, then claps my shoulder. "Let's get you over to the ring. If you have questions—"

Only one comes to mind. "Uh, do I have to sign a waiver or something in case of severe injury, or, I don't know, death?" That last word, it comes out with a cringe. Wouldn't that be funny— unsuccessful suicide attempt, then killed during the rehab phase: unintentionally so. *#FateIsABitch*

Mr. Langen shakes his head in mock despair. "No, Everly, we are trying to not injure you here. Besides," he adds with a sheepish look at me, "when I spoke to your mom I took care of all that."

At Trader Joe's? "Sure," I reply. Whatever. I'll seriously take over shopping duties from now on. Safer for me.

Once we arrive at the ring, Fire stops his hamster routine and drops into a cross-legged seat in front of us. Since the ring is up to my upper stomach, that gives me a good look at his muscular chest. Stupid costume and attitude or not, he is well built, gotta give him that.

He waves at me. "Hey, Everly." Maybe it's my imagination,

but he sounds guarded.

"Fire," I reply, then grimace right after. "Wait. What's your real name?"

"Fire's good," he says, shrugging.

Fire's good. "Oo-kaay…" I stretch. Weirdness scale? Needs to be adjusted.

Mr. Langen pulls on the lower rope. "It's a wrestling thing, Everly. Many wrestlers go by their gimmick only. Ever heard of the Million Dollar Man?"

"Can't say I have."

"A wrestler in the eighties and nineties. Rich, according to his gimmick, and that man lived it. Even when he wasn't wrestling, he would pay for everybody in every bar he visited or carry a whole wad of cash he could throw up in the air, just like on TV."

"Oo-kaay…" Weirdness scale adjusted even further.

"You'll need to come up with a ring name as well."

"Sure thing." When hell freezes over.

Mr. Langen chuckles at my obvious lack of excitement. "You still have time. I suggest you have a ring name once you need to perform what you've learned. Anyway, Fire goes by 'Fire,' I often go by 'Ben'—and that reminds me. When we're here, please call me either 'Ben' or 'Clark.' One is my gimmick, one is my first name. I trust you can figure out which one is which."

I blush. "But I can't—"

"Yes, you can. We'll be training together, and I bet at one point, I will wrestle you and you will wrestle me. That means there has to be trust between us, even more than we already have. Same goes for Fire and you. Without trust, injuries happen, so…" He lets go of the rope. "Have fun, kids."

And with that and a small wave, he takes off, leaving me alone with Fire.

Silence.

"So," I say, rocking back on my heels.

"Yeah." He draws in his legs and wraps his arms around them but then rubs a hand over his neck, an odd gesture while stuck in a full body suit. "So, want to start with the basics?"

I grab the rope and hoist myself up onto the outside of the ring. Ugh. Harder than it looks. "Good place to start." *#awkward.*

Fire jumps up to standing and lifts the second rope up while stepping on the lowest one, opening them up for me. "Come on in." He lets go of the ropes as soon as I've ducked under. "Now, wrestling one-oh-one… I think it's best to start with safety. Ring safety and performance safety. You might have noticed wrestling involves lots of throwing the other person, and that person taking a bump." He cocks his head at me.

"Yeah." I'm loving this already. So much fun. Can hardly contain myself.

"Okay. First things first. Rolling and falling. You'll need that when you're tripped, are falling, or are being thrown. It's something that should come out reflexively. Like this."

In one smooth motion, he executes a forward roll and comes back to standing. "Rolling is usually the hardest for people—"

I hold up a hand. "Let me try." *#BeenThereDoneThat*

His eyes narrow behind the mask. "I'll break it down for you—"

"Because you think I can't roll? I think I can handle it." I throw one look around—any phones, anybody recording?—but no, everybody is busy doing their thing. Nobody pays me even an ounce of attention. Huh. Feels… weird, and at the same time *#liberating* because then I won't have to worry about posts of my ungainly roll tomorrow. That's a feeling I haven't had in a while.

I blow out a puff of air. Okay then. Taking one step forward with my right, I let body memory take over and lead me into a right forward roll, and velocity carries me up to standing. *#BrownBeltJudo #BeenAges #StillGotIt*

I swear Fire's jaw drops behind his mask. "That was… really good." He chuckles and scratches his head—well, his mask. "Actually, that was pretty awesome."

I tuck a strand of hair behind my ear. "Took some judo when I was younger."

Something lights up in his eyes. "*Some* judo?"

"Brown belt."

"Nice!" Respect shines through, and it gives him his first bonus point ever. "So that means you know how to fall."

"I knew at one point." Although I'm pretty sure I can still pull it off. Somewhat.

He rubs his hands together. "Do me a favor—can you do a hard fall break onto your back?" Without warning, he throws himself back and lands flat on his back with a BANG.

Oy. Well, no time like the present to see what I still can do. Deep breath in—and *boom!*—I land on my back.

Fire laughs out loud. "Awesome! Okay, this is going to be fun!" He reaches down, offers me a hand, and helps me up to standing. "If you're comfortable falling—and looks like you are—this is a whole different ballgame."

"C-Cool." I wipe my palms on my thighs. Falling did hurt a bit more than I remembered. Could be the ring versus tatami mats, or just old age and less cushion on my bones, but I'd be damned if I admitted that.

"It actually is. Cool, I mean." Fire looks over my shoulder in the direction Mr. Langen went. "I'm not supposed to show this to you on the first day, but… Want me to show you something you'll need this for? Because it's cool?"

"Uh, sure?"

"Know what a clothesline is? And no, not the one to hang your clothes on."

I shake my head.

"Duh, surprise, guess what—it's a wrestling move. Usually, moving in against a standing opponent, the attacker's arm is clotheslining them off their feet so that they have to take a hard fall backward. Like this." He takes my right arm by my wrist and lifts it until it's in a position as if I'd high-five a hand above his left shoulder, with my elbow touching his chest "Hold it. Strong. Pretend it's a wall nobody can breach. When you feel contact with me, push your arm and body forward to keep it in position."

"Wait, what—"

"Go with the flow, Everly!" Fire steps back about half the distance to the other ropes, then runs toward me.

I squeak, but within like a millisecond, he's already charged me and run himself against my arm. He grunts, and *boom*, lands on his back, as if my arm had taken him off his feet.

"Holy cow!" A laugh breaks free, and it comes with a surge of some kind of… well, almost glee, I haven't felt in a while. "I didn't do a thing besides hold out my arm!" *#RockingThis*

Fire pops up to his knees and grins at me—even his eyes smile. It makes him… nicer. "Fun, eh? That was teamwork. As it always is in the ring. We can work on selling it—that's a two-way street—and making it look more realistic."

I scratch my chin. "Selling it." He sold it well for sure, because cool as it was, it wasn't me executing this. It was all him. As hard as it is to admit, it was awesome, just because... I don't know. Because it worked? *#MindBlown*

"Yeah, selling it. The matches are scripted up to a degree. This is not the UFC. Doesn't mean it's easy, though. From a certain point of view, it might even be more difficult because matches can suck if somebody doesn't know how to sell. We'll see if you're good at it. You have two advantages already: knowing how to fall, and long hair. Emphasizes the action."

I pose and put a hand to my hair, sixties-style. "Why, thank you. I—" Out of the corner of my eye, I see Mr. Langen slip his hands into his boxing gloves next to the heavy bag at the far end of the gym.

#Idea

I hold up a hand. "Fire? I have a plan."

"You do?"

I step closer and keep my voice low. This is perfect. *#PaybackIsABitch.* "I do. Can you please clothesline me? I want to scare Mr. Langen. *Ben,*" I correct.

"What?" His eyes pop wide.

I nod like a bobblehead figure. "You do it to me. I take the fall. And sell it. Mr. Langen kind of tricked me to take wrestling—"

His eyes narrow. "He tricked you?"

I wave a hand. "Him and my mom. Details don't matter, but I want to get back at him. So clothesline me." *#EasyPeasy.*

"No!" He shakes his head. "Geez, no! I'm not clotheslining you—"

I put both hands on my hips. "Because you think I can't do it? I aced that fallbreak!"

"N-No! Yes, I mean, yes, you aced it, but I just... It's that... I can't—I—not you—I can't. I..." He turns away from me, his shoulder heaving up with a deep breath in and out as his hands ball to fists and then relax. Once he faces me again, he sounds much more in control. Calmer. "Never mind. You got the fall breaks for it and you want to tease Ben. We can do that. Let's see if you've got the chops to sell it." He looks everywhere but at me for this.

#UncomfortableMuch, but I'll take it.

Mr. Langen circles his arms, then does some shadow boxing next to the heavy bag, so I'd say it's now or never before he's too immersed in his boxing. "Work with me," I whisper—then shove him into the chest so hard, he has to stumble back to keep himself from falling. "What the heck are you saying?" I yell at him so loud, his eyes pop wide. "What's wrong with you?"

"I- I didn't—"

Ugh. I roll my eyes and whisper under my breath. "You said sell it, so you better start!" Then, louder, accompanied with a harder shove, I add, "I don't want to hear any of this shit again!"

Something lights up in his eyes and he stomps his foot, throwing his hands up in the air. "Oh, really? Shouldn't have come here then!" Ta-daaah, Fire caught on.

Mr. Langen has abandoned his workout and strides over with large steps. "Guys, take it easy—"

I rush at Fire. "Go screw yourself!" And *boom*, I shove him so hard, he stumbles into the ropes. One quick glance at me, one quick nod—and he bounces out of the ropes and charges me with a roar. I have half a second to brace myself and *BAM!* his forearm hits me square in the upper chest.

"Ugh," I grunt, throwing myself back. I land flat on my back with a bang and curl into a ball, groaning and moaning.

Mr. Langen yells out. "Shit! Fire! What the hell are you doing?

Are you out of your mind?" He slides into the ring on his belly.

And I burst out laughing.

"Got you." I giggle. "We got you." I raise two fingers spread into a V.

"Got…?" His gaze darts from me, giggling on the ground, to Fire standing above me, shoulders shaking from laughter. The moment Langen gets it is the moment he rolls his eyes and lets himself drop flat onto his stomach. "Guys. You can't do that to me. I died about a million heart attacks right there and then." He rolls onto his back. "You gave me grey hair, Fire."

Fire still laughs. "Hey, it was Everly's idea—"

"Tattletale!" I wipe some tears of laughter from my eyes and sit up, still grinning like an imbecile. "That was payback for luring me in, Mr. Langen."

My teacher rolls his eyes. "I'll give it to you, you one-upped me. But honestly, that performance ten minutes after you entered the ring? That just bought you a nice change of assignment. Forget three moves, blah blah. After this, I want to see a full match at the end of the semester. Choreographed, worked out, professional. It can be short, but it'll be a match. You brought it on yourself," he adds with a twirl of his finger.

A whole match…

Fire winks at me. "And I promise you, she'll rock it. Relax, Ben, the risk was minimal. She pulled off her fall breaks like a pro. Get over yourself." He holds out a hand for me. I look at it, and in that very moment, something shifts inside my mind. As my hand slides into his, it's as if the costume and mask gained substance and became a person. A nice person, with a warm voice and awesome body, a person who backed me up when I asked. A person different than I thought he was.

Fire pulls me up, and I could swear he holds on to my hand a second longer than strictly necessary. "Welcome to pro wrestling, Everly."

CHAPTER FOUR

#BlastFromThePast

"Ah, a Lucha mask," Hazel says as she stuffs the first load of her books into her locker. "That makes sense."

"It does?" I open mine and look for the homework folder I was sure I brought to school.

"It does. Many wrestlers with Mexican roots wear these masks. It's supposed to be a secret who's under them. The true professionals don't even take them off when at home."

Sheesh. "That would take some getting used to, but to each their own."

"Don't judge, Ever. It's a culture."

I raise both palms facing outward. "Hey, no judgment. Made that mistake right when I walked into Mr. Langen, and I won't do it again. Kind of ironic the gal who hated people judging me online was quick to do the same herself, so… Done with that."

Haze grabs some chewing gum and stuffs it in her pocket.

"Yup. How'd it go otherwise?"

"Besides that? As well as could be expected, I'd say, considering that I wanted to get back at Mr. Langen, and Fire clotheslined me for tha—"

"He did *what*?" Hazel blinks and shakes her head. "He freakin' *clotheslined* you on your first day? WTF?"

"Shush, Hazel." I throw a nervous glance around. The hallway is busy, and while most students are doing their thing, the walls have ears. "I asked him to do that. And not everybody needs to know." Actually, nobody does.

She rolls her eyes. "Know what? That you got assigned wrestling? Get over yourself, Ev."

"It's just that—"

Hazel tilts her head to the side and cocks an eyebrow at me. "Everly. Really. It's cool. I promise you ninety percent of the guys in our year love wrestling. Maybe half will admit to it. And the girls…" She shrugs and throws her locker door shut. "I like it."

"But you've got three brothers." All older. Watching wrestling and doing *#BoyStuff* was her life until puberty hit.

"See? But who cares why I like it? Who knows why many others do? My point is, don't care about *them*. We're kind of done caring about *them*, right?" She lowers her voice on that last part of the sentence.

Are we? We, i.e., I, should be. It's just so freakin' hard to not feel under observation. I sigh. "Kind of. I think so. Working on it." One day at a time, with more or less success. I mean, take today. We're halfway through school, and so far, everything's going pretty we—

"Everly." A hairy forearm enters my vision. "Man. Really good to have you back." Ford Rodgers, football player extraordinaire, leans against my locker, his wide frame blocking my view of basically everything else. Even without his football gear and shoulder pads Ford is massive for a Senior, but in a good way. Muscular. Athletic. Cute, too, especially with that lazy smile gracing his face and bringing the blue in his eyes to an even more striking shine. Amazing how well that goes with his buzz-cut light blond hair. There isn't a single stall in the girls' bathrooms that doesn't have his name smeared onto the doors with Sharpie, no matter how often the janitor tries to remove it or paint it over.

"Everly?" He kicks one corner of his mouth up some more until a dimple pops out.

Oh. Crap. Conversation! "Ford," I squeak. He really said *my* name, right? So he's talking to *me*, and I'm not dreaming this, right? *#PigsAreFlying*

"I missed seeing you." The hand not supporting his weight on my locker taps my shoulder for emphasis.

My gaze flickers up to his, then down to the ground. So weird, weird, weird to know he knows I tried to kill myself. It's Ford. One of the hottest guys in school. I'd rather he didn't know. "Oh. Well, th-thanks, I…" I'm not sure what to say. *I was recovering from blood loss? #SelfInflicted.* Or should I go with *It's good to be back* and overplay it?

Ford doesn't give me time to come up with a reply. He wiggles his eyebrows at me. "You look as beautiful as ever. New hairstyle?" He reaches for my hair and tugs on a red lock.

I think I hear Hazel make an exaggerated gagging noise. My cheeks flame up. As beautiful as ever? Ford thinks I'm beautiful? Since when—I mean, he never said anything! "Yeah, the hair, maybe, a little." Meaning, no. Same hair as always, but whatever. Guys.

Ford gives my hair another playful tug before he drops it. "Well, it looks really good on you."

"Th-thank you." I wish it came out stronger, and I wish I could believe it more, but TeeVee has spoiled that for me.

#

Janey_08:
I like your hair, @MatrixGirl!
#RedRocks

#

BigD:
Ugh. #UglyAsHeck Who wears hair like that?
#UglyGoKillYourself #SpareUs

#

SkinnieMinnieWINS:
LOL! Like a doll! The kidn that look like they ahd an accident.
#uglyasheck

#

Ford leans against the locker some more, personified coolness. "I heard there's a new petition on TeeVee: Bring back MatrixGirl. From what I saw, it has seventy percent of its five thousand-vote ceiling already." He winks at me. "Still as popular as ever, Everly."

A small grunting sound escapes me. A petition to bring me back? I suck in a harsh breath. "N-No, didn't know that. Thanks for the info." My heart skips a painful beat. A petition to bring me back at seventy percent already… it feels great. I'm not forgotten. Offline, but not forgotten. I still have followers and fans. I still matter.

Unfortunately, that warm feeling gets a cold shower when a sharp pang of doubt shoots through my soul: How many of them are *#truefans*? How many want nothing else but their online punching bag back? Their source of entertainment?

Yeah, those seventy percent… they taste bitter. Of deceit.

If I have learned one thing over the last year, it's that in the TeeVee community, the spotlight can turn on you at any time, and I don't mean the good kind of spotlight. Everybody gets negative attention here and there, sure. There are always idiots and trolls. But once the community decides the tables have turned… they have turned. Period. There's no stopping the snowballing of that. Thank you, *@Moonsaulting_Spaceman*, for starting the downward spiral that got me to slice open my radial artery.

Ford taps my shoulder again. "And speaking of bringing MatrixGirl back. I know it's only your first week back at school, but… but I wanted to make my move before the masses descend on you." He gives me a cute look from under his lashes. Gosh, he's such an attractive guy. Always was. Proudest moment of my life when I was fifteen and had just lost some twenty pounds was him commenting under my petition to have the city supply help-needed-buttons to seniors over eighty. *Leave it to @MatrixGirl to know what's really #ImportantInLife*, he wrote, and I was knighted right there and then.

I clear my throat. Stop daydreaming, Everly. "What do you mean?"

A little twinkle lights up in his eyes. "Masquerade, Everly.

We're twelfth graders. It's our year to host the Masquerade. Our year to shine." He pushes himself off the locker and wiggles excited jazz hands in front of my face.

Right. "Masquerade. I'd totally forgotten." But he's right, it's that time of the year. Senior class organizes, and all tenth, eleventh, and twelfth graders celebrate an *evening of masquerades and mystique*, complete with classy costumes and all-you-can-eat buffet. I had a blast last year and posted at least ten updates throughout the night. This year… I hadn't even thought about it. *#ObviousReasons*

"You might have forgotten it, but I haven't." He takes my hand in his and goes down to one knee. "Everly Aldaire, will you do me the honor and be my date for the Masquerade?"

What the—

People stop in the hallway and stare at us. Some point, some giggle—nobody openly, because this is Ford, but…

Dang it, somebody pulls a phone out of their pocket and aims it at us.

Hazel steps to block their view. "Dude, seriously, stop—"

I rip my hand out of Ford's and hiss at him. "Get up, Ford! What are you doing?" I cross my arms in front of my chest and turn my face away from the crowd. The humiliation in front of Ford, of all people, is still better than in front of tens, or hundreds of thousands. My knees are wobbly and I hate that I'm overreacting, but—

Ford chuckles and stands up. He works one hand through his blond, short hair and grins. "I'm doing it properly, what else? I was hoping you'd be back in time for the Masquerade, so, you know, I haven't asked anybody else."

Heat invades my cheeks until they burn. "I don't even know

if I'm going." I don't even know why he's asking me. It's me, after all. *After* all my fame.

He places a hand over his heart in *#MockShock*. "But you have to! Wouldn't be the Masquerade if you didn't go."

I release a slow, controlled breath. The students standing and watching disperse one by one, now that there's nothing spectacular to be seen anymore, but the bitter taste of my reaction, my fear, it stays. "I—"

"She'll think about it, bud." Hazel lays both of her hands on my shoulders from behind and steers me to the left past Ford. "Excuse us. We've got places to be."

Ford moves aside. "Let me know, okay? Don't blow me off. We'd be fantastic together, Everly. You and me, hundo p! Call me." He raises his thumb to his ear with his pinky extended, like a fake phone.

"Sure—"

"Yeah, will do, thank you, Ford." And just like that, Hazel has maneuvered me away from him and down the hallway. "Unbelievable, that guy. Seriously. No *how are you*, no nothing, but making a show out of asking you to the Masquerade? What. The. Hell?" She stomps her foot and grazes the shin of a passing junior. "Oops, sorry." After one quick smile at the poor victim of her outburst, she focuses back on me. "You're hopefully not thinking of going with him. Right? You're not?"

I harrumph. "I hadn't even thought about it in general." But the Masquerade was my favorite school activity the last two years: Nobody recognizes *#BeverlyBacon* behind a well-chosen mask, so she can come out of her shell. Nobody recognizes *#MatrixGirl*, either, and she can party unafraid of people posting her ungraceful dance moves.

Hazel hooks her arm in mine. "Well, duh. You're going—just not with him. I don't trust Ford. What a phony."

"He supported all my campaigns on TeeVee." I noticed, believe me, I noticed. Ford has always been nice to me in a distant way, despite the all the rumors TeeVee brought up about me. In fact, he never commented on them once.

"So what? So did thousands of others. They were good campaigns!"

Heck yeah, they were! "Thanks. Told you, he never posted anything bad."

"That you know of."

My reply is stuck in my throat. She's right—there was nothing under his official profile, but he could have easily had two or three profiles. Or he could have shared one with somebody else, like his buddy, Arlo. Many people our age do to share the cost. Yeah, it's as little as a penny per like and ten cents per support or share, but depending on how active you are, it can get expensive.

I deflate. "True, but still, my point was, maybe we're on the same page about many things, and going with him would be fun."

The glance I get in return is loaded with skepticism. "Or maybe he's just an idiot, Ev." Because he didn't give me the time of day before I became MatrixGirl, she means. But then, I was a different person before MatrixGirl. *#BeverlyBacon.*

I pat her hand on my forearm. "Possible. As I said, I haven't even made up my mind about the Masquerade. Last year, I couldn't have imagined not going. This year, I honestly can't imagine actually going." As we pass a group of younger students looking our way, I pick up on whispered words: *Suicide. Loony bin.*

Heat creeps into my cheeks. Yeah. That's me. Hi.

Somebody else's voice cuts through the murmur of gossip, louder: "Holy crap, isn't that MatrixGirl? Why the heck did she come back? Six feet under looks better on her."

A chill snakes around my insides. *It could be worse, it could be worse, it could be—*

Somebody laughs out loud. "Oh my god! What a loser!" The word shoots through my defenses like a bullet, bouncing around in my heart. Loser—

More giggles. "Yeah, spot on. Loser—mute loser!"

Mute—

My eyes snap up to the source of laughter, a group of six or seven students, standing in front of a locker and pointing at it before they laugh some more and walk on. Once they're out of the way the source of their amusement is clear: Somebody has printed a picture of Freddy Krueger and taped it to a locker. *Stay home, fucking nightmare,* it says under the image.

Empathy lodges in my throat. "Is that Calan's locker?" My voice breaks with the last word.

Hazel nods. "The janitor usually removes that crap over lunch. They've been doing stuff like that since the beginning of the school year. It's getting old."

No. I shake my head, PTSD squeezing my heart to the point of pain. It never gets old. Every time, it hurts the same and it only gets worse, like a wound that isn't allowed to heal.

He doesn't deserve this. Nobody does.

But... I can't change it.

In my mind, courageous me breaks out of Hazel's hold, stomps over to the locker, rips the paper off the door, and tears it into pieces.

In my mind, courageous me screams at the guys trying to stop me: *One more word and you and I are going to have a problem. If I see you or anybody else either put something up on Calan's locker or laugh at it, your life will take a turn, and I don't mean for the better. Got it?*

In my mind, courageous me types out my anger and sends it into the world. *#FuckingMorons*

But in reality, I do no such thing.

I drop my eyes and look the other way, acid churning in my stomach. There's nothing I can do, not without a backlash. Not without bringing attention to myself, and *#BeverlyBacon* doesn't get noticed. It's better for everyone involved. And *#MatrixGirl…*

She died as soon as the knife touched my radials, and with her died all the fight I had in me.

#RIPMatrixGirl

#

"Backpack, please." Mom adds a little wiggle of her fingers when I don't slip out of the shoulder straps fast enough. "Today, Everly."

Goodness, what a welcome. I grunt and let the backpack fall into her hands. "Not quite sure what you're looking for, but it's not there."

She pauses and cocks an eyebrow. "So whatever I'm looking for is somewhere else?"

Ugh. "No, Mom. There is nothing to be found is what I'm saying." Sheesh.

"Uh-huh." Funny how my mom can put such a disdain in a grunt, and it rubs me the wrong way.

"What is it?" I prop both hands on my hips. Because that

grunt, it spells displeasure, disappointment, and a whole buttload of nouns starting with *dis*-something. I'm the master of grunt-translation when it comes to Mom. Welcome to my life.

"I'm looking through your backpack, as we agreed," Mom replies, half-stuck with her head inside the big zipper compartment.

"Not what I'm talking about." She was pi—I'm sorry, *annoyed* with me already when she opened the door. I know that expression. Very well, actually, although to be fair, she usually wears it after talking to Dad.

She sighs and straightens to look at me. "You really want to have that discussion now?"

"Sure." Better now than having that Sword of Damocles hang over my head for who knows how long. Doc Shamus said to get problems aired out quickly because if I don't, they wear me down and make me do stupid things. So look at me, being all mature and stuff.

Mom shrugs. "Okay then: I found food in your bathroom trash."

My heart sinks. Oh, crap. *#Busted.* "I… I wasn't feeling very well." Not lying. I'm okay with small portions, but if it's too much… I dunno. I get this pressure inside of me, like I did something bad. It comes with a shitload of shame, too, because I couldn't control myself and ate *too much*. Ergo, to avoid that I eat the portion size I feel is appropriate. Not the one Mom puts out for me.

Obviously those sensations are alien to my mom. "Oh, I *would* think you weren't feeling very well when you're not eating, Everly." She drops the backpack next to the shoe rack and crosses her arms in front of her chest. "*Again?* Are we back to this again?

I thought we were over the hump with that. You're going to therapy, you realized how wrong your behavior was—how unhealthy and dangerous—and now you're doing it again? After a few days of school?" She jabs a finger at the backpack, as if that old thing was responsible for my actions.

"Mom—"

"Don't *Mom* me, Everly! This is exactly what Dad was worried about when I let you return to your old school: your old patterns!"

"So, wait, are you mad at me for not eating or mad that I make you look bad in front of Dad?"

She glares at me. "I care about his opinion way less than about your health: You have to eat!"

"I am eating—"

"Oh, please. I'm watching you for whatever little bite it is you're eating. Don't tell me you've had much lunch. Did you?"

"I—"

"So, nothing. As I thought. And I checked the school menu. They served Bosco Sticks today."

Oh, come on! "And you're telling me that's healthier? Eating Bosco Sticks?" Because Bosco Sticks aren't exactly healthy. Are they delicious? Do I love them? Heck, yeah! Should I eat them? Heck, no! They're filled with liquid cheese and a myriad of calories!

Mom rams the door into the lock behind me. God forbid the neighbors hear us argue or something. "I'm telling you eating *something* is healthier than eating *nothing*. The old Everly would've had a double serving today."

Ouch. Tears shoot into my eyes so fast, I have to blink to keep them from falling. The old Everly, the one Mom refers to, is fourteen and not yet on TeeVee. She's a *healthy eater*, as Mom would say, or a chunky monkey, as my Grandma would. She's the one nobody sees at school. The one whom Ford never would've talked to. The one who became Beverly Bacon after the brunch on our eighth grade field trip.

I don't want to be her again—ever.

Sucking a shaky breath in I straighten up. Easier to pretend I'm not rattled by her low blow. "I'm not the old Everly, Mom. Things happened. I changed—"

Mom's angry frown melts into a visage of pity, and all of a sudden, her voice changes from snide to soft and caring. "I know, honey, I know. And you changed again. You're not that person anymore." She cups my cheek. "You're not that easily influenceable girl who stopped eating because of what others thought. You're done with that. You've learned their opinion doesn't matter. Ours does. Yours does. Screw them, Everly. So please, don't start falling into old patterns again. You're done with that."

I get a pat on the cheek, another motherly look, and then she drops her hand and turns toward the hallway. "I'm making lasagna for dinner. We can eat early. You have about"—she scans the Apple Watch on her wrist—"thirty more minutes before it's ready. Go freshen up and take care of your homework." And with that, she leaves me standing in the hallway because in her mind, we're done with this conversation.

So, so typical.

Neither Mom nor Dad get it. They've always been skinny. I'm the one who wasn't, for whatever reason. Thanks, genes. And yes, I know all of their actions come from a place of worry, but they don't understand it. To them it's unfathomable how a cookie can't make me feel better but ruin my day. And no, in the beginning I didn't get it either. It just *happened*.

Everything just happened, and once I realized I had a problem… well, I had a problem.

Last week, before Doc Shamus gave me the final thumbs up to return to school, she called it the new normal for my generation—*a mental downwards spiral triggered and fueled by social media leading to anxiety and personality changes.* She told me how I was one of many—somebody she wouldn't have considered at risk for an eating disorder or self-harm if it wasn't for TeeVee's influence on me. Somebody who suddenly found themselves under so much pressure and in so much pain, their mind needed control and relief and took it the only way it could: by controlling eating. By cutting. And while it sounds simplified, like, *oh yeah, it's a common pattern, we see it a lot, social media is at fault*, there is a certain truth to it. Still, I don't think my parents get it.

I slip out of my shoes and tippy toe up the stairs to my room. Maybe it's a generational thing. If my parents had spent one day in my shoes, they would understand. But no, they can't even imagine how my life works, or worked. How much school sucked. How much other kids sucked. Until I found TeeVee, that is. My parents and the Doc condemn it for what happened later, and I get it—but they don't see how it saved me in the beginning. TeeVee gave me a voice. It made me be heard. It gave me power, popularity. It made me see that once you remove the face-to-face interaction, people can like you for who you really are.

I let myself fall onto my bed. Nobody knew who MatrixGirl was, at least in the beginning, but they liked her campaigns on TeeVee, her opinion, and then they grew to like her. Grew to like *me*.

Gosh, I miss that. I miss it so, so much. That sensation of

community, of belonging, of being heard… Of course my parents wouldn't get that. To them, my suicide attempt and fearing whether I was going to make it or not was the hardest part, even for Dad, new family or not. To me it wasn't. Returning to life is harder. Attempting to kill myself was a decision made in pure despair and agony so deep, it cut my soul in two. Feeling the knife on my skin…

I close my eyes and suck in a slow, deliberate breath.

Feeling the razor blade on my wrist felt *good*. A hundred times better than on my deltoid, like I could drain all the sadness and pain out of my body. But yeah, clearly my parents see that differently, and I can't blame them too much for it. I do blame them for their *solution to the problem*, as they call it, their logical solution to take me completely offline, because it protects me from what drove me to try to kill myself. Thanks for that as well, *Spaceman*—but anyway, that's not it. I know the comments are there, especially now that I know about the petition to bring me back, the one Ford mentioned. That thought alone makes me all jittery, because I can't log in and read through these comments! Dang it!

I ball my fists and punch them into the mattress under me. So, so frustrating! I grunt and give the mattress another punch for good measure.

All I can do is lie here and… be.

That's it.

Nothing else to do.

One Mississippi.

Two Mississippi.

Three—

My room is dead quiet.

No purring of a hard drive. No soft hum of a fan keeping said hard drive cool. No pings or alarms to announce new likes, posts, or goals achieved.

It's my room, but it isn't.

I blow out another deep breath and fold my arms behind my head on the pillow. At least my bed is still the same. Not much else is. Somewhen between my suicide attempt and coming back home my mom must've gone through every square inch of my room. Every corner, drawer, or box. Every lousy old backpack, school bag, or purse. Every book, folder, or binder.

Nothing is at it was.

My room used to be painted in the slightest hue of purple, although not much of it was visible thanks to the dozens of certificates I pinned to my walls: TeeVee's *First Campaign, First Win* certificate after I completed my first campaign with them, about three years ago. TeeVee's *Most Supporters For A Single Cause* certificate for having over fifteen thousand people sign my petition to end antibiotics use in rural farming. Their *Rocking-Someone's-World* Certificate for completing the campaign that brought me national attention, improving conditions for incarcerated youth. They and all the others are gone. I haven't dared to ask what she did with them because I'm not quite sure I could control my reaction if she threw them away.

My gaze drifts over the bare walls, now painted white, as if Mom was trying to cleanse this room of its past.

Well, she succeeded. I feel about as much at home here as I did in inpatient psych. Even my books are gone—not my school books, no: my regular good old books, the Harry Potter, The Hunger Games, and Lux Series. Why? I don't know. Maybe Mom doesn't either, and it was her attempt at creating a blank slate for me to start anew. And blank it is all right: the desk is empty, the laptop, iPad, etc., all gone, I think she even cut Wi-Fi on the top floor, just in case I could produce an internet device out of thin air. This is my room, and yet it isn't. What am I supposed to do here? Homework? Sure, because nobody needs internet for that these days. And, just FYI, I did get that done without problems even when I was still on TeeVee. Mom said my online activity distracted me, but I beg to differ. It taught me to prioritize and how to be time efficient. I knew I had to get my homework done, but I also needed to check my posts and ratings. Groom my feed. If you want to be successful at both, you gotta streamline stuff. And I did.

Deep breath in, deep breath out.

Again.

Deeper.

Relax, Ever. Let your mind open up and your thoughts flow.

Deep breath.

Can't believe Ford asked me to the Masquerade. I mean, no way I can go with him. Way too much attention on me, and he's probably just inviting me to be nice—which is nice, for sure. If things were different… If I were a tiny bit more like MatrixGirl in real life… yeah, I'd go with him. I'd ignore everybody else, I'd enjoy myself, I'd maybe even look okay in a dress.

Oh, well. *#OneCanDream*

I stare up at the ceiling. Look at that. My room's do-over stopped where the walls met the ceiling: The cracks are still the same as they were when I was younger. Huh. Looks like the only new ones are in my heart and soul alone. I wonder who put them there. TeeVee? Spaceman? My parents? Me?

Once more: deep breath in. Deep breath out.

Again.

Again.

Boy, how long can you just lie there and breathe? And listen to that: I'm almost out of breath—from breathing. Pathetic. I'm out of breath from breathing, while Fire yesterday… He pulled off that hamster-routine without even breaking a sweat. As much as I can tell at least, with that costume and mask, I mean.

Yeah, that mask. What's up with that? I mean, fine, if he wants to wear it, apparently he's taking wrestling pretty seriously, but he's lucky I'm *#MsOffline* at this point because usually I would've started a petition already, just for fun.

\#

MatrixGirl:
Help me #demask @Fire! Meet the #ManBehindTheMask. All proceeds go to local wrestling school.
#MatrixGirlRocks #PlayingWithFire #BenBulletsWrestlingSchool

\#

I'd post a picture of him as he's flying off the rope in that backflip-thingy of his, all lean muscles and limitless power and energy, and I bet I would've gotten, let's say… five thousand supporters in less than six hours. Huh. Maybe I should've set the goal to ten thousand, just to give Fire a kick out of it.

I grin to myself. That would've been fun. I would've gotten the votes, he'd been surprised—and flattered, of course—he'd have taken off his mask, smiled at me, and maybe we'd—

My eyes pop wide.

Whoa, hold it right there, Everly! Excuse me, why exactly are my thoughts going there? I blow out a harsh puff of air and sit up. Sheesh. Seriously. Where'd that come from? I lean forward and bury my face in my hands. So this is what Doc Shamus warned me about. Not quite the existential malaise she referred to, but my thoughts leading down a rabbit hole I might not expect once I got to spend time with myself and away from the interwebs. Maybe I should call her and tell her she was spot on—ah, forgot: no phone.

One should think at least an old-fashioned flip phone or something would have been okay. You know, to call my shrink in case I need to? To call my mom if I'm in trouble at school? But nope. Mom didn't have—or need, apparently—a phone on her person when she was my age, so I don't need one either.

Ugh. I wish—

There's a knock on my door. "Everly?"

"Come in, Mom." And thanks for knocking-slash-pretending I had a choice in that matter.

Mom opens the door, and I instantly regret not faking I was asleep because she's holding her iPad in her hands. The only reason I don't groan out loud is because it would get me another lecture from both parents, separately, probably. *#ChooseYourBattle*

"Everly, Dad would like to talk to you." She hands me the iPad with a look of pity mixed with satisfaction, and that look… It gives her away. It's not the weekend and Dad's usual call time, so she must have called him, and if Mom called her ex, it can only mean she wanted backup. *#JustGreat*

I scoot up to sitting and take the iPad. "Thanks, Mom. Hey, Dad." Better pretend all is fine. Shortens the agony.

"Everly. How are you?"

"Fine, Dad. How are you?"

"Not quite awake, but I'm getting there." My dad raises a cup and takes a sip. It's what time in Shanghai now? It's the afternoon here, so there it's… early morning, tomorrow? I think? I could ask, but I'd only get a lecture how I should've internalized Shanghai time at this point. And you know what? If I cared, I would've. But I don't.

Dad takes another sip, maybe waiting for me to talk, maybe just oblivious to the awkward silence. He's sitting in his home office, the curtains still drawn in front of the window behind him. If they weren't, I could see a pretty impressive skyline, kind of the only thing I ever see when we Skype. He doesn't take the pad anywhere else in his apartment. He doesn't bring my half-siblings to say *hi* to me, either. Good thing I don't care. They all speak better Mandarin than me anyway, and none of them speak English. Our relationship is *#LostInTranslation*, for sure.

Eventually, Dad sets the cup down again. "I hear you're back in school."

He hears. Sure. He's on Principal Gunn's daily mailing list. I blink, I sneeze—he knows it. Still, I force a smile. "Yes, I am. It's going really well." *Fake it, fake it, fake it…*

"It is? Your mother tells me you're not eating."

Knew it! She told on me! I keep that forced smile up so hard, my cheeks hurt. "Misunderstanding, Dad. She's making lasagna now. My favorite." Or at least, used to be, before I knew how much heavy cream was in it.

Dad nods. "I remember, you always liked that one. Ate more than me already when you were still in preschool." He chuckles, as if the idea of little overweight me was such a highlight in his memories, but alas, at least I wasn't *#TooSkinny* then in their opinion.

He plays with the cup in his hands. "Oh, and I hear you're taking after your old man after all."

Excuse me? I try not to, if I can avoid it. "What do you mean?"

He offers a mischievous grin and eyebrow wiggle that do nothing to make him seem younger but rather more desperate to seem so, wrinkles and grey hair and all. "You're taking up wrestling."

Ah. Of course. "Yeah. School project." My cheeks are about to explode from their smile-workout.

"With a real performance at the end of the semester, I hear."

He hears way too much for my taste. "Not sure if I'm going to do that."

Dad's face falls. "Why not? You always were athletic." *Despite your weight*, I hear, even though he doesn't say it.

"Not my cup of tea, Dad."

Pause.

He looks into the cup as he swirls the liquid in it some more. "Remember how I wanted you to transfer to that school with therapy and supervision?"

I flinch. "Yes."

"I'd still prefer you there, Everly."

Nuh-uh-uh! "You said if I did well in school, I could stay—"

Dad looks up into the camera. "Well, *in school* means in every aspect of it, Everly. And that includes the wrestling assignment. But I know what you think about that boarding school, so…" A triumphant half-smile rises on his face. "Okay then, here's the deal. You show me you can be a part of regular life like everybody until the end of the semester—and I'll back off. But that includes going to school, completing your assignments, *and* performing that wrestling show."

"What?" My jaw drops. "You're kidding, right?"

"Not in the least, Everly. You want to be treated like an adult? Be responsible. Act like one."

I can't believe him. "By performing a wrestling match in front of the whole school? Do you even hear yourself?"

"Ever—"

"And to top it off, in front of the whole school, who all have TeeVee accounts? Do you know what's gonna happen, Dad? Because I do! It's all going to be online the minute I'm done, and I can guarantee that it's not going to be compliments, no matter how well I might do!"

He takes another sip from the cup, stalling. "You're being overly dramatic, Everly."

Somebody, let it rain brains! Dad needs one, *#STAT*. It takes me a good five seconds to calm myself enough to not *really* yell at him. Nonetheless, my voice hardens to stone. "Overly dramatic? Really, Dad? Do you remember what happened a few months ago? Do you?" I hold up my left wrist and with it the slightly pink, jagged remainder of *that* day. Dad flinches, but hey, some people need a visual. "Yeah. Right. That happened because of comments like the ones coming my way if I do this wrestling thing, if you remember. I would prefer to never get back to that emotional state—"

Dad's eyebrows pull down into a V. "Oh, I agree. Here's an outrageous idea: maybe Dr. Shamus could help you with that."

What the...? "Uh, she is?"

Dad grips his cup so tight, his knuckles turn white. "Right. And I'm sure it's going well, especially when she tells me your participation could be better. You're not talking much."

"What?" I ram my left palm into the mattress. "That's doctor-patient confidential—"

"Relax! Do you think she gave me any details? No, she didn't! I asked about my daughter's well-being, as I'm allowed to, and that's all she said!" He sets the cup down so hard the screen shakes.

Keep calm, keep calm… He's just pushing your buttons… I fist the blanket to keep myself from exploding. "I'm talking as much as I'm comfortable with. It's fine. Just let me move on, Dad!"

He picks up the poor abused cup once more and swirls the liquid in it. "All right, then the plan is set. You want to move on and we want you to move on. You show that you can, you stay. You can't keep attendance up, your grades decent, or don't perform—it's the boarding school."

I stare at my father, wide-eyed. How can he not get it? How, how, how? *#DifferentGeneration* "Dad—"

"Everly! Lasagna is ready!" Funny how my mom's yelling can penetrate walls of concrete from the ground floor, but when I cried for her after a nightmare as a kid, she didn't hear it in the room next door. For once, though, I don't mind it.

Dad must've heard it too. At least he rolls his eyes, a standard move when it comes to his and Mom's communication. "No, Everly, discussion time is over. I want you in the boarding school, you don't want to go. I'm giving you a fair chance."

"Fair chance?" Now I do raise my voice, sue me. "Nothing about that's fair—" I snap my mouth shut and lift one hand, partially blocking the camera's view of me. "You know what? Never mind, Dad. Gotta go. Mom's lasagna is ready. Bye."

And *tap*, I've ended the conversation.

Ugh.

Letting myself fall backward onto my bed, I drop the iPad on my chest. It lies there, weighing a ton and making breathing hard.

What an idiotic idea of my dad's. I mean, I know why he's doing it. *#Blackmail.* He's hoping I'll back out and he wins, no matter what I do. I don't wrestle, I go to the boarding school, he wins. I do wrestle, he gets the satisfaction out of me being his mini-me or something, he wins as well.

#Puke.

"Everly! Get down here! *Now!* Lasagna is ready!"

"Yes, Mom," I yell back, then sigh. No escape. This is my life now. Cut off from my social life and forced to comply: wrestling. Eating. As if nobody really cared what's going on inside of me: let's fix the outside and the rest will come! If she eats, she must be doing better! If she wrestles, she must be doing better.

But what do I want?

I—

A slow smile spreads across my face: What *do* I want?

I know what I do *not* want: I don't want lasagna. I don't want to go to boarding school.

Funny enough, that opens a door for me. And the best part? My parents can't complain because they're the ones who wanted me to do this.

#TeenageRebel.

CHAPTER FIVE

#PowerToMove

"That's it, Everly! Attack the ropes. Don't be afraid!" Fire claps his hands twice. "Harder!"

Harder—yeah, right. I'm running Fire's hamster routine from one side of the ring to the other, throwing myself into the ropes and using the rebound to propel me forward. Surprise: it's not as easy as it looks, and dang it, they hurt! Depending on the angle I'm hitting them at, my flank and kidneys, or whatever else I'm hitting, feel like they've been struck with a bat. Ow.

Whose idea was it to train instead of staying at home? And the gym is almost empty at this point. *#BrilliantIdea*, Everly!

We've gone through all kinds of rolls and fall breaks—which was somewhat easy—to a repetition of the clothesline move and are now working on basic ring movements. *#HamsterInAWheel.* Seriously.

"More bodyweight!" Fire yells. "Trust the ropes, trust your

moves. Use them!" He runs into the rope opposite from me and bounces right out again, leading with the right foot as he showed me.

He makes it look so easy.

I lean forward and support my weight on my hands, breathing heavily. "When can I finally throw you?" Because that sounds like fun. More fun than the hamster routine, and way less exhausting. *#FoSho.*

Fire leans himself back into the ropes, spreads his arms, and relaxes, as if he were in a comfy chair. Why his back doesn't hurt like it'd been whipped, I don't know.

"If you give me one minute of good runs, then we can start working on something else." He uses his chin to point at the ropes across from me.

"One minute?" I pant. Aw, man! I'm out of breath as it is—how long have we been doing this? A *million* minutes? Full power, and not half-assing it, as he said?

A mischievous glint lights up in his eyes. "Not enough? Then make it two." He rubs his hands together like an evil mastermind.

I groan. "You're worse than a gym teacher." But I straighten up and start running. Why? Because he thinks I can. Because he doesn't baby me. Because he treats me like a normal person, not like somebody fragile recovering from a myriad of issues, including, but not limited to, an eating disorder, some cutting, and oh, let's not forget, a failed suicide attempt.

"Call me that if you must, but we have to work on the basics before we move to the other stuff, Everly." He claps his hands again. "Faster!"

I throw myself into the ropes with all I got, the recoil sending me out as if I'd been fired by a slingshot. Paying attention to lead with my right foot I give it all the speed I've left in me, but my legs are so heavy, they have a hard time keeping up with what my brain commands them to do. I stumble—

"You got this, Everly! Keep it up!"

I got this—

Another stumble.

Man, it's hard to breathe—

"Come on, come on! Two more! You can do it!"

Ropes—throw myself in—use the speed—

I trip over my feet and fall flat on my stomach, barely getting my hands up in time to not completely *#faceplant.*

And I stay down. Panting. Waiting for the swooshing sound in my ears to tone down. For the world to stop spinning.

"Everly! You okay?" Fire's next to me in a frantic heartbeat, rolling me on my back. "You dizzy? Anything hurt? Are you okay? Everly!" He shakes my shoulders much harder than strictly necessary. "Everly!"

I grunt. "Sheesh, Fire. Ow. I hear you."

He blows out a big puff of air. "Well, thanks for acknowledging that. I was a tad worried after you fell and didn't freakin' move!" He gives my shoulders another little shove, but gently so, before helping me sit up and leaning me against the ring's turnbuckle.

One more deep breath. Feels good. Leaning back is awesome. I hold up a hand. "Just a tad out of shape." It comes out chopped, thanks to my panting.

"I can tell," he deadpans. "Although I'm wondering: when did you eat last?"

I shoot him a glance from under my lashes. Eating? Well… The answer is easy since I used wrestling training as an excuse to sneak out of having Mom's lasagna: this morning, when Mom cooked eggs and watched me eat them. Since then… I scratch a spot behind my ear. "Might've been this morning." *Spot on, Fire, spot on.*

"And nothing since?" He points at the clock hanging at the near end of the gym. "It's almost 7 P.M., Everly. And we've been at it for two solid hours."

Ah, that would be why I feel the way I do. *#RunDry*

I give him an apologetic smile and shrug. "Oopsie."

Fire looks to the ceiling in mock despair. "Oopsie, indeed. Give me a second." He rolls to his side and under the rope out of the ring, landing on his feet. He has such an ease with all these moves, it's fascinating to watch. I used to be like that in judo, when I still had strength, before I lost weight. With Fire, everything is smooth and fluid, like he's practiced a million times, and maybe he has.

"Fire?" I call over as I wave.

"Yeah?" He stops at his gym bag in the corner and digs around in it.

"How long have you been wrestling?"

He grabs something and jogs back over. "Forever. I can't remember not wrestling." The last words come out muffled as he slides into the ring on his belly, then sits up next to me. "Why?"

"Just wondering. You look good." *Wah! #Phrasing!* Insta-heat assaults my face. "Y-You look good in the ring, I m-mean. Your technique. Like, your moves." Crap, my cheeks turn red.

"Ah, sure. My technique," he says with a sly smile and a wink.

Dang it, I brought that on myself. Only way out is forward. *#Counterattack* "Well, I can't really tell anything else because of your mask." I raise one hand and give the flame stitched to the side of his face a small tuck. "What about taking it off—"

"No." He all but swats my hand away. "It stays on." His shoulders turn rigid as he fixes the mask on his face.

"All right, all right." I withdraw my hand and hold both up, like in surrender. "You're taking this pretty seriously." As in *#OverreactingMuch*.

His lips press into a thin line. "Part of the deal. You heard Ben. Anyway. Back to you. Food." He holds up a granola bar. "Not much, but it will give you some energy at least."

Ugh. Granola bar. Full of sugar and calories. "No, thanks—"

"Nuh-uh." Fire opens the granola bar. "You want to throw me?" He takes off his left glove and breaks off a piece.

Do I want to throw him? Duh. "Yeah."

"Good. Then you eat." He holds the tiny piece of granola bar right in front of me and gives it a small, enticing wiggle.

"Thank you, but really, I'm fine. Just a bit winded, but I'm better. See—" I'm about to jump up, but Fire's hand shoots out to rest on my arm.

"Jesus Christ, woman. Don't make it so hard on me. Come on. I can't wrestle you when I have to worry about you fainting on me. One bite." He scoots closer, so that our legs are touching, and holds the piece of food right in front of my mouth. "One. Bite."

One bite. And the way he's holding it it's clear that... Boy, it's warm in here all of a sudden. I swallow dry. "One bite," I whisper, and then I lean forward, taking the granola piece out of his fingers with my lips. My heart hammers like a steam train, so loud, he must hear it.

I'm not looking at Fire as I withdraw and chew. Can't. Too... personal. *#Intimate*

The Adam's apple in his throat bobs up and down. "Actually, I've changed my mind. One more."

All protest dies right off the bat when he breaks off another piece and holds it out for me in the same manner as before. I swallow and take the next bite out of his fingers. A soft sound escapes his lips, and that sound, it brings something to dance behind my navel.

"One more." His voice is rougher than before, lower—and this time I'm braver.

I look up from beneath my lashes, right at him, and hold his gaze as I take the bite. My lips brush over his fingers, and for that split second, I swear his pupils widen and he stops breathing.

To be honest, so do I.

Breathing is overrated anyway. All I focus on is my heart, pumping hard enough to punch a hole in my chest, and I don't think it's because of the exhaustion.

Fire breaks off another bite and feeds it to me.

Another one.

Another.

I don't keep track of the bites, only of his hand, the warmth it brings to my face, and his eyes, his gaze bouncing back between the bar and my lips. It's like a spell I'm under. Take a bite, chew, swallow, repeat. Maybe it's that whiff of body wash adding to the sensation of floating, but man, I'm *#floating*, all right.

Only when he crunches the empty wrapper in his hand is the spell broken. "There you go," he whispers, and while he drops his hand after the last bite, I feel it lingers longer at my mouth than strictly necessary. Or maybe it's just my imagination.

Fire throws the wrapper out of the ring. "Thanks, Everly. Makes me feel better. I can't make you work out and have you break down on me. If it had been any busier, Ben would've been here and I would have been in trouble. Anyway." He wipes his hands on his thighs. "By the way, how come you were back so early? Ben said two classes per week, didn't he?"

I shrug. "Who says I'm going to be back after this one? I might just want to get them out of the way for this week."

Fire chuckles and rubs a finger across his chin. "Yeah, right. If I didn't know better, I'd say you were bitten by the wrestling bug."

"Good thing then that you do know better. Puh-lease." I give an exaggerated exasperated look to the ceiling. "Pro wrestling. I'm still coming to terms with that assignment. I mean, don't get me wrong, yes, so far it's more fun than I expected and I'm sure I'm going to like the judo part of it, but overall… I don't know." As long as I can ignore reality and ignore that at one point everyone in school is going to know and the inevitable is going to happen… then I like it. But not once my higher brain functions kick in and do their best drawing a very realistic picture of what the comments are going to look like, especially if I have to do that performance thing. *#FakeBitch*

Fire's jaw drops in comic overacting. "Oh, no! You wound me, Everly. Full of pro wrestling prejudices."

"I'm not the problem," I mumble. "It's everyone else." Which is what I'm worried about.

"Ah, ye, the unfaithful." He shakes his head. "Believe me, most guys think wrestling is cool. My buddy Ronan and I—" He flinches and averts his gaze.

"Huh?"

Fire recovers with a quick smile. "Never mind. Buddy of mine I used to wrestle with. Not important." He scratches his neck through his mask. "What I wanted to say is that for guys in general, wrestling is right up our alley. Magical realism, if you want to call it that."

"Wow, you're throwing storytelling one-oh-one at me?"

"Well, yeah. Wrote an essay about it in eighth grade, actually. Wrestling takes fantastical elements, like weird and wild acrobatic and over-the-top attacks, and places them in a world of fighting, feuds, and honor. It's the perfect soap opera for guys, I'm telling you." He taps my leg for emphasis.

"Soap opera." Not the phrasing I would have chosen.

"Totally. You know what? Gimme a second." Fire rolls out under the ropes, sprints to his bag and returns—with his phone in hand. "Give me your number. I'll text you some YouTube links for wrestling videos. Look them through, or at least at one or two of them, and tell me what you think." He unlocks his phone, thumbs hovering, waiting.

"Uh..."

"Number?"

Embarrassment floods me as if powered by a tsunami. "I-I don't have a phone right now."

"You don't have—" He looks up from his cell, the same question in his eyes anybody our age would have, like, why the heck don't you have a phone?

I give his hand holding on to the device a little shove. "I just don't have one right now, okay? It's a family thing."

Something flashes in his eyes, gone so quickly, I can't name it before this lips curl into an unhappy line.

#SheCrazyWithNoPhone

"Sorry," I tag on, scrambling for an excuse. "M-My family isn't much into phones. We like to spend more time talking to each other." Blatant lie, of course, but come on, what am I supposed to do? Fire is, right now, the only person who doesn't look at me like that—like I was either crazy or weak or easily breakable. I'm sorry, but telling the truth is not in the cards.

But instead of rolling his eyes or whatever, he simply puts the phone down. "Okay," he says, like it was the most natural thing that I didn't have a phone. He comes up with a quick shrug. "Your family sounds more sane than many. And just FYI, I'm limited to phone use when I'm out and about. Not in school. Not at home. My parents' policy, not mine."

"Really?" I perk up. Normally, I'd say that's crazy because who's gonna post and update their feed only during a select few hours of the day, but maybe, just maybe, I find the idea a tiny bit appealing.

"Really." He smiles at me, and that smile—kind of the only thing visible behind his mask if you don't count the eyes—that smile makes me feel safe in a certain way, because it carries no judgment, no prejudices.

And boy, is that a feeling I haven't had in a long time.

Fire jumps up to his feet, holding a hand out for me. "You know what? Idea. I'll bring my iPad next time and we'll check out some wrestling of the stuff I've downloaded. It'll give you a good idea what you might like to work on. Okay?"

I take his gloved hand and let him hoist me up. "Okay. If you insist."

"I do. And I also insist that we watch that before training, and that you share a smoothie with me. I never finish them; it's a waste." He winks and gives my hand a slight squeeze, and my insides forget which way is up or down.

Still doesn't cause me to miss what's important here. I blink. "Share a—"

"Smoothie. Yup. Healthy stuff. Loaded with vitamins, some protein. Gluten free, lactose free. Just the right thing before a workout. Easy on your stomach."

Sucking in my lower lip, I drop my gaze to the ground, Fire's hand still holding mine in the periphery of my vision. "I don't think I should eat before—"

The hand gets another tuck. "Smoothie, Everly. It's not eating; it's drinking."

Well, drinking is better than eating, but—

"And I make the smoothie myself; it's my favorite one. I call it Powerslam because it's such a great mix and well, you know…" He steps from one foot onto the other. "A Powerslam is also a wrestling move."

The way he says it, a bit sheepishly, a bit shy, and a whole lot cute… The way I could swear he blushes under his mask… I can't help but laugh. What gives? It's a drink. "Well, then. Can't refuse a Powerslam, can I?"

His eyes light up. "No. No, you really can't." He brings my hand up to his mouth for a fake hand kiss. "I'll see you tomorrow then?"

Tomorrow already again? That'll be my third time within—

"Please?" He looks at me from under his lashes, and honestly, what's a girl supposed to do? *#qt*

"Tomorrow. Deal." I curtsy. Seems appropriate with a hand kiss.

His lips quirk up into a satisfied smile. "Awesome. Same time, same place." And with that, he lets go of my hand, steps onto the second rope, and lifts the third up for me to climb through. "See you tomorrow."

"See ya." I exit the ring and walk over to my bag, every muscle sore, but with an odd, light, and slightly bubbly feeling in my chest I can only identify as... I stop dead in my tracks. Wait, is that... Is that *happiness*? I think this is happiness—and ain't that weird? Here? Now? Why?

Fire whistles a tune as he pulls a sweater over his outfit, stretching his lean body through the openings for the head and arms. Fire. How did he do that? I mean, not the whistling or getting dressed, duh, but getting me to feel *#HappyForOnce*.

And as he packs his stuff and I do the same, keeping an eye on him in the corner of my eye, I wonder how he knew what to say. Why he gave a rat's butt whether I ate or not. How he knew I'd rather agree to a smoothie than actual food.

Am I that easy to read?

And why didn't he make fun of me not having a phone?

I wonder why.

CHAPTER SIX

#GymClass

It's my favorite time of the day: PE time.

Yay.

J/k, obvs. I'd rather sit through math again than go through PE, but to be fair, that's because of my issues, not because of the exercise. I used to like PE. Way back. Before Beverly Bacon, before every class became a torture session with judgment, bullying, and self-doubt, before I became thinner and thinner, but felt fatter than I ever was, as if every derogatory glance, every mean comment, every rude gesture put another pound on my body.

Working through the trauma that was PE… Doc Shamus could probably pay off her mortgage from that money alone.

And worse, PE after *#UglyGoKillYourself*? Forget it. A different country—heck, continent—sounds like a good idea right now.

I pull my already long shirt longer and over my butt as I finish my tenth circle run around the indoor court. The others have done almost twice as much, but me… guess I'm still special. Panting like an ancient dog, I stop next to Hazel. "Made it." It comes out chopped, but she gets it.

"Made it—for now."

"I love your optimism. Really do." I bend forward and support my weight on my knees. Only for a second, no more. Sophia took her phone into class with her, and one never knows. I've been running with my chest out and upper body straight, like a Forrest Gump-imitation. Probably looked like an idiot, but what if she took a picture of me running? All ten laps it felt like I was under observation. I could practically hear their thoughts about what I'm wearing, what my body looks like, what an idiot I am… So I ran faster—upright, to look better in case anyone was taking pictures, but I ran.

Which is why I need that *#SecondToBreathe*.

I wipe the sweat off my forehead as Haze points at Coach P. "My pessimism is warranted, oh dear Everly. We've been working on gymnastics. Floor, mainly. I can't say that's where my talent lies, so…"

Ugh. I deflate. Last thing I want to do is roll. Not today at least. Pushing up to standing, I massage my lower back and flanks. "I'm with you there. I'm so, so sore." Somebody laughs behind me, but I doubt that was because of me. I think. I hope.

An evil grin lights up on Hazel's face. "Sore from…" She lowers her voice to a conspirator whisper. "Wrestling? Or… from Fire?"

My gaze whips up to her. "Haze," I hiss.

"What?" She blinks a few times, *#innocence* personified. "Excuse me, he fed you that granola bar by hand, you said. Right?"

Something coils low inside my stomach, turns into

goosebumps and rises higher and higher, until my cheeks heat up. That granola bar…!

"*Right,* Ever?"

I refuse to take the bait. "Yes, he did, but whatever, Haze. No big deal. And FYI, your attempt at an innuendo didn't work."

"Well, too bad, so sad, but you get my point. And no, sure, of course it's not *a big deal,* he fed you that bar. He probably does that to Mr. Langen too, when he's hungry. And I'm sure you're only beet red because of, you know, running. PE." She folds her hands in front of her chest the same way she does when she has bested her brothers at something, proud of herself.

Ugh. Way to go being annoying. "Whatever, Haze. Yes, I'm red because PE, and I'm sore from… working out."

"From wrestling. Say, it, Ever. It's not difficult to pronounce."

Gah! "Yes, from wrestling, you most annoying friend ever." I step closer. Really, no need to announce it to the world any sooner than I have to. "Fire made me go through a few drills, and let's put it this way: after the few minutes on day one, I was sore. Today I am… sorer." Actually, when I got up this morning I was pretty sure I was paralyzed. Couldn't move. Ow, ow, ow. Took me fifteen minutes under the hot shower to get to the point where moving seemed like it could be doable. Of course those fifteen minutes cut into breakfast time, which means Mom was pissed from the get-go today. Beautiful day.

"Everybody, pay attention!" Coach P blows his whistle and the whole class groans collectively. Nothing good has ever started with those words or the whistle. He glares at us, arms propped into his hips, like he is ready to challenge every single student in here. Hint: nobody would dare to. Coach P is a massive human specimen with a tendency for ignoring that we're highschoolers, not fellow participants in his Mr. Universe training drills. "Three groups; you know the drill. Group one: basketball, practice your shoots. I want to see clean technique and good movements. Group two: rope climbing. If you don't have a burn on your palms, you haven't tried hard enough. Group three: over to the mats and floor time; you're with me."

The groan intensifies, although I'm sure we all have different reasons for the complaints. Mine is general. I'd like to not move, please. Three hours of wrestling… ow.

"Come on, Ever." Hazel grabs me by the arm, as Coach P falls into a surprisingly elegant jog toward the mats, considering his size. "You're with me, basketball. If we're lucky, he loses track of time. The first round always takes the longest." Meaning, we're lucky we're not starting with tumbling.

She pulls me past the unlucky groups one and three. I spot Calan jogging over to the ropes. Ouch. He got the worst one right away. I have yet to see him interact with anybody. We share lots of classes, but I've neither heard him speak nor seen him participate in any way. The fact that he is actively taking part in the torture that is rope climbing… Not where I would have chosen to break out of my shell, but to each their own. Like me, he's wearing a long-sleeved shirt and pants—I never wear short sleeves, not since I cut myself for the first time. Now I have another reason to cover up: the scar on my left wrist. I slide a finger under my sleeve and trace the rough, irregular line. Feels weird, because the area closer to my palm is still numb and might stay numb forever, the doctors said. So yeah, those scars are my reason for the choice of outfit, but Calan? Everybody else opted for shorts and tank tops, so I wonder… I mean, I wonder if what happened to his face… Could he look the same on his arms, or anywhere else? What is that anyway? Genetic? No, it looks too… I don't know. The normal left side of his face looks just that—normal. An injury? Burn? I turn toward the basketball court. "Hey, Haze? Do you know why Calan's wearing—ugh."

As if I'd run into a wall, I freeze, the sudden halt and inertia bringing me to a stumble I barely catch.

"Jesus, you all right, Everly?" Sophia puts her phone into the side pocket of her leggings, reaching out for my arm.

"Y-Yes, thank you. Just… tripped." *When I saw your phone aimed at me.*

Sophia frowns. "Don't I know it. PE sucks, right?" Her smile is so warm, I start to sweat.

"Y-Yeah." I swipe a strand of hair out of my face and pick up the basketball Hazel rolled over to me. "Better get it over with." With one small wave at Sophia, I step away from her and closer to Hazel.

She narrows her eyes. "What was that about?"

I spin the ball in my hands. "Nothing."

"Uh-huh. Right."

"She had her phone out and I thought…" No need to finish the sentences. Hazel knows.

"That she took pictures of you?"

I nod. Wouldn't be the first time, but I do remember the actual first time when a picture of me popped up on TeeVee I didn't know had been taken. They posted a screenshot of one of my posted pics next to one from gym class, with that annoying lightning-shaped speech bubble TeeVee adds under every posted picture.

#

Cheering4Lyfe
@MatrixGirl: Expectation and reality. LOL.
#SaveTheWhales #BeverlyBacon #DefinitelyWithFilter

#

It got two hundred likes and thirty-three shares in one hour until I decided to not check the post's progress anymore.

"Assholes," Hazel grumbles under her breath. "Want me to accidentally throw a ball into her face?"

I chuckle. Having a friend like her is great. "No, thank you. I'm not even sure she was taking a picture. I'm just sensitive right now."

"Rightfully so, after everything. We don't need pictures online. No fodder for the idiots." The way she frowns, I know which very specific idiot she means.

My hands still, and so does the ball in my hands. "Is _he_ still there?"

"He?"

"You know whom I'm talking about."

Hazel sighs. Yeah, she does know, just like I knew who came to her mind. "He's there, but I can't say I'm following his activities. I don't get it why they didn't block his account after… you know."

"After he drove me to kill myself?" I can say it out loud at this point. _#Progress._

"Yeah. That." She throws the ball so hard, it bounces off the opposite wall and rolls over to the area where Coach P is working with the poor souls starting with gymnastics.

"The email Dad got from TeeVee when he asked for the email address connected to Spaceman's account, or the IP or whatever, was that company policy was to not give out these things." That was when Dad had flown in from China after Mom had discovered me half-dead. He was furious when he found out what had been going on on TeeVee, and that's putting it mildly. He wanted somebody responsible, somebody to pay, because to him every problem is fixable. And while I have to give it to him for focusing on the right problem, i.e, Spaceman, he still doesn't get it overall. Plus, it didn't lead anywhere. "TeeVee said unless he had a warrant, which Dad didn't, no luck. He thought about going to the police, but then he had to leave, because, *reasons.*" Typical Dad. Swoop in, try to save the day, fail, retreat, leave us alone.

Well, that being said, we're better off alone. Anyway. "They also wouldn't block Spaceman because he was one of many and *his actions were not clearly enough correlated to my suicidality.*" I make air quotes with my fingers.

"Says them. I say, he should be off TeeVee. For, like, ever."

I happen to agree, but… "I'm not surprised. I've been trying to keep him away from my posts for an eternity, and nothing happened." Not that I was the only special snowflake. *#OnlineHate* is a general problem, and TeeVee is not exempt from it, or maybe it's even worse on there. Dissent is encouraged because it's a political platform. People campaign for their projects, and not everybody agrees which projects are worth supporting. It can get pretty heated at times, and yeah, dissent can morph into something else.

Case in point, half of my feed.

"But something should've happened, Ever. It should've! They should have taken it seriously. Should have taken *you* seriously! But no, not even after what he did. What a freakin' asshole. Add that whole grooming aspect, I mean, who does that? Pretends like he's your friend and then stabs you in the back," she adds, shaking her head. "Doesn't matter if it was real or a game to him—"

I hold up a hand. "Don't remind me." Maybe that's why it hit so hard. Moonsaulting_Spaceman was an avid supporter of my campaigns. Fair to say that without him, I wouldn't be where I am now.

Well, that came out wrong.

Suicide attempt aside, I wouldn't have gotten to where I was with TeeVee if it weren't for him: In the very beginning, he shared and brought in hundreds, if not thousands, of new supporters. He commented, he liked, we even DM'd a few times—he was awesome.

#

Moonsaulting_Spaceman
Hey, everybody—awesome cause by @MatrixGirl! Think about chipping in!
#FoodForEveryone #ItsNotWaste #MatrixGirlRocks

#

DIRECT MESSAGE:
MOONSAULTING_SPACEMAN
Thursday, 5:17 p.m.: How do you come up with those ideas of yours? Respect. I like it.

MATRIXGIRL
*Thursday, 5:18 P.M.: *blush* t/y. Just something I'm passionate about.*

MOONSAULTING_SPACEMAN
Thursday, 5:18 P.M.: Seriously. Great ideas!

\#

Yeah. He was awesome.

Until he wasn't anymore. Or maybe he never was. Maybe it was just a game to him.

Like he had split personality disorder or something, the messages changed. Some were normal, like before, and others… weird. Creepy. And when I stopped responding because he really, really creeped me out… Yeah. From one day to the next, the tables turned. Not just one-eighty, but upside down. There were no nice comments anymore, not a single one.

\#

DM:

MOONSAULTING_SPACEMAN
Tuesday, 2:33 P.M.: Can I get your number.

MATRIXGIRL
Tuesday, 2:43 P.M.: No, sorry. You can DM me, though.

MOONSAULTING_SPACEMAN
Tuesday, 2:43 P.M.: You a baby, or what? Don't own a phone?
MATRIXGIRL
*Tuesday, 2:56 P.M.: *eyeroll**

MOONSAULTING_SPACEMAN
Tuesday, 2:57 P.M.: Come on. Don't be like that.

\#

DM:

_MOONSAULTING_SPACEMAN_
Wednesday, 5:44 P.M.: How bout you tell me a little something about yourself?

MATRIXGIRL
Wednesday, 5:45 P.M.: Sure. What you wanna know?

_MOONSAULTING_SPACEMAN_
Wednesday, 5:45 P.M.: Bra size. Lol.

MATRIXGIRL
Wednesday, 5:49 P.M.: Har-har.

_MOONSAULTING_SPACEMAN_
Wednesday, 5:50 P.M.: No, rly. Do you sometimes touch yourself?

MATRIXGIRL
…HAS LEFT THE CHAT…

#

DM:

_MOONSAULTING_SPACEMAN:_
Tuesday, 12:45 P.M.: Send me a picture of your boobs. Bra is ok. Pussy too. NIFOC!

_MOONSAULTING_SPACEMAN:_
Tuesday, 3:32 P.M.: Come on. I supported all your campaigns. A little thakns, plz?

_MOONSAULTING_SPACEMAN:_
Tuesday, 5:11 P.M.: Wow. Bitch. Way to show your thankfulness.

MOONSAULTING_SPACEMAN:
Tuesday, 9:12 P.M.: Fuck yourself.

#

Moonsaulting_Spaceman:
*Gag. Another tearjerker by @MatrixGirl. Know when it's too much.
#OneTooMany #SameOld #MatrixGirlSucks*

desperate_idiot:
Right, dude. #MatrixGirlSucks

JennaTheHyenna:
Yeah. @Moonsaulting_Spaceman calls it as it is.

#

Moonsaulting_Spaceman:
*Yikes. Fat ass. @MatrixGirl needs to watch it. Who dresses like
that?
#SaveTheWhales #MatrixGirlSucks #TakeAHint #WeightWatchers*

JennaTheHyenna:
*That's what I thought! Too much bacon, fatty!
#BeverlyBacon #LeaveSomeForOthers #SaveTheWhales*

#

I sigh. "He's just an example of many, Haze. Every campaign
I ever started, every post I ever made, the trolls are there."

"But he—"

"It felt more personal with him because we had a connection,

I know. At least until he started hitting on me in that weird way." A shudder runs down my spine. Complete failure on my part. Usually I'm good staying away from creeps, but with Spaceman… Once I realized he wasn't who I thought he was the damage was done. "You know, I listened to some of what my shrink said when I was inpatient. She said that him not being able to handle my rejection is his problem, not mine. My mistake was taking this personally—"

Hazel throws up her hands. "Mistake? Come on, Ev—he made it personal! About the campaigns, yeah, whatever, diss them. Not everybody is of the same opinion. But he dissed *you*, as in you, the human standing in front of me! And that's not okay!"

Her outrage is like a soothing cool blanket over the burn Spaceman and the idiot trolls left on my soul. "You're right. It's not. My mistake was letting it get to me, but it's damn hard not to." I pick up a basketball and haphazardly throw it in the general direction of the basket. "You know, the thing with all the bullying is it's always going to be a part of me. How can it not after it drove me to try to kill myself? For my mental sanity, I have to try to forgive them, though. If I hold a grudge, they still have control over me, and I can't have that. The nightmares and PTSD are enough to deal with." I catch a ball Hazel is passing me and dribble it. Half the work is looking busy so Coach P won't notice me.

"Wise words," Hazel comments. "If only—"

"Sup, Ladies?" Ford swaggers over to us, basketball spinning on his right index finger. "Y'all looking good today, like a splash of color on a boring day."

Hazel makes an exaggerated gagging noise. "I'm fine with boring, if it means you'll stop those comments."

"What? My charm too much for you? Everly likes it." He

throws the ball up and catches it with ease and a simultaneous wink at me.

I feel my cheeks heat up. "Uh…"

"Have you given the Masquerade a thought, Everly? I stand by what I said. We'd make a great couple."

He's really-really asking? It's the second time, so… I throw a skeptical glance at him through squinted eyelids. "You mean that?" Because it's weird. The attention, I mean.

He covers his heart with both palms. "Everly. I mean it. Do I look like I'm joking? Actually, let me make it clear to you." He steps closer, wraps me in a tight hug, and whispers in my ear. "You and me, slow dancing at the Masquerade. Maybe there are some drinks somebody smuggled in, maybe not, but we'll have fun." His hand slides down my back and brushes over my butt—

"Excuse me." Hazel pushes Ford's shoulder back with one hand and mine with the other, separating us. "You better tell me that hand only slipped, my friend, because I'm starting to think I don't like you."

Ford's jaw drops in a slightly comical way. "Hazel. Please. You know me. Would I ever?" He makes a *tsk-tsk*-noise with his tongue and rolls his eyes up to the ceiling. "But in any case, sorry, Everly—"

"N-Never mind," I mumble, clenching my butt cheeks. What an unexpected rush of goosebumps erupting from that spot, even though the touch wasn't on purpose. Clearly not. He wouldn't just go ahead and touch me *there*—

"Uh-huh," Hazel says and cocks an eyebrow. *Not convinced*, it says.

Ford ignores her skepticism. "Okay then, back to the Masquerade. Think about it, Everly." He steps back and winks once more, so confident, I envy him for it. Me, on the other hand… I can't help the quick assessing look around. Who has seen us? Oh, like, nobody, only half the class: Sophia, mouth wide open, her hand reaching for something in her pocket, most likely her phone. Alexis pointing at me in a way I'm sure she thinks is inconspicuous while she whispers something into Aluna's ear, and Aluna is staring at me like she couldn't believe it, while Nevaeh, the leader of the everybody-loves-Ford-gang, looks like she ate something sour.

Just like before. The same looks, the same silent judgement, the same girls dishing it out.

Acid rises in my stomach. Too much, too soon. *Way* too much, *way* too soon. *#UnderObservation*

I want their glares to stop. I want them to not look at me, to not—

Nevaeh's high-pitched fake laugh stabs into my brain like a knife. "You don't say!" She covers her mouth like in surprise with fake wide eyes. The next sentence comes out even louder. "Seven thousand people signed that counter petition? Seven *thousand?* What's it called again? *Let MatrixGirl Rot?* Sooo funny, good campaign, really, I—"

Let MatrixGirl Rot? My stomach twists into a figure eight, and it comes with more acid up my throat. There's a counter petition to Bring MatrixGirl Back? Called *Let MatrixGirl Rot?* And *seven thousand* people signed it?

I feel dizzy.

Nauseous.

Can't breathe.

Nevaeh laughs again, and Alexis joins in. "Some people just don't get it, you know? So thick, it's unbelievabl—"

"Shut up, bitch!" The ferocity in Hazel's voice is enough to shut them up. "Come on, Ever. We'll take a break. So long, Ford." She takes me by the hand and pulls me past Ford and some others.

Of course they stare. Of course I see them whisper to each other.

Doesn't make the nausea any better.

Seven thousand people would like me to rot. Seven thou—

"Breathe, Ever. You're not looking well."

"I'm not feeling well, either." I stop halfway to the changing rooms and bend forward, like I did after the run, only this time it doesn't make breathing easier.

It never stops. *They* never stop. I might be offline, but apparently, my legacy continues without me. *Seven thousand* people.

Do they ever take a break and think about what their comments do? What their votes do? Do they—

A group of students breaks out in howls and applause over at the ropes. "Harder! Get him, Arlo!"

My attention is drawn to the commotion—and to Calan up on the rope, almost at the top. That alone deserves some applause because who can climb these things anyway, but that's not what's making the others clap.

Nope.

It's Arlo trying to shake Calan off the rope. The more he flings that bottom end of the rope, the more he jerks and yanks it, the more Calan's hands slide. A group of at least ten others are standing at the bottom, moving out of Calan's potential fall zone, some looking over to the gym mats, where Coach P is helping somebody stabilize from a backwards roll into a handstand, i.e., is being distracted.

Arlo doesn't waste time. He runs in short spurts from left to right, all the while manhandling that rope even more, trying to get Calan to lose his grip. "Come on, Nightmare! Jump! They'll put you in a whole body cast. It'll improve your looks!"

And everybody laughs, while Calan is clinging on to the rope for dear life. How he can hold himself there and not fall is anybody's guess. One hand slides—

"Nightmare, last warning!" Arlo gives that rope the biggest yank yet, and it does the trick.

Calan's second hand slips, and—

"Shit," Hazel hiss-whispers next to me because Calan falls. Not in the spectacular, arm-flailing way, more an uncontrolled slide, him trying to regain control of the rope to no avail. It happens so fast, everyone watching can only suck in a sharp breath—

And then Calan hits the ground with a resounding thud.

"Calan!" My outcry comes simultaneously with Coach P's yell, his voice cutting through the gym's noise with ease. "What the hell do you think you're doing, Bucking?"

Arlo lets go of the rope and steps back, holding his hands up. "Nothing, Coach. Just holding the rope for Calan. Dude had some trouble."

"Right." Coach is wearing his *don't-BS-me* expression. "Of course. Twenty five burpees. Now! Go, go, go!" Coach jabs a finger at the corner of the gym and jogs over to Calan on the ground.

Is he okay?

"Sir, on my way, sir." Arlo salutes, then saunters to the corner for his punishment.

Coach helps Calan up. "You all right, son?"

Calan nods, looking at the palms of his hands. They're red and chafed; I can see that from here.

"What happened, son? What did Bucking do?" Coach lays one hand on Calan's shoulder.

Calan looks at a spot somewhere over Coach P's shoulder. His response is spoken in such a low voice, I can't make it out.

Coach tilts his head. "You slipped. Really. I'm supposed to believe that?" Judging by Coach's tone his BS-detector is definitely working well, because heck, that wasn't a slip! That was an *#AssholeMove*! Never have I liked Coach P more than in this very moment. One look at Calan and everybody should know that boy is athletic. He may be wearing a long-sleeved shirt, but even I can tell there are muscles underneath and he knows how to move. He must, or else he couldn't have gotten up or stayed up there for that long. Coach, Mr. West Coast Universe of somewhen in the nineties, isn't stupid. He knows that too.

Keeping his hand on Calan's shoulder he steps a bit closer to him, saying something in a low voice. For a moment, it looks as if Calan considered talking, but then he gives a short shake of his head instead and drops his gaze to the floor.

Coach P sighs and claps Calan's shoulder. "If you change your mind, you know where to find me. And now go clean your palms and feel free to change. You're done for today." With one more clap, he dismisses Calan and turns to jog back to the gymnastic mats at the other side of the gym.

Good to know at least some teachers are #ProStudent.

Hazel tugs on my hand. "Come on, Everly. We already knew they were assholes. Nothing new." She pulls on me again, but I resist. I can't look away. Just can't. Something in Calan's eyes… that resigned, broken look… it draws me in. I know how he feels.

I know what being at the receiving end feels like. This is how it started for me. School. Everybody's disapproval. The bullying. The spiteful comments. And even though I have seven thousand people hating on me right now while Calan quote-unquote *only* has to handle our students, it makes no difference. Every bit of hate and bullying breaks something in you, no matter if it's one person or a million. Whether they laugh in your face or mock you online, you can feel pieces of your soul dissolve in real time. *#Traumatized4Ever*

As he passes him, David, some idiot from our year, shoves Calan hard in the back. "Fuck off, loser," he hisses, and while the shove doesn't make Calan fall, it does make him stagger. He catches himself, pauses, and stands up straight, his eyes closed, his face frozen in a mask of anger. His hands ball into fists, and my entire body tenses. Is he going to fight back? He clearly could, athletic as he is, yet he takes the names, the insults, without any fight.

But no, one second later, he relaxes his hands, opens his eyes, and walks away from David, who checks for Coach P's whereabouts first before he flips his middle finger. "Go back to Amityville, Scarface. We don't want you here."

Oh, hell—

I'm about to step forward, but Hazel holds me back. "Don't, Ever. Don't." Her eyes plead with me to let it go. David is an idiot, but one with a large following. In our school, not online, that is.

I get what she's saying, but hey, how much worse are a few more haters going to make my life?

Huh.

My shrink would be kind of proud of that statement. Shaking Haze's arm off, I step into Calan's path. "Calan. Hey. Are you—"

Like I slapped him in the face, he looks away from me, drops his gaze to the ground and makes a comically wide berth around me before slipping into the guys' changing rooms.

I stare after him open-mouthed. "Well, okay then." I guess we're not bonding over *#mutualenemies* then.

What an odd boy.

Odd yet living the same type of life.

And somehow, that makes me feel strangely connected to him.

CHAPTER SEVEN

#NotOnTopOfThings

Surviving PE once a week is a challenge; surviving it a second time two days later is no more a given than it was the first time. Since I had to see Doc Shamus yesterday and didn't go to wrestling at least I wasn't too sore during today's torture that is physical education, but my stamina is still in no better shape. Duh, how could it be, right? *#Drained* At least it's over. Thank whomever for small favors.

Hazel points a thumb over her shoulder. She's even sweatier than me, courtesy of running about three times as many laps as I did. "Let's go get changed before we have to help." And by *help*, she means stacking the mats against the wall and collecting all the basketballs scattered over the complete width of the gymnasium, either of which is going to make us late to the next class. In the far back, Calan has been unlucky enough to be roped in by Coach P before he too could flee the scene.

"Maybe we should help—"

"Nuh-uh. I feel I've worked out enough, and you don't need to be marked late, no matter what the reason. Hint hint, your dad?"

"Ugh. Yeah. Gotcha." Any excuse to take me out of school will probably do for him. Way to go overcompensating his absence with oppressive management of my life from afar. I throw one more look at Calan doing his best to maneuver the crash pad closer to the wall all by himself and with his hands bandaged from yesterday's quote-unquote accident. Sorry, man.

We're about to sneak out of the gym into the locker rooms when Ford saunters over. Have to say, he's got that easygoing, laissez-faire attitude down. Maybe that's why he never jumped on board the everybody-against-MatrixGirl-train.

"Everly, my darling." Ford holds his hand up for a high-five. I'm just glad it's not one of those intricate boy handshakes I never seem to get right, so I hit it.

"Hey, Ford."

He holds his hand out to Hazel for a high-five, which she ignores. Shrugging, he uses the same hand then to wipe the sweat off his forehead. His shirt is drenched too. "Exhausting class, huh? Gotta take a shower before class and hope not to be late for Mr. Stephan. I've had detention once already this year thanks to him."

"Ouch. Well, he'll understand. Let him talk to Coach P; he'll tell him you were the shining star today." Gotta pay respects when they're due—Coach P used Ford to show us every single gymnastics exercise we worked on today. From handstand over handstand into a roll to some weird combo that included a backward roll into a handstand that nobody besides Ford could pull off. Maybe Calan, but he only had like thirty seconds before

Coach concluded class.

Ford bows Renaissance-style. "Thank you, my lady. I got assigned gymnastics as my sport in Mr. Langen's health class. Guess it's paying off." He pushes up on his tippy toes and spreads his arms wide, the exaggeration of a ballet dancer, the sweaty shirt clinging to his abs like a second skin, emphasizing every muscle.

"I'd say it is." A slight grin pulls on the corners of my mouth. Not sure if I meant his dancing routine or the abs. Maybe both?

Ford sinks down onto his feet again. "It better. It's not a sport I would've picked, but I guess that was the point. What did you get?"

#OhShit. It's an innocent question wrapped in barb wire.

I shrug and try to shove my hands in my pockets, forgetting I don't have any in these pants, meaning, I look like an idiot. "I… You know, I came in late to the school year." A hot flush steals over my cheeks, spreading way down. Let him make his own assumptions from that statement.

Unfortunately, Ford gets the implication a tad too much. "Wait, don't tell me you got off without an assignment. You lucky bastard, really. Cora has scoliosis *and* gave him a doctor's note, and he still made her pick a sport. Wow." He shakes his head. "The others are gonna be pissed they had to do it if you didn't."

Ouch. And pissed means posts and posts mean nothing good for me. *#DamageControl* "Oh, no, no. Sorry, that came out wrong. I meant, I came in late, so I had to take what was left." Please don't ask, please don't ask…

"Ah, okay. Makes sense. What did you end up with?"

Dang it.

One-Mississippi.

Two-Mississippi.

Three—

"Everly?"

I blow out a harsh puff of air and with it the word I don't want to say. "Pro wrestling." It comes out in an off-pitch voice that makes me wince.

For a moment, I think Ford's going to laugh, but he doesn't. He wiggles his eyebrows at me, though, a twinkle of humor shining from his eyes. "Nice. So you're going to be our new Becky Lynch."

"Huh?"

Hazel elbows me into the side. "A wrestler, Ev."

I come up with a fast and fake grin. "Oh. *Right.* Yeah, working on it."

Ford sucks in his lower lip and gives me a shy glance. "I bet you're gonna rock your outfit. Like you always rock the dress code at the Masquerade. And speaking of... Has the prettiest girl in the year thought about allowing me to take her to the ball?" He bows again, this time complete with one hand pressed horizontally over his stomach and the left held away from his body.

I cringe. Prettiest girl—who is he kidding. Au contraire to Mom's thinking, I'm nowhere close to my ideal weight. Not anymore. "Ford—"

He holds up both hands. "Sorry. I mean, I don't want to be pushy or anything, I just... I dunno, I just wanna know, you know? I was so sure you'd be back in time, I didn't ask anybody else. Didn't want to. So... don't leave me hanging, Everly. Please?" It comes out so sheepish and so unlike Mr.-Football-Star-Ford, and... He hasn't judged me for pro wrestling. Plus, he believed in me coming back, and he waited. Let me savor that for a minute or so: Ford, who could have gone with anybody, waited. For me.

#YOLO, right?

I stand up straighter. Maybe it's time to start a normal life again. "Okay then. Let's do it, Ford."

Hazel's jaw drops. "What the what?"

"Yes!" Ford pumps a fist. "Perfect! We're going to have a great time at the Masquerade, Everly! You won't regret it. I—" He stops, narrows his eyes for a second, and then, quick as lightning, shoots forward and kisses my cheek. "We have only a few more weeks. I can't wait!" And with that, he winks at me and whirls around, vanishing into the changing room together with Arlo.

Like in slow motion, I raise a hand to the cheek he kissed. "Did that… Did that just happen?"

Hazel grumbles. "Which part? The part where he kissed you without consent or where you agreed to go to the Masquerade with him?"

"Both?" My cheek feels the same, but I don't. I'm not MatrixGirl anymore, and yet… and yet Ford wants to go with me. *Me.* He even waited to ask. Waited for me. "I guess I'm going to the Masquerade." With Ford.

"Hmph." Hazel opens the door for me. "Not the biggest fan of Ford, if you remember. He thinks of himself as the GOAT. Doesn't work for me."

I let the changing room door fall into the lock behind me, abandoning Calan to his lonely fate of cleaning up. "I see where you're coming from, and I get it. But you know what? Maybe it's time for me to break out of my regular Everly shell. Just a bit. Before TeeVee, I wouldn't have gone with him—"

"And he wouldn't have asked."

"Maybe. But he did now. He noticed me after my fame. I think that's worth a shot." Maybe there is a *#LifeAfterTeeVee*.

After humiliation. After bullying. After a failed suicide attempt.

Hazel pulls her shirt over her head and drops it into her bag. "Okay. Sure. Let's give it a try. Just… Just be careful, Ev, okay? I… I don't want him to derail you."

My answer comes out in a whisper. "I don't want to be derailed, either." Because we've seen where that path leads me, and to be perfectly honest, I'm scared to give anybody the power to get me back to that low point in my life.

#MorePowerToMe #DefensesUp

#

Two hours later, PE is forgotten, and so is me going to the Masquerade with Ford.

Why?

Oh, easy: it's lunch time, a.k.a., *#CatwalkTime*

Hazel and I got a table a bit off the beaten path, which might be part of the problem. Nobody would normally look this way, so every glance, every head turned, I notice. Seriously. I feel their stares boring into the back of my head. More like *drilling*, actually.

Maybe it's not even about me, but I can't help thinking it is. I shift in my seat, but the uncomfortable sensation stays. *#WhatsYourProblemNow*

Hazel takes a bite of her pasta. "When are you going back to wrestling?"

"Huh?" I blink twice.

"Wrestling, Everly. You know, that sport that you're doing with that guy who knows how to move, if I'm to believe you?" She waves a hand in front of my eyes. "You in there?"

I swat her hand away. "Yeah, I am. I just hate lunch."

"Tell me something new. What about it?"

I wave a hand at her corn dog and my salad. "Everything. The food, to begin with. Why would I put that in my body? Do you know how many calories that portion has, and how little nutrition? Then the people. Their phones. Hate it. I feel like everybody is connected besides me. I can't keep tabs on anything or anybody, and it's driving me crazy."

Pity lights up in Hazel's eyes. "You haven't been online at all since you were hospitalized, right?"

"Not a single second." And while it was good in the beginning, it started to make me antsy later on. Right now it's completely unbearable.

Haze hesitates for a second, then takes her phone out of her back pocket. "Do you… Do you wanna check something?" She shrugs. "I get where you're coming from. You can have twenty seconds, Ev, no more. Your mom and my mom teamed up against me and told me to never ever let you use TeeVee on my phone, and I won't. I'll open the app and scroll: You wouldn't be using it, as they said."

Hope and fear spring alive at the same time. "Would you let me see?" I really want to check my feed, or what's left of it. Or, wait, do I? What if the comments are still the same? What if they're still as bad? Not even during my suicide attempt, as I was literally in the process of slicing my radial arteries, did they stop.

ChanMan:
Is #BeverlyBacon dead yet? Finally food left for the rest of us in the cafeteria. #UglyGoKillYourself #MatrixGirlSucks

#

Chrunchy18:
*Lol. Good one. Fake. Nobody bleeds like this. #Faker
#MatrixGirlSucks*

#

HarleyMarleyT:
*Good @MatrixGirl. Making the wolrd a better place withpout you.
#death #MatrixGirlSucks*

#

What if that all is still there? Can I handle it? With shaking fingers, I reach for her phone.

"Nuh-uh. I do the scrolling. I don't want to wrestle you to the ground to get my phone back." Hazel lifts the phone up and out of reach for me. "And remember, I have two big brothers. Right now I still know more about wrestling than you."

I kick her under the table. "Shut up with wrestling and unlock your phone, Haze!"

She grins. "As you wish. But..." The grin disappears. "If I don't like what I see, I turn it off and you're not allowed to get mad at me. Deal?"

"Deal." My heart hammers like crazy. Maybe the analogy Doctor Shamus used wasn't too bad: I am an addict, or rather, was. Doesn't mean I'll become addicted again just because I'm taking a peek, right?

Hazel unlocks the phone and swipes until she finds the

TeeVee app. On my phone, it was the only app on the home screen; on hers, it's buried between tons of others. "Here we go. Twenty sec—"

A popup blinks twice on the screen. "Airdrop from— unknown? Who the heck wants to airdrop me?" She looks over her shoulder, and so do I. Nobody seems to be looking at her or us; everybody is focused on their food or friends. *#ThankGodForSmallFavors*

I shake my head. "Maybe it's not for you. What is it?"

"A video, the way it looks."

"Don't take it. Malware, spyware, whatever."

She taps decline and opens up TeeVee. "Agreed. Some people… Here we—ugh." The same airdrop request pops up once more. "Look. They changed their phone's name to *PlzUHAve2CThis*." She turns the screen for me to read it better.

"Really? Desperate much?"

Hazel makes a duck face and smacks her lips. "You know what? I'm curious." And before I can keep her from it, she's accepted the video.

"Say goodbye to your phone." I wave at it. I downloaded a lot before I learned my lesson. Granted, that was off TeeVee, but it still cost me two iPhones before I learned-learned my lesson.

"Hey, I'm saving the number this is coming from in my contacts. If this is crap, I'm telling you, I'm gonna track them down." She lays the phone down between us, and as soon as the transfer is complete, a video pops up and begins to play.

I squint at the screen. "What is that? Where is that?" All I see is white-grey, like—

"A floor? Who sends a video of a floor?" She turns up the volume. "I hear voices. Come over." She pats the seat next to her, and as fast as I can, I slide next to her, pressing my ear close to the phone she holds between us.

"You nailed it, bro," a guy's voice says.

Somebody snickers. "I did, didn't I? Half the year probably thinks I'm crazy."

"Is that… Ford?" I whisper at Hazel.

"Could be." She pinches her eyes closed, focusing on the voices.

The second voice continues. "I'd call it the best plan ever."

"You want to hashtag that?"

They both laugh.

"Totally. Wait till I show up with her at the Masquerade. They'll—"

As if punched in the gut, I jerk. "Masquerade?"

Hazel nods. "Shit. Yes. Could be Ford, and—"

The first guy laughs, about what, I have no idea. I can't think. Can't focus. Can barely hear what they're saying, and not because the volume is too low, but because the blood in my ears is swooshing louder than any river.

"—and I got the stuff already."

"Shit, dude. You're fast."

"Got my sources. You might not need it. She's, like, totally into you. But if you do, they say she'll be completely willing and out of it for at least two hours."

They both laugh again, and each snicker cuts like a knife, way deeper than my razor blade ever could.

"Arlo," Hazel presses out. "That could be Arlo."

I'm too frozen to nod, too frozen to move.

The next person speaking is Ford again. "Should've done that when she was still the queen of TeeVee." He sighs.

"Don't worry, man. Once you post that, you fucking MatrixGirl will get you like a couple of thousands of followers, and then boom. Contracts."

Something claps, like a high-five.

"You know it. I bet you I can get that video without drugs. Would be a pity if she didn't remember. I could give it to her so hard—"

Hazel drops the phone, her face white as the wall, her eyes black bottomless pits. "Holy shit." She taps the screen several times, each and every time missing the icons until she's found the right ones. "Come on, pick up, whoever you are." She scans the room, presumably looking for whoever sent this video, but nobody looks at a ringing phone.

"Fuck!" She hangs up. "Then I'll text them. I want to know where they taped it and if it's really Ford and Arlo." Her fingers fly over the keyboard. "And then—Ever?" She stills, then lays the phone down on the table and wraps one arm around me. "Ever? Hey. Hey. It's okay. It didn't happen. And I wouldn't have let it happen. You know that."

I nod once. I'm numb with fear and panic, so numb, I can't even move. Can't cry. Can't even feel the pain I know should be there.

He didn't want to go out with me. He wanted likes.

And he would have taken them, like me, by force, if necessary.

Nausea rises, bringing bile with it.

The next breath comes in wheezy, and the one after doesn't carry any oxygen at all. He would have drugged me, if I didn't play along. Drugged me, and who knows, raped—

"Ev? Hey. Everly. Come on." Hazel shakes me the slightest bit. "Let's get some fresh air."

No. No fresh air. No walking. No moving. Can't.

I drop my head between my legs, or else I'd faint. Somewhere in the depth of my soul, the tiny, ice-thin layer of trust I started to build breaks open and splits into a thousand pieces.

Yet it doesn't hurt.

It doesn't hurt.

Maybe if you die once, you can't die a second time.

Maybe I'm dead already.

#

"Everly, you *will* eat that bacon." My mom glares at me while pointing at the pile of bacon on my plate. Seven strips. I counted.

Nausea roils inside my stomach. I can't eat seven freakin' strips of *bacon*, of all things, and she knows that. Not today, not any day, but especially not today. I can't. I had two strips already *and* an egg. Both are weighing me down like lead, adding to the stomach-turning feeling Ford brought on. Yet I still ate them. Cut me some slack here!

I move the bacon from left to right on my plate. "Mom, today wasn't a good day at school—"

"Do you want me to tell your father that when he looks over the next doctor's report and sees you haven't been gaining weight, or worse, you've been losing weight? *Oh, she had a bad day at school?* Sure, then we can start the countdown until I have some expensive lawyer's paperwork in the mail, and you'll be in that fancy boarding school in no time!"

I deflate. "No, that's not what I mean. Today—"

She throws up her hands. "Okay then! Everly Aldaire, what's so hard to understand? You're going to eat that bacon, or—"

"Or what? *What*, Mom?" I stand up so fast, my chair topples back, only to be caught by the windowsill behind me. She's losing her patience with me, but I'm losing mine with her as well. She doesn't freakin' listen to me! And she knows it's difficult for me to eat! She knows it! But obvs it doesn't mean she understands it. *#ParentingFail*

"*What, Mom,*" she mocks me and rips the plate away from under my nose and tosses the bacon into the trash. "You know what? I don't care. Don't eat. Whatever. I'm done with this shit. You want to continue killing yourself, go right ahead." She slams the plate into the sink so hard, it shatters. "Fuck!"

Tears shoot to my eyes. This is not my mom. It hasn't been her since my suicide attempt, but this… My throat clogs up. *You want to continue killing yourself, go right ahead.* The first tears spill over and I dash out from behind the table and out of the kitchen.

"Everly! Everly, wait! I didn't mean—"

But I'm up the stairs already, running from her frustration that mirrors my own, her helplessness that feeds into mine, her sadness that tears me down. I'm sick of it. I'm sick of being the one who broke our little family, the one who's still considered broken, the one who can't be trusted anymore.

So, so sick of it.

I slam the door closed behind me and fall onto my bed, tears flowing free. *#TodaySucks*

How can one single day derail me so much? I worked *#FreakinHard* to not let that happen. My defense was up, and still Ford's plan shot right through it and left a mark. He isn't the first one, and he won't be the last, I know that.

#

Josiah_Is_KinG:
Hey, @MAtrixGirl, lets meet and post pictures together. With me, you can double your followers! FBFBFB

#

Kev33:
She's uptight. Idiotic campaign.

#

Tunnel_To_You:
I'd like her tight. Lol. #YoungGirls #CU46

#

Kev33:
Lol. Me, too.

#

There were always disgusting areas of TeeVee I tried my best to ignore. It worked well in the beginning, but obviously not so well later on, when the hits just kept on coming. Meaning, I know crap like this is out there. The world isn't all unicorns and rainbows.

But what Ford did…

Anguish racks through me.

It's always worse when it's personal. That's when the hits really hurt. And that's also why it's so hard Mom isn't getting it. Isn't getting *me*.

A familiar ache and yearning inside my chest crank it up a notch until they're at a solid, scolding burn. I grit my teeth. I'm over it. I don't do this stuff anymore.

NoCuttingNoCuttingNoCuttingNoCutting.

I ball my hands to fists and stuff them under my legs so I won't be tempted to reach for my nightlamp. Won't be tempted to fumble and check for the razor blade taped under it I'm hoping Mom didn't find. Won't be tempted to relieve this pressure, this pain, this weight on me the only way I can.

Because I won't let them do that to me anymore.

CHAPTER EIGHT

#HighsAndLows

Today isn't really a good day, either, even though Ford wasn't in school: out sick. But instead of feeling relieved by his absence, it made me antsier, more nervous, like I was missing something. The urge to run home, to finally take that razor blade, to glide it over my skin… Yeah. That's how freakin' bad today is. So, logically, the safest place I could think of that wouldn't let me cut myself—cue the sarcastic laughter—was Ben Bullet's Wrestling Studio.

#KillMeNow.

Oh, wait—I tried. Didn't work out so well.

I rub one hand over my temple. Can't focus today, even though it's finally quiet in the gym. Everybody else has left about fifteen minutes ago, including Mr. Langen. It's late, probably around half past eight or so. Maybe that's why my concentration is shot. "Fire. Wait, what? I didn't get it." I feel too drained, too used, too… I don't know. *Not well* is the summary.

Across from me, Fire sighs. "Earth to Everly. Are you here today? I mean, I see you, but have you mentally checked out of the gym already?" He reaches forward and knocks two knuckles against my temple, gently.

I swat his hand away and stick out my tongue, a weak attempt to cover up my distraction. "Shut up, Fire. Just show me again."

He cocks his head and gives me a look that tells me he doesn't buy it. "As my queen commands." He bows deeply, a move that looks the way he probably intended it to look—quite mocking, in his costume. As he comes back up, he rolls his shoulders backward. "Collar-to-elbow lock up. I was talking about locking up before a match. The ref starts the match; we start circling each other. When I stop circling, you stop, when I walk forward, you walk forward and we meet. Got it?"

"Yeah." Walking in a circle shouldn't be too hard, even for me, even today.

Fire moves to his right, then his left, and his right again, giving me a thumbs-up as I mirror his moves.

"Nice. That's pretty easy. Now, the actual lock up isn't too hard, either. You'll need that during every match because every match starts like this. It's part of our universal spot—"

"Huh?" Chinese? French? What's he speaking? "Explain, please?"

"I was getting there, Ms. Impatient." He pretends to smack me over the head. "Our universal spot is the first few moves strung together. Kind of your opening sequence. There will be other spots throughout the match, other highlights, so to speak, but the more that's internalized and automatic, the easier remembering the match is."

"Cool." Easier is fine, especially today. I'm not really at my best.

"Okay, onward: step with your left leg forward, and as you shoot in, you wanna grab my neck like this." Fire's gloved fingers fumble for my left hand and place it around his neck, like a one-handed embrace.

Uh—

"Perfect. Grab my neck and pull me in. That's the *collar* part of the lock up. Feel how my body resists the pull, and you do the same." His hand reaches around my neck and pulls. *#HolyMoly*—basically, we're so close, I can feel the warmth radiating off him. His typical Fire-scent is even more pronounced, something warm, like vanilla, mixed with something spicier. And, I mean, that outfit, it doesn't hide much to begin with, but from this close… I clear my throat and look up. Our eyes meet, and I swear his pupils widen. I bet mine do, too, at least if that little butterfly-sensation in my stomach is any indication.

His thumb brushes across the skin of my neck—or maybe that's just my imagination. I can't seem to focus. Fire surrounds me and floods all my senses. He's all I see, down to the grey specks scattered in his dark eyes.

I hear him swallow, then clear his throat. "Like this, right?" He yanks my neck a tiny bit, which prompts me to shake it.

Wake up, Ever! "Y-Yeah, got it."

"Good." He nods. "Now, you wanna have some control and feel how I'm moving. Your other hand can go on my elbow that I have on your neck. Collar-to-elbow lock up." Fire fishes for my other hand across from his body and lays it on top of his.

And just like that, I have him around the neck, one hand on his arm, and vice versa. *#SlowDancing* is what would come to mind in this position, not *#ProWrestling*.

"It's a nice, clean lock up. You feel me move, I feel you move, and nobody's accidentally headbutting anybody."

"Sounds perfect," I squeak. Besides the part where I don't want to wrestle him but stand perfectly still and enjoy his presence. Somebody cue the music, please. *#NotQuiteNormalEither*

"Right? Now, make it look dynamic. First we circle, then lock up and wrestle for the upper hand, so to speak." Fire lets go of me and begins to circle. So what other choice do I have other than to play along?

None.

We do this for at least thirty minutes. Circle, lock up, break the lock up, circle, lock up… It's a mesmerizing rhythm we fall into, and it's a welcome distraction. I don't think about anything but the next move. Not school, not Ford, not MatrixGirl. Nothing is on my mind besides Fire and wrestling. I don't even realize how exhausting it is until Fire holds out a gloved hand for a high-five.

"Awesome job, Everly! You got it down!" I hit his extended palm and he flinches. "Ouch. Still too much energy. Must've had lunch today, huh?" He winks at me.

Not really. "Maybe you're just a bit sensitive today," I tease him. Don't wanna talk about eating. Wrestling is an issue-free zone.

"Maybe. Injured my palms." He gives me excited jazz hands. "Wrestling can be tough."

"I guess so." Although I'm at a loss how you'd injure your palms. Fall break gone wrong? But wouldn't that hurt the wrist? And he's always wearing gloves. Oh, whatever.

I let myself slide down against the turnbuckle until my butt hits the ring and take my sweatshirt off. It's warm in here.

Fire eases himself down into a cross-legged position across from me, so close, our legs are almost touching. Almost. "But seriously," he says. "You're advancing much quicker than anticipated." He reaches to pat my shoulder—and freezes, hovering over my left upper arm, his stare fixed right there, something like disbelief or surprise flickering across his face.

Crap—My shirt! The sleeve of my shirt has ridden up on my left side, exposing the horizontal scars crossing my deltoid. I yank the arm away and straighten out the sleeve so he doesn't see the proof of how much I'm screwed up on the inside. And that's why I don't wear short sleeves, dang it!

Fire drops his hand into his lap, his gloved fingers pumping into a fist and loosening up again. Silence hovers, and with us being the only ones left in the gym, it feels absolute.

After half a minute or so, Fire lets go of a harsh breath and takes my left hand in both of his. "You know," he says, his voice so soft, I couldn't hear him if anybody was working a heavy bag, or on any of the machines in the gym, "sometimes we all do things we're not proud of. At the end of the day, it's how we recover from them, right?" He turns my hand over so my palm faces up—and I swear my heart stops for a few beats as his index finger smooths over the thin scar above my left radial artery.

A small gasp escapes me, one I'm not sure is coming from the fact that his touch feels like he's gliding a live wire across my skin, or the fact that... he seems to know.

He *must* know.

I yank my hand—

And lightning fast, he holds on to it. "Don't," he whispers.

For a moment, it's a tug-of-war, him holding on to my hand,

me pulling back—

"Ever. Don't."

I give in. *Ever.* It's the first time he shortened my name from "Everly" to "Ever." His hold on my wrist eases up, and the same finger traces the scar again gently, with the slightest shake to it.

A series of shivers spreads over my skin. My heart kicks against my ribs as if it were trying to escape. Fire stays silent, moving his finger up and down the inside of my wrist. Such a light touch, but I feel it everywhere in my body. Everywhere.

I can't take my eyes off my hand in his, the proof of my own fallibility looking right at him. I swallow hard, and somehow, the words bubble up from the depth of my soul and escape me before I can rein them in, before I come back to my senses and keep them locked up for all eternity. "I was in a dark place when I did this. A bad place," I whisper.

He closes and opens his eyes once as a means of reply.

My voice shakes. "There was no other option, as stupid as that may sound. But at that point, at that time, it was true."

Even through the mask, I see the look of pain on his face, of pity. "Ever…"

"None, Fire." Tears sting in my eyes. When you think you hit rock bottom, and yet you don't stop falling… it's not something I'd wish on my worst enemy.

Fire stays silent, watching, waiting—and maybe that silence is what breaks the dam. I'm not good at talking. At all. It took me weeks to talk to Doc Shamus at least a little bit after the suicide attempt. I doubt my mom knows all that has been going on. Dad doesn't get it anyway. Hazel knows a lot, but by far not everything. I couldn't talk about it because it's darn hard to talk about, and not just because it hurts to revisit all the pain and humiliation, but also because it hurts just the same that I let others bring me down to a point of—almost—no return. They all asked and prodded and talked and counseled and dug—but nobody did it on my terms. Nobody sat and waited for me. Nobody.

Fire does.

His finger keeps its tender movement. He doesn't get up. Doesn't walk away. Doesn't call me crazy.

He waits until I'm ready.

And it's everything I need.

"I used to be on TeeVee a lot—the app, I mean," I whisper, glad we're alone in the gym. For this, I need privacy. "Kind of an influencer. Over two hundred K followers." I'm not saying my user name. I don't want him to look me up and see my video. Too personal to share with him.

The apple in Fire's throat moves up and down as he nods.

"First it went well. New campaigns, I got lots of support, but then…" I don't know what exactly changed, but it did.

#

King_of_Queens:
Hey, @MatrixGirl. Come out, come out wherever you are!
    #ShowYourself

#

BibiDos:
#MatrixGirl better not be some old fart.
#ShowYourselfOrElse

#

TeeVee doesn't allow real-life profile pics. Their company philosophy is to pay attention to the cause, not the pic, which is why all they offer is the option to choose the color of your monogram, and, if you're high tier, the font. And I didn't post pictures in the beginning. I loved the anonymity, I loved the focus was on what I said, not on how I looked.

But yeah, I got it, people eventually wanted to see the real me. No biggie, right?

#

FANtasticFox:
Given that @MatrixGirl is getting our money with our support, I want to know if she is real. I've lost, like, fifty bucks already to some phony in Oregon. #NeverAgain Can you plz #ShowYourself

#

So I did:

#

MatrixGirl:
Hey, guys, thanks for supporting #MatrixGirl! It's very much appreciated! Hope we can change the world some more, for good! #MatrixGirlRocks #PositiveChanges

#

And I posted a picture of mine below. That was when I was fifteen, almost sixteen, and in retrospect I'd say it marked the beginning of my almost-end.

Funny, right? Funny that I thought I was an influencer, and by definition—and by my paycheck—I definitely was, but I bet I influenced people less than they influenced me.

My shoulders heave up and down with a heavy sigh. "I started to get comments. First, just a few. How I should lose some weight. How my hair wasn't cool. Whatever. I ignored it. Mostly, at least. Then it got worse."

#

Nick_On_Tour_666:
Since when is #MatrixGirl an expert in this? Who the fuck does she think she is?
#LittleGirlKnowsNothing

#

LLK-99:
Hello? Still waiting to see #boobs. Or are they too ugly to show, @MatrixGirl? Lol.
GNOC!
#MatrixGirlBoobs #sex #porn #CU46

#

ForAlllllEternity:
Go an d fucking kill yourself, you moron! Your disguting and a liar!
#MatrixGirlSucks #EndThis

#

Fire's hand clamps down hard on mine. I don't think he notices.

I blow out a puff of air through pursed lips. "Over a couple of months, it got worse. Everything I did was wrong. Everything got picked apart and dissed. It got more and more personal. There was one user..." Dang. My voice breaks, and I have to focus on breathing, or else those tears will fall. "One user, who was the most brutal and hateful of them all." To me, at least. There were others similar like him, but his comments *hurt.* Like I said, it's worse if it's personal, and with him, it was. Doc Shamus said he used classic grooming behavior, building me up for the fall to make himself feel better. "That person started a new hashtag for me. Actually two. One was recycled, *#UglyGoKillYourself,* and the other one was just for me. *#GoDieMatrixGirl.*"

That was the harshest wake-up call of them all. Looking back, it should've been my sign to tell somebody, to get help, but when it happened, I was too embarrassed and humiliated. I felt like they must be right since so many agreed I was an *#UglyBitch* with *#BirdNestHair*

I tried what I could. Controlled what I could. Ate healthier. Then less. Then even less. Changed my hair. Changed my makeup.

But to nobody's surprise but my own, it did not make things better. The hurtful comments kept coming and coming, like waves crashing onto shore, tearing down the dam bit by bit.

Nothing compared to *#GoDieMatrixGirl,* though. The first time I read the hashtag, it was in the middle of school, over lunch. I remember sitting there, disbelieving. Frozen in place, even when the bell rang. Haze was out sick, and I... I couldn't make sense of it. Just couldn't.

"They should've blocked him." Fire sounds raspy. Hoarse. "If he couldn't stop, it would've prevented *this*." My scar gets a tap before he resumes his back and forth motion over it.

"They didn't." But yeah, they should've. "I tried to ignore it, but online hate can really mess with you. And then you start believing it, believing them. *Boom*, enter self-doubt, downward spiral and then… It gets too much." I use my other hand to imitate slicing my wrist. It sounds so simple, so weak. *It gets too much.* But it did. When you're that far down, there is no light. There is no way out. It only gets darker. You only sink deeper. It only hurts more.

Fire closes his eyes for a few seconds, and when he opens them, they shine with moisture. "I'm so, so sorry, Ever. I mean it. So sorry." Pain swings in his voice, pain for me and what I've been through, and that empathy together with the lack of prejudice… it opens my heart to him. *For* him.

"Thank you, Fire. I like to think I'm over it, but… Sometimes I'm not." Sometimes those siren calls are still there, and as much as I hope I can ignore them in the future, I know that's not a given.

He lifts the hand smoothing over my scar and gives the thinner, more superficial ones over my upper arm the same tender touch before he drops it to my wrist again. "I can tell. You know, I… I get it. Sometimes we have to feel pain to know we're still alive. Sometimes we use it to punish ourselves. Sometimes… we see if we can bear the pain because it must mean we're not quite dead yet."

My throat turns dry. "Exactly," I breathe. Exactly. What is his secret to knowing so much? Is it firsthand; has he been there? Is it secondhand; does he know somebody who has? Or is it just that his empathy is measured on a different scale than my parents'?

Fire lets go of a shaky breath. "And sometimes we need something or somebody to take our mind off what hurts us. Sometimes, we need a sanctuary." His fingers weave between mine, the simple touch sending a ripple of warmth along my arm. "This is your sanctuary, Ever. A safe place. No judgment. You hear me?"

My heart stammers from the look he gives me and the words I hear: sanctuary. Fate must've sent Fire to make up for the crappy last year she made me go through. Sanctuary. Kind of mindboggling how much he is my sanctuary already. My timeout from reality. My safe haven. And now, despite knowing my story, he doesn't run screaming for the hills.

He offers sanctuary.

Is it possible to fall for a person you've never truly laid eyes on?

A rush of sensation hits me all at once, as if it were the answer to my question. And if that's the answer… Only one logical step can follow.

My chest rises and falls raggedly while I gather all my courage. "F-Fire? Will you go to the Masquerade with me?"

Fire's eyes pop wide.

I slap my free hand over my mouth. Stupid question. Stupid question! Of course I'm overinterpreting every little gesture and everything he says.

"Masquerade?"

A hot flush steals over my cheeks. Oh gosh, I've ruined it. Ruined. It. "N-Never mind. Just ignore me, I—"

A gloved finger presses ever so carefully against my lips and cuts me off. "Shush. Masquerade, I asked?"

Holy cow. My eyes cross to look down my nose and verify what I'm feeling—Fire's finger against my lips. He smiles, and my tummy flops.

"Masquerade," he says again.

Oh. Right. *Right,* he wouldn't know being from El Marino High, as Mr. Langen said. Oh my gosh, I do find ways to make things even more awkward. "Well, I... I wanted to ask... or, actually, I did just ask you if... if you had the time, if..." Sheesh. Deep breath. "Our school has a ball. Masquerade. Everybody comes in costumes, and I was wondering if you'd like to go with me." My cheeks are burning. *Burning!*

"Masquerade," he repeats, stuck on that one word. It carries so many meanings, depending on how I want to interpret it.

I nod, and his finger drops off. Pity, really. "End of November." Geez, why did I ask? Why didn't I shut up? It had been going so well here, not awkward at all, and I just had to go and make it cringeworthy. Why couldn't I—

"Okay." His voice is soft, and he taps each syllable onto my wrist.

Wait—he said okay? "Okay?"

"Yeah. Okay. I'd love to go with you. It sounds fun."

#OMGOMGOMG! He said *yes!* A wide grin spreads over my face. "You really said *yes!*"

He laughs out. "Yes, I did. Is that so hard to believe?"

Kind of. For both of us, #BeverlyBacon *and* @MatrixGirl. BeverlyBacon would have been without a chance, and MatrixGirl... yeah: What happened with Ford says it all.

Anyway, I'll take it. "Thanks, Fire. I really love the Masquerade; it's my favorite school thing. And not going would've been... sad." And I don't like sad these days. I've had enough of it.

The smile stays, but his voice turns serious. "I don't want you sad. Never wanted that." His throat bobs with a hard swallow. "Anyway." Fire jumps up and brushes his hands off his thighs. "Tomorrow, same time, same place? I mean, I'm here anytime—"

"So I've noticed. I could come over earlier."

"But this late, it's easier to get the ring to ourselves."

"Okay. S-Sure."

"Then it's a plan."

"It is."

He grins. "Good."

"Fire?"

"Yeah?"

"Why are *you* here all the time?"

He freezes with one leg over the rope, one still inside the ring. Then, suave, as if he hadn't stopped at all, he jumps out of the ring. "I'll see you tomorrow, Ever." And there he goes.

This is your sanctuary, he said.

But I'm coming to think that maybe… maybe wrestling is a *#sanctuary* for us both.

#

"And you just asked him to the Masquerade? *You* asked *him*?" Hazel slurps another sip of Coke, never taking her eyes off me.

"Yup." I chew on a slice of my apple I brought for lunch. *#ImEatingMom*

"And he said *yes*?"

I punch her in the arm. "Hey. That was way too doubting. Yes, he said *yes*. It sounded like he really wanted to go."

Her eyes narrow as she slurps louder over the noise of the cafeteria. "And you've seen him how often since?"

135

"Three times." And it hasn't been awkward at all. Unfortunately, there hasn't been any more non-wrestling touching, either, which is really a pity.

"And you've done what, those three times?"

"Wrestling, Haze. A snapmare—"

"Hairgrab—and throw."

"Correct. Some other basic moves like arm drag, which is like a shoulder throw spiced up."

"Wow, Ever." She looks me up and down as much as she can while sitting down. "You're getting your wrestle on. This Fire guy…" Haze lets go of her Coke and drums a rhythm onto the lunch table. "This Fire guy has gotten you good, Ev."

"What?" I almost spit out my water.

She shrugs. "You know what I mean. You're at wrestling so much, I rarely get to see you outside of school. *Before* you were obsessed with TeeVee, now you're obsessed with F—"

I cut her off with a fast flick of my middle finger. "Yeah, no. Don't even go there, Haze." It's *so* not as if I had replaced one obsession with another, come on. I used to be on TeeVee a lot, like, a whole lot, and now I spend that time—

At wrestling.

Ahem. Maybe Hazel's got a point: All those afternoons I spent online, I now spend at the gym. And I can't honestly say I would be that committed if it weren't Fire I was working with.

Heat rises to my face. She's right, dang it. *#DidntEvenRealize*

Hazel acknowledges my gesture with a cool glance. "Don't even go there? Why not? Fire is changing you. You asking him out. You learning wrestling. Most importantly, you having fun. I like it."

I take a sip of my water. Thing is, I like it too. So much that I can't wait to go back to wrestling. To Fire. I don't even mind the smoothie before we wrestle because we're sharing it. Sometimes a little of his scent clings to the cup and then transfers to my skin. I like that, too. In fact, I like a lot of things about Fire. "He *knows*, Haze. He understands me. I told him about TeeVee, and he didn't freak out." *#MajorBonusPoints*

She slurps some more Coke and pushes the tray with her half-eaten spaghetti to the side. "And he still hasn't taken off the mask?"

"Nope." And to be honest, at this point, I don't know if I want him to—or if I need him to. I'm not missing seeing his face. Fire is Fire, no matter if he has a big nose or a small one, acne or not. Maybe that's what I learned from years of TeeVee interaction: It's about the content. The quality. Not looks.

Huh. Maybe I should listen to my own gospel, at least once in a while.

The apple is gone, so I start picking at my orange. *#FruitSaladDeconstructed.*

Hazel tears open a bag of apple slices. "Gotta give it to him; that man's dedicated to his gimmick. And everything you tell me about him sounds *good*, Ev. Meaning, you need to introduce me pretty soon because all our girl-time has mysteriously turned into wrestling time at this point. I want to meet the guy who steals you away from me."

"And you will." Eventually.

Haze sticks out her tongue. "Ah, not ready to share, are we?"

Heat invades my cheeks. "Don't know. Right now it's going so well with him and me alone at the gym—"

"Why are you always alone?"

"We're not *always* alone. Usually some of the guys are still working out when I get there, so we start with warm up and theory, because the ring is taken. Fire says, and he is right with that, if we train at certain times, we're more likely to have the ring to ourselves."

"Uh-huh." She rolls her eyes. "And no chaperone."

"Hey!" I punch her in the arm again lightly. "He's not like that. At all."

"Okay, okay, can't blame me for looking out for you after the whole Ford-debacle. He—" Her eyes pop wide. "Don't turn around."

A spike of adrenaline rushes through my veins. "Why not?" Nothing good has ever started with those words.

"Because guess who recovered from the flu or whatever kept him out of school lately? Ford." She makes a disgusted face. "And gee, is he, like, the devil, mention his name and he pops up out of nowhere?"

I sit ramrod straight, blood swooshing in my ears. "What's he doing?" I haven't seen him since the video. Haven't talked to him. Not that I wanted to—or could have, without a phone, but also, I really, really don't want to see him. Out of sight, out of mind. It's healthiest for me right now.

Hazel squints. "Taking his tray and sitting down with—nope, looking around—ugh." She cringes. "He's coming over to us."

"To us?" I squeak. "No. Not happening. I don't want to see him." I scramble to stand up, banging my knee against the table in the process, but I'm too slow.

"Whazzup, ladies?" Ford sets his tray with spaghetti down next to mine, unaware of the fact that I was trying to flee him.

I freeze. Getting up was a tactical error; it brings me face-to-face with Ford, and way too close as well. So close that he completely misinterprets it.

"Good to see you, Everly." Too late does my panicking brain recognize what his outstretched arms mean. Before I can help it, I'm wrapped in an embrace—an embrace I neither want nor asked for, and for once in my life it fuels me. Powered by disgust and rage, I push him away from me. "Fuck off, Ford!"

I swear, the cafeteria turns silent. Dead silent.

Ford's arms sink down in slow motion as his face mirrors the surprise of most likely half the present student body. *She pushed Ford away? Is she cray-cray?*

My heart hammers at an unhealthy pace. I lift my hands up, palms out toward the guy who wanted to use me. They shake, and so does my voice. "Stay away from me, Ford."

His brows pull down into a V. "What's going on, Ever? Is it something I said?" He's got the caring tone down as he reaches for my shoulder, but I turn away. No touching. Never. Never again.

Hazel stands up too, straight, her arms crossed in front of her chest. "We have bad news for you, bro. Everly is not going to go to the Masquerade with you. Or anywhere, really."

Ford blinks. "Why—"

"Because we heard about your plan. You know, the whole drugging her and potentially date-raping her to post it on TeeVee-thing? A complete turn-off, if you ask me."

If it weren't so sad and, well, disgusting, it would be comical to see the questioning look on Ford's face get replaced by dawning understanding. The moment he gets it is the moment he counters.

"What the hell are you talking about?" He steps back from me, a muscle in his jaw popping.

"You know exactly what I'm talking about." Hazel's voice is calm and strong, stronger than mine would be. "But if you'd like me to, I don't mind repeating the details, especially the ones that involved using date-rape drugs on Everly." The last words cause some head-turning at the tables around us, and for a moment, Ford is quiet, but the type of quiet that comes before the storm.

His lips press into a thin line, and a vein in his temple pops. *That's* when his decision is made, that the opportunity he was working toward is lost. "You bitches are crazy," he calls out, loud enough that Mr. Robles, the teacher assigned lunch monitor duty, perks up and works himself out of his chair. "Should've taken the hint from everybody else, but no, I thought you'd be normal. Fuckin' bitch—"

"Mr. Rodgers! Language!" Mr. Robles sprints over—well, wobbles over. He *is* on the heavier side, and neither athletic nor at least somewhat in touch with current style suggestions. Or maybe he just likes corduroy pants and ill-fitting tie-dye shirts. It's a possibility.

Ford ignores him. "You're still as crazy as when you tried to kill yourself, but you were too stupid to even get that right!" Anger distorts his features. "Oh, and by the way," he adds in a lower voice, only for us to hear. "I'd be careful what kind of fucking lies you're spreading, bitch. It might come back to bite you." He makes a dismissive hand motion, grabs his tray, turns around, and walks away without looking back. But still he's getting thumbs-up from some guys at the tables nearby as he passes until he sits down with Nevaeh and Soph.

Mr. Robles abandons his pursuit, out of breath.

I press both hands onto my stomach. "I'm going to be sick."

Lightning quick, Hazel is next to me. "No, you're not. You're not going to let him see how much he got to you." She takes my hand and squeezes it once. "In fact, I want you to take what's left of my spaghetti and dump it over his head."

That gets my attention. "What?" I can't do that.

"You heard me right, Ever. Come on." Her eyes shoot fire.

"No. No, I can't do that." My knees give in, and I sit my butt back down into my chair. I'd get in trouble. I'm sure somebody would post it. Can't.

Hazel's mouth opens—and then snaps shut again. She sighs but sits down again, reaching over the table for my hand. "I know. I know you can't. It's not your style. I'm sorry, Ev. Got carried away by that asshole."

Misery lodges in my throat, threatening to choke me, but I stay seated.

I won't let them get to me.

Or at least I won't let them see that it does.

CHAPTER NINE

#WTF

"**N**o, sir, we only have audio. More or less." I turn the cell so that Principal Gunn can see the screen and hit *play*. Listening to the whole conversation again, for the umpteenth time, is giving me the *#heebiejeebies*

Hazel is right; going to Gunn is the right step, though. What if Ford tries something like that with somebody else? Plus, at the end, the whole *careful-or-else* one-liner… that sounded like a threat. Ergo, we're reporting him.

It's a risky move, since Gunn might notify my parents—and then that little story might be the straw that breaks the camel's back: hello, boarding school. It's all Dad would need to make good on his threat of sending me there, which is exactly why I'm handling this myself and without his or Mom's involvement. Big Girl pants? I'm wearing them.

Gunn's brows furrow as he listens to the whole thing, even

tilting his head as if it'll help him see more than the camera captured in the boys' changing room. When the recording cuts off, he looks from me to Hazel, then sighs. "And nothing happened. Do I get that right?"

"You mean, nothing of what he said happened?" I blink. "No. Because I'm not planning to go to the Masquerade with him."

The principal nods, looking at Hazel's phone in my hands. "I'm not convinced. This could be anywhere and it could be anybody. Without witnesses to identify those voices, my hands are tied. There is nothing I can do."

Hazel rips the phone out of my hands and shakes it in front of Gunn's nose. "Oh, there is! For example, you could investigate whose number this was sent from!" She dabs a finger at the paused video. "That's the person who recorded it! They are your witness!"

Principal Gunn folds his hands over his considerable belly. "Hazel. Everly. Let me tell you this straight up. One, we're a school, not a police academy. We're not *investigating* anything because two, there is nothing to investigate. This's nothing but showing off. Bragging. Locker room talk. Boys will be boys, no harm done." He makes a dismissive motion with his hands, and my jaw drops.

"No harm done?" I ask, then louder. "No harm done? Do you even hear yourself? Ford planned to use drugs! If—"

"Ms. Aldaire!" Gunn sits up straight and leans forward, glowering at me. "You're accusing a student who has been nothing but exemplary so far of a very serious crime! Who's on the football team! You could ruin the student's career!"

My jaw drops. "His career? *His*—"

He makes a slicing hand motion. "We're done with this. Nothing happened and there is no proof."

"The proof is right there!" Like Hazel, I jab a finger at the phone, but to no avail. "The school has anti-bullying regulations, and—"

Principal Gunn grunts. "You teenagers with your drama. This is nonsense. No bullying. Everything was said in private, not to you. Nothing happened and nothing will happen because this is a safe school. And now leave. You're late for class."

And just like that, we and our worries have been *#dismissed*.

Way to go making me feel inconsequential.

#

Two days later, Ford is far from my mind, and for a reason. No, not because Principal Gunn grew a pair, but because it's not healthy to cling to that stuff. I feel lighter ignoring it. Otherwise, I'd just get mad, or depressed, and that's not better, either. For a while, I considered asking Hazel to start a TeeVee petition, something along the lines of *help to identify student planning a rape*, maybe, but I didn't. Too much drama, and I couldn't live with the backlash surely coming if Gunn's reaction is any indication.

Anyway: wrestling.

Fire switches his iPad off. "And that's kind of what I want to work on with you later and/or tomorrow. Suplex. Power Slam. I'm probably going to use Ben to show you. Easier when you see it first, before you work on it." He extends an arm through the ring ropes and points at Mr. Langen doing his warm-up, some shadow boxing and kicking against a heavy bag. Three other people are working out on the machines in the front of the gym, so considering we're usually alone this late, it's pretty busy.

I kinda miss having Fire to myself today. I mean, we had a great workout, but I feel he's more relaxed when we're alone. Can't fault him for that, because so am I.

Leaning forward, I rest my forearms on my crossed legs. "Can't say I find the idea of you power slamming my teacher unappealing." Although I have other teachers in mind who'd deserve it more. *coughcoughprincipalgunn*

Fire chuckles. "I'll give him a good bump. And then you do it to me." He takes a sip from what's left of his smoothie and plays with the cup in his hands. "You know the basic throws, hip toss, arm drag, etc. It's time to move on to higher and better things."

"Hey, you guys." Sergey, one of the taller wrestlers in this gym, puts his kettlebell down next to the ring in front of us, using a towel to wipe the sweat off his massive neck. "You guys staying in zzere, or can ve ozzers use it, Kel—"

Fire tenses. "It's *Fire*, Sergey. Get with the program. And actually, I was going to have Everly work on something. Give us twenty minutes?"

Sergey shrugs and drapes the towel over his broad shoulders. "Sure. Vy not?" His accent is Russian, or maybe German, I don't know. What did he start to call Fire? Kel? Kelvin? Kelley? Kel-something?

My pondering is interrupted when Fire hands me the smoothie. Clear shift of priorities, because… Oh, that smoothie. Mere seconds ago, Fire's lips were wrapped around that straw. *#Sigh*. I love the ease we have sharing, but man, it brings my hormones to a boil.

"Thanks, Sergey," Fire says, then directs his attention back to me. "Anyway. Suplex. Power slam. You can do it."

Cocking an eyebrow at him, I take a sip from the straw.

"Looks tough."

"It's not."

I frown at him. "Uh, 'scuse me. Not tough? I have to lift you up." And over my shoulder or head, depending on the move, before I throw him. Lifting Fire up isn't quite what I would call easy. That guy is solid. I'm... not.

Fire rolls his eyes. "Ever, you've been wrestling with me for how long now? A couple of weeks? You should know that if I'm selling taking the bump, I'll have to do most of the work. You're gonna see when I do it to Ben. He's definitely heavier than me. It's gonna be fine. Don't worry. Plus, there's *this*." He leans forward from his cross-legged position across from me, takes the smoothie out of my hand, and brushes a gentle gloved finger over my biceps. That touch... dang, it shoots through my body as if I'd touched a live wire.

"There's what?" I squeak, looking down my arm. Unbelievable how such a little touch can throw me off. Fire has that effect on me. Not always, I'd like to emphasize. I don't turn into a raging ball of hormones when we wrestle, for example. But when we're not, it's a different story, like his touch meant more then, during our off-times.

Fire takes a slow, slurping sip from the smoothie, then wraps the fingers of his other hand around my upper arm, a strong muscular grip encircling my not-quite-so boney arm. "This. Muscles, Ever. Muscles! They... They look great on you." He sucks in and bites onto his lower lip.

Air lodges in my throat. The way he said it, his voice deep and low, and the tiniest bit rough... I swallow dry. This might be the first time in two years I'm proud of having gained weight. Because *he* likes it. Maybe it's pathetic, maybe it's a light at the end of the

146

tunnel. I choose to see it as a good thing.

Those two fingers are still around my arm. I suck in my lower lip, just like he did. "Fire…"

"Yes, Ever?" Slowly, like in slow motion, he wraps the remaining three fingers around my arm.

And smooths his thumb over my skin.

That slight touch packs a *#shitload* of sensations, but the dominant one is the need for more. More of Fire.

I see him swallow. "Ever," he repeats, my name barely audible over the noise of the gym. I wish the others weren't here. I wish—

"Uh, Earth to Fire and Everly? Hello?" Out of nowhere, Mr. Langen pops up in front of the ring and waves a hand through the ropes, then uses it to hoist himself up onto the ring, cheeks slightly red from his warm-up, but shirt not yet sweaty.

Both of us startle. As if burned, Fire lets go of my arm and scrambles up to standing. The smoothie cup catches on the rope—

—and the lid tears off, the content of the cup spilling over Mr. Langen.

"Ugh!" Ben tries to jump away, but it's too late. His shirt is already stained in beautiful strawberry-banana smoothie-pink.

"Crap." If it weren't for the mask, I could swear Fire turned red. "So sorry, it was an accident—"

Ben's shoulders slump forward. "I sure hope so. Wouldn't be very nice if it weren't, Fire." He gestures down his shirt. "Oh, well. Not as if I needed it." In one smooth motion, he takes off his shirt and throws it on the ground in front of the ring, leaving him in his wrestling shorts and shoes. Okay, plus elbow- and kneepads. Basically in full clothing, for a wrestler. Still, only because I've seen him a couple of times shirtless do I not think it's awkward.

Okay, well, maybe it is. A tad.

"Anyway." He ducks under the ropes into the ring. "You needed me for a Power Slam, Fire?"

"Uh, yeah, we—I mean, we were starting to… The Power Slam—"

Mr. Langen pats Fire's shoulder. "Easy, Fire. No biggie. Remember the time Nicco puked on my shirt after a belly flop? That was way worse." He winks at him. "But before you move Everly on to the more advanced moves, I need to check how she's doing with the basics. Up, up."

I scramble up to standing. "Wait, what? Now?" I didn't prep anything, I—

"Yes, now. Don't worry, I'm not grading you. I just want to make sure you're safe to advance. You know, I do carry the responsibility for you here, right?" I get a questioning glance from him and nod. "And you *all* know what that means, in *every* regard. Right, *Fire?*" This time, he directs his glance and raised eyebrow to Fire, who drops his gaze.

"Got it," he mumbles.

"Wonderful. Also, as a reminder, the performance is coming up in December, so you better keep practicing. I hear your father is very much… *interested* in it."

I freeze. "How'd you know *that?*"

Mr. Langen shrugs with a mischievous half-grin. "Got my sources. But anyway, let's go." He claps his hands and steps forward into a fighting stance.

Oh. Okay. I guess we're doing this *now*.

Blowing out a big puff of air through pursed lips, I jump up and down twice. I can do this. My stamina is better, and Fire just felt my muscles—*muscles!*

Dropping into my fighting stance, I raise my hands. In the

periphery of my eye, Fire unfreezes from the shock of dousing my teacher in his smoothie. He rolls his shoulders and mimics grabbing somebody. "Okay, Ever. Start with the universal spot, just like we practiced. Lock up."

I nod and burst forward, my left hand seizing hold of Mr. Langen by his neck, my right taking control of his elbow when he does the same to me. Together, we move back and forth, each pretending to be fighting for the upper hand.

"Ropes, then hip toss," Ben instructs me, as if I could forget the moves we've been working on for forever until they became second nature. He lets go of my neck and swings me into the ropes by my arm instead.

I hit them like I was taught and bounce out again—right into Ben's hip toss.

Boom!

I hit the mat with a thud and groan—not because of pain, but because of, well, selling it.

"Nice, Ever!" Fire claps. "Let him lead you up. That's it," he comments as Mr. Langen guides me up by the head. "And… Lock up! You're up!"

Lightning fast, I grab Ben the way I'm supposed to, even tug on him to get him closer, and growl. After all, now it's my turn.

"Nicely done!" Something lights up in my teacher's eyes at the same time as a couple of fast flashes brighten the periphery of my vision. "You've got talent, Everly. Good sell."

For one tiny, split second, I look up to meet his eyes, the praise shining from them lifting me up and making me soar. Then it's back to business. Time to shine. "Thank you. Upper cut," I call out under my breath—and *boom*—I've upper-cutted my health class teacher under the chin. He sells the punch like a pro, stumbling back, holding his mouth, anger flaring in his eyes—and charges me with a roar, arm held high for a clothesline.

The second the arm makes impact against my chest, he pulls it, but I've practiced this enough to throw myself backward and look stunned on the ground.

Fire claps again, this time more enthusiastically. "Nicely done, guys! That's how you do it!" Like with Mr. Langen, I hear the pride in his voice, and I'd be damned if it didn't make me float even more.

Fire walks over to Ben, taking one hand and holding it up. "And the winner is… Ben Bullet! Undefeated against MatrixGirl."

MatrixGirl—

As if punched in the gut, I jackknife up to sitting. "Who told you about MatrixGirl?" I don't want to hear that name here—not here, of all places, not at my sanctuary.

Not from Fire.

Fire's entire body tenses. "Wha—"

"MatrixGirl. My username. Who—" I work my way up to standing, the elation of a tiny completed match against Mr. Langen gone, replaced by jitters and nerves.

Mr. Langen lays a hand on my shoulder. "Everly. You've been saying it." He squeezes my shoulder once.

I blink. "Oh. I have?" When? Odd. Must've slipped out. Shows how much I'm still MatrixGirl inside. *#DangIt.*

"Yes, several times." He gives me a slight smack against the back of the head. "Getting old, huh?" Then, he looks at Fire, with more annoyance on his face. "You, too, apparently. Anyway, both of you, out of here. It's late, and somebody has health class tomorrow morning." That's when I get a pointed look.

I lift up both hands. "I'm gone. I don't want my favorite

teacher mad at me." I bow down to slip through the top two ropes and out of the ring.

"Brownnoser," Mr. Langen calls after me, laughing. "Everly, you go home and think about a ring name. It's about time. Fire, you stay a moment. I want to go over some… stuff with you."

The pause before Fire replies says it all. I guess he's going to get chewed out for that smoothie-incident after all. "Of course, Ben. I'll stay." It sounds resigned.

I throw one last glance at the two in the ring, grab my bag, and make my way out the gym, ducking out from under the gate into the night.

"So. That's how MatrixGirl spends her time these days." The female voice comes out of nowhere in the dark, startling me. *#HeartAttack*

"Geez!" I twitch, a hand flying to my chest, then I look to the right for the owner of said voice. "Nevaeh!"

Nevaeh raises one hand. "Yeah." She's dressed in a skin-tight, all-black outfit, melting into the shadows as she's leaning against the wall of the gym, one hand in her pocket, the other one holding a cell she's looking at.

My heart leaps into my chest. Why is she here? How does she know I'm here? Coincidence, right? She didn't see me. She can't have. She wasn't even inside. Must come up with something—

I give her a haphazard smile. "Hi. I was just… you know, looking for someone. Uh, in there—"

Her thumb swipes over her cell before she turns it for me to see. "You can stop the pretense, Everly." The picture she shows me freezes the blood inside my veins: me. Mr. Langen. In a lock up. Dizziness sweeps over me. Not good. *So* not good. "How did you get that?" I wheeze. It's taken from above, like she used the small windows under the high ceiling.

She pats the bag over her shoulder. "I came prepared. Zoom can be helpful in life." She pauses and gives me a critical onceover. "So now that you don't have your internet fame to help you through school anymore, now you're sleeping with your teacher. You're disgusting."

"*What?*" I all but scream it out. "What the hell, Nevaeh? I'm not sleeping with Mr. Langen. This is for school. It's my assignment—"

"Sure, it is. Which is why Mr. Langen doesn't wear a shirt. And why you're hugging him."

Holy frack. "We're not hug—"

One more swipe of her thumb, and the next picture pops up. From this angle and how she zoomed in and cut it… It looks like I'm about to pull him in, like for a kiss or hug, with my hand around his neck and the other on his arm.

And it doesn't look good.

Honestly, I didn't even notice anymore that he was shirtless once we started, but it's the first thing that springs out from that picture: Mr. Langen, shirtless. Me, holding him around the neck.

"Aw, you look so happy, dear Everly," Nevaeh coos, and she is right. In this picture, I'm beaming at him.

"He told me I did a good job," I whisper. That's why I looked like that: proud.

Yeah. *#PrideBeforeFall*

"*Pft.* Good job blowing him or something." She makes a gagging noise.

The ground opens beneath my feet. No, no. She's making it sound all wrong, and I know where this will lead. The accusations. The rumors. I've seen it before. Nausea sweeps over me. "It's just wrestling, nothing else. Please delete those pictures—"

"You crazy? The others have a right to know why you're getting an A, don't you think? Ford was right when he said there was something fishy about you. If this is what you do with him when people are watching, what are you doing when they don't?" She pockets her phone.

Ford— The others—

No, no, no. I reach one shaking hand out to her. "Nevaeh, please—"

She moves her shoulder out of the way. "Don't touch me, bitch!"

"Hey!" Like an avenging angel, Fire shoots out from under the rolling gate, pulling himself up to his full height in front of Nevaeh. "You have a problem with Everly?" He says it calm and even, but the threat in his voice is thinly veiled at best.

Nevaeh frowns. "Who the fuck are you?"

"Who the fuck cares? I'm the one to tell you to get the fuck off our property, and if you come back here, we will call the police." He steps in front of me, hiding me from view, a welcome distraction from the horror unfolding in front of my inner eye.

Nevaeh huffs. "Sure. Whatever. Bunch of idiots." She pushes off the wall and saunters over to her car. As she gets in, she pulls her phone out of her pocket and wiggles it in the air. "I got what I wanted anyway. Wasting my afternoon following you here paid off. Have fun, losers." She sticks out her tongue and closes the door behind her.

I think that's when he gets it: Fire's eyes widen in what I'd call a comical way if I weren't fighting with every breath against the uprising panic. His body tenses as he sprints forward, but he's too late. She revs the engine and accelerates, showing him the middle finger as she passes him by.

"Fuck!" he yells, throwing two punches to the air. "That bitch. Fuck!"

Little spots dance in front of my eyes. I bend over and support my weight on my knees. Everything's so surreal. Like it's not my life, but someone else's.

Truth is, I knew it had gone too well for a while. Too well with Fire. With life.

And I guess I'll have to pay for it. Something like this was bound to happen. I don't deserve to be happy.

Never did.

#

"Honey, Hazel is here!" Mom sounds muffled yelling up from downstairs. "Fifteen minutes, ladies! School day tomorrow, and Everly, you barely came back from wrestling!"

Hazel.

I look up from the book I was trying to read—*trying* because I couldn't focus. I'm surprised I made it home in one piece because all I kept seeing was that picture of Ben Bullet and me. All I kept thinking about was what Nevaeh will do with it, meaning, I'm trying to convince myself she isn't going to post it. Because no way. We're not friends, but up till now I had no reason to think she'd hate me, either. She's probably going to show it to her clique of friends, and they're going to make fun of me tomorrow in school. Annoying, but survivable. Right?

Right?

TFW you realize you're deceiving yourself: Hazel is here.

At nine-something at night.

That screams emergency until proven otherwise.

I try to swallow, but my throat is too dry. Maybe she just wants some girl time. We have so little of it these days.

Yeah. *#FatChance.*

I hear Hazel stomp up the stairs, turn down the corridor to the right, and—

She barges in, throws the door shut, and leans against it as if she were afraid my mom was going to follow and force her way inside. "Now, usually, I'd complain that you didn't give me a heads-up, but I know you don't have a phone or anything, so never mind. Still, the amount of pop-up notifications on my screen the last hour were kind of heart-attack inducing."

I close my eyes. *Shit.* There goes the hope for girl time. "The last hour. *That* bad." It has begun, no doubt about it, and we're not talking about making fun of me in school. Not only, at least. It feels like the bed I'm sitting on has dissolved into nothingness. Ground gone. *#OneBigSwallow*

She holds her phone up, the home screen filled with pop-ups. "Yeah. That bad."

"Well, at least you're not sugarcoating it." I force a smile, but it's nowhere near credible. Hazel shrugs out of her jacket and lets it drop to the floor. Mom made her take off her shoes already, as always, so she sits down on the bed next to me, her legs crossed. Her thumb hovers over the TeeVee app.

"Let me see." I lean over to her and reach for her phone, my heart skipping a couple of painful beats.

At the last second, she snatches the phone away. "You know what? I'll show you, okay?" Worry coats her voice, and because I know she's only watching out for me, I let her. Doesn't change the anxiety. Actually, it makes it worse. It's out of my hands.

Literally and figuratively.

She opens the app and taps until she pulls up *that* post. Even without seeing the details, I recognize the picture of Mr. Langen and me, and the purple frame around the post, indicating it's a *hot topic* with at least five thousand likes, comments, or supporters.

"Shit," I whisper again, although that word is way too tame: Nevaeh got to five-k in, like, one hour. I don't want to imagine where this post will be when people are up and awake.

Hazel turns the phone for me to see better. Our heads are stuck together over the screen.

\#

HeavenSpelledBackward:
@MatrixGirl making out with her teacher.
#cheater #affair #teachersex #bitch #MatrixGirl #sex
#goodgradesforsex #blowjob #teacherlife #UglyGoKillYourself
#MatrixGirlRot #Zaddy

\#

"Holy crap," I breathe. "How many hashtags did she use?"

"About a million," Hazel growls. "Using *#sex* and *#blowjob* probably brought her post half of the interactions."

My finger shakes as I reach to move the thread up to see more.

\#

GiGo4_44:
Good for that teacher. He's one lucky guy.
#teachersex #blowjob

\#

MightyAndTrue:
Which school? She blow me too?
#teachersex #sex #porn

\#

JRR:
Fuck #MatrixGirl. Actually, fuck me, @MatrixGirl. DM me.
#FuckMatrixGirlForReal

\#

DeadInsideAtHome:
I'd do her too when it's dark. lol.
#BDSM #teachersex

\#

My vision narrows. *Deep breath, Ever, deep breath. No fainting.* "It's… horrible." I keep on reading. Maybe somebody will say it looks like wrestling—

I recognize his handle the split second my eyes fall onto the post and gulp in air.

\#

Moonsaulting_Spaceman:
Matter of time. Surprised it took her so long.
She—

"Fuck." Hazel rips the phone away from under my hand. "You weren't supposed to see that."

But I did. Shock freezes my system to standstill. "Spaceman... he's still there."

Haze shoves the phone into her pocket, as if that could protect me. "Never left."

That's not what I meant. I knew they never kicked him off TeeVee, and if they did, he could have easily gotten on with a different email again, but I didn't know he still took... an interest in me. He got me where he wanted me, down, out for the count. "What... What is he posting?"

"Nuh-uh. We're not talking about that asshole. All we're doing is letting you know that stuff happened on TeeVee, and that you need to brace yourself for that come tomorrow morning. A glimpse—the glimpse you just had—is enough. You don't need more details. Nobody does. They're disgusting. People are disgusting."

"Yeah," I whisper, letting my head hang, smoothing out some of the wrinkles in my sheet with my hand. "I can't believe Nevaeh posted it. What did I ever do to her?" *Nothing* is the answer. *Nothing.*

"Wrong question, Ever. What did you ever do to Ford? I'm telling you, either he put her on this, or she took it on her own to avenge the poor guy."

"Nevaeh said something about Ford when she confronted me at the gym."

"See? It's not about you. I mean, yeah, it is, but Ford's the reason. I'd say because... well, lots of reasons. Because he chose you for the Masquerade—"

"But he only did that because—"

"She doesn't know his plan, does she? Gosh, at least I hope she doesn't. I'm thinking she just knows he didn't choose her, but the weirdo, i.e., you. No offense."

"None taken." Weirdo is one hashtag I don't mind applied to me.

"So, it could be because he didn't pick her, could be because you had the audacity to blow him off—how dare you, right?—or could be because you accused the poor, innocent baby of something he surely didn't do. Pick one."

I bang my head against the wall behind me. "Don't want to. And it doesn't matter. The pic is posted, and by tomorrow morning, the whole school will know." When will it become boring? *Ah, another pop-up about MatrixGirl. Meh. Whatever. Moving on.* Soon? Never? Like, now would be fan-freakin-tastic. "Do you think they'll see it's wrestling? I mean, some of them know that Mr. Langen—"

"Even if they do, it's more fun if they pretend they don't. I wouldn't get my hopes up."

No, of course not. I'm not that stupid. "Yeah."

"Welcome to the age of internet. And yes. Tomorrow… Tomorrow will suck. I'm sorry, Ever. But at least you can brace yourself, right?" She lays a hand on my knee and squeezes.

Like that's gonna make a difference. "Yeah. Sure."

She sighs and moves in to hug me. "Let's meet in front of the school, okay? I'll update you then?"

I nod into her shoulder. "Yeah."

"Cool." She lets go of me and shrugs with one shoulder. "Sorry, I gotta go. It's late."

"Yeah."

"Bye, Ever." Hazel slides off the bed, picks up her coat, and waves.

"Bye."

The moment she closes the door behind her and I hear her footsteps pitter-patter down the hallway, I feel like my sanity, my hold on the world, is leaving with her. Without it, all that's left is this feeling of being stuck, granite on either side, and it's pressing down on me until I can't breathe, can't think, can't *live*.

I hear the front door close downstairs, then the engine of her car start and rumble, and I envy Hazel. She can move. Freely. She can drive away from here, do her thing, and I—

I can't.

Sheblowmetoofuck#MatrixGirlfuckme@MatrixGirlI'ddohertoo whenit'sdarksurprisedittookhersolongsurprisedittookhersolongsurprise dittookhersolong

Curling up into a ball, I let myself fall to the side. Those words on the screen made no sense. They can't be about me—and yet they are. By people who don't know me, but judge me.

Surprisedittookhersolongsurprisedittookhersolongsurprisedittookh ersolongsurprisedittookhersolongsurprisedittookhersolongsurpriseditto okhersolong

The words are razor-sharp, chopping away at my insides until nothing is left but shreds. Every breath I take hurts, like barbwire was stuck in my lung. My heart beats, cramping with every contraction to the point of pain.

I'm hurting. I'm really, really hurting on the inside, and there's nothing I can do to stop it.

I suck in one sharp, harsh, burning, stinging breath—

I mean—

There's one thing—

No.

But—

No.

But the sheer thought alone makes me feel lighter. What a relief it would be. How much better I'd feel.

But still, won't do it.

Won't.

Do.

It.

Breathe.

Breathe.

Breathe.

No use: pressure rises in my stomach until my whole body is one tense, curled-up ball of pain with the weight of the world on my shoulders.

It's all too much.

FucksHerTeacherEatThatBaconSheBlowMeTooFatBitchBlowJob DieMatrixGirlUptightSaveTheWhalesGiveItToHerGoodLetMatrixG irlRotFuckMe@MatrixGirlSixFeetUnderLooksGoodOnHersurprisedi ttookhersolongsurprisedittookhersolongsurprisedittookhersolong—

Stop.

I have to make it stop, or it's going to get worse and worse, and tear me apart, like it did before.

I have to make it stop. *#StopStopStop.*

Slowly, like through a fog, I push myself up to sitting, then reach for my nightstand lamp and turn it over.

Relief floods me. I knew she wouldn't have checked there. Not in that little groove underneath the curled-up power cord.

Fumbling until I get to the tape holding the used razor blade stuck to the bottom of my lamp, I sit up straighter, as if energized.

The blade feels cool between my fingers, a soothing icepack for my soul.

I stare down at it and swallow hard.

Make it stop.

It's the right thing to do. It'll make me feel better. It'll help.

Then I glide the blade over my left deltoid until the skin pops, and warm, red blood spills from my body.

With every drop of blood running down my skin, with every millimeter I cut, I feel the release, like I opened a pressure valve on a hot water tank, and the weight on my soul lessens.

Fingers shaking, I let the hand holding the blade sink and lean back, careful not to bleed onto my bed. My heart stutters once, then finds a steady, calm rhythm when I close my eyes.

Better.

Much, much, better.

#ThankYouOldFriend

Thank you.

#Relapse

Needless to say, I didn't sleep last night. Not a single bit. How could I have? Nevaeh posted that picture on TeeVee, and my life is over. *Again.* A teeny-tiny part of me is holding on to hope that people are going to see it's not what she makes it to be, but experience has shown they'll see what they want to see. *#BeenThereDoneThat*

Still, when Mom checked in on me, like, ten minutes after Hazel was gone, she found me quote-unquote reading a book and in a good mood, because, *puh-lease*: she finds out about this, Dad finds out about this. And if that happens… Yeah.

And: the damage is done. No need to add insult to injury.

As soon as Mom left I gave myself over to worry and speculation again, so really, it wasn't a good night, and it's not a good morning, either.

Mom takes a sip of her coffee when I make it into the kitchen, feeling more dead than alive. *#PunIntended.*

"Good morning, Everly." She regards me over the rim of her cup. "I've got a nice breakfast for you."

My stomach cramps. The last thing I want to do is eat. If I had anything in my stomach, I'd love to shove a finger down my throat and bring it back up. I haven't had those thoughts in a while, but right now, in this very moment, I want that relief that comes with getting rid of all the food, all the ballast. Like I was getting rid of guilt and bad feelings as well. Soothing.

I close my eyes and swallow hard, bracing myself for the fight about to come. "I'm not really hun—"

"Got up early today and drove out to Porto's for you." Lowering the cup, she gives me a warm smile. A peace offering. "Brought you Besitos."

Besitos. My most, most, *utmost* favorite pastry in the world. From Portos. That's, like, twenty minutes from here. One way. And I was so trapped in my own horror show, I didn't even hear her leave.

She brought me Besitos.

Tears spring to my eyes, and granted, maybe it's 'cause I didn't sleep. Maybe it's the fear of what's been happening on TeeVee in the last few hours. But mainly it's because my mom did something so thoughtful and nice for me, and I can't handle it.

I can't handle it.

I'm still trapped between a rock and a hard place, and no matter where I go, I'm going to run into a wall and hurt myself.

The first tears fall, and with them comes a heavy sob before I slap my hands in front of my face to hide. My capacity for holding in emotions has been surpassed, clearly.

"Everly!"

I hear Mom's chair being pushed back, and two seconds later, her arms encircle me, cocooning me, as she rocks me back and forth. "Baby. Shh. It's okay. It's okay. What's wrong?"

What isn't? For a moment, I consider telling her but then dismiss it. She doesn't mean what's wrong with TeeVee anyway, she means what's wrong with the Besitos. *Besitos.* Another sob escapes me, and Mom sighs—the worried sigh, not the annoyed one.

"Hey. What's going on, Everly?" She gently takes me by the shoulders and moves me out of her embrace, for once, no frustrated expression on her face.

It's quite disarming, to be honest.

I sniffle and wipe a sleeve across my eyes. "Mom… Why did you go to Porto's? Why did you have to do that?"

Confusion crosses her face. "I thought you liked—"

"I love Besitos, Mom! I love them! And now they're here, on my plate, and you went through all that trouble to get them, and if I don't eat them, I'll make you feel bad, and I don't want that, but if I eat them, *I* will feel bad because I ate them, and I don't want that, either!" I throw myself forward into her arms.

The last few weeks I did so well. Smoothies. Some more food. I didn't look into the mirror. I didn't go to the school nurse and check my weight on their scale, since we don't have one at home anymore.

No.

I did what I had to to stay strong for wrestling. For Fire.

But I don't feel strong today. At all.

Sobbing spells wrack my body. I don't care that I'm behaving like a baby in my mom's arms. Life is mean, so, so mean. She does something nice for me and I want to appreciate it, but I can't.

I just can't.

I'm such a weak, stupid baby. Useless. A pain. Maybe they're all right about me.

Surprisedittookhersolongsurprisedittookhersolongsurprisedittookhersolong—

Mom sighs once more, rocking me back and forth, gliding one hand over my hair again and again. I feel her kiss the top of my head. "Everly, it's fine. You don't have to eat it. And it's my mistake. I… I saw you ate more, and I figured…" Her shoulders lift and drop. "I figured you might like Besitos. I didn't think it would be so bad."

And how could she have? Yesterday I might've been happy about them, even shared them with Fire.

Today is not like yesterday, though, but she doesn't know that.

I squeeze my arms around her waist. "It's me, Mom. Not you. And I'm sorry. I'm so, so sorry." I'm not sure whether I mean the Besitos, or the last two years.

Mom nods. "Me, too, honey. Me, too."

After that, she stays silent, making me wonder if she, like me, wasn't quite sure whether she meant the Besitos or the last two years.

Or maybe she meant having me in the first place.

#

Way before she sees me, I spot Hazel waiting in front of the school gates. I want to wave, but that would mean others might pay attention to me too, and I'd rather they didn't. The fact that Hazel is anxiously looking around tells me enough attention has been paid to me already.

I rush to her and take her by the arm, dragging her off to the side. "How bad is it?"

She jerks. "Gee, Ev. Wrestling turned you into a sneaky ninja, or what?" Still, she follows me over to where the apple trees are and takes her phone out of her pocket. "We're up to a red frame—"

I suck in a harsh breath. Those words, a punch to the gut. "Red frame?"

"Uh-huh."

Crap. A red frame indicates a *scalding hot topic* with at least fifteen-K interactions.

I guess that answers my question where Nevaeh's post will be when people are actually up and awake.

Working on a hard swallow, I feel over my left deltoid, a little sting shooting through the cut I covered with a Band-Aid this morning. "Not good." It comes out scratchy and hoarse.

Hazel pats her phone in her back pocket. "No. But look, Ever: you're gonna get through this. I'm right here. With you. I won't go anywhere else but stay next to you, all day."

"But your classes—"

"Always wanted to try trig instead of art. I bet Mrs. Rocheleau won't say anything." She winks. "But the point is, you're not alone. Ignore them. TeeVee isn't real life. Those people aren't real life. You are better than them. You. Are. Better."

Nice words, but I still want to run. Need to run. I can't face them. "I think I'm going to go home," I whisper.

"And tell your dad what when he finds out you were MIA?"

Crap. *#GoodArgument*

I deflate. "I want this to be over."

"It will be. Soon. Look, maybe they haven't even seen it. Or not many people have."

Right. Out of fifteen-K. "Nice try, Haze. They've seen it, all right—but why do they believe it? I never got that. Those guys in there"—I point at the school—"they know me. Kind of. They shouldn't just blindly believe what they read on the internet. They taught us that in elementary school!"

Pity shines in Hazel's eyes. "I know, Ever. But they choose to believe it, or at least to run with it, because it's what everybody does. And it's *fun* to them—it doesn't hurt them, does it?"

"No, it doesn't. I just wish they'd pause and think at some point."

Haze hooks me under the arm and guides me to the entrance of the school. "Amen, sister. So let's go. Head up, eyes straight ahead. Engage fake smile."

If Hazel hadn't hooked me under like a clingy octopus, I'd run. Once we're inside, that option is gone, though, unless I wanted to fight myself out of her hold, which is a bad idea since it would mean even more attention for me.

And it's bad enough already.

The first few yards nothing happens.

But then they see me.

And the whispers start.

"Is it true that—"

"... for grades? You're fucking kidding me."

"... is disgusting..."

"I heard she also—"

We pass into the next hallway. *Sneaky looks, hushed whispers, sly finger pointing.*

"Shit. Brave to come here—"

"Poor Mr. Langen. He had to ride that."

"—think she's easy. She'll prob—"
The next hallway.
"Ew. Yuck. She's—"
Boom!
The sound of a body being slammed into the locker makes me twitch, then look to the left.

It's Arlo—Arlo shoving Calan into a locker. Calan's hands are up, as if to defend himself, but all he does is cower behind them.

"Let's keep moving, Ev," Hazel hisses under her breath and speeds up to pull me past that scene.

Arlo shoves Calan into the locker again, harder, then rips off the other boy's cap and throws it on the ground, exposing the lack of hair on his right temple and forehead.

For the shortest of seconds, I'm about to stop Arlo and help Calan.

But I don't.

I should say something. Do something.

But I can't.

Everybody is watching me. I feel their eyes on me, hear the words they whisper.

"Ever," Haze hiss-whispers at me. "C'me on!"

Arlo slaps Calan across the face, and I look away. *I'm sorry. I can't.*

"We talked about this, Nightmare. You—" He picks up on the mood shifting around him, on the noise calming down and the whispers getting louder. The moment Arlo sees me more or less right in front of him, a slow, malicious grin spreads across his face. The hand ready to hit Calan sinks down in slow motion. "Look at that. If that isn't MatrixGirl. Heard you're quite *active* these days. Why not me, huh? Want some of this?" He pumps his hips forward in a suggestive manner. "You know what? We have five minutes before class. You, me, janitor room. Let's go." He grabs my forearm and pulls hard.

"Hey!" I try to yank away, but he's got me good.

Hazel tries to slap him and get his hand off me. "Let her go, you fucking moron! You—"

Arlo laughs. "She gives it out for free—oh, sorry, for grades. But I'll give it to her for free." He yanks harder, his fingers digging into my skin, pinching me.

Calan chooses that exact moment to make his escape and move forward, but instead of ducking off to the side and getting away unscathed, he makes the mistake of bumping his shoulder into Arlo's.

And Arlo is not pleased. "Nightmare, what the fuck? I told you to stay." He drops my arm and instead grabs Calan by the shirt, shoves him into the locker, and rams his fist into the poor guy's stomach. With a grunt, Calan doubles over—

"Ever, come on!" Frantically, Hazel pulls me away from Arlo and the boy who, I could swear, wears a smile as Arlo continues to beat him up.

#

By the time we have health, the sweat stains under my arms have grown to epic proportions. My only saving grace is wearing black. Oh, and sitting in the second-to-last row. That helps too. *#CountYourBlessings*

One would think the last years had given me enough experience and foresight to anticipate how bad this would be, and *#congratulations*, they did. To some degree. But they didn't give me nearly enough strength to survive a day of school under this kind of siege and constant attack. At this point, I can honestly say I have not heard a single word in class besides the ones I should probably ignore but can't.

I thought the girls would be worse, like they were before, but it's the boys showing what pigs they are. Arlo wasn't the only one. Every time we switched classrooms, I heard those comments because they were never meant to *not* be heard. Somebody pinched my butt, and when I turned, they were gone. Some guy the year under us grabbed me from behind and dry-humped me until one of the teachers saw him. Then he ran off, high-fiving his buddies, leaving everybody laughing around me.

Oh, such a hoot.

I pull my long sleeves down my arms, all the way to my knuckles. Seeing my skin now might only tempt me to run home and cut myself, and there's no doubt that's what I'm going to do once I'm home. Nevaeh's post has opened up a wound so big, the only way to close it, as paradox as it sounds, is to cut myself. I need it. Hazel is right; I have to get through this, but the only way I can is by grounding myself.

Quiet and smooth like a fox, Calan slides into his seat to the right behind me. He's gotten his cap back and pulled down into his face, as always. Him and me, we're both trying to hide our scars. I look back, attempting to catch his eye, but he ignores me.

Better than the opposite, I guess.

Mr. Langen enters the room. "Good morning. Everybody, sit, be quiet." There's no sign of the usual easy smile he carries, no matter how annoying the class behaves. His back is straight and his body rigid, his lips pressed into a serious line, which is probably why everybody complies pretty much right away.

Mr. Langen's gaze roams over the class, lingering only for a split second longer on me than on the rest of my classmates. It must be a full minute without a single word of his, but what would normally make us crack jokes or laugh has everybody on edge because of the way he looks at us: disappointed.

After what feels like an eternity, he begins to talk, but not in his trademark fun and exuberant way. More quiet. Subdued.

"By now, I assume you've all heard about *the* post on TeeVee from last night. And just in case you've been wondering, my last twelve hours have been hell. More than I ever thought they could be from one single post. To be honest, those last hours have given me a pretty good taste of what some of you have experienced before." His glance drifts over to me and I sink lower, my face burning. Not because he referred to me and my issues with *#TeeVeeFame*, but because I didn't even stop to think how Nevaeh's post could affect him.

There were two people in the picture, literally, and I disregarded one completely.

Mr. Langen continues. "I've had complete strangers send me hate mail or post death threats on my TeeVee wall—and yes, I do have an account." What normally would have drawn laughs doesn't. The whole class is dead silent. "That alone is very much disturbing by itself, but what is even more disturbing is the fact that other people congratulate me. Call me a stud. Want to know more about *it*. About *us*."

A muscle in his jaw pops. "Now, to everybody who knows me, and I would assume you guys do, it shouldn't come as a surprise that there is no *us*. That nothing happened *between* us—but lots of things happened *to* us. I got woken up at four in the morning and had to explain myself to Principal Gunn, who in return had been woken up by the District Superintendent, whose daughter had alerted him to the post. I can consider myself lucky I still have a job. I can also consider myself lucky I'm not one of your peer group, or else I assume I'd have heard more of the comments and laughter behind my back than I already have. I'm not that old. I'm not deaf. And don't any of you dare get offended because I said that."

Nobody breathes. A needle falling to the floor would be heard into the farthest corner of the room.

Mr. Langen paces in front of the class. "I might have underestimated the herd effect and the stupidity of said herd, though. See, Everly didn't have much of a choice when it came to choosing a sport for her assignment. She ended up with pro wrestling, and while she's been a great sport about it, she was worried from the beginning what you all would say when you found out. I told her not to worry, after all, what could happen? But as I said, I underestimated the effect one single post can have when liked by the wrong people, or when adorned with the wrong hashtags."

He stops his pacing and looks straight at Nevaeh. "You entered a property you weren't supposed to be in. Took the fire ladder to climb up to a window of a building you had no business of being in. Took pictures while we were unaware. That all is wrong to begin with, but what you chose to do after is even worse."

Nevaeh's face is beet red. To her credit, she's sitting upright and looking straight ahead. Not at Mr. Langen, not at us. But also not crying.

Mr. Langen takes one slow, controlled breath in. "You saw us wrestle. You saw there was nothing else going on besides that. Yet you chose to lie, to make up a story, to bully one of your classmates, to play with the lives of two people who had done nothing to you or anybody else. I could have lost my job, but more importantly…" He pauses. "More importantly, you know what can happen to a person when things get out of hand. You've seen it. And yet you chose to disregard all decency, common sense, and safety, and instead threw that same person into an even worse situation."

I blink hard. *Hard.* Tears threaten to fall, but I won't let them. *This*, what Mr. Langen said and how he said it… It gives my soul a crutch to hold on to, to help it clamber up out of that dark, black place it's been hiding in, and peek into the light.

I could've used that a few months ago.

Nevaeh isn't quite so lucky as I am. Her lower lip trembles as the first tears fall. "I-I—"

But Mr. Langen isn't done. "No. I don't want to hear it. You chose to post this picture regardless of the consequences. Was it for the likes? The exposure? The money you made with every like and share and comment? I hope it's worth the fallout from all this." He shakes his head. "We all make mistakes in our lives. Tons. That's not what should define us. How we recover from them, on the other hand, should. Obviously, some of you have not recovered well. Others…" His glance brushes over Calan, I think, then me. "Others are working on it."

Walking over to Nevaeh, he takes a folded red paper out of his pocket. "Nevaeh, you're to report to the principal. Your parents have been notified and will pick you up. I don't know how this will play out, but you might not be returning to our school. I'm sorry." Because he is Mr. Langen, he does actually sound sorry, credibly so. I'm surprised Gunn is actually taking action—ah, right: the District Superintendent is involved, and Nevaeh isn't the school team's football star like others. *#SuccessProtects*

Everybody else is frozen in shock, staring at Neveah, me, or Mr. Langen. There's no whispering. Only wide-eyed glances being exchanged, the non-verbal equivalent of *holy shit*. I shoot a glance from under my lashes at Ford. He might be the only one faking disinterest, staring at his pencil he's bouncing between his fingers.

Nevaeh's face, on the other hand, loses all color. "But—"

Mr. Langen shakes his head. "It's out of my hands. Please take your belongings and see Mr. Gunn."

The whole class watches Nevaeh gather her things with shaking hands, trying to suppress the sobs and failing. Can't watch it. Her misery displayed for everybody to see, it's too close to home. I look over my shoulder—

—directly at Calan staring at me. His eyes lock with mine, and a myriad of emotions flashes through them, each and every single one of them confusing and yet familiar.

And they all make it pretty clear: Mr. Langen's speech about mistakes not defining us wasn't just for me.

It was for Calan as well.

CHAPTER ELEVEN

#Changes

I stuff my books into my locker next to Hazel's. "Today feels different."

She takes out a pack of gum and offers me some. "Whaddaya mean?"

"Not quite sure. Being here feels different." I take one piece of gum and pocket it for later. The whole day has been weird. I mean, it's day two after *the* post, and yesterday I'm being grabbed by the ass and laughed at, Mr. Langen gives his speech—and today... not. Okay, not so much, at least. I didn't expect that. Plus, I've been officially outed with the whole wrestling thing, and so far... nothing.

Still. I sigh. "It feels a bit like when I came back that first day. Under observation." Like they didn't know how to react around me. "Honestly, I'd rather have them carry on with it instead of having to wait for the hammer to fall. Feels like I have to keep my defense up all the time."

Hazel looks over her shoulder, scanning the masses of students roaming the hallways. "When in doubt don't trust them. Agree. Maybe—"

"Nobody has said anything about pro wrestling," I hiss-whisper over to her.

"I guess it's not the shocker of the day, Ever. Told you, people don't mind it as much as you thin—"

"Hey, MatrixGirl!" Some guy forces his way through the students toward me, bumping into people left and right without minding them. He holds something in his cupped hands, carrying it like the Holy Grail, a way too self-assured and arrogant expression on his face. "I'm ready for you to fuck me! Come on! I'll give you the best fuck of your li— ugh!"

The guy trips over some girl's leg and goes flying face-forward onto the ground. Just in time, he gets his hands out to brace his fall, at least twenty condoms spilling out of his cupped hands onto the floor, one of them sliding up to the tip of my shoes.

The students around us stop whatever they're doing and stare—but for once… not at me. But at the girl. The guy. I've seen her around, she's a year under me, him… no clue. Probably too.

She stands there, hands on her hips, shoulders back, like she was fresh from a fight. "Oops." She offers me a hesitant and shy smile as she swipes a strand of dark-brown hair behind her ear. "Didn't see him. So sorry. Really." With a slight shrug, she turns and continues on her way, leaving me staring after her. *Didn't see him*, my butt. That was *#OnPurpose*.

She did that on purpose.

My throat feels insanely tight and my heart does this flutter-thing inside my chest, where it feels like it doesn't pump any blood at all.

On purpose.

She didn't look away. She didn't enable him.

She freakin' *tripped* him.

Something unfurls in my stomach, some kind of emotion I have no experience naming.

But it gives me wings.

Looking down at the condom at my feet and the guy about two yards away from me, doing his best to recover gracefully from his stumble and fall, I make a decision.

I cock one eyebrow, then give the condom a shove with my foot so it slides over to the guy. "I hope you have a healthy right hand, because the only one *giving you a fuck* is you." Making a jerk-off motion with my left hand, I close my locker with my right and walk away, my heart beating like crazy.

Four steps later, Hazel catches up with me. "What just happened here?" she murmurs under her breath.

My heart hits my ribs with every single one of its rapid beats. "No clue," I whisper back. "Absolutely no clue."

Because not only did somebody stand up for me, but most importantly, *I* stood up for myself. Not with the greatest one-liner of all times, but it's a start.

It's a start.

#

"Hey, honey." Before I can even insert the key, Mom opens the door for me and steps aside to make room. "How was school?"

It's been three days since the TeeVee incident, and she knows. Mr. Langen called her and explained before the rumors could make it to her. That night Mom opened a bottle of wine for herself, something she rarely does.

And as far as I know, Dad has not been added to the circle of trust. I'm still here, am I not?

"School was fine, Mom. No problem." I slide out of my backpack and hold it out for her.

And hold it.

And hold it.

Mom's mouth opens and closes as her gaze darts back and forth from the backpack to me. "You know what, never mind," she says. "Take care of your homework and... let me know if you'd like something to eat."

And with that, she leaves me standing in the door and walks back to the living room.

I blink twice.

Shake my head.

Actually slap my cheek.

Yup. I'm awake.

And if I'm not mistaken, that was my mom starting to trust me again.

#

It's around dinner time when I come down the stairs to find Mom sitting on the couch, her iPad propped up on the coffee table in front of her. She looks up and waves me over. "Yes, Everly is here, Jason. Give me a sec." She slides out from between the sofa and table and gestures for me to take her place.

Aw, come on. No, no, *no*. I grimace and hiss-whisper, "Mom, I don't want to talk to Dad." Either he found out himself about *the* post or Mom told him—doesn't matter which one. I still don't want to talk to him. The way Mom looks at me I'd say the risk of Dad blowing a fuse and sending me to that special school he so loves for me is low, but can't say that fact alone would make me look forward to talking to my sperm donor. All things considered, I'm having a good day, and Dad has a way of undoing that. Special talent of his. *#PatronusNeeded*

Mom rubs my upper arms, unknowingly brushing over my not-quite-healed cut deltoid. "I know, honey," she whispers back. "But then he's going to call again tomorrow and the next day until he talks to you, and that's not going to make it any better. You know how he gets."

Yes, I know. It's surprising what a man on a mission can get done over here when living in Shanghai. Still, I don't get why an absent parent gets that much say about me, or why the court seemed to think his presence in my life would be valuable. *#ValuableMyButt*

I grunt and let my shoulders droop forward. "So I better get it over with." I don't care if he hears me.

"You better get it over with." Mom does, at least she lowers her voice. I get an encouraging pat on my shoulder and a little shove toward the couch. Falling into it, I draw my legs up onto the cushion, sitting crisscross-applesauce. "Hi, Dad."

The corners of my father's lips move up into the slightest smile ever seen by mankind. I don't get it. If you're not happy to see me, leave me in peace.

"Hi, Everly. How's life?"

Har-har. Is he really asking that? Okay, two can play this game. "Good."

Pause.

Somewhere in the background, kids are screaming and laughing. Two of my half-siblings, I presume, although I'm surprised they're up at this time, since it's… never mind. I don't care enough.

He sits straighter. "I hear… there was an issue with TeeVee."

That's mildly put, and for a moment I have to think if he might mean something other than *the* post. "Uh, yeah."

Pause.

"And you're feeling okay?"

"I'm fine."

He tries out a wider smile. It doesn't work, even though I'm sure it cost him. Who knows what kind of magic Mom worked on him before I joined the party. "Glad to hear it. Also glad to hear you seem to be doing well in all your classes."

Well, thank you for really taking the time to find out how I feel. Not that I want him to get all worked-up about that stupid post, but uh, hello? *And you're feeling okay*, is all I get? It's not even a question! It's leading the witness at its finest—the expected answer is *yes*! So, so typical: change of topic, back to the important stuff. All that counts for him is school, as always. "Guess you don't have to put me in a boarding school then."

He deflates. "Everly, I'm only suggesting what I think is best for you."

Oh, sure. "How would you know? You don't live here."

"I call—"

"Big, f-ing deal, Dad. That doesn't give you the right to mess with my life."

Dad takes in a deep breath and releases it slowly. "Heard also you're doing well with wrestling. I must admit, I didn't expect that."

Wow, it gets better and better. Not that I didn't know he made that specific requirement to win his argument, but hearing it out loud… "Thanks for the vote of confidence, Dad. I did take judo for several years, you know."

"But that was before you stopped eating to get my attention—"

"*Excuse me?*"

That man outdoes himself with everything he says. I drop my legs off the couch and scoot closer to the edge of the couch and iPad. "You think I stopped eating to *get your attention?*"

He gives me a blank stare. "Well, yes. Maybe there were some other factors—"

"Heck yes, there were, Dad! Newsflash: not everything revolves around you. Actually, nothing in my life does! And please, enlighten me. You think I sat down and thought *aw, I wish Daddy would pay more attention to me, 'cause it's always so pleasant when he does*, and then I gave myself an eating disorder? Uh, no, that didn't happen! Newsflash number two: your opinion doesn't matter that much to me." The opinion of thousands of strangers on TeeVee, combined into one powerful voice of disdain and negativity on the other hand… Enter one of the more unhealthy ways to cope with stress, anxiety, and depression: F50.82 in medical speak, otherwise called an avoidant restrictive eating disorder. Okay, with a tad of F50.02, purging, but it's not my main problem. *#Medical Coding #ImNotJustADiagnosis*

"Ev—"

"Or did you mean my suicide attempt? Trying to kill myself so you'd pay more attention to me? Newsflash number three: had it worked as I intended it to, your attention wouldn't have mattered! But no, I survived, and now I have to listen to you!" *#JoysOfLiving*

There's a loud crash coming from the speakers, followed by a piercing scream and crying after.

Dad's gaze darts over his shoulder then back to me. "Ever—"

I lift both hands. "Never mind, Dad. Saved by the bell. Your real family needs you. Let's not pretend, okay?" I pause, letting my words sink in—but nothing. No *but you are my real family, Everly,* no denying of what I implied.

And man, it makes me mad.

To him, I'm nothing but a task to be checked off, always was—nothing he ever did felt like he genuinely cared about me. It was—and still is—him going through the motions, as if he had a manual on his lap titled *How To Handle Your Teenage Daughter from Afar,* and he was reading off it like a kindergartner without intonation and without understanding.

How is that fair? He has his expectations of me I need to fulfill—but what about my expectations of him?

That thought opens a door in the corner of my mind where I've stored most of my fears—a trap door. It opens wide and drops all those worries about the looming wrestling performance into a trash compartment and locks them in, away from my soul and heart.

A slow smile spreads over my face. Screw him. He thinks he's got me all figured out? Well, this is me extending my mental middle finger to him because he ain't got nothing figured out. "Oh, Dad, before you go? You can look forward to seeing a video of my wrestling performance in December. It's gonna be rad, just FYI." Because what is a pro wrestling performance to a girl who survived a point so low in her life that she wanted to kill herself? To a girl who has been *fucking her teacher,* according to the interwebs? To a girl who's pulling through with the help of her friends?

Hint: it's not the end of the world, no matter what they post. Maybe, if it's not getting old to them, it's at least going to get old to me. I have a *#sanctuary*, and it's both a location and a person.

My heart and soul shake hands and drop into a fighting stance, preparing themselves for the backlash my decision might bring. *Ready*, they shout, and I hear them.

Dad looks taken aback, then catches himself as he pushes his chair back and stands up. "We'll see about that when we get there, Everly. But I hope for your sake you're going to be ready or—"

I reach for the red button and, in one of the more *#ballsy* decisions of my life, hang up on my father in mid-sentence.

Why?

Because I can.

Because I'm done taking what he dishes out.

Because I like wrestling, I like Fire, and both are giving me the strength to face what lies ahead, be that a wrestling match in front of the school or my father's disapproval.

Guess what, Dad? Your opinion isn't the one that matters most to me.

#CaughtOnFire

CHAPTER TWELVE

#Masquerade

I shift my weight from one foot to the other, doing my best to see over the crowd of at least two hundred students, many of them taller than me. "Do you see him?"

Despite the Venetian mask covering Hazel's face, her eyeroll is epic. "No, Ever, I don't. And unless your Fire comes in here wearing the outfit you described to me, I wouldn't have a clue whom to look for."

I deflate. That's exactly my problem, too. "I don't know what kind of costume he's going to wear." We talked about it. I showed him the flyer, he said he got it and that he knew exactly what to wear. Okay, then, gotta let the man do as he plans to and cut him some slack. I'm not about to *#micromanage* Fire. Not when I'm not only happy he's going with me, but thrilled.

Giving my corset-style black dress a tug, I sigh. "Do you think he's going to come?"

"He'd be stupid if he didn't. He'd be missing out on you." She wraps one arm around my shoulder and leans her head against mine, our masks knocking against each other. Both of us chose large, butterfly-style masks with intricate decorations and swirls all over. Mine black, matches my dress, hers red, matching hers. As they do every year, many students went overboard and came in outfits worthy of a true masquerade held somewhere other than a modified high school gym. So far I've seen Venetian joker masks, full-faced golden devil masks—some even with horns—one full-faced cat mask that must've been super expensive, and lots of full-face white, solid Venetian style masks with different decorations. Some of the girls opted for the smaller eye masks, leaving more of their faces exposed, but not me. I'm *#DoingThisRight*. My corset is part, well, corset, part Rococo, like most of the dresses at the Masquerade. I love that it emphasizes my figure while hiding it at the same time, if that makes sense. The most remarkable detail about my dress though is the fact that my arms are uncovered. Translation, that nothing is hiding any of my scars. And the kicker? I don't feel exposed. Talk about personal growth.

I press a kiss against Haze's mask. "Thanks, bestie. If Fire doesn't show, I'll dance with you."

"Puh-lease." She lets go of me. "I'll be busy with the guy over there, the black velvet suit and red bird mask. Who do you think it is?"

I follow her gaze. "No clue. I can tell you he's not Ford. Not wide enough."

She shudders. "Yuck. Yeah, good. No dance for Ford. Or Arlo."

"I don't want to think of either of them." Since Nevaeh got kicked out of school, the others have calmed down somewhat. The school district's lawyers got TeeVee to remove the post, so there's that. Of course screenshots exist, but they're harder to find and bound to be buried under tons of other stuff. *#LuckyMe* I still get stupid comments and whatnot, but less. Or maybe I care less, after Mr. Langen's speech in my support.

Hazel sighs. "Anyway, could be any of the guys. Almost everybody is here tonight."

I'm not so sure. "Do you think… Do you think Calan is here?" I'd love to talk to him. In school he avoids me, and I can't blame him. His social standing is bad enough. Associating with me won't improve it. But here at the Masquerade, we'd both be free to talk. Free-er. Free-ish. But still.

"Calan?" Her voice turns up at the end.

"Yeah, you know… I figured he might want to use the Masquerade—"

"To hide, like you did? Like you do?"

It sounds stupid when she says it like that. "Yeah."

"Ever, he isn't you. MatrixGirl's haters were online; you didn't know who they were. You could come here and pretend everything was fine. Like you this year, he knows exactly who has bullied him, which is like, everybody. Why would he want to do that to himself without a trusted bestie next to his side, like you have?" She bumps her hips into mine.

Up on the stage, Principal Gunn takes the microphone, the first eardrum-splitting squeak of the PA system shutting down all conversations. "Welcome, students, to another Masquerade! As a reminder, since the dances the last few years have gotten a bit too much… *fun,* please keep it civil. Teaching staff is here, easily recognizable by the red harlequin masks." He points at several spots in the gymnasium, and if I'm not mistaken, the person he points at close to the stage is Mr. Langen. I know Ben Bullet's well-built upper body.

Gunn holds the microphone farther away when another squeak shoots through the speakers. "Sorry 'bout that. Furthermore—"

Goosebumps erupt down my spine. Like drawn in by a magnet, my gaze drifts from Gunn and the stage over to the right, toward the entrance, to the person whose way of moving I'd recognize anywhere, no matter what. I suck in a harsh breath and fumble blindly for Hazel's arm. "He's here," I whisper.

Her head whips around. "Phantom?" she asks, after following my gaze.

"Yeah," I whisper hoarsely. "The Phantom of the Opera."

"You sure it's him?"

"Hundred ten percent." I have no trouble recognizing him. Who needs to see a face when you know the other person that well? The way they stand, the way they walk, the way they hold themselves? The way they pick you up for a body slam?

Hazel whistles through her teeth. "He looks hot."

And I have to agree. Dressed in black slacks and shoes, he has forgone the Venetian frock or suit most guys chose. Instead, he went for a white dress shirt and black vest, both fitting his body like a glove and emphasizing his strong frame. A cape is tied around his neck, and he's holding a single red rose in his gloved hands. The mask, though, is what completes the outfit. Like the Phantom of the Opera, his mask is bright white and covering most of his face up to into his hairline. His eyes, lips, and part of his chin are visible, which is why his smile when he spots me in the crowd...

It hits me right in the feels. Funny how a simple smile can

have that effect. *#Butterflies*

While Gunn is droning on, Fire weaves his way through the students until he stops right in front of me. "Hi, Ever," he says, and even though it can't be more than a loud whisper, it's enough to carry over Gunn's voice, and it's all I hear.

"Hey, Fire," I reply. Yay for theses masks, or else my blush would be really, really obvious. I guess there's a difference meeting him at the gym versus here.

At the gym, we're there to wrestle.

Here, he came for me.

Fire's standing so close, I have to look up to him, and when I do, he meets my eyes with such intensity, his gaze ensnares me. Seriously. Like I lost most of my vision, the periphery is non-existent. All I see is Fire. Only he stands out in twenty-twenty.

He brings the rose up between us. "For you."

As I take it, my fingers land atop of his gloved ones, the connection bringing my heart to a stutter, no matter the thin layer of fabric preventing true skin-to-skin contact. "Th-Thank you." I suck in my lower lip. A rose. He brought me a rose. *#RomanceAintDead*

Hazel clears her throat. Oh, uh, right. I step aside and gesture from her to him and back. "Fire, meet Hazel, my best friend. Hazel, meet Fire, my…" My *what*? Crush? Yeah, but ain't gonna say that, though. Wrestling teacher? Sounds stupid. Friend? Yes, but sounds weird, too, after calling Hazel my *best* friend. Maybe—

Fire steps forward and holds out his hand to Hazel. "Hi. Fire. I'm the reason why Ever is sore every morning." Mischief sparkles in his eyes.

Hazel laughs as they shake hands. "My friend, you have no idea. Nice to meet you, finally. I've heard a lot about you." The way she emphasizes *a lot* is way too telling from my point of view.

I give her a *#WTF* look behind Fire's back. "Well, I was keeping you up to date with my progress—"

"That you were as well, true." Hazel tilts her head and points at Fire. "How long have you been wrestling?"

He shrugs. "Forever. Can't remember not wrestling." Same answer he gave me.

"Who's your favorite wrestler?"

Oh sheesh, we're starting the Hazel-interrogation.

"Of all time or currently?"

Hazel purses her lips. "Good reply. Both."

"All time, I'd have to go with Ric Flair for his lifetime achievement in wrestling, if you will. Currently—definitely Ricochet. You?"

Hazel smacks her lips. "Ricochet, huh? Interesting choice. Quite the highflyer. Finishing move a double moonsault."

I cringe. That word gives me PTSD.

Fire laughs. "Yeah, I wanna be him when I grow up. Don't think I have the agility down, though. My frie—" He stumbles over the word, coughs, then starts again. "A guy I wrestled with broke a leg with a wrong landing. I'm trying to avoid that. But you didn't answer my question. Favorites?"

Hazel holds out one finger, then a second. "Best of all time, the Great Muta. Obvs. Favorite current wrestler—Kenny Omega."

"Interesting choices." Fire echoes her earlier comment. "You know your wrestling one-oh-one."

"I do, and I have a bunch of older brothers. Meaning, I know how to apply a Stone Cold Stunner in case somebody pisses me off." She puts her hands on her hips and steps closer, raising her voice over the applause of Gunn finishing his welcoming speech and the dance music starting. "And I get really pissed off when people misbehave around friends of mine, if you catch my drift." She gives him a challenging look.

I groan. Gee, I'm right here. Hello? Slightly *#embarrassing*, Haze?

Fire holds her gaze without blinking. "Good thing then that I don't intend to misbehave. But if you don't mind, the music started playing and I was told this was a ball." He turns to me and bows. "If I may have this dance?"

I curtsy. "Of course, dear sir."

Fire holds out his hand, and as I lay mine into his, a wave of tingles spreads from my hand all the way to my chest. The DJ's playing some kind of mid-tempo song as Fire leads me through the crowd and onto the dance floor, the soft pressure of his fingers around mine an anchor for my soul starting to take flight.

This moment, I don't know why, but it holds an infinite tenderness I didn't expect from a guy who lives and breathes wrestling. The way he takes my hand. How he guides me to the dance floor, turns me once, then smiles at me. "Ready?"

Since words have left me, I nod. *#AsReadyAsCanBe*

He holds up his left hand, like for a high-five. Uh—

When I don't react, a slow smile tugs on the corners of his lips. "Like a collar-to-elbow lock up, Ever." He drapes my hand around his neck. "Just closer." His other hand finds my waist and tugs me in.

In the name of all that's holy—

I've wrestled with Fire. We've locked up a million times at this point. He has thrown me, taken me into headlocks, and I've done the same to him. This isn't the closest we've ever been, but it's by far the most intimate. Our faces are separated by scant inches, and his fingertips sear through the thin material of his gloves. I swear my skin burns where he touches me, and even though he's holding me in a formal dance position, it feels anything but formal.

He nods his chin over to Hazel. "You got yourself a good friend in her."

I beam at him from under my mask. "The very best. The type that gets you no matter what. She's always in my corner, and, of course, I'm in hers."

Fire dances us into a tight turn to avoid crashing into some other couple. "Ah. Your wingman." It has a wistful ring to it.

I shoot him a glance from under my lashes. "Who's yours?"

He looks at a spot somewhere behind my right ear. "Used to be Ronan. He wasn't into wrestling as much as me, but hey, he gave it a try for me. Called himself *Ronan the Barbarian* in the ring." He chuckles softly, but it comes with a nostalgic undertone.

"What happened?"

He shrugs. "Been a while now. Half a year, maybe? Not quite? We had a difference in opinion. Wasn't the first time, but the last time it happened it was a biggie. Had to choose between him and what's right, so…" He raises and drops his shoulders again. "No wingman for me, I guess."

I pat his shoulder once. "I'm sorry, Fire." He sounded sad, and don't I get it. I'd be heartbroken if Hazel and I ever had a falling out. But anyway: "Sounds like he didn't leave you a choice and… you did the right thing."

His lips tug into a half-smile. "I'd like to think so." His hand on my waist slides over my side before he takes a stronger hold of me again. A small gasp escapes me. Was that… on purpose?

Swaying us to the beat of the music, Fire takes a look around.

"So this is the famous Masquerade. Fun idea."

"Uh-huh." I lost the ability to form coherent sentences the moment Fire's hand trailed over my side.

He regards me with silent intensity. "What is it you like most about it?"

I make tiny fists with my toes. That question… It shoots right down to my *#problems*. I've been honest with Fire, but it's hard to keep putting my issues out there.

Hard, but doable. *#trust*

Sucking in one big breath, I look him straight in the eye. "Because… Because it's nice to not be seen for a while." The Masquerade is a time to just be, no matter the hashtags attached, no matter what they want me to look like, no matter the pressure to conform to norms that don't fit me. Being hidden by a mask is pure, soul-soothing relief.

Fire closes his eyes for an eternal second. "Yeah. I… I get what you mean. But you *should* be seen, Ever. You look wonderful tonight. The dress suits you." He lifts his arm and mine with it, his left hand giving me a slight push until I twirl once, then land back in his hold.

The dress suits you.

And I was worried I looked too fat in it.

He lets go of my waist and glides his hand to my side, the simple caress sending a ripple of warmth all through my body. "Actually, the dress looks wonderful. But you… you're perfect."

A rush of sensation hits me all at once. "Fire—"

"Nuh-uh." He lets go of my waist for as long as it takes to place a finger across my lips. "Perfect. Don't let anybody ever tell you anything else. The fact that you can learn a wrestling move in five minutes. That you didn't judge wrestling. You didn't judge me. So don't you dare protest when I say you're perfect, you hear me?" He drops the finger from my lips and holds me by my waist again.

Blood swooshes in my ears. Perfect. Me. I'm so far from *#perfection*, it's ridiculous. But the way he says it, the way his voice breaks at the end of the sentence, the way he looks at me—he means it.

To Fire, I'm… perfect.

The warm sensation growing in my chest is hard to describe for somebody who has spent the last years feeling inadequate, no matter what. Judged, no matter what. Criticized, no matter what.

"Thank you," I whisper. I doubt he can hear me over the sound of the music, but he for sure can read my lips.

"Just saying the tru—"

Somebody bumps into me, bringing me to a stumble, Fire barely catching me before I'd have fallen.

A high, sharp, and completely unnatural laugh pierces my ears. "Eight thousand likes to let MatrixGirl rot? Nice."

The voice responding belongs to a guy—Ford! "To me, she looks dead already. Rest In Peace."

They both laugh as they dance away from us.

Fire stiffens. "Fuckers." He lets go of me and is about to storm after them, but I yank him back in, closer. We haven't practiced lock-ups for nothing.

"Fire, don't."

His eyes widen in surprise as he's pulled back into me, and just in case, I repeat myself. "Don't, Fire." I tug on his shoulder. "Don't. It's not worth it. *They*'re not worth it."

I feel his hand ball into a fist under mine. "It would be worth it, believe me." He sucks in a choppy breath. "Words… Words have power. Every single one of them. They're weapons, and they clearly used their words as an attack."

Warmth fills my chest. Having Fire in my corner, having him understand… it means the world to me. "But it's not an attack if there's no target."

His gaze snaps to mine. "What?"

"There's no target. I've decided I'm done with that." Since I hung up on Dad the other day, I've felt different. Not like a passive sitting duck, awaiting whatever came her way, but… active. Like I could shape what comes my way—or if I can't, then at least I could shape how I react to it.

Doc Shamus wanted me at this point months ago, but it looks like everybody has to get to where they need to be at their own pace.

And I've found mine.

"Done with—"

"Yup. Done with that. I've been a target or been made a target long enough. I refuse to stay this way." They're not going to stop. Ford's mad Nevaeh is now transferred to a different school, or maybe still mad at me spoiling his sick hustle for TeeVee likes, who knows? And if it isn't him, it's somebody else. It's not about them. It's about me. "Let them talk. I don't care. In one ear, out the other. Because it's not important what they think. I'm starting to realize that. Right now, in this room, there are only three people whose opinion of me counts, where I'm coming from. One." I jerk my chin in the direction of Hazel. "Two." That would be Mr. Langen standing watch at the makeshift bar. "And three." I look him straight in the eye.

Fire's eyes widen. "M-Me?" he asks, the apple in his throat bobbing up and down.

The music changes to a slow beat, and yet we're not moving; we're standing still smack on the dance floor, mesmerized by each other. "Yeah. You."

I swear the pulse in his neck beats as fast as mine, if not faster.

Slowly, inch by inch, Fire reaches for my hands and drapes them around his neck, gliding his fingertips down my naked arms until his hands come to rest on my waist on both sides. My scars feel knighted by his touch. He gives me one tug, and we're flush pressed into another. A small gasp escapes me, one I had no chance to suppress, but also one nobody will have heard over the sound of the music.

My breath hitches as a strange flutter dances low in my stomach.

I take it back. *This* is the closest we've ever been. Chest to chest, my cheek on his shoulder, every inhale bringing a fix of his scent, a mix of vanilla and something typical Fire.

He holds me tighter, and I feel his chest rise and fall with a sigh. "Just for the record," he whispers in my ear. "We could have totally taken them down." His breath caresses over my skin. *#Heaven*

"We could have?" I don't care about them. But I do care that Fire is talking to me. I love the sound of his voice, especially tonight. A bit husky, a bit rough. A whole lot Fire.

"Of course. One, when you kept me from going after them right now, I didn't—because you locked me up, Ever. Nice work. You've got the power for those wrestling moves, in case you had any doubt. Two, what do you think wrestlers do when their partner's crap and doesn't play along? They *make them* go along." He stretches the fingers of one of his hands out over my lower back. "We'd start with a kick to the midsection, and when they double over, elbow to the neck, to soften them up."

He lowers his head so that I swear I feel his lips brush over my ear when he speaks. "Then a Body Slam. Boom!"

A small chuckle escapes me. "You do the Body Slam. I have a hard time with you, and you're cooperating. I'd probably just knee them in the face." While I have the stamina now, I still lack the strength for the big-big moves. Doesn't mean I wasn't proud of how far I'd gotten.

I feel the chuckle in his chest. "I like the way you think."

Aww. "And I like that you like that." *Ugh.* Pitiful but true, and it's out.

Fire's arms tighten around my body. "Who needs the others, right?"

Who needs the others. Not me. Not Fire. Not *us.*

I snuggle myself closer to him, savoring each breath that brings his unique scent, and for the first time in years, I'm at peace.

Light.

Free.

Because with Fire by my side, I can handle anything life throws at me.

Anything.

CHAPTER THIRTEEN

#ToughLuck

It's been two days since the Masquerade. Two very long days because I didn't get to see Fire at all. Mom had me visit her, like, hundred-year-old great-aunt in the nursing home with her, and there went my Sunday wrestling session. On Monday, she insisted we go shopping and have a mother-daughter-day, and well, couldn't really say *no* to that, either.

Especially when she was willing to spring some serious money on clothing—and I surprisingly felt in the mood to stock up on some nicer sports outfits.

Plus, she was so mellow and nice and mom-like I would've felt bad rejecting her.

But, since I didn't want Fire to think I ditched him, I had Mom text Mr. Langen that I wouldn't be wrestling those two days due to family obligations: Mom texts Mr. Langen, Ben Bullet texts Fire, and we're good. *#Sneaky*

So today the second school's out I'm rushing over to Vista Verde. My little Vespa's engine isn't purring as usual—it's screaming at me, probably trying to tell me it was never made for such speed. Alas, it needs to suck it up because I have a severe case of Fire-withdrawal.

The moment when I pull into the parking lot and see his car? *#Butterflies*

The moment when I duck under the gate into the gym and spot him in the ring? *#Breathless*

The moment he sees me and his eyes light up under his mask and he gives me the most wonderful, loving, Fire-smile ever? *#HeartStops*

Leaving the guy he was working with alone in the ring, he jumps out, and as cliché as it sounds, my mind chooses this moment to go all movie-scene on me: I swear the ceiling light focuses on him alone, darkening the rest of the gym. Sound doesn't obey the laws of physics anymore, either, because all the chatting and the normal work-out noise, it's gone, replaced by the swooshing of blood in my ears. And as if that weren't strange enough on its own, my mind slows Fire's jog over to me to a mere power walk. Like in slow motion, like I had all the time in the world, I get to appreciate every muscle flexing and stretching under his outfit on his way over, and with Fire, there's a lot to appreciate.

He comes to a standstill right in front of me. "Hi." His voice is soft, deep, and it stirs something inside of me. The way he looks at me makes my knees wobble.

"Hi," I whisper. Can't get my voice to turn it up, not with my heart fluttering more than beating, and my lungs obviously not doing a good job, or else I wouldn't be so dizzy.

Fire sucks in his lower lip, then wraps me in a tight yet gentle hug. "I missed you this weekend."

I melt into his embrace. So, this is what people mean when they say they continued where they left off. Despite the two days where I had no chance of contacting him, it feels like no time passed. "I missed you too." Every single second.

He hugs me tighter before he lets go, a mischievous look on his face. "I've got something nice planned for us for today."

Everything we work on is nice, as long as it's with Fire. "Looking forward to it."

He wiggles his eyebrows at me. "Meet me in the ring when you're ready."

"Okay." I watch him jog back over, this time in real time, and because I'm *#desperate*, I slip out of my second layer within a few seconds. That's why I change at home: Not a second to waste when I could spend it with Fire.

It's busier than usual here, reminding me why we usually train later. But sue me, I didn't want to wait today. I wave at Mr. Langen lifting weight at the biceps machine, then drop my bag in its usual corner, and because I'm feeling exuberant, I slide under the first rope into the ring on my belly. Gosh, is that Fire giving me this energy, or… breakfast? Lunch? All of it?

How nice when things are going right in all aspects of life, for a change: My morning oatmeal sat well with me *and* my mom, lunch was Greek Salad—healthy and delicious—nobody made any mean comments to me in school, and I'm sliding into the ring next to the feet of the coolest guy in town. *#Hallelujah*

I'm about to pop up, just as Fire drops to his knees next to me. "Nuh-uh, stay down. Today we're working on ground moves."

"Ground?" My heart thumps triple-time. Ground means… lots of Fire, really close.

A corner of his mouth lifts into a crooked smile. "Ground. I figured it's a good topic for today. We'll start with the basics, and to be honest, they're more judo or wrestling moves anyway. Side headlock. Armbars. You should find them moderately easy. Once you've got them down, we can advance to the more flashy and pro wrestling ones, like figure-four leg lock, or the Walls of Jericho or so." He moves closer to me on his knees. "Ready? Then if you don't mind, lie down."

Holy cow.

I've done ground in judo. Lots. But hearing Fire ask me to lie down, seeing him move into position next to me, feeling his arm sneak around my neck and his body pressing into my side… It's different. Way different.

He tightens his hold around my neck and keeps my right arm locked in front of his body. "Now, I don't need to tell you how to properly put this one on. If I'm not mistaken, this here is the judo version of it. Right?" He looks at me, our faces so close, I see nothing but Fire.

He pops his biceps under my neck twice, bringing my head to bop up. "Hello, Fire to Ever. This is the judo version, right?"

My cheeks warm. "Uh, yeah. Kesa-Gatame. It's called Kesa-Gatame."

"See, there you go. You know how to get out of it?" He leans himself back, transferring more weight onto my stomach, and I recognize it as what it is: an invitation for an escape.

I forgo a verbal reply and instead swing my legs up and turn my body so that I can wrap one leg around his neck from behind. The speed of the movement combined with the power of my legs forces Fire down backward as I twist underneath him, releasing my leg from around his neck and sliding into a side mount position on top of him.

Holy cow. Just to clarify: *I'm lying perpendicularly over Fire's chest*, controlling his left arm, and keeping my head down, the way I was taught. What I was *not* taught was that this position lets me feel every breath he takes, every heartbeat of his. *Dub dub, dub dub, dub dub,* as fast as mine.

One-Mississippi.

Two-Mississippi.

Three—

"That… That was good, Ever." He swallows. "Let's see how far we get. Work with me. Easy flow." Before I know what he means, he's used his bodyweight and strength to pop me up and get some space. He brings up a knee between us and shifts his body, shrimping, until he can push me into his guard, otherwise known as *between his legs*.

Oh, how I wish I had one of those masquerade masks again. I'm not blushing. Nuh-uh. Turning beet red is more like it, but hello, I'm between Fire's legs. He's wrapped around my waist.

Between.

Fire's.

Legs.

"Your move," he rasps, his pupils wide and dark under his mask. I'm definitely not the only one affected by this position, and that knowledge, that whatever is developing between us right now is mutual, it secures and fuels me at the same time.

I use my elbow to dig into the soft part of the inside of his thigh until he loosens his hold around me. Pity, I liked it a lot, but as it is, we're wrestling here.

Or officially, at least, we're wrestling, because unofficially… Unofficially, something else is in the air, something charged and electrifying, and with every move, with every touch, it gets stronger and stronger.

We fall into an easy rhythm of ground work. Submission, escape, reversal, escape, rolling, armbars, chokes… It becomes one fluid, smooth back and forth of techniques, all executed slow and clean.

Slow. And. Clean.

There's no rushing through it, no fast exchange of techniques. No, we're both taking our sweet time, meaning, I feel *everything* during those techniques. I'm surrounded by Fire, his body on me, under me, pressed into me, his hands finding the correct spots on my body to execute a technique, mine doing the same to him—

And neither of us says a single word.

It's ground work, yet it's so much more.

After about ten minutes, Fire comes up on top of me from a reversal, his knees close to my armpits, his weight not quite sitting on my stomach. I appreciate that.

He peers down on me with soft eyes. They must have a direct line to my heart or something because it skips a beat or two. "Nice job, Ever. Unfortunately, I'm afraid we've got to make room for the others." He points to some of the guys sticking very closely to the ropes of the ring, trying to give us room. I swear I didn't see them come in. I was a tad distracted—excuse me, focused. Yes, focused.

Fire presses his knees together, giving my ribcage a little squeeze. "Unfortunately," he repeats. Regret swings in his voice.

"Agreed," I whisper. Glad we're on the same page here.

He stands up and holds out a hand for me, helping me up.

"By the way, cool new outfit." He gives my tighter leggings and shirt an appreciative nod.

#OMGHENOTICED "Thank you," I say, pretending it's no big deal, while heck, it's a ginormously big deal! Just looking at this outfit after I picked it out gave me the jitters. Old me would have been terrified parading around in it, especially in front of potentially judgmental teenage boys. New me, on the other hand, trusted Fire. And? Trust well placed, there you go.

Fire scratches the side of his head through the mask. "We should work on something else, like a—"

"I'd love to see you try the double moonsault."

Fire cocks his head in surprise. "You would?"

I nod like crazy. "All we've been doing is working on my stuff. I mean, I even have a finishing move." Hazel's favorite, a Stone Cold Stunner, to the rescue. "But I haven't seen you do any of that." Besides on the first day, when I thought he was an obnoxious showoff in his costume and pulling off some kind of backward flip off the ropes. Fair to say I've changed my mind on that assessment.

His smile lights up his whole face. "I'd love to. The moonsault has been my dream move since I was like three years old. Not sure if I can pull off the double—"

"Like Ricochet." Look at me: I do pay attention.

The smile turns into a grin. "Like Ricochet, but I'll try. I'd say I'm sufficiently warmed up. Thanks to you." I get a wink before he turns away, but I'm pretty sure under his mask, his cheeks turned the same shade of red as mine probably turned right now. *Warm* isn't really the correct word. *Hot* is more like it. *#HotAsHell*

Fire walks over to the corner, exchanges a few words with the other guys, and when they make room, he climbs up the ropes.

That alone to me is a view I wouldn't mind checking out every day.

In my mind I see it, the perfect post: a picture of Fire as he's standing on the third rope, his arms spread wide, his black-and-red costume fitting him to perfection, emphasizing his wide shoulders and slim waist. If I were still online, I'd post that picture. Betting right here and now that would be up to fifteen-K likes in no time.

#

MatrixGirl:
True #power.
#MatrixGirlRocks #PlayingWithFire #BenBulletsWrestlingSchool

#

Up on the rope, Fire bounces up and down, testing its elasticity. Then he readies himself, jumps up high and off the rope—

—and pulls off a double moonsault like a pro, landing on his stomach and bracing his fall with a perfect hard fall break.

"Yes!" I punch one fist up in the air. "That was awesome, Fire!" Elation shoots through me. Simply amazing how he got height with his jump, how he curled up into one lean ball of muscle, then stretched out just at the right moment—

Too lost in thought, I don't watch where I'm going. My right foot catches on something—

"Ow!" I roll my right ankle, a sharp pain shooting through the outside of my foot. "Crap!" I can't bear weight and drop down to my knees.

"Shit, sorry—you stepped right into me." One of the other wrestlers, I forgot his name, bends down and regards me with worry. "Rolled it?"

"Ever!" Fire darts over and kneels next to me, reaching for my foot. "What happened?"

I was too distracted swooning over you and didn't watch where I was going. "Rolled my ankle," I press out through clenched teeth. Man, this hurts!

Fire's already untying my shoelaces. "Greg, can you get us some ice, please?"

The guy I stumbled over nods. "On my way."

Ever so carefully, Fire takes off my shoe without moving my ankle, then removes my sock. I don't even care that I might have stinky feet, that's how much my ankle hurts. Please don't let it be broken, please don't. I don't want to sit out wrestling.

Fire flinches when his eyes fall onto my ankle. "Ouch." He glides one careful finger over the swelling. "That's bruising already."

And it hurts! I cringe. "Is it broken?"

He shakes his head. "I don't think so. Rolling your ankle happens quite often in wrestling, and this is typical, the swelling, the bruising, I mean. Not broken, I think."

Thank goodness.

Greg is back with the icepack, and with him Mr. Langen. He slides into the ring as Fire takes the ice from Greg and presses it against my ankle. "How bad is it?"

Fire lifts the icepack for him to see, and Mr. Langen makes the same flinching expression Fire did before. "Ouch." He reaches for my ankle. "May I?"

I nod. Mr. Langen feels around my ankle and tests its movement. "Nasty sprain. Can you stand on it?" He nods at Fire, who grabs me under my arms from behind and helps me up. As soon as I put weight on it, a sharp pain shoots through it.

"No," I push out. "No way." Dang it. Dang it, dang it, dang it!

Fire changes his hold to one of support and guides me to the ropes. "Come on. I'll help you down."

Mr. Langen holds the ropes open for me while Fire supports me from the other side, then jumps off the ring and extends both arms toward me. Accepting his invitation, I lean forward and let him help me off the ring and set me down gently. I keep my right foot off the ground, though.

Mr. Langen jumps down next to us. "Honestly, Everly, you can't ride your Vespa like this. Fire, can you take her—" He grimaces. "Never mind. I'll get changed and drive you home, Everly."

Aw, wait, no. I don't want to be driven home by my teacher. "It's all right, Ben. You don't have to do that. Maybe Fire—"

"No, Everly. *I'll* drive you home." He nods at Fire, something passing between them that makes Fire grunt in frustration before Mr. Langen walks off to get changed.

Without a word, Fire drapes my arm around his neck and helps me over to a bench in the corner, next to my gym bag. He sits me down and kneels to feel my ankle one more time, his lips pressed into a thin line. His whole body is rigid and coiled, radiating tension.

I reach out and tap his shoulder. "Just in case you're wondering, it wasn't your fault."

He jerks up, like from deep thought. "Wha-What?"

"Wasn't your fault. I wasn't watching where I was going. Too mesmerized by your moonsault," I joke, trying to lighten the mood, but Fire doesn't react. He stares at me, blinking, his mouth slightly agape, as if he couldn't process what I said. I get it. I'm frustrated too. Lowering my voice, I bend forward, closer to him. "I was hoping he'd let you drive me home. I mean, nothing against Ben, but… I'd like you to be with me."

Fire looks at me with this strange expression, then licks his lips, presses them into an even thinner line, and holds his breath. When he lets go of it, he keeps his eyes glued to the floor. "It's better if Ben drives you, really. I… have to check on something. Feel better, okay?" I get one more gentle pat on my foot, and then he's gone in the direction of the changing rooms.

Sheesh. Awkward. I really hope he doesn't fault himself for my clumsiness. His only fault was executing a perfect double moonsault—

Huh. Look at that.

I didn't even cringe saying the word moonsault. Not once did I think of @Moonsaulting_Spaceman, not once did I get triggered. A proud smile spreads over my face, no matter the throbbing in my ankle. To be honest, I'd take a busted ankle any time of day if it meant I got my demons under control at last.

Any time of day.

CHAPTER FOURTEEN

#DownwardsSpiral

Today is day four after I sprained my ankle.

Day four that I wobbled to school on crutches.

Day four that I sat out PE.

Day four that I didn't go to wrestling.

And day four that I didn't hear from Fire.

I get it. I don't have a phone. But I do have a home. He could ask Ben Bullet where I live. He knows. After all, he drove me home after I was stupid enough to injure my foot. Or he could ask Mr. Langen to tell me to feel better, to say *hi* from him. He is my teacher, and I see him every day.

But nope.

Haven't heard anything from Fire, and of course I don't have any means of contacting him, phone-less as I am.

Doesn't mean I didn't try: *I* did tell Mr. Langen to say *hi* to Fire—I just didn't get any greetings back. But what else am I supposed to do? I don't even know his real name! And no, Ben Bullet doesn't spill the beans. *#LuchaSecret*

Frustrated, I push myself off my bed and fumble for my crutch. I feel much better already, but the doc said to stay on the crutches and off my foot as much as possible to heal faster—and I do want to heal faster. The performance/match is coming up, and since the cat's out of the bag, I'm actually kind of looking forward to it. Hazel needs to record it and then I can send it to Dad, as a big, fat, middle finger right in his face.

So yeah, I want to get back to wrestling. To Fire.

Although I gotta say, the silence coming from him bothers me. A lot.

I hobble over to the door and out into the hallway. "Mom? Can I use the upstairs phone, please?" I call out loud enough for her to hear downstairs.

"To call whom, honey?"

"Hazel." Because I need to vent. STAT.

"Of course. Tell her I said *hi*." Mom has been very lenient with my landline phone use over the last four days.

"Will do." I turn and crutch down into the other direction. We only have one landline phone upstairs, and it's in the guestroom. *#Oldfashioned.*

Hazel picks up after the first ring because *she* has a smartphone. "Whazzup, girl?"

"The usual." I sigh into the receiver.

"Fire trouble," Hazel concludes.

"I'm just so frustrated. Like, I feel like we hit it off. We—"

"Sure looked like that at the Masquerade." I hear her unwrap something in the background, knowing her, probably chewing gum.

"It did, didn't it?" And that's exactly my problem. "Haze, I'm telling you, it wasn't just me imagining things. The Masquerade was wonderful, and before idiot-me twisted her ankle, wrestling was great. I mean, we did ground—"

"Which, by the way, is super-hot." She starts to chew ferociously.

"Exactly! It was! There's no way I'd have imagined him liking that, no way!"

Hazel calms down her chewing speed. "Could it have been too much too soon? I mean, maybe he doesn't want you to see how much you affect him."

I grunt. "Well, he's doing a fine job because right now I'm thinking I don't affect him at all."

"Ev, you know that isn't true. He came to the Masquerade for you."

"Maybe he was bored."

"Right. So he decided to drive cross-county from wherever he lives in the area of El Marino High to join you. In an outfit he surely had to buy. Sure. Why not?" I can hear her eyeroll through the phone. "I'm telling you, he's into you, but there's something holding him back. Right now, I'm thinking he's overwhelmed or something. I mean, clearly, that guy has... issues."

"Why would you say that?"

She stops chewing. "Let me see... because he goes by Fire, didn't give you his first *or* last name, and *maaaybe* because you've never seen him without his freakin' mask on?"

I deflate. "Well, yeah, there's that."

"There's that, indeed. Look, Ever, all I'm saying is, don't freak. It doesn't have to mean anything. Maybe he also feels guilty and doesn't know how to approach you. Could be."

That was actually the theory I tried to convince myself of. It sounds much better than the one where I'm thinking he's just not that into me.

I swallow hard. "You know what? I really like him. That's why it hurts so much to sit here and wait for him. It makes me think of all the times on TeeVee I let somebody's opinion of me ruin my day, and right now, if I even think I misinterpreted everything and Fire isn't into me at all… it makes me feel… empty."

There's a pause at the other end of the line before Hazel speaks again. "Define *empty*."

"Not well. Like something's missing. Well, empty. It's not that hard of a word."

I hear her spit out her gum. "Empty, meaning, do I have to rush over and sit next to you to make sure you don't starve yourself or cut yourself, or—"

"Kill myself?"

She sucks in a harsh breath through her teeth. "Yeah."

I sigh. "If it makes you feel better, I haven't thought about that at all—for any of it." Truth. Despite Fire ignoring me, I have been eating. *Not* restricted—much—or vomited. *Not* cut myself. *Not* even felt the need to do any of that. I've come a long way in the last weeks since I started school again, and even more so since the Nevaeh-debacle. *#GreatSuccess*

"That does make me feel better. So, what do you wanna do about feeling empty?" That's Hazel, she likes plans.

"I'm supposed to stay out of PE until Monday, so once I'm cleared, I'll return to wrestling and then… we'll see."

She pauses. "Do you want me to check in on him?"

A jolt of electricity rushes through me. "You'd do that?"

"Well, duh, why else would I say it?"

Hazel's offer is more than tempting. Seductive, actually. But... do I want to be the kind of needy person who sends their friend to check in on somebody who isn't even their boyfriend? I mean, since I'm considering it, I probably am that kind of needy person—but I don't want to be her.

I shake my head, even though she can't hear it. "No, thank you. I think it sends too much of a controlling, pushy message. I'll be fine."

"Okay, but let me know if you change your mind."

"Yeah."

"Ev, I've gotta go. I have tap practice."

"Huh? Since when do you do tap?"

Pause.

When she speaks again, her voice sounds funny. Weird. Rougher than normal. "I was wondering when you'd ask."

"Ask what?" What am I missing?

"Which sport I got assigned in Health."

"Oh." I feel my face warm up. "S-So you got tap, huh?"

A heavy sigh comes over the phone. "Yes, Ev, I got tap."

Pause.

"And I gotta go."

"S-Sure thing, uh, sorry to bug you, and thanks for listening. I'll... I'll see you tomorrow." Well, that took a weird turn pretty fast...

"See you tomorrow. Love ya," she says, smacking her lips to blow me a kiss. It sounds like she said it with a smile.

"Love ya too," I reply before hanging up the phone. Was... Was Hazel mad I never asked? But she could have said something, too, right? I mean, we're friends—besties. Granted, I should have asked. I mean, sorry I didn't, but come on! When I got my project assigned, it was like, *pro wrestling*, which I imagined to be much worse than it turned out, but still, I was distracted. Had other priorities. And after that… I dunno. It didn't come up. But heck, she could have said, like, *hey, Ever, I have tap today, by the way*, or something.

I scratch the back of my neck. Whatever. Not a biggie. Like I said, we're besties. We love each other, no matter what.

That word, the *#LWord*, stirs something deep inside my soul, something that's been there quite obviously over the last few weeks, only I didn't dare to truly acknowledge it.

Love ya, I said to Hazel. So easy to say. Problem is, she's not the only one I love. I'm pretty sure at this point I'm *#InLove* with Fire as well. And not just as in having a crush. No. The way I feel is pretty clear if I let myself truly look at it: I'm *in love* with Fire. With the guy who ghosted me over the last days.

I let my head fall forward into my hands and groan.

Fate sure likes to have some fun with me.

#

Returning to Ben Bullet's Pro Wrestling School feels exactly the same as about ten days ago.

The moment when I pull into the parking lot and see his car? *#Butterflies*

The moment when I duck under the gate into the gym and spot him in the ring? *#Breathless*

The moment he sees me—

He ignores me completely.

Misery lodges in my throat. Maybe I didn't imagine it. Maybe something is off.

I take off my sweat suit, leaving me in leggings and a tight shirt, the same new outfit he complimented me on last time. Then I wait.

Standing in front of the ring, I watch Fire and Eric wrestle, and they're taking their sweet time. I mean, Eric is rarely in since he became a dad, so I guess he needs to take this opportunity and make the most out of it. But man, how much longer can it take?

After about five minutes I clear my throat. Eric's long, dark hair flows in a commercial-worthy way when he looks at me and gives me an acknowledging nod.

Fire on the other hand ignores me.

I cross my arms in front of my chest.

Fire lets Eric escape from submission.

I start to tap my foot.

Fire gets up from a power slam that should've finished the fight.

I put my hands on my hips.

Fire moves in for a lock-up—

And Eric steps back. "Fire, dude. I'm spent, and, uh, I think Everly is waiting for class." He gives me a small nod.

Fire chews on his lower lip. "Yeah, I guess so."

I guess so?

What is going on with him?

I pull myself up and step into the ring. "Hi, Fire."

"Hi." He doesn't look at me.

"O-Okay, what's going on with you?" I cross my arms over my chest again. Makes me feel stronger.

"Nothing."

"Sure."

Fire blows out an exasperated breath. "Look, can we just get on with it and wrestle?"

My jaw drops. "Can we—" What the *#FingHell?*

"Just wrestle, Everly. Come on." He steps into a position to initiate lock up. No *how are you.* No *how's your ankle.* No *good to see you.* No freaking-*nothing.* What's wrong with—

He makes an impatient hand gesture.

Oh, okay. That's how we're playing it. Anger rises, and it wants an outlet.

I storm forward and into the lock up. Fire grunts when I slam my arm harder around his neck than strictly necessary. You don't like this? I didn't like being ignored, either!

I move him in the lock up, then feel him loosen his grip to throw me into the ropes.

Okay, fair game. I let him whip me into the ropes and bounce right out—

Fire readies himself for a clothesline against me—

Oh, heck, no. I'm way too mad to let him dictate the match.

I duck under his lifted forearm, bounce into the rope behind him, and come out swinging. My ankle protests the stomp I make, but I ignore it. I'm *mad.* Fire barely has time to react to the elbow I'm throwing at him. He sells it—and I grab him by the fabric of his shirt, pull, and throw him in a wonderful Morote Seoi Nage, or shoulder throw. A ripping, tearing sound mixes with Fire's grunt as he flies over my back and hits the floor, bouncing off and landing again—that's how hard I slammed him down. Anything to snap him out of his funk.

"What the hell, Everly?!" He jumps up to his feet. "What was that about?" He darts one angry finger at the surface of the ring.

"I don't know, Fire!" I yell back as I throw my arms up. "Maybe I wasn't so happy about the way you ignored me, or that you didn't call—"

"You don't even *have* a cell phone!"

"But I do have a landline and there's these things called *internet* and *phone book*, where our family is listed, believe it or not!" I stomp closer to him, steaming on the inside.

He pulls himself up to his full height, a good head taller than me. "Whatever, Everly. I—"

My gaze falls onto his chest and I suck in a sharp breath: right where I grabbed for the shoulder throw, his shirt is torn, and the skin—

"Fire," I breathe. "What—?"

The skin under the ripped part of his outfit is bright red and crisscrossed with thick scars. What happened to him?

His spine stiffens as his eyes widen, but other than that, he doesn't react. Doesn't move. Doesn't breathe. Then he slaps a hand over the exposed few inches of skin, the muscles in his neck bulging. When he speaks again, his voice has dropped low and every word is clearly enunciated, free of emotion. "You know what, Everly? This here is obviously not working out. Any of it. You and me. Leave me alone."

Wait, *what?* "Fire—" I take one small, lonely step forward, but he's already jumped out of the ring.

"I'll let Ben know he'll need to find somebody else to train you. I won't be here when you do, so no worries. It was nice meeting you, Ever." His tone is not ungentle—harsh, yes, but not ungentle, the last part even spoken with some affection to it, but the meaning is clear, no matter the tone of voice.

#CrystalClear.

"Fire—" My world begins to spin. This isn't happening.

But Fire doesn't turn back. He walks to his bag, grabs it, and leaves the gym, never once looking back.

Never once seeing me standing there, too frozen to react, too shocked to understand I just got *#dumped* before we ever were together.

CHAPTER FIFTEEN

#OutForTheCount

Today sucks.

Like yesterday.

The day before.

Everything sucks when nothing makes sense and the only question is *#WHY.*

I walk into the first period room with Hazel next to me. She knows. She's heard it all. Listened to everything I needed to get off my chest, like the best friend that she is.

Doesn't mean it helped.

It didn't.

Fire's dismissal still hurts, and the most fucked-up thing is, I still miss him. A lot.

A bunch of students surround my desk, several of them scurrying away when they see us come in, some snickering, some looking uncomfortable.

Hazel stops dead in her tracks, and me with her. She sucks in a harsh breath through her teeth—

Oh.

That's why.

Bacon.

A loaded plate of fried bacon on my desk.

Hazel storms forward. "You fucking morons! Who did that?"

Somebody snickers.

Somebody takes out a phone.

Bacon.

Hazel is throwing the bacon on the floor and yelling.

I observe the scene as if I'm not even there, like something is separating me from them, a fog of sorts, a barrier. I'm here, but I'm not.

Bacon.

It's never going to stop, is it?

It's never going to stop.

Never.

The question is: how much do I even care anymore?

#

That afternoon, I'm lying on my bed, staring up on the ceiling, doing breathing exercises.

In. And. Out.

In. And. Out.

In—

Dang it. Not working. I rub a palm over my eyes. Gonna look even puffier now, not that it matters. I looked puffy the last three days, and it's not as if anybody besides Hazel noticed. If they notice me at school, it's because I'm *the girl who tried to kill herself* or because I'm *the one from TeeVee*, but I'd never be *the girl who looks like her heart was ripped out.*

I groan and roll on my side.

Pathetic.

Nothing happened between Fire and me besides some slow dancing. That's hardly enough to give me any claim to his heart—obviously.

Then why-oh-why does it feel like my soul was ripped in two?

Easy: because I felt he understood me. Because I opened myself up and let him see the real me—and then he rejected me.

That's why.

It always hurts more when it's *#personal.*

Maybe I'm too fat for him. Too crazy. Too many issues.

My chest is tight with pain. He'd be right: I'm not at my best. I've gained weight. I have too many issues. I'm broken, complicated, and, let's be honest, probably unlovable. Ask my classmates: All I'm ever going to be is a source of amusement, their punching bag, their way of making themselves feel better by putting me down.

I squeeze my eyes shut until stars appear.

I wouldn't want to date me, either.

To give myself some credit: I've gotten better. Maybe because I've been here, done that, but despite not thinking about killing myself, everything's just so much right now.

So.

Much.

A pang of longing slices through me, different from the pain that has been my constant companion since Fire wanted nothing to do with me anymore.

Relief. I want relief. I *need* relief. I want the world silent for a while, obeying my command instead of using me as a pinball in a game I didn't choose to play.

I swing my legs over the edge of the bed and sit up, reaching for my lamp and turning it over. When things get too much, when crying isn't enough, there's only one way to feel better. "Hello, old friend," I whisper as I glide one finger over the center of the shiny razor blade.

Whatever the world does to me, it can't take *this* from me. I have *this*. *This* is mine.

I pull the tape off the blade and free it from its prison under the foot of my lamp. The mere act of holding it, feeling its cool steel in my hand… My heart beats faster, anxiously awaiting the kick and relief it knows is only one cut away.

I press the edge of the blade against my left upper arm, just below the scar the last cut left.

But I don't cut.

I don't cut.

Pressure builds inside my chest, bringing my hand to a shake—

With a pitiful, choked-off cry, I throw the blade across the room and bury my face in my hands.

Then I sob.

#

"Everly, could you please stay for a moment?" Mr. Langen waves me out of the stream of students leaving his classroom. He's dressed spiffy as always, but as I get closer, I pick up on a whiff of perfume or so, something masculine with a hint of fresh grass. He curls his index finger at me to make me move faster, but despite him wearing a neutral expression and, well, being Mr. Langen, I don't want to.

"I have English—"

"I'll give you a late slip."

"Oh." Okay. I give in to fate and wait until the last student has left the room. What does it matter anyway? It's not like I was paying attention in class.

For a moment, Mr. Langen looks at me, then sighs. "What's been going on with—"

"Nothing," I interrupt him.

"Right." He drums a rhythm onto the desk with his fingers. "I heard about the bacon."

A lightning bolt of red hot embarrassment shoots through me. I close my eyes. *Must not let it affect me. Must not let it affect me. Must not—*

"How are you doing? Everly?"

The concern in his voice breaks through the walls I've been working hard on keeping up. Higher walls mean fewer hits will go through. Doesn't mean the hits wouldn't chip away at my defenses.

"You haven't been at wrestling for a while." He says it without accusation as he slides onto the desk surface and folds his hands on top of his lap.

"Didn't feel like it," I whisper.

"That's interesting. It's the same thing Fire said when I asked him why he was only showing up sporadically these days."

Fire.

I don't care. "I don't care." I do. *I don't.* I don't care.

Mr. Langen regards me with a look of empathy. "I don't think that's true. Rather the opposite. And the same can be said of Fire."

A dismissive snort escapes me before I can hold it in. "Yeah. Right."

Mr. Langen regards me silently, his eyes slightly narrowed, his mouth a worried line. "You know, all I'm saying is that sometimes things are more complicated than they seem. Fire… Fire has been hurt before."

My gaze snaps up. "What happened?" *Hurt* as in emotionally, or *hurt* as in physically? Because I can't forget those scars. As if he'd been whipped. Whatever caused them, it must've been something big. *#LifeChanging.*

He cringes. "It's not my story to tell. But anyway, the reason why I held you back was I wanted to let you know something. As Ben Bullet talking, I'd like to say we all miss you at the gym, so please come back. As your teacher, Mr. Langen, I have to remind you that you will still need to complete your assignment, i.e., the wrestling match, at the end of the semester, and as your friend, who's seen you grow since you returned to school, I want you to know that I'm here for you. And by here, I mean here at school, here at the gym, at any time, any day. You got that, Everly?"

I nod. This rollercoaster of emotions, it's giving me a run for my money: Fire, the bacon incident, Mr. Langen's care and worry about me—I don't know what to feel.

But maybe… Maybe that's good.

It for sure beats the sensation of nothing but overbearing sadness.

#BetterThanNothing

#

Coming home from school is soothing. Being at home limits the potential battle zones, and to be fair, there haven't been very many in the safety of our house. Actually, none for a while now.

After dinner Mom catches me before I can make it out of the living room and up the stairs. "Honey, come here." Mom pulls me into a tight hug that feels good. The clasp of her fancy blouse she wore for work today presses into my chest. "You're making an effort eating, you're going to school, you're talking—you're doing everything right, but I feel like I've got a robot for a daughter."

I squeeze my eyes shut and snuggle closer. This robot has been working hard—*#ExtraHard*—to get to this point. I'm considering it a win. "It's fine, Mom." The dull ache that has been taking up residency behind my eyes for the last few days cranks it up a notch, calling me a liar.

She sighs. "No, it's not, honey. When you're hurting, I'm hurting. I was blind to your pain once before, and I nearly lost you. I'm not going to make the same mistake again." Keeping me in the hug, she walks to the couch, leading me there backward until my knees hit the cushion. "Sit. Stay. I'll make us some tea, and then we'll talk. No judgment, just mother and daughter. Okay?"

Just us? My mom is actually… I mean… I swallow once. This is different from *before*. A tiny flame of something not grey and dark and heavy springs to life inside my heart. Tiny, but there it is. "That… That would be nice. Thanks, Mom." It's what I missed *before*. *#MommyAndMeTime*

She bends forward and kisses my hair. "Anytime, honey. Anytime."

As she's on her way to the kitchen, the doorbell rings. "I got it," she calls out, so I sink back into the couch cushions and close my eyes. I'm sick of this heavy, sad feeling. It's just *there* and won't go anywhere. But I'm stronger than the emotions threatening to drown me. Stronger than the urge to cut myself to feel something other than my soul being torn apart, and too strong to make myself throw up, to feel better.

I draw in a shaky breath. Who am I kidding? Every minute is a struggle. I'm on a slippery slope, on the black diamond run of emotional runs, without a clue how to get down in one piece. The temptation to give in, to find relief, is close to overbearing. See, I'm at this point because of Fire: heartbroken because of Fire. Suffering because of Fire. But the weird thing is that I'm also strong because of Fire. Not because he trained my body over the last few months, but because I refuse to give him the power to get me to hurt myself in any form, be that cutting, restricting, puking, or whatever. It's bad enough I can't get my heart out of its depressed funk. I won't let him hurt my body on top of things.

My mom's surprised voice and short laugh come from the door about five seconds before she closes it behind whomever. She's *really* making time for me and hearing me. I like th—

A tiny shriek cut off by a strangled sob breaks me out of my funk. I sit up straight. "Mom? Everything all right?"

The moment she comes into the living room is the moment I know it isn't. Like she wasn't quite aware she was walking, she stumbles in slow motion, her eyes fixed on the bouquet of white flowers in her one hand and a black-rimmed card in the other. Her face is white, like the flowers, and her eyes watery.

She scares me.

I scoot to the edge of the cushion. "Mom? What… What is it?"

Her mouth opens and closes as she blinks rapidly. But she

doesn't say a single word.

"Mom?" Seriously, it's freaking me out.

She blinks harder, the bouquet in her hands shaking. "It… They… They—"

The doorbell rings again—

And my mom, in a completely uncharacteristic move, drops the flowers where she stands and returns to the door.

Holy cow…!

As soon as she opens the door, several people start talking—

I get off the couch and kneel on the floor, picking up the abused flowers. The card falls open, and my heart stops:

Our sincerest condolences on the passing of your
daughter, Everly Aldaire.
May she find the peace in heaven she couldn't
find on Earth.

CHAPTER SIXTEEN

#Condolences

I'm mad.

Flipping, stinking, ginormously mad.

Granted, that's an improvement from where I was a mere two hours ago, but overall, I'm not feeling much better.

At all.

At least fifteen bouquets of flowers crowd the couch table. Could be more. I stopped counting after ten, and it's not like I cared. Or maybe I should. This is giving me a glimpse into the *#AfterLife*, into what would have happened if I had succeeded in killing myself over the summer.

Well, good to know my passing would get my mom to drown in flowers.

Every card on every bouquet carries a variation of the same condolences. None of them are sent by people we know, which is why—

The doorbell rings, and Mom jumps out of her seat. "The police are here."

Exactly: which is why the police are here.

Mom hurries to the door, and when she comes back, she's followed by two police officers in uniform, one guy, one gal.

"You must be Everly," says the guy-cop. He's probably around Mom's age and looks like he's in good shape. Not the classic donut-type of cop. This one could actually hunt somebody down and tackle them successfully. "You look very much alive to me." He winks.

Mom sucks in a harsh, shocked breath—

And I smile. "Rumors of my death were greatly exaggerated."

Mom releases the breath she held, and I get it. A few months ago, this comment would've thrown me into a fast and furious downward spiral of depression. Not anymore, though. I'm stronger than this.

Stronger than them.

And stronger than Fire.

Anyway. I sit up straighter as the officers take a seat next to each other on the smaller sofa across from me. The lady officer, Officer Goldstein, according to the embroidered patch on her uniform, takes out a pad and pen. She's definitely younger, more like late twenties, and with the short blonde curls peeking out from under her police cap she looks more like a model for police recruitment than an actual officer. I wouldn't let that fool me though, because she has a super athletic build. "Ms. Aldaire, we got only a one-liner from dispatch. So you're getting condolences and flowers sent to your house and all are about your daughter passing—who is clearly healthy and in one piece." She nods at me.

"Correct," Mom says, her arms crossed in front of her chest.

"Do you know any of the senders of the flowers?"

"None."

Something cramps inside my stomach. *I might, but I'm not sure I want to open that Pandora's Box…*

The officer's eyebrows turn down into a V. "Nobody? But why would people you don't know think that Everly died and send you flowers? That's out of nowhere."

A new voice comes from the living room doorway: "Actually, it's not."

My head whips around. "Hazel!" Hazel and— "Mr. Langen?" That's… unexpected, to say the least. I was too distracted calming Mom down to call Hazel. And Mr. Langen? That's just odd.

He raises a hand. "Uh, hi. The door was open and…" Before it becomes awkward, my mom jumps out of her seat and darts over to him.

"Thank you for coming, Clark."

And she hugs him.

#WTF

Hazel's eyes pop as wide as mine as she inches away from them, as if they'd give her the cooties. She weaves past the officers and sits down next to me, leaning over and whispering into my ear. "Ran into Mr. Langen as I was coming over, had I known *that* would happen…" She makes a gagging noise. "I don't think I can unsee that."

Neither can I. Mom and Mr. Langen have stopped hugging, but he still holds her by her upper arms, his head bent low as they talk in hushed voices.

Once they sit down—Mr. Langen beside Mom—the guy cop, Officer Travis, gives us a questioning look. "Okay, resume, please. We're still trying to figure out—"

"Oh, yeah, sorry, got sidetracked." Hazel makes a yuck-face, probably referring to Mom's and Mr. Langen's hug, and takes out her phone. "I can tell you why you're getting all these flowers. Or rather, why people think you died."

I knew why the moment she took out her phone. To be honest, I feared it once the first shock had worn off.

There's only one explanation, and it lies in the one app on Hazel's second home screen.

She opens TeeVee. "So, this popped up earlier today on Everly's wall." She holds out her phone for everybody to see.

#

MATRIX-GIRL
Everly Aldaire
passed today, suddenly and unexpected.
May she rest in peace.
Well-wishes and prayers for the family welcome.
1812 Obama Blvd, Santa Azul, California

#

Mom stares at it, her pupils so wide, her eyes look black. "I thought you weren't on TeeVee anymore."

"I'm not, Mom! No internet, no nothing!" Since *that day*, the only glimpse I had was when Hazel let me see that stupid picture Nevaeh posted.

"So why does it still say MatrixGirl there?" Mom asks.

Mr. Langen lays one hand on her knee. "Because Everly didn't delete her profile, Ash. She could go back to it anytime, but right now it's abandoned, which you can see by the little dot next to the profile picture. It means MatrixGirl hasn't logged in in several months."

"Oh," Mom says, a slight blush on her cheeks that probably has nothing to do with her inability to understand TeeVee, but everything to do with Ben Bullet's hand on her knee.

Officer Travis leans forward. "May I?" He takes Hazel's phone without waiting for a reply. Must be nice to be a police officer.

He scrolls and clicks through a couple of things. "If I'm seeing this right, and correct me if I'm wrong, you guys know TeeVee much better than me, obviously, but the person who posted this only posted this, meaning—"

"It's a fake account," Hazel says.

Officer Travis shoots her an annoyed glance. "You're stealing my thunder here."

Hazel turns beet red. "Sorry," she mumbles.

"Huh." Officer Travis scrolls some more. "So, if this is a new and fake account, why did this go more or less viral? We have… fifteen thousand interactions with this post, if I'm not mistaken."

"That's because it really blew up after the post got shared." Hazel scoots around on the edge of the seat. "And in this case, the post was shared by somebody with several thousand followers, who then shared it, and then their friends, which is why we're now at over fifteen-k views within a few hours for that post—"

"And a police car in front of our door. Splendid." Mom claps her hands in biting sarcasm. "Details, please."

Hazel scratches her neck, a dead giveaway she's not only uncomfortable, but not happy in her skin at all. Join the club. "Well, you know how you can share a post—"

"I do have a Facebook account and dabbed into TeeVee, Haze." My mom gives her *the* look, the *don't sell me for stupid* look.

"That's not what I meant."

"We need to see a list of people who shared." That's Officer Goldstein. "If the person knew you were alive, this is clearly harassment and cyberbullying, and we do have a case."

"I'm sure you can get a list," Hazel squeaks, avoiding my eye—and in that moment, I know.

I just know.

"*He* shared it, didn't he?"

Hazel deflates. "Yes. Yes, he did."

I close my eyes. Of course. Did he laugh as he shared it? Did he hope I'd try again and kill myself for real this time? Did he think nothing? Or did he do it for the shares, the interactions, the money that comes with it?

"Who now? What?" Officer Goldstein readies her pen while Hazel taps around on her screen.

"This guy. Moonsaulting_Spaceman. He—"

Mr. Langen chokes and coughs with a wheeze, prompting my mom to lay a hand on his shoulder. "You need some water?" All I'm missing is the *honey* at the end of the sentence.

"No, thank you. Sorry." He wheezes and waves a hand. "All good. Carry on."

Hazel raises a brow. "Sure. Anyway. Spaceman doesn't have quite the amount of followers as MatrixGirl, but still a pretty decent number. So when he shared it—and he was the first to share it, by the way—it got the exposure that brought it up to fifteen—" She glances onto the phone. "Sorry, sixteen-K interactions."

Officer Travis looks at the profile I know only too well, although I can see even from afar that he has changed a few things. Different color for the profile monogram, different font. So he put lipstick on a pig.

"Do we know who this is?" The officer nods at Spaceman's profile.

"No," my mom says with a heavy sigh. "But that person messed with Everly's head before. That's him, right, honey?" She offers me the maternal look of worry, and I nod.

"Yeah. We used to interact a lot on TeeVee." Abracadabra, best supporter to fiercest critic in no time. It hurt—and still hurts—to know there's a person out there who truly hates you. Who apparently still wishes you were dead.

Mr. Langen looks up from his phone, which he's been checking. "From a quick scan, I'd say there are at least five or six students of Everly's High School on here who shared as well, or commented."

The police officers look at each other. "Wasn't there another incident with a student and cyberbullying recently at the local high school?"

Langen's cheeks turn crimson. "Well, yes. I'm a teacher there. A student posted a picture of Everly and myself wrestling—"

"Wrestling?"

"Pro wrestling. For school. Anyway, that student posted the picture implying there was a sexual relationship between us, which obviously there isn't."

My mom pats his upper arm, and Officer Travis shoots a questioning glance from Mom to me and back.

Geez. Now my cheeks are heating up. *#SuperAwkward*

The officer lifts and drops one shoulder. "Okay then. We'll contact the cybercrime unit and let them do some digging. They should be able to figure out the IP address of the person who posted this via the fake account, and then we'll track down everybody else. This clearly falls into their territory, and these days we don't take cyberbullying, or any kind of harassment, lightly." Both officers stand up. "Keep us up to date if anything changes, and we'll be in touch later today."

Mr. Langen jumps up. "I'll get the door for you."

Mom smiles up at him. "Thank you, Clark." That scene has something so domestic to it, I wonder how often he's been here already without me knowing. Has he? I've been wrestling so much, I could have missed him. Why else would he be here tonight if they weren't somewhat close?

She turns her attention to me. "Honey? How are you holding up?"

How am I holding up? Good question.

I look at the bouquets, the cards, Hazel's phone with the app open, and it doesn't bring on the sensation of overpowering greyness, of the ground opening for me and pulling me under, trying to drown me. Not like it did when this happened before, when I tried to play the game: first, the hunger for acknowledgement and the highs when I got it. Then the lows when I got disapproval instead of validation.

I close my eyes, recalling the feelings that were part of my life—that were me—for such a long time. The way I felt to be at the mercy of others, addicted to and depended on their opinion of me, their likes, their approval. And when that didn't come... Or worse, when the opposite happened and everything I said or did was picked apart and ridiculed... When it became personal...

I remember how that felt all too well.

"Honey?"

When I look up at Mom, her eyes are glistening. "I know it's a lot—"

"Actually, it isn't."

"It isn't?" Mom and Hazel say at the same time.

"Jinx. You owe me a soda," Hazel mumbles under her breath, then gives me a onceover. "You look... *angry*, Ever. Not like you're going to retreat into your shell, like you used to."

"That's because I *am* angry. And believe me, I'm using it." I feel the anger growing in my chest, swirling around like a dissolving bath bomb—but it's healthy anger. The vanilla bath bomb of anger. Anger that keeps me afloat against the weight of sadness trying to drown me.

Isn't there a movie called *You Only Live Twice*? If there is, they're right: You only live twice.

My first life ended when I woke up in the ICU, broken, confused, a shadow of my former self.

My second one started bit by bit over the last few months, as if it had to piece itself together with the building blocks it found along the way. I'm not the same girl who tried to kill herself anymore. I'm the girl who resists temptation and doesn't cut herself. I'm the girl who knows she'll get better at one point, even though Fire ripped out her heart.

I'm the girl who knows she's still insecure and easily rattled and shaken, but I'm also the girl who doesn't back down anymore.

The girl who doesn't give in.

Because she's stronger than that.

Maybe I need to mean the words I said to Fire: I refuse to be a victim any longer.

And I'm not.

Backing.

Down.

CHAPTER SEVENTEEN

#Scars

For the first time since I returned to school after TeeVee fame and a botched suicide attempt, I don't walk in trying to blend in and become invisible. Well, I'm not making a grand entrance, either, but I also don't lower my gaze. Don't walk in the shadows. Don't keep my voice down.

I walk in as me.

Do I hear the whispers? *Condolences... Heard she died... So funny... Should really kill herself... Genius idea...*

Yeah, I do hear the whispers.

But they bounce right off my defenses.

Okay, okay: once in a while, one pierces through, bringing a sharp pain with it that I do my best to ignore, but that's it.

I'm not a shivering mess and I'm not running. I'm here to stay.

During lunch, I eat half my portion of pasta, and I even like it. Kind of. Still a success.

237

Hazel puts down her fork. She's close to finishing her pasta. "You gonna go back to wrestling today?"

Ouch. Yeah, that one pierced the defenses for sure. "I don't think so."

She cocks her head. "You have to. Mr. Langen called you out on not meeting your requirements for the last two weeks. That was weird," she adds in a lower voice.

"Totally weird after the way he was in our home yesterday."

"Did your mom say anything?" She gives me a curious glance.

"Nope. After you went home, Mom opened up a bottle of wine for them and I took that as my hint to go up to my room. And I haven't spoken to her this morning."

Hazel grins. "Well, at least Mr. Langen was wearing different clothes than yesterday, so…"

"Ew!" I punch her in the shoulder. "Don't give me visuals like that!" Okay, my mom's quote-unquote old enough to date. Dad has been gone for ten years, and besides him meddling in my private life, there's not much we see or hear of him. So from that point of view, her dating is fine—but it had to be my *teacher*? Really?

Hazel leans back. "Have the police said anything?"

"Last thing I heard is that they cracked the VPN or something and have an IP address and an idea where the owner of said address was when they posted about my untimely death. Mom says they're going to get warrants or something for some potential suspects or so." It sounded all a tad confusing in its technicality, but also very official and pretty scary. On the one hand, I pity the person who did this. The fallout is not going to be fun. On the other hand… think before you post, idiot. *#HindsightIs2020*

Mixing what's left of her pasta with her sauce, Hazel frowns.

"Do you think it's somebody from school?"

We both look up at the same time.

"You thinking what I'm thinking?" Hazel points her thumb over her shoulder in the general direction of the other students.

I blow a raspberry. "As revenge for not going out with him or for calling him out on his idiotic plan? Or because we got his fangirl #1 quote-unquote kicked out? Nevaeh? Maybe. But he'd be stupid—"

"To be honest, Ford never struck me as smart."

Well, she has a point. "Then I'll let the police figure it out. I wish people stopped buying into all the crap that's online, but if wishes were fishes… Sometimes I just wanna delete everything and get a fresh start. Or reset. Like, forget all the crap that's been said. Look at me, here, in person, not at the stuff that's online, and form your own opinion. That's all I'm asking."

"So, basically you want the impossible. A fresh start either way and you're expecting people to not show their worst side online. Lol. You funny, girl." Hazel takes a bite of pasta.

"Yeah, right? Well, I try not to worry about it, if I can help it. It's healthier. Plus, they pronounced me dead. That plus my suicide attempt… This dead girl is done letting them ruin her life."

"Wise words," Hazel comments. "But I doubt your wisdom extends the whole 360: wrestling? Fire?" she adds and raises one eyebrow.

I drop my spoon and let myself fall back into the chair, mirroring Hazel. "You had to bring him up again, didn't you?" *Grr.* "Are we being honest?"

"Well, *I* am."

I roll my eyes. "Okay, here's the thing. Like I said, I'm okay right now. I'm in an okay-ish place. Fire's behavior hurt me, and it still hurts a lot because—"

"Because it's personal and just like on TeeVee."

"Yeah. Exactly. And for a moment, for a short while, I was about to go down that same path. The depression, the sadness—all that was right there. Calling to me."

"But you didn't answer." She holds an extended thumb and pinkie to her ear, phone-style.

"Nope. But that call is still there, and not answering is hard, depending on how loud it is."

Hazel picks a noodle from her tray and drops it onto the plate. "So to stick with that analogy, you're saying seeing Fire would turn those calls into sirens and it might be too much."

I point a finger at her. "Exactly. It's called self-protection." Or rather, self-preservation. It's not weakness avoiding something if it has the potential to throw my mental health into chaos, but rather a strength to admit that. That's what Doctor Shamus said, and I've finally decided to see it that way. *#MentalSanityRocks* Maybe all her talking does bring something good after all.

"So you're saying seeing Fire would hurt you more than some idiot posting a fake death announcement."

I cringe. "Yes. Yes, I guess that's what I'm saying." Tucking a strand of hair out of my face, I lean forward again. "Fire is a good memory. A *really* good memory. It's... It's been a while since I was that happy, you know?" I draw a random pattern onto the table with my finger. "Maybe it makes me pathetic and shows how needy I am, but with him... I felt safe. Physically when wrestling, and emotionally. Having that safety taken away after I relied on it... yeah, that's worse than some idiot who hates me anyway spewing some of the same venom. Nothing new there. Haters gonna hate." Doc Shamus would be so proud right now.

Hazel takes a sip from her Coke, regarding me with her head tilted to the side. "You had it bad for him."

Maybe it's the evenness she says it with, or maybe the fact that she's right, because I *still* have it bad for him, but I feel my eyes tingling with tears. Damn it, I miss him. I miss our wrestling, I miss… *us*.

And there is no *us*.

Probably never was.

I push my chair back. "Haze, I gotta get some fresh air. Tears in the cafeteria are not part of my plan for today." The wink I give her comes close to letting a tear drop.

Her expression changes into one of empathy. "Ugh, sorry, Ev. I never learn, do I?" Like me, she stands up, leaving her tray on the table. A no-no for normal days, but for today… I'll take getting written up if I can get some air, please.

We walk past the rows of tables until we hit the double-doors to the schoolyard. I don't pick up on anybody hating on me or making fun of me, but I'm not stupid enough to believe it's not happening.

No, they're just hiding it better for the moment.

As soon as the cool December wind hits my face, I feel better, like it washed away some of the dark fog that was clouding my soul. As if synchronized, we both wrap our arms around our bodies to keep warm without jackets and stroll down the schoolyard past the tables nobody's sitting at in the direction of the basketball court and grassy area. One lone tray with half-eaten food sits on one of the tables, the wind about to blow the salad's leaves off the plate.

Haze gently bumps into me. "You know what? Let's ask Mr.

Langen if he can come up with a plan, like, a schedule for you. He can run it by Fire and make sure he definitely isn't at the gym at that time." We pass the basketball courts and turn around the corner of the school building toward the grassy area. "Plus, you've been there so often for the last few months, if we add it up, it should come out to the twice a week as he requested. Easily. Ri—"

Voices. Yells. Laughter.

We both come to a standstill at the very same time.

We're not alone in the farthest corner of the schoolyard.

Not by a long shot.

A group of what, maybe fifteen or twenty students, male and female, all upper years, stands around a tree, clapping, laughing, howling from fun.

"Harder!"

"One more!"

"Yeah, you got him good!"

"Blood! Blood! Blood!"

My heart skips a few beats as I narrow my eyes. "Is… Wait, is there somebody standing against that tree?" I take one hesitant step forward, nauseating flutters churning inside my gut. "Are they beating somebody up?"

Hazel grabs my arm. "Let's go, Ev. We don't want to be here."

I shake her off and take another step forward. What—who…?

Dark hair.

A black baseball cap thrown over the crowd into the grass.

"… fuckin' Nightmare—"

"Calan," I breathe. They have Calan.

"Shit," Hazel rasps. "Let's get a lunch monitor—"

"No." I ball my fists at my side.

"No?"

"Takes too long. Let's go." I march forward, every step sure, every heartbeat ready.

"Ever, wait! No! We can't—Ever! We can't." Hazel grabs my shirt and yanks, but with one quick pull and twist, I've released myself.

"Oh, yes. We can. We have to." I've stood by for too long, endured them for too long, let them play their cruel games for too long.

Because I was afraid.

Well, I got declared dead yesterday. How much deader can I be?

When I'm about ten feet away from the group I yell out. "Hey!" Only a few students on the outskirts turn. Some ignore me, some alert their neighbors. "Hey! Idiots!" That gets more attention. Part of me notices people are holding out phones, recording what's happening to Calan—but also recording me.

Once I see them, I can't unsee them: phones are everywhere, following the action. Of course. In my mind, I hear the little ping of a successful upload. Sweat breaks out and runs down my neck. Breathing becomes more difficult.

I have tried to be popular. It backfired spectacularly, and I still carry the scars to prove it. Maybe it's time I try my hand at being unpopular—and being okay with it. But still, the reflex to run is so strong, I have to counter it by storming forward, or the flight instinct would take over.

The first few students jump away as I stomp right through the middle of the group.

The next few don't, so I grab them by whatever I can and shove them out of my way. They protest, most of their words getting stuck as soon as they realize who manhandled them.

"What the…?"

"MatrixGirl—"

"Lunatic."

But nobody shoves me back, nobody keeps me from walking right into the clearing in front of the tree—into the scene of a horror movie.

Arlo and some other douche have each grabbed one of Calan's arms and twisted them back, so that he's pressed against the tree, facing the third person, who's unleashing a swing into Calan's stomach that lands with a thud. A strangulated, cut-off groan breaks from Calan's throat as his body wants to double over from the impact but can't because of Arlo's and Douche's hold.

Calan's not looking good. At all. His shirt is torn at the shoulder, only staying in place because the attacker has a good grip on the fabric. The left side of his face is red and purple from a nasty bruise, his eye on that side swollen already. With the cap missing, the extent of all his scars on the right side of his face are more visible. Where his hair is missing on his temple and right forehead, the skin looks angry, welted, and red.

The third person winds up for another punch, making a show out of it, circling his wrist and blowing onto it. "Gonna make your face look even, Nightmare!"

Ford.

What the actual fuck?

I dart forward and grab the arm lifted for the punch. "Stop it, Ford!"

Ford freezes as a shocked gasp comes from the onlookers. For a moment, his body tenses, and I ready myself for a blow to my face instead of Calan's, but no. Ford lets his hand sink and turns to face me. "Look at that. Crazy girl has joined the party. Heard you were dead." The gaze he tries to level me with is cold and hard.

My pulse kicks into overdrive. I can take it. I can take it. He's not messing with my head.

I can take it.

And I can't show weakness.

I let go of his arm, shake my hands out, and wipe them off on my shirt, as if he had the cooties. Counterattack. "And I heard the only way you can get a girl to make out with you is if you drug her." I don't look away from him, instead stepping forward and in front of Calan, my arms on my hips, my chin raised high. Still, I hold his gaze, which is why I see the anger light up in them.

"You're a fuckin' liar, bitch. Go back to killing yourself—"

"Oh. Well. Sorry. Must have mixed up your voice then." I look back at the others. "Maybe you could help me with that?" I look for the one person I know who'd never let me down—and there she is, fists balled, in the middle of the others, ready to go. "Hazel?"

Hazel catches on and pulls out her phone. "Yeah, really. I thought it was Ford, too. And Arlo. Let's clear this up once and for all. Here's the audio—and, by the way, no use trying to take this away from me and deleting it because this is up in the cloud and several teachers have a copy." A lie, at least part of it, but good insurance. She turns up the volume and holds the phone out.

As the audio begins to play, Arlo and douche let go of Calan, exchanging worried looks as they move closer to listen to the recording.

Ford tries to hold them back. "Just keep him there—"

"He can't go anywhere. I wanna hear this," Arlo says, and right he is. Calan's only way out is through the crowd of students in front of him. The bushes planted next to the tree are too thick to run through and too high to jump over.

As soon as the Arlo/Douche-duo lets him go and Ford's attention is on the video as well, he bends over, one hand on his knees, breathing hard, the other shaking hand feeling for the swelling on his face. I gently take him by the shoulders. "Hey. Calan." I help him up and keep my hands on his shoulders. He lets his head fall back against the tree, his eyes squeezed closed, his face turned away from me. His chest heaves up in irregular breaths, but I can feel his body coiled under my hands.

Damn it. What. Have. They. Done. To. Him.

I whisper at him. "We can get you out of here, okay? We're going to walk through them and not care. They won't beat up all three of us." I hope.

Calan's breath comes out in an unsteady rush like a suppressed sob, its tremble letting part of his torn shirt fall open, exposing—

Scars.

Large, thick, crisscrossing scars on his chest—scars I've seen before, scars I'd recognize anywhere, because they look like something big happened.

My mind short circuits as it adds one and one.

Calan. Fire.

Fire. Calan.

How could I not have known?

#Flashback: what did Sergey start to call him before Fire cut him off? Kel. Yeah. Not *Kelvin* or *Kelley. Calan.* Calan, spoken with a Russian or German or whatever accent. Ugh.

I blink hard. Again. My fingers cramp into his shoulders. "You," I whisper. "It was you."

Calan sucks in an unsteady breath, his eyes wide, shimmering with a myriad of emotions, the most prominent shooting like a dagger to my heart: fear.

One single tear falls from his eye and runs down the scarred side of his face, and it breaks something in me. What have they done to him? What happened to him that *this* is his life when he's at school?

I reach up and gently swipe the tear with my thumb. He twitches and turns away—

"Don't," I whisper. "It's okay. It's me. Let's get away—"

That's the moment the video ends.

Ford huffs loudly. "What a fake. Doesn't even sound like me."

"Not at all," says somebody else.

"Fake news," yells another.

I hear the self-confident smile in Ford's voice. "And I guess we still have some business to continue."

Before he can surprise me from behind, I've turned around, planting my feet and staying protectively in front of Calan, my arms spread out.

Ford snickers. "Oh, that's cute. You protecting the Nightmare? I mean, he's so weak, even protection by a girl is doing him good, but..." He lifts both arms to a bodybuilder pose. "No chance."

Sweat breaks out and runs down my neck. Not good. People still have their phones out. Aimed at us. At me.

I force a slow breath out. *Please, heart, calm down. Not helping.* "Move out of the way, Ford."

"Nuh-uh." He saunters the few steps from Hazel over to Calan and me. "This is defamation. Slander. You accusing me of this shit. I don't like it." Ford stops about a yard away from me, Arlo on his side. Douche is nowhere to be seen. In fact, some of the students are leaving, their heads close together, talking, throwing looks back at Ford and Arlo.

But most stay and watch, their phones silent witnesses to the situation.

A nasty expression grows on Ford's face. "You know, now that I think about it, you coming here and accusing me. It's pretty aggressive. Plus, the way you grabbed me earlier. I have to defend myself." He punches his palm twice.

Oh, dear.

Arlo snickers next to him and moves closer, threateningly.

They're gonna beat up both of us. They're going to make us—

#Epiphany: make *us*?

No. We can make *them*.

"What do you think wrestlers do when their partner doesn't play along? They make them *go along,"* Fire said.

We only have one shot at this. I reach back with one hand until I find his, then throw one glance over my shoulder. "Fire? The show's on." I squeeze his hand twice, hoping—no, *praying*—that he gets it. His ring name should give him a hint.

Ford sneers. "Yeah, it's definitely on, you little—"

Fire squeezes my hand back. Let's take that as a *yes*.

Adrenaline spikes as I drop his hand. "Now!"

There's a chance he'd leave me hanging, he'd leave me alone, but really, I needn't worry. As if synchronized, we both burst forward, me slightly to the left toward Arlo, him to the right, toward Ford.

Our kicks to their midsections land at the same time, and they both double over. The audience breaks out in hushed, surprised whispers that turn into louder yells as both our elbows crash into their faces simultaneously.

Fire grabs Ford, lifts him up high, and throws him on to his back in a perfectly executed choke slam. Me, I grab Arlo by the hair and ram my knee up until I feel resistance.

Arlo drops to the floor next to Ford.

I exhale roughly and ready myself—

Ford and Arlo lie on the ground, groaning.

Nobody else comes storming at us.

Now's the time.

"Fire." I hold out my hand to him, the look in my eyes probably as wild as in his.

He slides his hand in mine, and together we run.

CHAPTER EIGHTEEN

#ComingClean

I run faster than I've run in ages.

Without the fear of Ford and the others catching up with us, I'd never run that far, that fast. And without wrestling, without eating better, there's no way I could sustain this run the way I am. *#Progress.*

Fire doesn't say a word as he keeps himself slightly behind me, his hand in mine, following. He's moving choppier compared to normal, less smooth. His breath comes out harsher and more irregular than normal too, and he stays silent.

I don't say a word, either. I need all my energy for the flight away from these idiots.

Doesn't mean I'm not thinking about all the stuff I'd like to yell in his face right about now.

I lead us down Main Street to the only hideout I know that's close by and, well, out of view. At one point, we stop running because it gets more crowded on the sidewalk and it's just plain weird to be weaving through all these people. Plus, we're so far away, I'm pretty confident to say they're not chasing us down.

Fire stays silent and a step behind me. Like a mom pulling a belligerent child with her, I walk us down Second Street and cross Ocean Front until our feet hit the sand. I drag him down the beach to where the pier crosses the sand out into the sea and pull him with me under the large, wooden structure.

Our little seaside town has two piers. One smaller and narrower one, and one larger and wider one. This one is the wider one, at least twenty yards, with thick wooden pillars supporting it every three yards or so. No matter the tide, the water never comes up all the way under the pier; there's always room to stand or sit in the sand and gaze out into the Pacific. Typically during the summer, lots of photographers like to hang out here and catch the sundown out in the ocean, but this is December. It's cold, for our neck of the woods, and windy. Nobody's here besides us.

Good.

I drag Fire until we're smack in the middle under the pier, a good six yards away from the water's backwash. It's noisy here from the waves breaking and rolling out under the pier, but it comes in handy for me.

Because I intend to yell.

Like a madwoman, I push Fire against one of the wide wooden pillars by his shoulders and glare at him. "What the heck, Fire?! What the actual heck?! I don't even know where to start!" I squeeze my eyes shut and suck a big breath in. Why did he never say he was Calan? Why did he dump me like he did? Out of fear that I'd discover who he truly was? And would it have been so bad if I had? The fact that he obviously didn't trust me enough to confide in me *hurts*.

I trusted him.

But obviously, he didn't trust me.

I deflate and let go of his shoulders. "You didn't trust me enough to tell me who you were." Instead he stuck to his ring name. Even Mr. Langen did—and he obviously must've been in on it. I wonder why he complied with Fire's request, I mean—

"It's complicated." Fire's words are spoken so low, they're barely audible over the sound of the crashing waves.

"Well, try me." I cross my arms in front of my chest.

A muscle thrums along his jaw. "What do you think? I can't say I'm Mr. Popular with others these days." He gestures at the right side of his face but keeps his head slightly angled, so I see most of his intact, non-scarred side.

These days. Is this something new, something moderately recent? I swallow my anger and try empathy. "What happened?"

The muscles in Fire's jaw are working overtime. For a long moment, I fear I overstepped and he won't answer, but then he keeps eyes trained to a spot somewhere out in the sea behind me and swallows hard. "Car accident. My buddy was driving. Got distracted, crashed into a tree, car started burning." His face is tense and hard. "He got lucky, got out fast. Me, I was stuck. If it weren't for some courageous people, I would've burned in there."

Holy. Shit.

I mean, yes, I figured it must've been something big, but this… "You could have died."

Pause.

"And sometimes I wish I did." The way he says it, level, calm, with a certain defeated attitude… I know it too well.

"And I'm glad you didn't." I uncross my arms and stuff my

hands deep into my pockets for warmth.

His gaze whips up to mine, surprise and doubt shining in it.

I give him a little shove on his shoulder. "Still. You could have told me, Fire. That you're Calan."

He laughs out dry. "Yeah, right. If Fire had told you he was Calan, you're telling me the next day you would've come to school, high-fived me, and we'd been having lunch together?" Anger flares in his eyes, and I deflate.

"Well—"

"Yeah, That's what I thought." He sounds bitter. "You wouldn't even look at me in school."

Aw, come on! "Not true! I tried many times, and all you did was walk away or ignore me!" I tried! Eventually, I tried!

His brows narrow into a scowl. "Oh, but I remember you from the very first day you came back to school, when you looked away when those idiots threw wet paper towels at me. You looked away, like everybody else."

Shame assaults me, pushing bile up my throat. "I know," I whisper. "I should've had the strength to say something, but... I wasn't in a good place at that point." Not until today did I dare to strike back. To be unpopular, and to not care what other people think.

Behind us, the waves are washing up the sand, some crashing, some rolling in more gently. Somewhere seagulls do their thing, shrieking and calling. Together with the wind and cold, it makes for a somber mood.

Fire lets his head drop. "It's okay. To be honest, I didn't expect you to go between them and me. Didn't expect anybody to do that."

I squeeze my hands inside my pockets until the pain from my

nails on my palms grounds me. How alone must he have felt if he expected nobody to stand up for him—and worse, when he was proven right, when nobody did stand up for him? "Why did you never fight back yourself? You can fight, Fire. You did today. Why did you never show them what you can do?"

A soft, dry chuckle breaks from his throat, and it leaves a sad, resigned smile in its wake. "I hadn't paid my dues yet."

What the what?

"Fire—"

"Well, now you know." He pushes off the pillar. "Time for you to go back to school and work the crowd. You can go back to ignoring me. I'm sure Ford is going to forgive you."

My mouth drops open. "You didn't just say that."

He shrugs. "Who are we kidding? I'm not good for you, in any way. Add me to your history, and they're never gonna let you live that down. I know how it works," he adds with a bitter undertone.

I shake my head twice to clear it. "Clearly, you know nothing, Jon Snow."

He lifts an eyebrow at my *Game of Thrones* reference. "Oh, believe me, I know."

Sheesh, what an arrogant bastard! I kick up sand in frustration. "Really? I don't think you have a clue. I told you about my problems, my insecurities and believe me, I expected you to run. Guess what? You didn't. Not only did you not run, but you supported me, you helped me. And the moment something not perfect gets revealed about you, the moment I see your scars, you drop me like a hot potato? You didn't even think I would extend the same courtesy to you that you showed me? That I might be on your side?"

He shrugs his shoulders, like he doesn't care. "I'm sure you would've been thrilled to find out Fire looked like Calan."

A frustrated groan leaves my throat. "You don't get it, do you?"

"Oh, no, I get it just fi—"

I shove him back against the pillar, the impact driving the air out of his lungs. "No, you don't!" In a move so much braver then I feel, I cup his face, one palm on soft skin with stubble and a bruise, the other on rougher, scarred skin. "In fact, you're being an idiot," I whisper. My heart beats triple-time. I trusted him once, and he almost broke me. I pray to whomever he doesn't break me again, because I'm done with breaking. *This*—this is about fixing.

Both of us.

Fire twitches from the unexpected touch and sucks in a sharp breath. "Ever—"

"Shush," I say.

Then I lower my mouth to his in a soft kiss.

At first I feel him stiffen under me, his body going rigid, his hands flying up as if he wanted to rip me away from him.

But he doesn't.

Instead, after a moment of hesitation, his body relaxes, and the breath he held is released with the softest, smallest sigh ever, the sound of it shooting right into my soul, spreading tingles all over my body.

Then, with a tentative brush of his lips, he returns the kiss.

#ButterflyAssault

Fire's hands come to lay on my shoulders and slide down my arms.

OMG, this is real, this is happening for real!

And I want more.

I push forward into his body, the body I've felt close to me and even on top of me for the last few months, but *this*, this is a whole new ballgame. I feel him differently, like I'm more alert, every nerve ending firing at triple capacity, every sense stretched to the max.

His hands move to my waist and pull me in, his thumbs circling over my flanks. I want nothing more than to drop my hands and to feel his chest under them, but I'm not sure he'd be comfortable. So I keep them where they are, my thumbs stroking the skin of his face.

Fire gently coaxes my lips apart with his tongue, and the moment our tongues meet, lightning crashes through me. Out of control, I wrap my arms around his neck and pull myself closer, deeper into the kiss. Nothing else matters. Nothing but Fire, but us.

A soft moan leaves his throat, and another one when I roll my hips into his. The kiss intensifies as I become hungrier for more. I glide my hands down his back until I reach his butt, leaving my hands half on his butt, half on his hips. Fire's hand shifts the slightest bit, mirroring my hand position. His teeth gently nip at my lip, giving me the courage to go further.

I slide both hands down over his butt, feeling the curve of his strong muscles. The moment I make the move, Fire mirrors it, and this time it's me who can't keep the moan suppressed. Fireworks light up inside my core, so strong, so bright, they drown out everything else. I use my grip on him to pull myself closer into him, circling my hips and feeling him use the same pressure against my pelvis, hard meeting soft, boy meeting girl. His entire body jolts, as if he'd been shocked.

Breathing out a soft, long puff of air, Fire breaks the kiss and leans his forehead against mine. "Ever," he whispers, giving my butt another squeeze before he moves his hands up to my waist again. "What does this mean?"

I smile, even though he's too close to see it. "It means I like you, idiot." I draw my hands back up to his neck, enjoying the feel of his butt tightening under my hands as they glide over it.

A little tremor rocks his body. "I like you, too."

"Cool. Then we're on the same page."

"Totally," he whispers, placing a soft kiss onto the tip of my nose.

We're both breathing heavily. That kiss, it was real. Raw. Everything.

I snuggle closer to him. I need more Fire against the cold. Funny, how it feels so natural to be held by him like this. Like we were made for it. Like we should've done this a long time ago.

He rubs his hands over my back. "We should go somewhere warmer."

"Not back to school."

A smile graces his face. "Didn't say that, did I? Come on." He holds out his hand and I take it. "Today belongs to us."

CHAPTER NINETEEN

#InternalBeauty

Fire leads me out from under the pier and up the beach toward the more residential areas. We walk silently next to each other, and even though it's similar to the way we got here—holding hands—it's a huge contrast to the way I dragged him over. This is comfortable, like Fire and I always have been. I do notice, though, that he walks close to the stores or fences, whatever we pass, keeping them on his right side, and it makes me sad. Yes, he is scarred, but I wish the world didn't treat him like that. I wish it treated him kinder.

After about five minutes, we arrive at a small, one-story house painted grey with a bright red door and cute little front yard. "Voila," Fire says. "Welcome to my home." He opens the gate for me and closes it again after he's passed through as well. "My parents are at work, so it's all ours."

After entering the code into the number lock, he opens the

door into a large open combined living area. Everything's in white, even the couch and coffee table in front of the floor-to-ceiling sliding doors to the backyard. On the right side, a kitchen is separated from the living area by a high island, also in white. Three full back bar stools are lined up in front of it. "Wow," I say. "This is… bright."

Fire slips out of his shoes. "My mom's an interior decorator; my dad's an architect. They used this house as their guinea pig." He waits for me to take off my shoes as well, then leads the way down to the left. "I didn't let them touch my room, though."

The moment I step into Fire's room, I laugh out loud.

"What?" Fire asks, closing the door behind us.

I turn around, taking in everything that is Fire's room. "I would've known this was your room without you saying so." Give me ten boys' rooms, I would've picked out his easily, no doubt about it.

"Huh. What gave it away?" He sits himself down on the bed in the right corner of the room, close to the window in the center of the wall.

I grin. "Oh, I don't know. Maybe the Ricochet poster?" I point at the poster over his bed, Ricochet performing what I guess is his finishing move. "Or maybe the Ingobernables de Japon towel pinned to the wall? If not that, the framed—and signed— poster of The Rock could have done it." Everywhere I look, little things that fit Fire like a glove come into view: framed autographs, pictures of him with wrestlers I don't know, him in a wrestling ring when he was younger. Most pictures on the shelf on the left side of the room of him are either of Fire in a wrestling ring or taken in different locations with another boy about his age, a blond guy with an infectious smile. "Who's that?" I point at one of the pictures.

"Ronan," he says, keeping his face completely level.

Ronan. "Your ex-wingman? Ronan, the Barbarian?" Hey, I'm a *#GoodListener.*

There's a moment's hesitation before he says, "Yeah. My former best buddy. We don't talk that much anymore since the accident. His parents moved him to his grandparents' in Ohio." He looks down at the hands folded in his lap, and *click*—my brain does the math.

"Wait—Ronan, this guy here, the guy you wrestled with—he was the one you were in the accident with?"

Fire gives a curt nod.

"Shit," I say as I put the picture down again. That would be a reason for a falling out—getting your friend almost killed.

He huffs dryly, then presses one palm into his forehead. "You can say that out loud. Sometimes… people develop in different directions, and with Ronan, that was the case. Always was, but the accident showed that clearly." His lips press into a bitter line.

"Always was?"

Fire makes a circling motion with his finger. "This. I was the wrestling geek to everybody for as long as I remember. The weird one. Never ran with the popular crowd, to put it one way. Ronan, on the other hand, was the king of the school. Classic jock. Girls fought over him even in middle school. Smart. Rich family."

"Wow." I look at the picture again with different eyes. Fire's wearing a John Cena shirt, while Ronan looks preppy in a collared Lacoste shirt, with a white sweater tied around his hips. The way they're standing, it looks like Ronan is in charge, with him standing more in the front, and the way he has one hand on Fire's shoulder. "I can see why girls liked him. Still think you're cuter though, then *and* now." And I mean it. Looking at the pictures I picked up on many things, but not the fact that they were all taken *before* his accident.

Fire lowers his gaze and looks to the side. "Well, at least one person in a fifty-mile radius thinks that. Good to know."

Dang it, my heart hurts for him. "So you changed schools after?" I change the topic somewhat. "And, wait—Mr. Langen lied! He said you were from El Marino High, but you're not even living in the district."

"Not a lie. Bending the truth. We used to live in that area. Moved here a while ago, and I was supposed to stay at my old school with a permit."

"But then…"

"But then the accident happened and my parents thought it was time for a change. Should've known the bullying is worse for the new kid."

"They're idiots. Not your parents. Other people, I mean."

"I know. Believe me, I know."

I pick up a framed picture of Fire, taken maybe two years ago. He's in wrestling trunks with a bare chest, already well on his way to the athletic figure I felt under his full-body wrestling suit. Something's printed on the side of his pants. "Kugelblitz?" I read out. What the what?

He blushes. "I was young. My first ring name. Thought it sounded cool."

I set the picture down again. "Fire came *after*." After the accident. After the fire.

"Yeah. I didn't use a consistent ring name before, just playing around with different gimmicks. But after the accident…" He shrugs, the shoulder under me bouncing me up and down. "I became Fire. The name fit—fit me and a wrestler. And so did the Lucha outfit. I didn't want to be seen."

An ache opens up in my chest. "I know how that feels." And I quote-unquote carry most of my scars on the inside. His are plainly visible for everybody to see, plus the ones his soul must be burdened with.

Sadness radiates from his body and rolls over to me in palpable waves, reverberating in my heart, my soul. The world was unfair to this boy.

The world is unfair, period.

I take a few small steps until I'm standing in front of Fire, then kneel down before him, placing my hands on top of his knees. "But I want you to know I don't see you as Calan, the guy with the scars. I see you as you, as Fire—the guy who's crazy strong and athletic, who's been a rock to me, who's making me feel the most sane while making me go crazy at the same time. I don't care about the scars, Fire. I care about you."

He lifts his gaze and meets mine, wariness shining in it.

I cup his face, my thumb gliding over his bruises and beard stubble on the left, and the scars on the right. Amazing how the cut-outs of his mask for the eyes and his mouth were perfectly fitted to cover any evidence of his burns. Yes, the scars reach up to his right eye but don't quite touch it. And yes, they're close to the right corner of his mouth, but again, not quite touching. When he was wearing a mask, I had no idea the scars were there. The perfect cover.

Yet I don't care about the scars.

I lean forward and place a gentle kiss on his lips. "You are you, Fire. It's *you* I like. I'm not afraid of the scars."

He harrumphs and turns his face away from me—always to

the right, so I won't see the scarred side.

I get it.

But I won't have it.

Gently, I reach up to his shoulders and push. "Lie down."

Surprise flickers over his face. "Lie—"

"Exactly. Lie down." I push once more, for emphasis, and Fire complies, letting himself fall backward but keeping both feet planted on the ground.

I climb up onto the bed and sit down next to him, crisscross-applesauce. "Trust me, Fire." I lay one hand on his stomach, only the thin, torn shirt separating my skin from his. His eyes pop wide, a small gasp breaking from his throat.

"Trust me," I whisper—and slowly move my fingers on his stomach lower, little by little, until I've reached the hem of his shirt. I look at him, his eyes wide, the pulse in his neck beating as fast as mine. "Do you?"

The apple in his throat moves up and down.

And then he nods.

That little nod, it knights me. It lifts me up, and gives me the courage to do what is new to me.

Ever so gently, I slide my whole hand under his shirt. As soon as I make contact, his abs tighten under my palm and he pulls in a sharp breath through his teeth.

I don't move for at least ten seconds, not until the muscles under my hand relax a bit. But then I curl my fingers, dragging my fingertips over his skin.

Fire lies still, rigid, his pulse beating overtime in his neck. I slide my hand a tad higher under his shirt, over his left side. Goosebumps cover his skin, erupting in the wake of my touch.

Not even inch by inch, but centimeter by centimeter I let my fingers wander over to his right side.

Even if I hadn't felt the change in skin texture, the roughness, the harder, raised scars, I would've known I'm in sensitive territory by the way Fire reacts. He pinches his eyes closed, his hands balling at his side, his body coiled so tight, it's basically coming off the mattress.

My heart pitter-patters, and I make a decision. It's only fair.

"Fire," I whisper. "Look."

Using both hands, I grab the hem of my shirt—and pull it over my head in one smooth move, dropping it behind me. I must look bolder or better than I feel because Fire's eyes pop. Like, literally.

"Ever—" He's trying his best to keep his eyes glued to mine and not let his gaze flicker to my goods on display for him, covered only by a black, demi-cup bra.

"Go ahead. You can look, Fire. I *want* you to look. I'm asking you to trust me, so here I am, trusting you." I gesture to my boobs, then turn the slightest so he can see my left upper arm and the thick, linear scars I caused there. "I never wear short sleeves, really. Not since I started cutting. It's not just about looks, but more like… it's too personal. Do I wish I didn't have the signs of my weakness written into my skin? Yeah. Sure. But they're there, a part of me—but a part I don't trust everybody with." I look straight into his eyes. "But I do trust you with them. With *me*."

Fire's dragging in a raged breath.

He sits up, swinging his legs onto the bed, so that I'm between them, and taking off his shirt in the same motion, discarding it to the side.

A flush rises in his cheeks, the smooth, but bruised, *and* the scarred one. His chest is heaving up and down in irregular breaths as he puts himself on display for me, watching my reaction with silent intensity.

Air hitches in my throat. Fire is… beautiful. There's a strength in the way he holds himself, in the way he opens himself up to me, that's beyond the physical. It's what makes Fire Fire. The scars are there, marring most of his right side, from his hairline down his neck, shoulder, chest, and arm, then vanishing under the waistband of his jeans. Some areas are scarred thicker, with raised lines crisscrossing or skin puckered in irregular circles, others turned in different shades of pink, but very little surface is not scarred at all on his right. On his right upper arm, some scars show the same parallel structure mine do, although thicker, more jagged scars disrupt what could have been a straight line.

And then, of course, there are the fresh bruises Ford and his idiotic minions left today.

His body tells a story, and I can't bear that it's a sad one.

Reaching out so slowly I'd give him ample time to move away if he wanted to, I glide a finger over one of the more prominent scars on his lower chest. "Why mostly your right side?"

He swallows hard, and when he talks, his voice is rough. "More exposed. I guess the way I ended up being trapped kept my left side against the seat, and the fire came from the engine in the front."

"Oh," I breathe. He must've been so afraid. In so much pain. I pull my hand away—

—and Fire catches it, pressing it to his chest. "Don't."

I feel his heart under my hand jackhammer against his chest as he lays himself back until his back hits the mattress, giving my arm a slight pull. "Come."

Come wh—

Oh.

Heat assaults my cheeks as I follow his invitation and climb up onto his lap, my legs straddling his hips. The moment I lower myself onto him, we both suck in a simultaneous sharp breath. We both freeze for a moment.

Fire lets go of my hand and places both of his onto my waist, the skin-to-skin contact shooting through me as if I'd been hit by a live wire. My entire world zeroes in on this guy, on Fire, lying under me, naked from the waist up, the longing flaring in his expression mirroring my own. I'm in deep with him. I knew that a while ago, but now… there's no escape. Not that I wanted to.

A muscle thrums along his jaw, his fingers digging into my sides. "Touch me," he whispers, then he sucks in his lower lip and closes his eyes. "Please."

Something in his words, maybe the combination of vulnerability and yearning, tugs at my core. My heart practically explodes with love for Fire, love I want to show him. Fingers trembling, I splay both my hands over his pecs. His body jolts up under mine, bringing me to slide forward over his lap.

I gasp. Did I—

Did I feel that right?

Holy cow.

I swallow dry, then let my hands continue their exploration down his body, caressing every square inch I can reach, making sure to not apply too much pressure to the bruised areas. His abs contract and tremble under my touch, and it comes with a soft moan. The top of his belly button is scarred too, making it look like somebody drizzled hot wax there, a bit dull-looking and thick. I circle over it, then follow the trail of hairs down to his waistband.

As if powered up by launchers, Fire jackknifes up to sitting, his arms sliding around me in an embrace. A throaty groan leaves his throat, his breath caressing over my jawline. He cranes his neck up and kisses me, gently coaxing my lips apart with his tongue, his fingers skimming upward on my back and exploring more of my body on the way down. For a moment, he hesitates before he pulls his hands forward and brings them between us, his thumb brushing the sensitive skin under my bra.

The sensation that hits me is so strong, so unexpected, I arch back and into his touch with a moan.

His throat bobs in a loud swallow as he breaks the kiss, looking up at me, keeping his eyes trained on me as he repeats the movement. My heart skips a good three beats before it remembers how to pump blood. Instinctively, I grind down onto his lap, a move that is rewarded by an upward push of his pelvis.

Something lights up in his eyes, and—*boom*—he has turned us so that I'm lying on my back with him between my legs. The way he shifts his hips… it brings pressure to just the right spot and stars to dance in front of my vision.

"Fire," I breathe.

"Yeah?" His reply is raspy. Hoarse. Out of breath.

"I trust you." I hold the gaze of the guy who's taught me how to be me again, who's helped me to overcome more than one hurdle, and cup his face with both my hands.

For a moment, the fear is back in his eyes, the fear of rejection, of putting himself out there, but it gets overruled by something else, something warmer and braver. His throat bobs in a loud swallow. "I trust you, too." He shifts his weight to the left and peels my hand off his face, placing it over his chest, gliding it over his scarred pec and down his side. "Only you."

CHAPTER TWENTY

#DefenseLawyer

When I arrive at school I don't need to look for Fire—I find him like I had my personal GPS set to his coordinates. He's standing next to the apple trees, a little off the side of the main entrance, blending into the background like I imagine I blended in when I was still Beverly Bacon. The sight of him brings the butterflies inside my tummy to somersault. Yesterday was magical. Fire and me were magical. Yes, the pants and my bra stayed on, but still... *#Magical.*

Amazing how Fire can have such a presence in the ring and when I'm alone with him, but be so... unnoticeable outside of it, like he had two different personas. The way he leans against the tree, scarred side of his face turned away from the path, cap pulled down deep over his face, hands buried into his pockets... It's a different Fire than the one in the ring. One-hundred-eighty-degrees different.

Fire scans the passing crowd the way a deer would look for hunters, but the moment he recognizes me, the apprehension and wariness on his face morphs into guarded joy. Dang, if that didn't fuel those butterflies for me. I practically dance over to him and wrap him in a tight embrace.

"Morning, Fire."

The first second of the hug, Fire's as stiff as a log, but then he deflates and returns the hug, molding his body to mine. "Morning, Ever."

I inhale a deep breath of his Fire scent. When exactly I began to associate it with comfort, with home, I don't know, but I do. Breathing in Fire calms me and excites me at the same time.

I let go of him. "You ready?" Funny, Hazel asked me the same thing what feels like yesterday.

His face falls. "M-Maybe we shouldn't. Maybe we should keep our distance. They'll—"

"Fire. We talked about this." I reach for his hand and take it in mine. "I'm done caring about them. Done. I care about you, and I'm making a choice." I squeeze his hand once. He needs to stop worrying. We've got this. Really, it's not school we need to worry about. What are a couple of hundred kids compared to thousands hating on you? And yeah, I'm not stupid. I assume it will take an hour max before a picture of MatrixGirl together with the Nightmare is posted online—but do I care?

No.

At least not about them uploading a picture. About the ignorant and hurtful comments, yes, but: there's an advantage to being completely *#offline*, and it's called blissful ignorance. It's all mine. And I would like to keep it that way.

Speaking of: "I would recommend you stay off social media,

though."

His pupils widen. "Huh?"

"Not so much Twitter or whatever, but... do you have a... a TeeVee account?" My stomach cramps. Guess that's what recovering addicts get when they think of their drug of choice.

"TeeVee?" His voice goes up at the end and breaks, like he was still in puberty. "N-Not really. I—"

"Awesome. Cool. No TeeVee. Good." I pat his shoulder like a praising parent, because *#Yay*, finally somebody who hasn't followed the siren call of TeeVee. "Then, please don't go and open an account today, okay?" And now off that wonderful topic, please, before I get sucked in again. I double-squeeze his hand in mine. "Ready?"

Fire chews on his lower lip, then nods. "Okay. Let's do it."

"Exactly. Let's show them we don't fear them."

Together we join the masses and walk up the stairs to the main entrance. Fire squeezes my hand like his life depends on it, but he keeps his head held high, walking tall and strong. This is Fire next to me, not Calan. At least mostly.

We enter through the double doors, the usual noise welcoming us.

Until the first pair of eyes falls on us.

And the second.

And the third.

One could think there was some kind of neuron-overload blocking speech when they see our entwined hands because as more and more people begin to spot us, the voices drop until the hallway is quieter than after John O'Connor slipped and bust his head open last April.

I ignore them.

Fire's hand tightens like a vise around mine, but he doesn't run, he doesn't hide. He stays with me, using me as his anchor. When I came back to school, Hazel did the same for me. Boy, what a messy school year.

We're about to turn into the hallway toward the health classroom, when Mr. Langen comes around the corner, giving us a nod when he sees us and blocking our way, making us stop in the middle of the hallway. "Everly. Calan."

Calan, not Fire. In retrospect, hats off, Mr. Langen, for being so smooth and for not giving away Fire's identity either here or in the ring. Mental note—ask Fire about that whole wrestling-Mr. Langen-thing. "Good morning, Mr. Langen."

Fire stays quiet, but I swear I hear him swallowing.

"So," Mr. Langen says, glancing at our hands, then at Fire.

Fire focuses on a spot somewhere over Mr. Langen's shoulder. "Yup," he replies. Nothing else.

Mr. Langen takes a slow breath in, a hint of worry on his face. It's adorable and much appreciated, but not necessary. We've got this.

I hope.

Langen scratches his temple. "Well, okay then. Anyway. Guys. You, me, Principal Gunn."

"What?" My entire body tenses. "Why?" I take it back; we haven't *got this* at all.

Mr. Langen gives me the look adults like to give small children when they ask stupid questions. "Oh, I don't know. Maybe because somebody forgot the real world isn't wrestling and fought two students on school property?"

Oops. I cringe. "But—"

Fire is faster. "They deserved it."

Mr. Langen's eyes soften. "I know. And that's why I'm coming with you. Felt it was unfair to have the principal bring up the fighting and skipping half the school day without somebody there to defend you."

I grimace. "Nobody called." I thought we were in the clear, because nobody called Mom, and I didn't tell her. I just... didn't.

My teacher cocks his head. "Doesn't mean the school didn't notice. Do I know why Principal Gunn decided to play it this way? No. But like I said, I also don't think it's fair, so let's go." He gestures ahead. "You know the way."

Unfortunately, I do. Unease squirms in the pit of my stomach. Last thing I want to do is face Ford and Arlo. Or Principal Gunn, for that matter. Somehow it's easier to walk through crowded hallways than to line up against those two in front of the principal.

Once we reach the admin hallway and the principal's door, Mr. Langen pauses, a hand on the doorknob. "Let me do the talking, if possible, okay, Fire?" Ah, we're back to *Fire*. Maybe because the pretense isn't necessary anymore: Calan is new to our school, but Fire's been wrestling with Ben Bullet for forever.

Fire nods, and so do I.

"Wonderful. And... Everly?"

"Yes?"

"Your father called and left me a voice message. He's requesting an update when we're done here."

Seriously? "Why does he know and not my mom? And he has no right—"

"You should ask Principal Gunn." Mr. Langen lifts a palm to the ceiling, as if to say, *Heaven knows.* "I'm not saying he's handling this well, but you know how your father has been putting pressure on all of the staff to be kept up to date with your progress.

Anyway. Calm down. I'm optimistic this will be going well here. I've got ammo." He pats the right pocket of his tweed blazer, then knocks and enters without waiting. "I have Everly and Calan here, sir."

Looks like I needn't have worried about Ford and Arlo. Neither of them is here. But boy, am I glad we brought Mr. Langen as reinforcement, because it looks like judge and jury are here, but somebody forgot to call in our defense lawyers.

Principal Gunn sits behind his desk, three adults in their fifties or so on the chairs in front of him, one male-female couple and one other male. All turn when we enter, and all look at us with cool anger.

These must be Ford's and Arlo's parents. Oh, great, even better than their sons. *#Sarcasm*

The man sitting on the left, a balding man in his fifties with more weight on him than healthy, makes a dismissive sneer. "These two beat up our boys? Hardly believable."

We do get a once-over by the impeccably dressed woman next to the other man on the right. "Well, my Arlo has the bloody nose to prove it. And he didn't do anything. This kind of aggressive behavior does not belong in school." Arlo's mom turns back with an arrogant twist of her body.

Principal Gunn jabs an angry finger onto the desk. "I completely agree, Mrs. Bucking. Inexcusable behavior. We do not tolerate any form of violence in our school—"

"Agreed," the other man, Ford's dad I assume, throws in. He is dressed in a formal and expensive-looking suit, and despite his balding head and being overweight I can see he used to look a lot like Ford when he was younger. Especially when he glares at us like his son did yesterday. "I assume they're going to get expelled."

Shock twists my stomach into a figure eight. Expelled? They can't expel us; we only defended ourselves! If I get expelled, I know where I'm going, no matter how much better I'm doing, because Dad won't care: It starts with *boarding* and ends with *school!*

Ford's dad taps on a stack of printed papers in his lap. "I have read through your school's regulations and it's clearly there. Chapter three, paragraph—"

Mr. Langen clears his throat. "Correct, Mr. Rodgers. The school's regulations call for dismissal of an aggressive student. I agree, it's only fair that somebody who hurts others and clearly is a disruption to the daily routine should not return to school."

What the what? That's not helping us!

"Exactly. Thank you." That's Arlo's dad talking. "And I mean, look at *him*. No wonder my son's afraid of this guy. The face of a thug."

For a moment, I can't believe he actually went there.

But, boy, he did.

Like a reflex to Mr. Bucking's words, Fire looks down to the right, hiding his face, and rage flares up inside of me. How dare he? *How dare he?* "Oh, wow," I say, propping the hand not holding on to Fire's on my hip. "Like father, like son, I guess."

"Excuse me?" Arlo's dad looks outraged, like I just ruffled his feathers.

Gunn slaps a palm onto the desk, then points a finger at me. "Ms. Aldaire, you're out of line—"

"*I* am out of line? Have you heard what he just said?" I jab a finger in the general direction of Arlo's dad. This is so not fair! All adults against Fire and me, come on!

At least Gunn has the decency to blush. "Well—"

"Everybody. Please." Mr. Langen interrupts the principal and steps forward like a referee in the ring, only the striped shirt missing. "I assume we all would prefer to let facts speak to punish those who did wrong, am I correct?"

All three parents nod, Arlo's mom the most vigorously.

"That's what I thought." Mr. Langen reaches in his back pocket and brings out his phone.

#OhShit. It's one thing talking about it, a whole different to have the carrot dangle right in front of my face. Cold sweat breaks out and trickles down my neck. Now it's me squeezing Fire's hand like crazy. I know what he's going for, and it's not that I thought this wouldn't happen—it's just that I hoped I wouldn't have to see it. *#KeepingMySanity*

From the angle I'm standing next to him, I can see the screen. He scrolls, taps on the TeeVee icon—

And I close my eyes and turn away.

I don't want to know.

I don't want to know what exactly is online.

What color the frame is.

How many likes we have.

How many upvotes.

How many dislikes.

How many hateful comments.

But gee, *I do want to know.* It's like a need opened in my chest when the phone came out the pocket. Apparently, talking about not caring and actually not caring when the temptation is right there are two different ball games.

Fire's thumb smooths over the back of my hand, grounding me in the present. A small movement I'm eternally grateful for. *He understands.*

Mr. Langen steps forward and away from me. Releasing a

shaky breath, I open my eyes again, my heart hammering like crazy. *#DodgedABullet*

"If you all wouldn't mind directing your attention to this video. Several students witnessed the whole thing, and I feel like we should know the extent of the violence before we come up with a sentence."

Everybody nods, and Mr. Langen hits *play.*

Fire and I can't see what's on the screen, and I don't want to— I don't need to. I hear the cheers, hear them rise with every punch Arlo and Ford deliver, hear their taunting, their name calling, and it makes me nauseous. Fire doesn't fare much better, if the way he holds on to my hand is any indication. We're both going to have bruised hands by the time this is over, seriously.

Arlo's mom gasps out loud. "That's Arlo—"

Principal Gunn looks from one parent to the others, clearly taken aback by what he's seeing. "But you said—"

Oh, dear. Seems like somebody is realizing just because Ford and Arlo are considered cool doesn't mean they're always right or telling the truth…

Mr. Rodgers is red in his face, the muscles in his jaw working overtime, as he is focused onto the small screen.

I hear my voice—ugh, *#squeaky*—and a short pause with the shouts and yells, then about ten seconds of surprised *whoas, holy shits,* and *what the fucks,* then the video stops.

Silence.

Arlo's mother is the first to find her words again, and to my absolute surprise there is no quiet, apologetic *sorry.* Instead, she snarls at Mr. Langen. "That's not what Arlo told us happened! He would never— That video must have been taken out of context!"

"Agreed!" Her husband reaches for her hand and squeezes it.

"I assume they provoked our boy and his friend somehow, and when they finally fought back, somebody recorded it!" The hand not holding his wife's balls into a fist.

What the what? "Didn't you see what happened?" I burst out. "What you see is what you get—they started it!"

"Sure. Nice try," Arlo's dad snarls.

Impressive how the tension in the room has grown hostile in less than thirty seconds. The only person quiet is Ford's dad, but he doesn't look any happier with his lips pressed into a thin line and eyebrows pulled down into a v.

Fire swallows hard, then clears his throat. "Actually, if you check @Alpha-Jesse001 you'll find how everything started. From the very beginning." His voice breaks at the end and he clears it once more, to overplay it.

What the what? My gaze whips over to him. I thought he wasn't on Tee—

"On it." Mr. Langen types and scrolls. "Ah. Here we go." He hits play and turns the screen around.

The first two seconds are static, or maybe the sound of wind against a microphone, then somebody snickers.

"Fuck me, he's so stupid. Sits there all alone." *Arlo.*

"Begging for it." *Ford.*

"Thought you told him to keep his fucking face out of your sight." That—That must be Douche, I think. His voice sounds as if he was closer to the mic. Must be his phone then, I assume. He's recording.

"Obviously he didn't understand the first fifty times I introduced my fist to his grill. Hey, Nightmare!" The last two words Ford calls out louder. "I told you to eat out of sight. You expect anybody to keep their appetite with your ugly mug around?"

Oh God. I close my eyes. That tone, the aggression, the phrasing—in that combo, it's the absolute trigger for me. Shudders run down my back, and the nausea that's been lingering for the last minutes flares up.

The sound of something clattering to the ground comes through the speakers, part of it drowned out by grunts—Fire's—and then Arlo's voice: "This time we're gonna put you in the hospital, Nightmare!"

Mr. Langen sucks in air through his teeth as he pauses the video. "I believe this is enough. At least I don't want to hear any more of this." He pockets his phone and works a shaking hand through his hair.

This time the silence is different. Deeper, if that makes sense. Heavier.

Arlo's father pinches his nose, a strangulated breath leaving his throat. "We thought—" His voice gives out and he reaches for his wife's hand, who wipes away a tear from her eye.

"He swore he was attacked unprovoked. And... and we believed him." She sniffles, and I kind of feel for her. Kind of. Must be hard to have a child who's a liar *and* stupid enough to underestimate the power of social media. There's always a different video somewhere, always a comment that states the exact opposite of what you read before. Always somebody who messes with you.

Welcome to the club of people who learned their lesson the hard way.

Gunn puts on a fast smile. "I... I mean, it's difficult to blame Calan and Everly at this point—"

The words leave my mouth before I can stop them. "Fantastic.

At least you're not ignoring this video like you did the other one. Ford isn't the saint you want him to be, and neither is Arlo."

Gunn turns purple-red. "Ms. Aldaire—"

"Speaking of video or my son being no saint." Ford's father's voice is calm, yet loaded with authority, and it makes Gunn's mouth snap shut. "I'm very much interested in hearing more about that. Does anybody have said video available?" For the last part, he turns to look at me.

The principal stands up. "I don't think that's necessary—"

"After what I have seen of my son here, I think it is very much necessary, Mr. Gunn."

Oh, I like Ford's dad. Way more than his son. Maybe he's going to see the video for what it was and not chalk it up to *boys bragging*, like Gunn.

Mr. Langen swipes over the screen. "I actually do have the video in question. And Principal Gunn, I also have an additional preliminary police report for you." He reaches into his right pocket of his tweed blazer and produces a double-folded paper from it. The *ammo* he talked about? "You might remember there was a death announcement against a student posted online, which the police filed as online harassment."

"I remember," Gunn snaps. "What does that have to do with the schoolyard incident?"

"Everything. Ms. Aldaire called me a few minutes ago: The police were able to track the IP address." Mr. Langen pauses. "And it came from our school."

Holy cow— How about breaking with the good news maybe *first*? And sorry, but *#LifeWithoutAPhoneSucks*, because Mom should've let *me* know right away!

"What? From our school? That... That must be a mistake, I

can't imagine any of our students—"

"Would do what, sir? Bully somebody online, like they do in the schoolyard?" Langen's tone has bite in it, and Gunn feels it.

"No. I mean… It's unfathomable—"

"Really, not so much. We looked into it and found the student assigned to the specific computer." He slaps the folded paper into his palm twice, then hands it to Gunn.

Wait—they know who did it? Who? *Who?*

Gunn takes it, a sour expression on his face. "I'll look at it later—"

"You might want to look at it now. Mr. Rodgers might also be interested in it. But—"

Mr. Rodgers might also be interested in it—Ford! It was Ford. No f-ing way.

Ford!

Can't take *no* for an answer, or what's his problem?

Mr. Langen continues. "—in the interest of privacy and time, I think we can dismiss Everly and Calan and have them return to class, since we have established they acted in self-defense, am I correct?"

That's what it must feel like with a personal defense lawyer with us. I'll take it.

All three parents nod, only Principal Gunn joining them a tad too late. I figure it must be hard for him, realizing the world out there is not as black-and-white as he thought it was.

Mr. Langen gives us a wink and nod. "Go, guys. Let the class know I'll be in in a few minutes." He ushers us out before Gunn can change his mind.

The door closes behind us with a loud click, and Fire and I release a simultaneous breath.

"Are you thinking what I'm thinking?" I say.

"That Ben is awesome?"

I chuckle. "Oh my God, yes. Without him we'd been overrun. Wouldn't have stood a chance. And if you hadn't known Douche posted that video…" It changed everything. And yet, the taste it left in my mouth is twice as bitter. "So you *are* on TeeVee." It comes out way more accusing than I wanted it to. Blame it on my sensitivities regarding that topic. Somehow I assumed he didn't have an account, the way he reacted when I told him to stay off TeeVee right before school today, or given the fact that he only takes his phone with him when he's out and about, as he told me.

Fire frowns and shakes his head, keeping his gaze trained onto the floor. "Not really, like I said. I have a throw-away account I don't do anything with. Sometimes I look stuff up, like after…" He sucks in his lower lip and points to his face.

"Oh." *Oh.* I got it. "Sometimes it's good to know what's out there, you're saying."

He shrugs. "Yeah. I mean, I wouldn't call it *good* to know, but… at least it gives you time to mentally prep."

Don't I know it. I'm such an idiot when it comes to TeeVee. *#Oversensitive* "I got it." I give his hand a gentle squeeze. I got it. "I'm sorry I—"

Hazel comes running around the corner. "Ever! Are you—?" Her glance drops to our entwined hands and her eyes pop open so wide, they're bulging. Stopping in front of us, she puts both hands on her hips. "And that's why you need a phone again, my dear. I'm not up to date with current events, it appears, since apparently your landline is also broken." *#HintHint*

Oops. I didn't call her back. Totally my bad, especially because calling—or rather, texting—Hazel would have been my number one activity about six months ago. To be honest, I probably would've posted about Fire and me as well. And yet none of those urges hit. None.

See? When temptation isn't right in front of my nose, I'm doing a great job. *#Maturity*

"Sorry, Haze. Yesterday was…" Wonderful. Mind-blowing. "Busy."

"Busy, eh? I mean, I figured the others didn't catch up with you, but man, a sign of life would've been nice. Or, you know, some obviously much needed girl talk, 'cause, you know, I'm a wee bit surprised here." There's that glance to our hands again—crap! Hazel doesn't even know half of it!

I tug on Fire's hand. "By the way, Hazel, you remember Fire, right? From the Masquerade? Fire, meet Hazel, Hazel, meet Fire. All official now."

Fire gives a small wave. "Hi."

Hazel's mouth drops open. "Wait—Fire—Calan—"

"One and the same." I make a circling gesture with my finger. "Long story." One we don't need to dive into standing in front of Gunn's office in the admin hallway.

"O-Okay." She gives Fire a skeptical onceover. "So, what do you go by then? Fire? Calan? What shall it be?"

"Fire," he says. "Calan is for the ones who don't know me."

Hazel cocks her head, and knowing her, she's about to point out that she doesn't really know Fire, either, so I beat her to the punch.

"Gunn had us called in. Wanted to kick us out of school for fighting on school grounds."

She throws one worried glance at the door behind us, then hooks one arm under my free one and guides the three of us down the admin hallway. "Yeah, that's what I heard and why I came running. Figured a video might help—"

"Mr. Langen was on top of it. He—"

"Okay, that's where he was? With you? Class has been thinking he's out sick, since he's like ten minutes late. If Chris hadn't seen him take you guys down to admin, I wouldn't even have had an idea—"

"Easy, Haze." I pat her shoulder. "Yes, Mr. Langen was with us and showed the video that's on TeeVee—"

She stops so sudden, I have to tug on Fire's hand to have him stop as well. "You say that like it's no big deal, but… It's literally all over the web, Ever. Are you going to be okay?"

Huh. Am I?

Seeing the app, it called to me. And yeah, thinking about what is going on online, without me monitoring it, it makes me nauseous. Knowing the hate is still pouring freely, only I don't know the extent of it. *#Shudder* Makes me feel helpless somehow.

On the other hand, I wasn't helpless yesterday when I didn't walk past Fire, but I stood up to the bullies. I feel the pull of TeeVee, but I'm resisting it, I'm stronger than I thought I could be. I'm currently sandwiched between my best friend and… well, my boyfriend, or if not that, then at least a special friend. And I just got cleared of wrongdoing by Mr. Langen.

Am I okay?

Surprisingly, I think I am.

Things have changed for me—*I* have changed. My attitude. As Beverly Bacon, I was insecure and I was bullied for it. An easy target. As MatrixGirl, I was stronger, successful—and I was targeted because of that. You can't win.

Or maybe you can, just in a different way.

A slow grin spreads over my face.

"Ever?" Hazel waves a hand in front of my face. *#AnybodyHome?*

"You know, guys," I say, tugging Hazel closer on my left and Fire on my right, "after everything I've been through and after everything Fire's been through, I'm thinking we're too good for them. And no matter how much they gossip and try to lift themselves up through that, we'll always be better. Because we're not stooping low to their methods. We. Are. Better." I bring Fire's hand up to my lips to place a kiss onto it. I have to work for it, though, as rigid as he is. I feel him. Reliving everything, it's stressful, but: "I like it when things work out for once. Us, one. Bullies, zero."

Hazel lets go of a relived laugh. "Yeah, for sure. Let it be known that bullies always pay for what they did, one way or another."

Fire twitches next to me—

"One way or another," I repeat, looking up to his eyes. We've got this.

A quick, forced smile appears on his face. "Y-Yeah," he stutters, forcing a visible swallow. "One way or another."

CHAPTER TWENTY-ONE

#DroppedABomb

"**Y**ou can do it, guys!" Hazel claps her hands. "Come on!" She claps some more, harder, and moves slightly to the right so she can keep a better eye on the ring—actually, on Fire. And, okay, maybe on me as well.

I blow out a big puff of air and wipe my palms on my leggings. I can do it. Hazel's right. I can do it.

Fire pulls himself up to standing on the second rope, facing me standing half-way in the middle of the ring. I swallow hard. I can do it. He cocks his head, waiting for my signal. We've been practicing this move for the last few hours, from the basics up. Theoretically, I should be able to pull it off.

Theoretically. Only one way to find out how well my training holds up in real life.

Here goes nothing. I nod—

—and Fire jumps off the second rope, as if he were a koala

baby jumping through the air ready to latch on to its mom, arms wide open, legs spread. For a moment, I'm afraid the velocity of his impact is going to throw me over, but no, Fire's that good. He timed the jump exactly the way he said he would, with more of a downward force than one driving me back, and that's what I'm feeling when his body crashes into mine. He anchors his hands together behind my neck to stabilize himself, one leg to the right of my shoulders, the other to the left. Lightning fast, I grab him by the hips, step back with one foot for a more stable stance—

And drop myself to my knees, slamming him down back first onto the mat in a not-quite-so-bad Powerbomb.

"Yes! Pin him!" Hazel yells. "Go, Ever!"

I scramble up and forward, driving Fire's legs back, and roll him up onto his shoulders. Something black-and-pink slides into the ring—

"One! Two!" Hazel slams her palm onto the ring's surface with each count. "Three! And the victory goes to… Everlywhoneedsaringname! That was awesome!" She pulls up on her knees and claps.

I have to agree. I take my weight off Fire and drop his legs—

One of his hands darts up and gets me by the neck, pulling me in closer. "That was really, really good, Ever." Pride shines from Fire's eyes as he sits himself half up, me in his guard. "And totally hot, if I may add." He brings his mouth to mine in a soft kiss, the edges of his mask scratching over my chin.

I swear, the ring flips upside down, and the world with it. It's been two weeks since *that* day. Two weeks during which we've done our fair share of kissing and… well, *stuff.* But there's no habit forming, no getting used to Fire's kisses or touch: I'm still as addicted as on the first day. Maybe even more.

That's why I push deeper into his kiss. He can't just tease me, come on! A throaty growl breaks from his throat when he feels my tongue gliding over his lips—

"Ew, guys. Get a room. I came here to see you wrestle, not to make out." Hazel adds a gagging noise, and man, what is a good girlfriend supposed to do? I break the kiss but lean my forehead against Fire's, the flame applications on it nice and cool against my sweaty skin.

"She's such a spoilsport," I whisper, just loud enough for Hazel to—

"I heard that, you know?"

Fire chuckles softly under me. "You guys…!" But he scoots a tad farther away for me to sit himself up.

Aw, man.

Anyway.

Hazel holds out a high-five for Fire, then me. "That was awesome, really. Wait, I think I said that already. Never mind, still was. Totally smooth. Only thing is, you need a ring name, Ever."

"I know." I'm still waiting for an epiphany.

"Then work on it, woman, or I'll choose one for you. But yeah, well sold, both of you. I mean, make it longer and this could've been a real match! I'm in awe, Ever." She lays a hand over her heart. "You are so set for the end-of-the-year performance. You have a couple of spots you can string together to a nice match. The things you can do…! Lock up, running ropes, clothesline, some trapping, some rolling, a Boston Crab, a Choke Slam, my favorite, a Stone Cold Stunner, and now a Powerbomb. I mean, add an angle—a storyline," she adds for my benefit, "and this is gold! Fan-freaking-tastic."

I feel my cheeks warm. "Thank you, Haze. I'm actually kind

of looking forward to it. Good thing there's no pressure at all."

Her eyes narrow. "What do you mean?"

"Nothing. Only that Dad freaked out with the whole Ford-Arlo-thing. Like, *now she's becoming violent as well.*" I guess I was naïve thinking I could keep my little *altercation* from Mom. Or Dad. Not with Dad on Gunn's speed dial list, or Mom on Mr. Langen's. Sigh. Dad's next facetime call wasn't exactly fun. "Took Mom a good thirty minutes to remind him that one, he wanted me in wrestling and pushed for it, and two, all I did was defend myself."

"Ugh." Haze lets her tongue hang out. "Your dad is special."

"Tell me about it," I mumble. Mom on the other hand is on *#TeamEver,* solid. Actually, correction: she's on *#TeamEverAndFire* since she met him the day after Mr. Langen bailed us out of Gunn's office. She thinks Fire is fantastic—which I happen to agree with—and while I do pick up on those motherly worried looks she sometimes gives me when she thinks I'm not paying attention, she's not lecturing me. I know she wishes I had *met him at a different point in my life,* translation, she's worried what might happen if something went wrong between Fire and me. But she isn't lecturing me, so I'd call that support. A whole different category than my sperm donor.

I pick some lint off my pants. "I think Dad's kinda waiting for me to fail so that he can stuff me into that boarding school."

Hazel makes a face. "Ew. But your mom—"

"Will try to fight it, but if he involved his lawyers and they make a good case, it could happen. She says if they bring up the bullying and weave it in with my past"—i.e., me trying to kill myself—"they could convince the court I'd be safer and better off in that stupid school."

"Ugh." Haze makes a gagging noise. "Well, not going to happen. One, Mr. Bully himself, Ford, has been expelled. Mr. Assistant Bully, Arlo, is on 24/7-watch by his parents and school, so he can't put even a toe out of line. We're safe. Right, Fire?"

Fire fixes a fast smile on his face. "Bully free since twelve-oh-three."

"Ex-act-ly." She points a finger at him. "Two, Ford's father will be donating all the money he made with his post from shares etc., so something good comes out of it. And most importantly, three, you were looking great wrestling. Ah, that Powerbomb…" She lays a hand over her heart.

"True that." Fire jumps up into a squat, then stands up. "Perfect ending for a perfect training day. You witnessed the great finale." He bows and slips out of the ring under the third rope. Holding on to the second rope, he sticks his head into the ring again. "Hey, Ever?"

"Yeah?" I scoot over so that I'm in front of him.

"You still coming with me to my place, right?" He looks at me from under his lashes, his mask doing nothing to hide the insecurity shining through his words. I swear, he still doesn't trust me that I like-like him. He still worries I'm going to fall in line with the other idiots and call him names and drop him.

I smack him over the head. Lovingly, of course. "Yes, Fire. I am. Nowhere I'd rather be."

A huge smile lights up his face. He jumps up once and smacks a kiss onto my cheek. "Awesome."

Aw. I melt a bit. *#Sappy*

Hazel looks after him as he saunters over to his bag. Funny thing is, these days, Fire is actually changing out of his wrestling costume into normal street clothes—now that I know he's Calan and he doesn't have to keep the pretense up anymore. He still prefers to wrestle when nobody else is around though, which is why we've been making good use of the Golden Hour of wrestling gyms: too late for people working out over lunch, too early for those coming to train after work. It's gonna get busier in the next thirty minutes, I predict.

"That boy." Hazel sighs when Fire bends down, his butt in the air. "I really wanna know what else you're working on." She sits down crisscross-applesauce next to me.

I misunderstand the innuendo on purpose. "I'm working on a moonsault." Jumping off the third rope, doing a flip, and landing on my opponent… It looks so easy when Fire does it. He's actually done the double-moonsault twice since that unlucky day I sprained my ankle. Me, I have a hard time doing a flip onto the crash pad. "Fire says it's almost easier to do it to him than into the crash pad, but…" I shrug. "It's damn high."

Hazel gives me a small shove. "Ya think? You've done so much more than I ever thought you would, no offense."

"None taken. Same here." I blame Fire, though. He's the one who ignited the flame for wrestling for me, pun intended.

She lowers her head and her voice after a quick glance at Fire taking off his kneepads and stuffing them into his bag. "I also didn't expect to see *this*." She tugs on my tank top and taps my three-quarter leggings. "You're comfortable around him, aren't you?"

I glide one palm over the scars on my left upper arm. "Yeah," I whisper. "I am. It just happened. You know me, I was most comfy in baggy clothing, but somehow… I don't know, somehow it changed, or rather, Fire changed it, and not that he said anything about my outfit, but maybe that's it. Maybe because he always accepted me the way I am, I felt I could let more and more of myself shine through, you know?" Maybe my baggy layers were like the walls coming down, little by little, the more I trusted him.

Hazel brushes a palm over the ring surface. "Speaking of accepting you the way you are. I didn't want to ask when Fire could hear me, but you said your dad was mad about the fighting-thing… how's he taking everything with Fire?"

Dad. Who cares? "Well, that's easy. I didn't say anything about Fire." All he asked was how school is going when we FaceTimed last week. Neither of us mentioned anything about the near-expulsion, probably because neither of us was in the mood to talk it out *again*.

"Your mom likes him though. So that's good."

"Better than good. And she didn't stand a chance not liking him." A grin steals across my face. "Did I tell you that the first time he came over to my house, he arrived at the same time as Mr. Langen?"

"Yikes."

"Yeah, that was awkward." Don't know for whom most, though. Mom hugged Mr. Langen, I hugged Fire, and both of us pretended this was normal, like we'd been doing this for years.

"Hey, at least she hasn't offered to share a pack of condoms yet." Hazel ducks out of the way as I pretend-swing at her head.

"*Yuck*, Haze! Yuck, yuck! I don't want those images stuck in my head!"

She cackles. "I wouldn't be surprised if she did though. Your mom has come a long way trusting you and letting go, to a degree at least. I mean, for example, I'm surprised you're here today." She taps the Apple Watch on her wrist and angles it for me to see, time and date popping up.

No need to read the screen to know what she's referring to.

"You mean because it's today, six months ago that…" I make a slashing gesture across my wrist, and Hazel nods.

"Exactly. I would've figured she'd keep you home today, since it's hard on her."

I know it is, but to be honest, for the last week or so I wondered if she was even going to mention the date. If dates had names, we'd call *that* day *Voldemort* and never speak its name again. *#TheDayThatMustNotBeNamed* "I think she doesn't want me to see how it's affecting her. She doesn't want me to feel bad or guilty or anything. But change of topic to something more uplifting, speaking of Mom-slash-moms: today I'm actually going to meet Fire's mom."

Hazel whistles through her teeth. "Big step, Ever."

"Agreed. I can't stop worrying about what she's going to say. I mean, what if she isn't thrilled that I'm together with her son? If she doesn't like me? I'm in a good place right now, but I don't know how I'd handle rejection."

She plays with the laces of her boots. "Speaking of good place… That means you probably don't… I mean, you probably don't want to know—"

"Heck no." The answer is out before she can finish her question, but it doesn't take a genius to figure out where she was going: online. TeeVee. I don't even want to think about that double-edged sword. I ball my hands into fists and relax them again. "Don't tempt me, Haze." I might hold up well right now, but that's because I am as far away from anything TeeVee as I can be. And I'm smart enough to know that a glimpse won't be enough, that I'll get sucked in, and that is the first foot into the downward spiral I know only too well.

Half the school blames Fire and me for getting Ford kicked out and Arlo on bad-boy-watch. The video doesn't matter, that's *#FakeNews*. And unfortunately, truth versus lie doesn't hold a candle to popular versus unpopular, and when it comes down to that, MatrixGirl and the Nightmare are going to lose every single time.

I know that.

I can't say I trust myself with TeeVee at this point. Handling everyday life is enough for me at the moment. I can only do one thing right at a time. Too many hits might penetrate the defenses. The crazy thing is that even though I know hate is pouring out over us right now, I still want to see it. Knowing it's there, happening in front of my eyes, only I can't see it—

A drop of cold sweat runs down between my shoulder blades.

Hazel fixes a quick smile on her face. "Figured. Never mind. Self-preservation, eh?"

"Self-preservation." I nod, shivering from the cold sweat running down my neck.

That's what TeeVee still does to me, luring in the shadows of my life, waiting to spring at me and tear me down when I least expect it. But hey, if I've learned one thing over the last few months, is that if that happened, if TeeVee jumped at me, I'll grab it and powerbomb it into submission.

#WrestlingToTheRescue.

#

"Mom, I'm home! Everly is here, too!" Fire closes the door behind me and drops his gym bag onto the floor in the hallway. He whispers to me, "Sometimes she sings along to the radio, and she's not the best singer. She appreciates a warning instead of ruining her reputation with people for all eternity."

An upbeat voice replies from the kitchen corner straight ahead. "Wonderful, honey! I'm trying to bake something." All I can see is a woman about my height with her back to us and her black hair pulled back into a ponytail, and loads of pots and groceries on the countertop.

"No singing," I comment.

"Lucky you." Fire winks at me and holds out his hand. "Come on." He leads us straight toward the kitchen. Having been to Fire's house twice before, I can honestly say it grew on me. It looked too white and sterile for my liking when I first came by, but on second glance, I find Fire's parents did a great job making it a comfy home underneath this modern façade. Little touches are everywhere, from family photos over decorative items to art. Must be his mom, the interior decorator.

Fire slides onto one of the barstools lined up in front of the kitchen island. "Mom, meet Everly. Everly, my mom."

Fire's mom turns away from the kitchen scale she was using, a warm, open smile on her face. There's definitely a family resemblance with Fire, no doubt. The same dark hair, the same eyes. It makes me like her instantly. #ByAssociation She dries her hand on a kitchen towel, then shakes my extended one. "So nice to meet you, Everly. I heard so much about you. Very happy I get to meet you, especially before my husband does. He'll be home in an hour, but it's going to bug him forever that I met Calan's girlfriend before he did." She makes a strike-gesture with her left arm.

Calan's girlfriend. My cheeks warm. "Uh, thank you, and it's very nice to meet you too, Ms. Adler—"

"Call me Ariel." She pats my hand in hers with her other one, then lets go and nods her chin past me, at Fire. "Don't forget, you have your follow-up appointment later at six… You know… at the…"

"You can say it, Mom. At the burn center. It's not like I could hide that from Everly." He gestures to his face and down the right side of his body, then explains to me. "I get physical therapy to keep my range of motion. The scars are still thickening, and I need to stay active, or they're going to limit what I can do. Wrestling helps, but the docs added the burn PT on top."

Wrestling helps—epiphany! "That's why you're at the gym like 24/7?"

Ariel laughs in a cute sarcastic way. "Good one, Everly. Calan has always been more interested in wrestling than in school, and he's just using what the doctor said as an excuse and reason to move in at Ben's wrestling school."

"Hey!" Fire lifts both palms up. "I'm doing what I'm supposed to do, Mother!"

"Yeah, yeah." She waves a hand at him. "That's what you're getting yourself into, Everly. Two skin transplants, several surgeries, and the first thing he did when the wounds were healed and he was cleared was have his father drive him to Ben's school."

"I call it determination," Fire says.

"I call it crazy," his mom retorts, "but it clearly did you good. But enough of your wrestling addiction. I don't want to be responsible for Everly realizing what a lunatic you sometimes are. Do me a favor, please, Cal? Would you mind going into the basement for me? There must be a box of frosting, you know, the Costco-sized one? Somewhere by the sugar. Would you mind getting it for me, please?"

Fire looks to me, frowning. "Mom, I—"

"Oh, impolite. I apologize, honey. You take care of Everly—"

"Meh. Don't mind me," I say as I slide onto the chair next to Fire's. "I can wait."

Fire grins. "You couldn't wait when I was ten minutes late this morning."

I wave a hand. "Puh-lease. Different ball game. I just couldn't wait to throw you around." Or to do ground with you. Or to kiss you. Or—

He meets my eyes with such an intensity, he must know what I was thinking. "I see your point, Ever." He slides off the chair. "Only one box, Mom?"

"Again, Costco-sized, honey. It better be enough. Oh, and if it's not by the sugar, it might be on the shelf in the garage. If it's not there either…" She taps a finger against her chin. "If it's not there either, try the Volvo's trunk. I'm pretty sure Dad took it out, but…"

"All right then. Going on a quest for frosting. A worthy cause." Fire squeezes my hand once, then lets go and strides out of the kitchen, leaving me alone with his mom.

And—it's not even awkward. Ariel stares after her son. "He *has* changed over the last few weeks." She offers me a warm smile. "Thanks to you."

The warmth invading my cheeks cranks it up a couple of degrees. "Thank you, but, you know, he's changed me as well." In a big way. *#SocialAnxietyGone*

"That's what good relationships do; they make us better." She winks at me, then tears open a bag of chocolate chips, offering some to me.

I wave a hand. "N-No, thank you." Can't eat right now.

Really, can't. I'm better, but unexpected food is not my thing.

Ariel pours a few onto the kitchen island in front of me. "In case you change your mind." She gives me a maternal, warm smile, then pours the remaining chips into the batter she's preparing and goes to work, using a handheld mixer blindly while reading the recipe open in a magazine on the countertop.

"So, what's it going to be?" I ask.

Ariel taps at the left side of the magazine. "Two-tiered chocolate-chip vanilla cake with strawberry frosting."

I whistle. "Sounds great."

"Sounds great, if I can make it work. It's my first two-tiered cake, and unlike my husband, I'm not an architect. I don't build things; I decorate them." She turns the mixer off and uses a finger to smooth the leftover dough off the beaters.

For somebody who is not a baker, she sure pulled out all the stops here. "What's the occasion then?"

A wistful expression crosses her face. "A day that should call for a big bottle of wine, or rather tequila, but cake is healthier. Somewhat, at least." She sighs. "It's six months today. Six months ago today I almost lost my only son in that car wreck."

Whoa. I blink twice. "That's *today?*" Fire's crash was *today*, six months ago? We're *#soulmates* by fate, seriously—we both almost died on the exact same day.

Ariel picks up the baking spray and two springforms. "Worst day of my life. Having the police pick me up at work, telling me my son's in critical condition in the burn unit..." Her shoulders heave up and down with another silent sigh. "I thought I had lost him. A feeling so horrible, it's beyond comprehension."

My throat tightens. Ariel and my mom share the same experience, but hearing it from Ariel, it feels different. Maybe because Mom isn't good at verbalizing that stuff, and all I felt was her anger in the beginning.

Ariel covers the inside of the first pan with nonstick spray, forcing a smile. "But luckily, he made it, and the more details emerged, the luckier he was he was intubated and wrapped in gauze head to toe, or that boy would've gotten a good spanking from me."

"Huh? Why?" I give in and pick a single one of those chocolate chips from the table and pop it into my mouth. One I can do. For the flavor.

Fire's mom lets the pan and spray sink low. "Because he was doing what we strictly forbade him to do. His friend Ronan was driving, and Calan was on his phone. Yes, I know what you're going to say, at least he wasn't driving, but he distracted Ronan with this stupid live stream on TeeVee he was watching, and it almost got him killed. At least Ronan got out—"

The rest of her sentence gets buried under the shock of hearing the word that was my world for so long until it almost became my death. "On TeeVee?" I choke out. Fire was on TeeVee? I thought he wasn't really on—

Live stream.

The words tie themselves around my chest and squeeze tight until I wheeze. *I* was streaming live that day.

But it can't be. He would've said something. He didn't watch me try to kill myself six months ago and then said nothing when we met. He didn't know who I was, and there are tens of thousands of live streams every day, or more!

Ariel's lips are pressed into a firm line. "TeeVee, yes. He and Ronan were obsessed with that app. Half their allowance went into their account on TeeVee, if not more."

I force the most insincere smile ever. That means nothing. Parents says *obsessed* so easily because they're not in tune with how social media works. They say obsessed, I say normal use. Doesn't mean her words don't leave a bad taste in my mouth. "I guess… I guess they're not the only ones. It's a popular app."

"Tell me about it. I don't think he's been on it since the accident at all, but before… All day nothing but that thing, unless he was wrestling."

Oh, okay. Soo… definitely more than average use. I scoot forward on the chair, a chill snaking around my insides. "Do you happen to know… I mean, do you know…" *Get it out, Ever!* I suck in my lower lip and bite it. "What was his username? Do you happen to know?" Really, I'm only asking out of curiosity. I know my frequent supporters, commenters, and yes, my haters. I'm just asking out of curiosity. There's no way I'll recognize Fire's username. Most likely we've never interacted on TeeVee.

Then why then do I feel nauseous?

Ariel picks up the second pan to be sprayed. "Of course I do. It's the same one from when we still controlled his social media and a typical Calan-and-Ronan choice: Moonsaulting_Spaceman. Boys," she huffs and she coats the pan in spray *again*.

Moonsaulting_Spaceman:
About time. Cut deeper, bitch! Show us this isn't fake, like you! #GoDieMatrixGirl #MatrixGirlSucks #FakeUntilTheEnd

\#

A wave of nausea threatens to overwhelm me.

No.

No, no, no, no.

Nuh-uh.

Impossible.

Fire can't be Spaceman—can't be. Not Fire, the most supportive, understanding, cool guy I've ever met. The first guy I trusted. The first guy I kissed. The first guy I allowed to touch me.

Bile rises up my throat.

"Excuse me," I push out, slapping one hand in front of my mouth and hurrying away from the kitchen.

Need air.

Need to think, need—

"Ever? What's wrong?" Fire comes up the stairs next to the entrance door, holding a large box of frosting in one hand, reaching the other one out to touch my shoulder.

I twist away and stumble back a step or two. "Don't touch me. Don't."

His brows furrow. "What's going on?" His gaze flicks over to his mom in the kitchen, who takes that as her cue.

"Is everything okay?"

"Yeah," Fire calls over, drowning out my softer "No," spoken at the same time.

My next breath comes out harsh, wheezy, and entirely too short. "TeeVee. You were on TeeVee."

His pupils widen the slightest bit—but nothing else. "Yeah. I told you I like to keep track once in a while. Why?"

He's lying—or, maybe he's not, but for sure he's deceiving me. Even worse. Nausea turns into real pain, stabbing my insides and bringing tears to my eyes. "You posted every day. You tagged.

Shared. Commented. You—" I close my eyes and curl up as a wave of pain hits. "It was you. You are Moonsaulting_Spaceman."

Click.

The moment he realizes I know, he turns as white as the wall.

It's all the confirmation I need.

With a loud crack only I can hear, my heart shatters into a million pieces. My pain scale overloads, the fuses blown by a surge too high to register. I'm waiting for the agony, the sorrow, the devastation—but nothing.

Only numbness.

Dull, never-ending, drowning, all-consuming numbness.

Fire reaches for me. "Ever—"

I step back.

And again.

Again.

Can't think. Can't cry. Can't breathe.

But I can run.

I feel for the doorknob behind me—

Rip open the door—

Turn around and run out of his house, run, run, run down the street, run as far as I can to get away from the boy who made me try to kill myself.

CHAPTER TWENTY-TWO

#Numb

It's been four days.

Four days I didn't shower.

Four days I didn't leave the house.

Four days I haven't eaten much or talked much or done much of anything else.

Four days. SaturdaySundayMondayTuesday.

Mom has been up here a lot. Dad tried to FaceTime me, but it ended up as a very one-sided conversation with him getting louder and louder when I didn't talk, which, big surprise, didn't make me open up to him, either. Then little Johnny, or whatever my half-brother's name is, needed a fresh diaper and Dad had to go. Perfect. That's the way it always is, and I don't care.

I have a long list of things I don't care about right now:

- Fire.
- Fire.

- Fire.
- Fire.
- School.
- Passing grades.
- Anybody. (Besides Hazel.)
- Fire.

But then, not caring is good. Not caring is better than caring too much. That only drives the knife in deeper. Pun intended.

Since I've retreated—because I won't call it hidden—to my room, I've circled through a *#shitload* of emotions, and they're changing so fast, it's giving me whiplash.

First, I was destroyed. Completely. Lost, hurt, wrecked, and heartbroken. My first real love, the person I trusted, I confided in—nothing but betrayal. He played with me and built me up only to tear me down.

Then came the fear: This is my life from now on. Nowhere to hide, nowhere to run. Any google search will bring up my video, anybody I ever meet will only be one click away from MatrixGirl and BeverlyBacon. I won't be able to move past it. *This is my life from now on.*

Then, resignation and guilt: that's what you get when you go online. My mistake. Why did I put myself out there? I invited it. My fault. My fault, my fault. Mine.

But after resignation—and that part was new—came anger. Bright, hot, energizing anger. Oh, sure, the pain is still there, and when I think too hard about Fire and what happened, it could get the upper hand again, but I'm not letting it. I'm keeping this anger because it fuels me. It helps me to not stumble and fall into that hole, the one with the razor-sharp edges that are going to leave new marks in my skin on the way down. Anger is the glue helping me to not fall apart, to not get my razor, to not make myself throw up.

It doesn't quite help me to go back to school yet, but eventually.

One step at a time.

Right now my brain is doing a *#MajorUpgrade* from Everly 1.0—the one who'd cut herself to feel better—to Everly 2.0—the one who deals with shit and handles it. Problem is, like with every update, there are hiccups, meaning, I really needed to have those days to myself. To sort things out. To get to the point where I *just don't care* for 24/7, because sometimes the programming's faulty and the old code takes over. Like I said: *#Shitload* of emotions. Whiplash.

It must be early afternoon when the doorbell rings and then the sound of footfalls comes up the stairs toward my room.

Somebody knocks—

"Knock knock. Incoming."

Hazel.

She enters without me saying a word, zipping open her jacket the moment she's in my room. "Ever. Gee, girl, what's going on with you? I mean, here I am at school thinking you're sick, but nobody knows. I call you, your mom says you're sleeping. You don't call back—okay, we gotta work on that, but whatever. Then, your end-of-the-semester wrestling performance is supposed to be in, like, a few days, but instead of training, you're about to get into trouble for your absences. Mr. Langen tells me he can't talk about a student's health, so I freak out of course, fearing like, the worst. Then I ask Fire, who looks like somebody died, and all I get from him is—"

Fire. "He is *him*," I bite out. Hello, anger. You're back.

"Huh?" Hazel unwraps her scarf and throws it on the floor onto her jacket. "Who is who—is whom?"

I draw my legs in and wrap my arms around them, bracing myself for the pain to set in again with my next words. It always does, no matter how often I say it to get used to it. One more thing to work on, I guess. "Fire is *him*. Moonsaulting_Spaceman. Has been him all along."

"What?" Hazel's eyes pop open wide as her jaw drops. "What the what? Did you say *Fire* was Spaceman—"

"Yup." I nod. I was so stupid. That realization hurts almost as much as Fire's betrayal because it was there all along. Fire knew I needed to eat, because my struggle with weight was obvious on my feed. Fire knew I had tried to slice my radial artery, because he had watched me do it. Fire accidentally called me MatrixGirl because that's who I am to him. Fire wanted to be alone at the gym so nobody would give his secret away.

Really, had I put an ounce of brainwork into it and not just surrendered myself to my surging hormones, I should have known.

Haze lets herself fall backward onto my bed. "Nuh-uh. I can't believe it. Calan, Fire—Moonsaulting_Spaceman? I mean… that doesn't go together in my head."

I huff dry. "Oh, no doubt about it. It was him. His mom told me."

"Just like, 'By the way, my son is Moonsaulting_Spaceman?'"

"Har-har. It just came up, okay? She said he hasn't really been online since the accident, but clearly, she doesn't know her son very well." Or at all.

The confusion on Hazel's face would be funny if any of this were a laughing matter. Her brows narrow farther. "He wasn't online and yet he posted—"

"Says his mom, Haze. As if she knew every time he went online. And he admitted he had an account, but *only to check on things*. Boy, I was so naïve. Oh, and you know what? It's basically because of me that he looks the way he does." That's another realization that came to fruition over the last four days. It made me feel guilty for a short second, then… I didn't care.

"Wait, what? You're speaking in riddles today." Haze sits up and crosses her legs, facing me.

"He was checking out my live stream, his buddy was driving, got distracted, *boom*, accident, almost burned." I want to think *serves him right*, but whenever I try to convince myself I should feel good about this revenge fate had on my account, a sting to my heart keeps me from it.

"Live stream. *The* live stream?" There really is only one that counts, Hazel knows.

Picking at my cuticles, I nod. "Yup."

"Oh, crap. That's messed-up."

"Ya think?"

She lets her head hang and massages her temples. "Fire was so nice—"

"So was Spaceman." In the beginning, at least. "Bipolar stalker."

"Huh? Stalker? But Calan wasn't at our school when everything with Spaceman happened."

"*Now* he is, so there you go."

Hazel rolls her eyes. "Not helping. I know he is. But, man, I can't see those two as one person, crazy Moonsaulting_Spaceman and Calan. That boy… That boy truly liked you, I felt."

A lump forms in my throat, the kind that makes breathing hard and won't go away with a million swallows. "Probably just part of his plan. Whatever. I don't care." Don't care, don't care, don't care.

"I don't think Fire would do anything to hurt you—"

"Oh, sure. Didn't you say Spaceman shared the fake death post, and that's when it blew up? There you go. He's good at sharing stuff and getting the numbers up." Spaceman helped me once, but he hurt me way more often with that. I dig my nails into my palms. Pain helps. Pain is good. It grounds me. My gaze darts over to my nightlamp—

No.

Hazel reaches into the pocket of her cargo pants and pulls out her phone. "That reminds me…" She taps something and scrolls.

I swallow dry. "Are you… Are you on TeeVee?"

She nods and continues scrolling, her brows pulled together into a V.

"Can I… Can I see?" My throat's all dry all of a sudden.

Hazel twists her body farther away from me. "No way, Jose. I'm just… Never mind." She clicks the phone off. "I'll talk to you later, okay?" And with that, she scrambles off my bed, grabs her jacket, and slides into it. "Don't do anything stupid or I'm going to kick your butt."

"No worries." Because I don't care.

I.

Don't.

Care.

#

I'm lying on my bed and staring at the ceiling when somebody knocks on my door. "Everly? Can I come in?"

Mom.

I grunt in frustration and snap my eyes closed. *Please go back downstairs. I really, really don't want to talk.*

The door opens.

And closes.

Silence.

Go back downstairs, go back downstairs—

Yeah, no: I hear a few hesitant footfalls until the weight on my mattress changes. Dang it. I keep my eyes closed. There's nothing to see here.

"Honey." Mom strokes my hair. "I've called Doctor Shamus. She has an appointment—"

"Not going." I shake my head just as much as it takes to have her hand drop off. I know what she's gonna say, and I really, really, *really* don't want to tell her everything about Fire.

Mom sighs. "You need to talk to somebody, Everly. The last time you didn't talk, you ended up—"

My eyelids fly open. "This isn't like the last time, Mom."

A sad expression crosses her face before she has herself under control again. "But how can I know? You're not talking, not eating, not going to school…"

I scoot back a little so that my upper body props up against the wall. "I told you. I needed some time. And I'm doing what I'm supposed to, keeping myself healthy." Because going to school too soon would definitely mess up my mental upgrade. All programs must be closed before updating or else the override won't work. Me going too school would have thrown me off, and I'm working really hard on not letting that happen, even though it *doesn't look* like I'm doing much, I know.

"Fire came by again," Mom says, trying her best to keep her

voice neutral. "He looks miserable."

A sting of something hot wrapped in barbwire shoots through my heart. *I don't care.* "Whatever." I grunt. Not feeling sorry for him—if he *is* even truly miserable. Maybe he's continuing the charade, that's all.

"He wanted to talk to you. Again. Like every day that he came by."

"Tough luck. *I don't* want to talk to him."

"I can tell. But maybe you should."

"Not going to happen." I press my palms against my ears and shake my head. The betrayal of the century—I'm done with him. Just because he's coming by doesn't mean I have to give him my attention, or that I have to listen to him or talk to him. Why would I? Is it going to make me feel better? No. Is it going to make him feel better? Possibly, but do I care? Nope-nopedy-no. He didn't care whether he made me feel bad or not when he posted all that crap. So why should I care?

Point is, I don't.

"And Dad called," Mom adds after a pause. "He saw you had two more missing days at school and no doctor's note."

Geez, will any of that stuff ever stop? "I don't care," I push out. Not caring is harder than I thought.

"That's what you say now, but I know you do. Honey, if you want to make this work, you have to go to school. You have to go to wrestling. You have to do that performance."

Hell to the no. "Also not going to happen." School, okay, I can see myself go back pretty soon. But wrestling—with Fire? That's a hard *no* from me.

"Honey, you have to. You're about to fail that class, and just because Clark and I..." She pats my head again. "Us being a couple won't save you from a failing grade, either, I'm afraid. And… you know your father is going to insist on that boarding school if you don't adhere to his conditions."

A sharp sting shoots through my heart. "I told you, I don't care." If that's the price I have to pay for sticking to my guns, for keeping my mind protected from more assault, then so be it. I'm done being everybody's playball. I can put my foot down, and the wrestling performance is exactly that. School? Sure. Wrestling? Nope.

And I'll handle the consequences.

"Honey…" Mom strokes my hair. It feels kind of like a helpless motion: She's afraid of what Fire did to me.

I rub a palm over both eyes and look at her. Like, really look at her. Her hair is a mess and she's not wearing any lipstick, a sure sign her mind is elsewhere. Dark circles line her eyes, and I can't remember the corners of her mouth ever being so droopy.

#Newsflash: I'm not the only one having a hard time here. And I didn't notice. But that's just the way I am, right? I didn't think of Mr. Langen, how he felt with Nevaeh's post, and I didn't think of Mom, either. Only about myself.

Update to Everly 2.1—major bug fix in the empathy department. Download and install.

So, well, I take a ginormous step forward, figuratively, and get over myself: I sit up, scoot forward, and wrap my arms around her. "I'm sorry, Mom." Sorry the last year was so hard for you, too. Sorry you had to go through this. Sorry the world is not letting us relax for one minute.

She holds me tightly. "Don't be sorry, Everly. Just promise me you'll talk. To somebody. It doesn't have to be me, doesn't have to be the doc. Can be anybody. Hazel. Anybody. But please talk.

It helps."

I let myself sink deeper into her embrace. It feels like home, like childhood, like boo-boos made better. "I will, Mom." Eventually.

When I'm ready, I will.

#

I still don't go to school the next day.

Fire comes by twice.

Both times he leaves after Mom talks to him. Once I see him from my window, cap pulled down deep over his face, as always. From up here, it looks like his shoulders were slumped forward as he left, but that was probably just perspective. Or he was sad he was missing out on more money without me. How much did sharing Ford's death thing make him? A couple of thousand? Ford had to donate the money—Fire should have do the same.

Whatever.

It's about seven in the evening when I sneak downstairs to get myself a tea, and when I say *sneak*, I mean I tiptoe down in my fuzzy socks because I really, really don't want another Mom talk. Or talk in general, period. So I wait until I hear the door to the bathroom close, then hurry down. The light's still on in the kitchen—

"Good evening, Everly."

My hand flies up to my heart as my head whips around toward the voice coming from the chair in the corner, next to the window. "Mr. Langen?"

My health teacher raises a hand. "Hi."

"Uh, hi," I give back. "You're... uh, here." Wow. Smart

assessment, Everly.

He chuckles. "Yes. Yes, I am. Your mom invited me to dinner." He holds up the glass of wine I hadn't noticed before.

Oh. Gee. Awkward because *she didn't freakin' tell me!* "That's… That's great. I mean, Awesome. I-I better get going—"

"Why don't you have a seat, Everly?" He points at the chair across from him.

"No, I—"

"Sit."

Darn it.

I pull out the chair and fall into it, in my sweatpants, fuzzy socks and with five-day-unwashed-hair. So much for sneaking into the kitchen unnoticed. Out of the frying pan into the fire. Fantastic.

One more try. "I really don't want to interrupt your dinner, Mr. Langen. I should—"

Pulling back the sleeve of his black button-down shirt, he glances at his watch. "Huh. Look at that. Not school hours. I'm off the clock. And I'm in your kitchen, on a date with your mother. Call me Clark, or Ben. Either works."

"Ben," I squeak. That's wrestling. I can do that. Clark is too… *personal* somehow. More than him being in my kitchen. On a *date* with my *mom.*

"Okay then." He twirls the wine glass between his fingers for a long half minute or so. "Wanted to tell you. Nevaeh's gotten officially charged with a misdemeanor for her post."

I suck in a deep breath. "Good." Because while it won't make the picture go away, at least she won't do it again. Won't try to get cheap revenge for a boy who doesn't deserve it, like Ford. Speaking of: "What about Ford? And Arlo?"

"I assume that's going to go the same way eventually, but it might be charged as a felony, since it's assault, but I'm no lawyer."

"Can't say I'd be sad for them. I just… I just want to put that crap behind me." I want it to stop.

Ben stares at the wine swirling in his glass. "Agreed."

So many emotions swing in that word… My stomach heaves. Let's give that empathy-upgrade a try. "The picture is still out there, isn't it?" I expect it to be. The internet doesn't forget, I know that. I just ignored it. It's healthier that way, if the way I'm feeling right now is any indication.

He shrugs, but it doesn't come across quite as carefree as he probably intended it to. "The school district paid for a company to remove the picture and all its traces from the web, but thanks to screenshots it jumped from TeeVee to Twitter, to Facebook, to TikTok, to GL… you name it."

So that means my picture is all over as well. I swallow down the sudden rise of nausea. "It will never stop, will it?" Any of it. The name-calling, the bullying, the harassment, the idiocy…

"I don't know. I'm still getting daily comments, same as before. All disgusting."

I breathe in through my nose. Hallelujah for being *#offline*. I can vividly imagine what kind of comments—been there, done that. When will people look at me and see me, not MatrixGirl, not BeverlyBacon, not the *girl who tried to kill herself* or the *girl who's sleeping with her teacher*? When will they feel I'm not theirs to use?

"I've missed you in school." Ben says it completely even, yet it rubs me the wrong way.

Hmph. "I thought you were off the clock?"

"Touché. Then let me rephrase it then: I've been missing you at wrestling."

I cringe. Not much better.

"You haven't been all week."

I cross my arms in front of my chest and stare at a spot on the kitchen table.

Ben takes a sip of his wine. "I wasn't the only one missing you."

My gaze whips up to his as his implication sinks in. "Tough luck."

"I hear he's been by a few times. Tried to talk to you."

"I wasn't interested in that." Not on the first day, nor on the second, nor on any other day he came by. It was only coincidental I sat at the windowsill and watched him come and go. Watched him look up to my window, as if he could see me behind the thick curtains. Totally coincidental.

"Have you thought about hearing what he has to say? No strings attached?"

Anger spikes, my newly found friend. "No, I haven't, and why would I? There's no excuse for what he's done to me, just like there's no way I can be around a person like him anymore!"

"What if—"

Oh, hell to the no, I've had it! "No what-ifs, Ben! That's it! Stop being on his side so obviously! You knew, didn't you? You knew from the beginning Fire was Moonsaulting_Spaceman, like you obviously knew he was Calan, and still you played this game!" I had a lot of time to think over the last few days, and Ben must've known. And still he didn't warn me. "You got me into wrestling, kept his secret—if it weren't for you, I'd never have started wrestling! I'd never have met Fire. You knew my history, and still you brought us together. That's so messed-up, I can't even!" I was okay with him knowing Calan was Fire, but this, hiding he was Spaceman—

Holy cow!

OMG and WTF, it just occurred to me. I look at him, incredulous. "You lied to the police! When they came to our house and you were here, they asked if we knew who Moonsaulting_Spaceman was—and you didn't say it!" Un-be-lievable! "You protected him from the police, even though he shared that freakin' death post!"

Ben smacks his lips. "Sorry to disappoint, but when I escorted them out, I did tell them. I'm not about to get myself into trouble with the law."

Oh. "Okay, fine—but why wasn't Fire arrested or whatever?"

Cocking his head to the side, he raises both eyebrows. "Curious, right? Maybe you should talk to him about that and find out."

"I'm not that interested in the answer."

The sound of the bathroom door opening and closing comes from the hallway. Mom to the rescue!

Ben swirls the wine in his glass. "You know," he says slowly, "there was a method to my madness. I knew he'd be running into you when I recommended he switch schools to yours."

I gasp. "Why would you do that to me?"

He stops swirling the wine and peers at me over the rim of the glass. "Or to him?"

I hear my mom's steps come down the hallway. She stops for a moment, then goes on toward the living room. Traitor.

Anyway. Gotta fend for myself, it seems, yet I still don't get it. "To him? What's it to him? He's the one who bullied me—"

"Have you ever considered you don't know the whole story?"

"No, and what difference does it make? None. I could be dead because of what he did."

Ben chews on the inside of his cheek. "You know, it's not my place to tell you otherwise, but some things are not as they seem. You of all people should know that. Your online persona was different from who you were behind the screen."

I throw up my hands. "What are you saying? That Fire is only an ass when he is online? That makes me feel better, really."

"What I'm saying is that every person is more than the sum of their actions. That every person can make a mistake, and that every person can change."

Tears spring to my eyes. "A mistake? What he did wasn't just *a* mistake! We're talking planned, deliberate bullying over months! Harassing me. Making me feel so incredibly bad, I still can't look in the mirror and not hear the voices criticizing me!"

\#

AEIOUS
Could look pretty if she did something with that mop of hair.

Gen03:
Nope. Can't make that look pretty. Maybe cut it off.

JimSalabimGoesPoof:
Maybe cut off the head, lol. Would improve her looks #fosho.

\#

And he was sneaky about it. Never too obvious, never the worst offender. But oftentimes the one who poured gasoline into the fire, pun intended. The one who instigated and kept poking and prodding, until the others jumped onboard. Until he delivered the almost deadly blow with the *GoDieMatrixGirl* hashtag.

Ben leans forward and holds out his hand, wiggling his fingers until I comply and put my hand in his. It could be awkward and weird, yet it's not. I've wrestled this man when he wasn't wearing a shirt. Him holding my hand in a fatherly way doesn't even register on the weirdness scale. Doesn't mean I'm not still mad at him.

"I know. And I'm sorry that I'm coming across as… I don't know, probably as a big douche, from your point of view, but…" He frowns. "It's complicated. You're complicated—no offense, you know what I mean—Fire's complicated, heck, *life* is complicated. And sometimes I just wish we could make it a bit easier for all of us, you know?"

I let go of a dry huff. "Yeah. Wouldn't that be nice." Not that I'd hold my breath for it.

Ben taps the back of my hand with one of his fingers. "So, to make a long story short, I want you back in school. Back at wrestling."

I shake my head so fast, it hurts. "No." No wrestling. Nothing that has to do with Fire. Can't do that. Just can't. He's been nice to me in person, but behind my back… Anger mixed with hurt roils inside my stomach. Fire's betrayal… it runs deep and on many levels.

Ben snaps his mouth shut, then thinks for a moment. "You know what? You're used to ignoring half the school; you can ignore him as well. You're a pro: When you're in school, ignore him."

Ain't that the truth. I'm a master at ignoring people, or at least at pretending I am. "Point taken." Fire himself, the one more additional person to ignore, wasn't what was keeping me from school anyway. And once I return, yeah, of course I'm going to ignore him, but wrestling—

Mind reader that he is, Ben lifts an eyebrow. "Plus, the end-of-the-year performance is coming up, and—"

Hard no. "I'm not doing it." I've got to draw a line somewhere, and I'm drawing it here.

"Ever." Ben squeezes my hand in his. "You're inviting trouble. I know your father—"

A sharp sting shoots through my heart. "Oh, I know, believe me, I know. Boarding school. But I've been thinking. It could be a fresh start. It's probably good for me." I'm going to miss Hazel. Mom. Even Ben. But my priorities have changed lately. I'd be free of all the baggage attached to my name. For the first time in years I'd just be… me.

Until anyone new in my life googles me.

Sigh.

Ben regards me silently for a few seconds, then squeezes my hand again, twice, like two little pumps. "Can I give you some advice?"

I doubt it's a question for which he'd take *no* for an answer. "Sure."

"Sometimes to move forward, we have to move backward."

"Huh?" Cryptic much?

"I'm saying that it's hard to move on with this anchor in your past. You need to be able to let go to move on, and right now I don't think you can. You want a fresh start, and for that, you need to deal with the old issues first."

I draw my hand out from under his and let myself fall back into my chair, hugging my elbows. "I've dealt with them."

"Clearly." The sarcasm in his voice makes me stick out my tongue to him, and Ben chuckles. "Tell yourself whatever you want, Everly. All I'm saying is that sometimes you have to be the bigger person, even though it feels like that's the last thing you want to be."

Good description. It feels *exactly* like the last thing I want to be.

My teacher/wrestling-coach/mom's-boyfriend looks at me with his head tilted to one side and a mischievous gleam in his eyes. "Don't worry. Nobody said you needed to do that on your own. You'll get some help along the way." With that, he raises his glass of wine at me and takes a sip, the conversation over.

And while everything he said was completely supportive, I can't help but feel a little shudder running down my spine. Those last few comments—what was he hinting at? What am I missing?

What. Am. I. Missing?

CHAPTER TWENTY-THREE

#ListenToYourFriends

It's Thursday, a.k.a., going back to school day, and it feels weird—surprisingly not because of school, though, but because of me: I've had my heart ripped out and stomped upon yet lived to tell the tale—but nobody sees the ginormous wound inside my chest. They all treat me like I'd been out with the flu or something.

Fine by me.

I've got my mental defense up from the moment Mom drops me off, and so far, it's working. I didn't cringe when somebody took out a phone, I didn't duck into the shadows when switching classrooms, and I didn't as much as move a muscle when Ford and Nevaeh's leader-less gang shot dirty looks at me.

My armor? Holding up.

At lunch, Hazel and I meet at our lockers. She looks left and right, then scoots closer. "How's your morning been so far?"

"Okay."

I can practically hear her frustration about my elaborate answer, but she keeps an upbeat voice. "Glad to hear it. So that means you're ready for the wrestling performance tomorrow?"

"Harr-harr. Nope. Not going to happen."

"Ever." She stuffs all her books into the locker, catching one resistant folder before it falls. "You need to do that performance."

I cross my arms and lean against my locker. "What is so hard to understand about that for everybody? I won't. I'm going to pretend Fire doesn't exist, and that means I won't wrestle." If that also means there won't be a multitude of videos and pictures of me wrestling online, I can live with it.

Hazel rams her locker shut much more forcefully than strictly necessary. "Okay, *what's so hard to understand* that I don't want you in a freakin' boarding school? Just because you have convinced yourself you don't care doesn't mean that *my* opinion doesn't count!"

My eyebrows shoot high. "Haze—"

"No, seriously, no boarding school, Ever!"

I chew the inside of my cheek. "But maybe I want it. A fresh start. Away from everything and everyone."

Hazel growls—actually growls! "A fresh start away from everybody? For one, how naive are you? For another, way to go thinking about others, Ever, like your mom, or even little old me! You know, maybe I should have pushed you more to open up during your TeeVee-time, but have you ever stopped to think about how I felt when I found out what happened? My best friend tried to kill herself, and I had no freakin' clue! None! You could've come to me, you could've talked to me, but no, you had to try to kill yourself and stream it freakin' live on TeeVee for me and the world to find out! Who does that?" She hammer-fists the locker, and I flinch.

"I… I thought you were on my side—"

"I am on your freakin' side, stupid! Always have been, and that's why it hurts me too when you lock me out, and it hurts me when you throw away what we have, just because you can't get over yourself and talk to Fire!"

Over myself—that doesn't sit right with me. Anger rears its ugly head. It's had practice the last few days. "So to summarize, you're saying I should get over myself and to do so, I'd have to wrestle with the boy who almost made me kill myself just so you can keep me here in school?"

Hazel rolls her eyes—*rolls her freaking eyes at me!* "I'm saying that yeah, surprise, I'd kind of like not having my best friend move away to some stupid boarding school. And I'm saying that maybe I know more than you in this case, and that maybe you should listen to me. Oh, and just FYI, Ms. They-Have-All-Wronged-Me, there are always two sides to *every* story, you know? I'm saying that you should check your assumptions at the door and give others the same courtesy you expect from them! You always complained people believed what they read about you, all the crap, and right now, sorry to say so, you're no better! I'm *not* saying what Fire did was right, not at all, but I *am* saying you're not making things easier right now!"

"*I'm* not making things easier?" Me? "Did I post all that nasty stuff—"

"Stop it, Everly!" Hazel stomps her foot. "Your life isn't online anymore, and yet everything still circles around it, and I'm sick of it! And I know I'm not allowed to be sick of it because nothing's happening to me and all that horrible stuff has happened and is happening to you, but man, it sucks the life out of me! Sorry if that triggers you! Live in the here and now, or at least try, would you please? I'm on your side and I always will be, but seriously, for once, do what you didn't do on *that* day and trust me!" She glares at me, then turns on her heels and walks away from me, leaving me standing next to my locker like somebody forgot to pick me up.

What. Just. Happened?

I blink a couple of times, but it doesn't change a thing: Hazel is still weaving through the crowd. Without me.

As I'm staring after her, another figure comes into focus. Tall. Slender, but muscular. Walking the slightest bit hunched over, with his head turned to the side. People let him pass and make room for him, as if his mere presence was contagious. Somebody says something, and the ones around them giggle and snicker, throwing knowing glances at each other and disgusted ones at *him*. *He* turns crimson red and speeds up, scanning the crowd for openings to slide through—

And then he sees me.

He stops dead in the middle of the hallway, several students bumping into him, shoving him forward—and although he stumbles to regain his footing, his gaze stays locked with mine.

That connection between him and me, it opens the door to the same *#shitload* of emotions I can't deal with right now. Don't want to deal with. Betrayal. Hurt. Anger. But also to something warmer, something softer, something I don't want to admit to myself, not now or ever again, and yet it doesn't let go of me, not until I've long turned away from *him* and gotten through another day of school I don't remember much of.

Even then, some of it stays, right next to Hazel's words, digging into my defenses until there's a hole I'm not sure I can close again.

#

Friday.

Yay.

I used to look forward to *#TGIF*, but today it leaves a bad taste in my mouth.

Maybe because I didn't sleep last night. Or at least not much. Obvs had nothing to do with what Hazel said. Probably the moon or something.

It's fine. It's probably one of my last days of school here anyway. Once Dad gets word I skipped the performance, I'll be out and on my way, knowing him.

Good.

I'll get my desired fresh start at that boarding school and leave the past behind me, so why I have to be here, today of all days, is anybody's guess. Would have preferred to not come at all, but Mom made me. What's the use? Because of the performances scheduled for today, our whole year is blocked for the afternoon starting at noon, and I'm definitely not sticking around for that, meaning, I'm attending half a day of school. What a waste.

Hazel catches up with me after trig and right before lunch, when I'm trying to figure out how to best leave. "Hey."

"Hey."

Awkward silence hovers. We haven't spoken since our fight yesterday. I couldn't text, I couldn't email, and calling… is weird. So I didn't.

But neither did she.

"Brought you something." She pops her shoulder up,

bouncing the blue-white backpack slung over her should up and down.

"Uh, thank you?"

She gives me a challenging glance. "That's the outfit you're going to wear for your wrestling performance. You and Fire are up first."

Adrenaline spikes, mixed with disbelief and sprinkled with annoyance. "What the hell? I'm not wrestling!"

Hazel absorbs my outburst without moving a muscle. Then, she lays a hand on my shoulder. "Ever. *Trust me.* Just *trust me* that I know what I'm doing here. Yes, you are wrestling. It's on the schedule, so it's happening. The ring is already here. Set up on stage in the theater."

"What?" I call out, then I lower my voice when people look at me. "What? Nobody told me—"

"That's what happens when you skip school, Ever. Get over it. You're doing this."

"No! Not with Fire, I'm not!"

"I said trust me. You want to wrestle Mr. Langen?"

"N-No!" Hell, no!

"Then you'll wrestle with Fire."

"I don't want—"

"But you will. You're going to take this bag, go change in room C2 behind the stage, and wait for me in the little hallway up behind the audience, and I'll give you instructions."

"Haze—"

She holds up a palm. "No. Stop it. You can do this, and you will do this. You won't go to boarding school because you're skipping this performance, and you won't let a good thing die because you're too stubborn to listen. You can't not talk and not listen, either."

What the what? "I—" I swallow dry. "What are you saying?" It's not like Hazel to push me like this. Not unless… "Actually, what are you *not* saying?" Because there must be something else behind her behavior, something that makes more sense, if that makes any sense? *#CompletelyConfused*

She shoves the bag into my arms, gently so. "I'm saying go change and I'll meet you in the hallway behind the auditorium. You *will* be fine."

"But—" I press that stupid bag against my chest.

"Still don't care about it." She turns me around and gives me a push in the direction of the theater. "I'll see you in five. You're doing this. Period."

#

Six minutes later, I've changed into the costume Haze gave me.

Why?

I don't know.

I could have run.

I could have taken that stupid bag and shoved it back into her arms.

I could have turned around at any point as I walked over to the theater.

But I didn't.

I took the bag and got changed into the costume, and I did it fast, with a little flutter in my chest that can't possibly mean I wanted to wrestle—or I wanted to wrestle with Fire—because I don't.

Nope.

Don't.

But then, why am I not fighting it? Why am I complying?

Good question.

Very good question.

I'll file it away for later.

Gliding one hand over the spandex material of my outfit, I look down my body. I'm dressed in black leggings and a tight, black tank top, both decorated with swirls of numbers in bright green, kind of like in *The Matrix*. Not sure where Hazel got it or if she made it, but it fits like a glove. She even got me black wrestling shoes, I presume an old pair of one of her brothers', because they're definitely worn and a tad too big.

But overall, given that the words *leggings* or *spandex-wrestling outfit* would have given me a *#coronary* about three months ago, she did good.

I get out of room C2, which we normally use for the string quartets or other musically talented people to practice, and step into the narrow hallway in front of it. It's empty as usual, since it's only used by students going to quartet or during performances for the actors to enter the auditorium from behind the audience. Both doors leading to the top of the auditorium are closed, but I can hear tons of chatter behind them. If the noise level is any indication, half the school must be there.

I swallow dry. So, so stupid. I seriously should've run while I had the chance. With shaking hands, I twist the doorknob and open the door just a smidgen for me to peek through. "What the hell—holy cow!" Not sure what I was expecting, but it wasn't this—wasn't the full *#BellsAndWhistles*.

Our theater is not small, by any means. We can fit the complete student body into the seats, and the stage has seen school musical performances of *The Lion King, Mulan,* and even one very ambitious production of *Les Misérables.* Meaning, it's a big stage.

Yeah. Not today. Today the stage looks tiny, and the reason for that would be the big, fat, wrestling ring set up smack in the middle of it. When did they haul it over? How? I didn't even know it was portable, or rather, transportable. The stage's curtains are drawn all the way to the sides to make its whole range accessible, and looks like that was a good call, since there's a table to the left of the ring, angled so that if two people sat there, they'd partially face both the audience and the ring. In addition, the retractable screen is out on the wall behind it, three large words projected on it together with a smaller sentence beneath them: *Health Class Challenge. Next performances in courtyard and gym.* The lights on top of the stage are on, illuminating the ring and a microphone lying close to the ring apron.

Oh, and when I mentioned the noise level? I hate it when I'm right, because almost all seats are taken. "Just fantast—"

"You ready?" Somebody taps me on my shoulder. I jolt and spin to the right—

What the what? "Hazel?"

Hazel grins and twirls once in her black pantsuit. "You like it? I think I rock it."

I blink twice. "Why are you—"

"Somebody needs to be the commentator. Duh. Ever actually watched wrestling, Ev?"

"You're going to comment on the match?" There's going to be a freakin' commentary? Wrestling alone isn't bad enough, it *has* to be commented on?

"That's what I just said, didn't I?"

"But—"

"Ever." She sighs and lays a hand on my shoulder in the same calming manner she tried on me about twenty minutes ago. "It's going to be fine. You learned so much, it's going to be a great match. Just… don't get distracted, okay?"

My head's swimming. "W-Why would I get distracted?"

"Oh, I don't know. One, Fire. Two, audience. Three, commentary. You've got options." She pats my shoulder twice, which is surely meant as reassurance but doesn't help at all. "But really, it's fine, Everly. Just… do me a favor and work with Fire here. You've practiced this. I'm supposed to remind you that *Heel controls the heat, Face controls the comeback.* You're supposed to know what that means."

I shake my head to clear it. Unfortunately, it doesn't do the trick. "Wait—why does it sound like you're in this with Fire?" I put my arms on my hips. Is that what I've been missing? "Okay, what is going on here? You, the costume you gave me—everything! Seriously!"

"It's not my story to tell. You'll find out soon enough. And like I said a million times, trust me. Once in a while I know what I'm doing."

Easier said than done. "Haze… I can trust you, but I can't trust Spaceman." Never again. Some things just can't be repaired.

She gives me a tight-lipped smile. "I know. And the only thing I'm asking you to do is to trust *Fire* inside the ring. Okay? He can and he will get you through this."

A desperate groan breaks from my throat. "That doesn't sound reassuring in any way. At all. Do I really have to do this?" Not sure what kind of an answer I'm expecting, but I'm stuck in whiny mode.

"Looks like it. I'm all dressed for the occasion, so you better."

So what? I could still choose to not wrestle. What's gonna happen? A few more comments on TeeVee? More bacon on my desk? Another death announcement? *#BigDeal*

My gaze scans over the crowd of students assembled in the theater. It's our whole year because their presence is mandatory, but since it's lunchtime and the weather sucks, I'd say about seventy to eighty percent of our school are present. Great. More witnesses to another humiliation. "I hate him."

Hazel pulls me into a quick hug, and after yesterday, it feels fantastic. "See, that's your problem. You don't. Quite the opposite. You wanted a fresh start. This is it. And don't we all deserve that? Including *him?*"

Including him—

Fire, responding why he didn't fight back against the bullies: "I hadn't paid my dues yet."

My mouth drops open and closes on its own account.

She gives me a pointed look and taps a finger against my temple. "See? The wheels are starting to work, eh? Anyway. I just have two directions for you. You wait for him to initiate lock up. You'll see where it leads. Do your universal spot in the beginning, but he'll lead you to the others. Let him call it in the ring, and you'll play it by ear. No biggie." She shrugs.

Aw, man. This is going suck big time. "Could you be any more vague?"

"Probably, but I'm good the way it is." She hugs me again. "You'll be fine, Ever. You both will be."

CHAPTER TWENTY-FOUR

#Wrestling

Click. The main lights turn off, leaving only the ring and the two aisles from the doors here in the back toward the stage illuminated. The audience, excuse me, my fellow students, let out an anticipating *wooh* sound. Some girls squeak from the sudden semi-darkness, some boys make weird noises.

The joys of high school.

Mr. Langen's voice comes over the PA-system. "Students, please take your seats. Even the seniors in the last rows… thank you. Much appreciated." As the chitter-chatter dies down, Mr. Langen steps in front of the ring, dressed like Hazel, surprisingly formal in a black suit. Not his usual style, but then, this Health Challenge thing is his idea.

He waves into the crowd. "Today marks the first annual Health Challenge day—the first, because believe me, it was a success, and we're doing it again. Juniors, look forward to it." A soft groan goes through the audience, making Mr. Langen smile.

"Ah, sweet anticipation. Anyway, we're going to start this year's presentations right here, right now, and we'll then move out into the courtyard for the archery demonstration. I would like to introduce the following show as, shall we say, a story that needs to be told, and before you laugh, if anybody has ever watched wrestling, it is the finest form of storytelling." He smirks, and the students laugh. "No, really. Not kidding you. But, without further ado, let's get started. This is the story of Moonsaulting_Spaceman and MatrixGirl."

Those two names mentioned together in one sentence—

A shock goes through my system at the same time the assembled student body bursts out in cheers, applause, and more than a few giggles and laughter. *The story of Moonsaulting_Spaceman and MatrixGirl*—I wish I hadn't heard this right, but the many more whispered repetitions of both our names I pick up on call that hope an illusion.

Dread forms inside my stomach, coiling tightly. Hazel, what the heck did you get me into?

Mr. Langen grabs the second rope and hoists himself up onto the apron, then bows under the third rope to enter the ring, joining—Wait, is that… Sergey? I squint. Yes, that's Sergey, from the gym, the guy with the accent. He's dressed in a black-and-white striped umpire outfit—okay. Okay. So we're going all out: ring. Referee.

Mr. Langen tugs his suit straight and raises the mic to his mouth. "Ladies and gentlemen, welcome to the very first George McMillan High School wrestling match!"

The *wooh*s get louder, but there's tons of laughter too.

I swallow hard and close the door a tad more so that I'm really, really not visible through the little gap I left. A superfluous concern, given that my name has already been announced and that I'm going to walk out there in a moment or two. *#Sigh.*

Like a professional ring announcer, Ben Bullet stands in the middle of the ring, holding the microphone in his hand. Now the black suit makes more sense. "The following contest is scheduled for one fall—"

Light shines into the semi-darkness from behind me, the only indication that someone opened the door from the other quartet prep room into the hallway. I peek over my shoulder—

Fire.

Only today he isn't dressed in his typical Fire wrestling outfit, but white, long wrestling pants, with white, shin-high wrestling boots, a tight, white Lycra shirt—and a Lucha-style mask in, big surprise here, white as well, with silver star applications. Translation: Fire has changed into the Moonsaulting_Spaceman.

He lets the door fall into the lock and jumps up and down, then twists at the waist. With the second twist to the right, his eyes fall on me as I'm about to melt deeper into the shadows, and for one eternal moment, our eyes connect. He freezes in mid-motion, and so do I. His chest lifts up in one big breath but doesn't lower, as if he's forgotten how to exhale. To be fair, I'm not doing any better. A thick, convoluted blob of emotion clogs my throat, making it hard to breathe. I have to stab my fingernails into my palm, or else one of those emotions might show on my face, and that's a big no-no after the betrayal of the century.

Out in the ring, Ben continues his announcement. "Introducing first, fighting out of Vista Verde, California, in the red corner: this man knows what he wants and how to get it. He is the current, reigning, and defending champion, Moonsaulting_Spaceman!"

AC/DC's "Highway to Hell" starts blaring from the speakers

as the crowd goes nuts. One, they're sitting here for a wrestling match, which is better than algebra or whatever, and two, they're all active on TeeVee. They know Spaceman.

They know *me*.

Fire blinks, breaking the connection between us, then closes his eyes for a short second, and when he opens them, determination shines from them.

He cranks his neck, shakes out his head—

And rips open the door wide, bursting through into the theater full of energy, like this wasn't our stupid McMillan Auditorium, but the freakin' Staples Center.

Me, on the other hand… my knees are wobbly. Seriously: wobbly.

Why? Another really, really good question. I'd like to chalk it up to performance anxiety, but I can't lie to myself that much. I'm afraid it has more to do with… with Fire. And not because of the match we're about to engage in.

Speaking of: out in the, uh, *arena*, Fire makes his big entrance, shouting, talking, and gesticulating as he strides down the stairs toward the stage. Some kid, probably a ninth grader, holds out a hand for a high-five—but Fire grabs the boy's baseball cap instead, makes a disgusted face, and throws it far into the assembled students, wiping his hands on his thighs as if he had dirtied himself.

The audience gets the hint and boos, which Fire responds to with more and louder yelling nobody understands, although I don't think being understood is the point. It's establishing himself as the heel, the bad guy.

I have to admit, he's doing a good job with it. How fitting.

Once he reaches the stage, he jumps up, takes two big steps

toward the ring, and hoists himself up and over the third rope. From there, he climbs onto the second rope, faces the theater standing straight, beating his chest, and, judging from his gestures, insulting the audience some more.

The boos crank it up a notch—

And Fire's music stops.

Oh, gee. My stomach cramps. That can only mean—

A feedback-squeak comes through the speakers when Ben Bullet turns on the mic again. "About to enter the ring, fighting out of Playa Grande and the blue corner, she is the contender, the newcomer, everybody's business—MatrixGirl!" Rage against the Machine's "Wake Up" blares from the speakers: my cue. That's my cue, and what a fitting choice of song.

Okay.

I hop up twice and shake out my arms.

Looks like I'm really doing this.

How do I enter— Well, I guess if Fire's the Heel, the bad guy, so I'm the good one. The Face. Sounds about right, doesn't it?

One more swallow, then I count myself down.

Three...

Two...

One!

#Showtime

Unlike Fire, I don't burst through the door, but walk through. This is my intro, and it sets the stage for the performance. I'm smiling, waving, as I'm picking up speed and skipping down the stairs toward the ring, where Fire is testing the ropes. The crowd applauds, some people whistle, and yeah, as I pass, I hear some fragments that could be *MatrixGirl,* or *psycho* but also could not.

I hop up onto the stage, slide into the ring on my belly, pop up, and do as Fire did, climbing the ropes in the corner and waving into the audience.

They cheer and clap—and to be honest, it feels… not bad. Not half as anxiety-inducing as I feared.

Well, the day is still young.

After another ten seconds of waving, the music stops, and I jump backward off the ropes and turn toward the ring. Fire strides over to Ben—

And shoves him in the shoulder, ripping the microphone out of his hands and throwing it out of the ring—

—to Hazel, seated at the table on the stage off to the left.

Doing a quick headcount, I guess I'm surrounded at this point. Even if I wanted to run, with Hazel, Ben Bullet, and Fire here… yeah. Not going to happen.

Mr. Langen stumbles back from Fire's push and, like he didn't know how to handle the ropes, falls into them and sinks to the ground. Sergey, as the referee, gesticulates wildly, pointing at Ben, then Fire—who shows him the middle finger.

The crowd boos.

Out of the corner of my eyes, I see Hazel sit down in her chair behind the table and raise the mic to her mouth. "Hello, McMillan High School. This is Hazel, and oh my, this match is off to a good start. What does Spaceman think he's doing? Arrogant much?"

Ben Bullet rolls out of the ring and makes a show of limping over to the table. He takes the second mic from Hazel. "And Ben Bullet here, commenting as well. I agree, Hazel. Whose idea was it to set up a guy like him against MatrixGirl? She's as sweet as they come, and him…"

The crowd cheers, but some laugh. *I don't care.* I keep my chin up and attention on what's happening—

"It spells disaster."

"You're right about that, Hazel." Mr. Langen sits next to her. "That guy seems pretty unhinged. But he wasn't always like this, was he?"

Fire walks around me, dragging a finger over my shoulder and back as he passes behind me. I let him, despite the shudder running down my spine. My heart hammers away at an unhealthy pace, yet I stand still and wait—we haven't really started yet. I'll know when to lock up. This is all set-up.

The lights dim even more, and the screen behind the ring, clearly visible for the audience, springs to life.

#

Moonsaulting_Spaceman:
Sharing for a good cause: Support @MatrixGirl's fight to improve conditions for incarcerated youth! Support your fellow brothers and sisters!

#MatrixGirlRocks #Sharing #EveryoneMakesMistakes #PrisonSucks

#

Holy. Cow.

Good thing I'm standing with my back to my fellow students, or else they'd all have seen my jaw go slack. What the—

Hazel: "You're right, Ben Bullet. If I'm not mistaken, he supported MatrixGirl in the beginning."

The post fades, only to be replaced by another one fading into view, a comparison of my followers.

#

MatrixGirl
December Statistics
December 1st   **December 5th**
2422 Followers   **15789 Followers**

#

#OMG.

Nausea rises, bringing bile with it. What have I gotten myself into? When they said *the story of Moonsaulting_Spaceman and MatrixGirl,* I didn't think they meant it that literally.

But you live and learn.

Should've run when I had the chance instead of following some weird tug in my chest out here.

Ben Bullet: "Told you. He shared, and the number of her followers skyrocketed. That was pretty cool."

I agree, despite my heart bleeding from the old wounds being ripped open. That was my big break. When Spaceman shared my post and I got tons of attention. With his help, I got up to higher numbers, until I had enough speed that I added followers on my own, without him.

Hazel: "Yeah, and don't forget, he defended her."

Fire looks me over, head to toe, as he continues dragging his finger over me while walking around me. The audience cheers something that sounds like, "Bring it on! Bring it on!"

The next screenshot pops up.

#

NERDY_JOE86
Where she goes to school? Wanna meet her.
#MatrixGirl #schoolgirls #LikeThemYoung #LMIRL

#

Moonsaulting_Spaceman
Watch it, @NERDY_JOE86. Reported.
#creeper

#

I blink. That was way over a year ago. Before stuff got crazy.

Hazel: "But, man, he should've gotten the memo, Ben. Felt like he was entitled to… I don't even know to what."

#

DM:

MOONSAULTING_SPACEMAN
Wednesday, 16:03 hrs:
We should be together. You and I. We'd blow up the internet.

MATRIXGIRL
Wednesday, 16:05 hrs:
Ha ha, right! Thank you, but no, I'm ok. I like you, but I'm not looking for a relationship. :)

#

Fire completes his circle around me and stops in front of me.

Ben Bullet: "Happens too often. Either you help, or you don't, but it's not quid pro quo, is it? He just didn't get the memo, like you said."

Fire takes a menacing step closer, and I know it's an act, but it's all I can do to keep my ground and appear unaffected. The posts, the narration with them, Fire and Spaceman rolled into one, right here, and to top it off, a judgmental audience for sure armed with TeeVee-enabled phones… All my weaknesses rolled into one event.

Hazel: "Look at him, the way he stares at her, Ben. I bet you he is planning something."

Fire glances at me from under his lashes—and I know what's coming. His hands ball to fists, he brings one of them to his mouth, biting it in anger as his breathing gets heavier—

#

DM:

MOONSAULTING_SPACEMAN
Tuesday, 22:03 hrs:
I supported you and that's what I get? Nothing? What a frigid biotch you are!

MOONSAULTING_SPACEMAN
Thursday, 14:01 hrs:
WTF? Now you're ghosting me?

MOONSAULTING_SPACEMAN
Thursday, 23:45 hrs:
Figid Bitch. You'r going to pay for that!

#

With a roar Fire charges me—

Ben Bullet: "Whoa! Look at that aggression! Where's that coming from?"

We lock up, wrestling for the upper hand.

I get Fire by the neck, but he slips out of my grasp, playing hard to get, so I speed it up, and *bam,* I got him hooked in a nice lock up.

"Look at MatrixGirl!" shouts Hazel. "She knows her stuff! She is not bowing to this guy!"

The students cheer and yell, and some call for blood. Fire releases his hold of me and directs me into the ropes with an Irish Whip. I take them as I was taught, bounce out, and duck under his clothesline.

Ben Bullet: "Nice reaction there by MatrixGirl—"

The audience *whooo*s and laughs when Fire, turns around, mad, ready to engage me as I'm coming out of the ropes again—

And he captures me and throws me in a perfect Body Slam. A big *oooh* goes through the audience as I land flat on my back and buck up in, uh, pain. *Acted* pain, of course. To be honest, despite the *#CrappySituation*, I'm a tad proud of that Body Slam. A tad.

Hazel: "Yikes! What a Body Slam! He's not going easy on poor MatrixGirl!"

No, he doesn't. Fire isn't wasting a single second. He grabs me by the legs and flips me over, keeping my legs locked between his arms, forcing my spine into an unnatural backward bend.

Hazel: "Walls of Jericho! Her back must be about to break!"

Ben Bullet: "And that after taking that Body Slam! The hits just keep on coming!"

I scream and throw my head back. The Walls of Jericho are supposed to be excruciating. The only way out would be to reach the ropes, since that would make the referee separate Fire from me.

Like Fire taught me, I drag myself forward, pretending I was working against severe pain and against a hold impossible to break. Since I'm crawling away from the audience, I can catch another glimpse of the screen, an old selfie I posted, scrolling over it, followed by several comments.

#

MatrixGirl
Hiking with my mom.
#MatrixGirlRocks #SundaysFundays #sunshine

#

Moonsaulting_Spaceman
SHARING MatrixGirl: Hiking with mom.
That was the #earthquake I felt. Lol.
#GoLoseSomeWeight #PoorTrails #ProtectTheWildlife
#WeightWatchers

#

GAGIK_HappY:
When will grils understand they're not attractive when there're fat?
#GetReal #NoGuyEver #FatUgly #GoLoseSomeWeight #ByeFelicia

#

Fin(n)MeansEnd:
Yeah, it's an #InstantTurnOff. #Liposuction.

#

It keeps on scrolling as I'm working my way to the ropes, Fire pretending to do his best to hold me, me working against him.

Ben Bullet: "If she could only reach the ropes, but he's putting his whole weight into his hold! I wouldn't be surprised if her back broke under this torture! It's too much!"

Hazel: "Agreed, it's too much! But MatrixGirl isn't giving up, maybe—"

I stretch… stretch… and my fingers wrap around the rope.

Sergey jumps between us—crossing his arms and pointing at me, then Fire, who lets go of me in more of a drop than a gentle release, like he was pissed I made it to the ropes.

As I flip onto my back so I can see him, all the while keeping the heavy breathing and show of visible exhaustion up, Fire throws a wrestling tantrum, i.e., sells how frustrated he is I made it out of his hold. He sees me scramble back onto my feet—

—and advances in with a side kick to my face, stopping and pulling it an inch before he'd actually make contact, his palm slapping his thigh at the point of quote-unquote impact for the added sound effect.

A loud *Ooww* goes through the crowd when I let my head fly to the side, like Fire kicked me for real.

"Holy cow, not cool!" shouts Hazel. "A side kick right to the face? What does he think he's doing? This isn't the UFC! MatrixGirl is taking a beating!"

#NoShitSherlock

I pretend I'm dazed, which isn't too difficult at the moment. Everything's so surreal. Me wrestling Fire. The posts on the screen… None of it goes together, and yet here I am.

Fire stomps closer and grabs me by the hair to pull me up.

Yeah. This is his time to control the Heat—and it's feeling very heated, I must say.

I scream out and cover my hair, making it look like the pain is unbearable. Sergey comes to the rescue, trying to separate Fire from me—but he gets pushed away.

The audience boos like crazy. "YOU SUCK! YOU SUCK! YOU SUCK!" and while Ref Sergey is quote-unquote recovering from the shove, Fire pulls me close—

"Fireman's carry drop," he whispers in a quick command tone. "Freeze when up. Once I throw you, you stay down. Come up when Hazel says, then Comeback."

What the heck have they planned now? This match isn't enough already?

But there's no time to think because Fire transitions smoothly, yanking me up to standing by my hair, and from there into a Fireman's Carry until I'm lying across his shoulders, wrapped around his neck like he was a rheumatic old lady and me the cat warming his shoulders.

Ben Bullet: "He's got her where he wanted her! This constant pressure, it's gotten to her. There's no way out for MatrixGirl!"

I catch a glimpse of the screen, a million hashtags moving across it, like the end credits of a movie—

#

#UglyGoKillYourself
#SpreadingHerpes
#MatrixGirlSucks
#MatrixGirlSlut
#UglyGoKillYourself

#STD
#UglyAsFuck
#SaveTheWhales
#UglyGoKillYourself
#WeightWatchersFail
#BeverlyBacon
#MatrixGirlBoobs
#GoDieMatrixGirl
#GoDieMatrixGirl
#GoDieMatrixGirl
#GoDieMatrixGirl

#

Hazel: "You're right, I don't think MatrixGirl will find a way out of it!"

Fire roars under me, holding me strong, rocking me up and down as he walks through the ring with me, like I was a trophy he won—

Click.

Fire freezes as the lights switch off, leaving only a single spotlight aimed at us from above. A murmur hurries through the ranks—

Hazel stands up, mic in her hand, facing the crowd. After about three or four seconds, they get that something is about to happen and stop their talking and their whispers.

Hazel: "Bullying starts harmless and out of nowhere, often without reason. It may start as teasing, it may start because the bully feels entitled to it. To them, it's a game. Fun. But what's fun for one person can destroy another, and the outcome can be disastrous."

The light behind me changes from bright white to something more colorful, less bright. I turn my head as much as I can without giving away that I'm moving.

Mistake.

A split second—hell, half of that—is what I need to recognize the picture up on the screen:

Me.

It's a screenshot of me, of my one and only live stream, as I'm leaned back fully clothed in our empty tub, makeup smeared from my tears, looking like life had left me with my eyes half shut and only the white visible.

My fellow students suck in a harsh breath as if they all had the same visceral reaction to the real kicker in that picture: the razor blade pressed to my wrist just on top of my left radial artery. Before I made the first cut.

God.

It seems so far away. Me doing that. But I remember that place. The misery. The despair. The hopelessness.

That picture shows the depth of my agony to the point where it's almost palpable. I'm surprised Principal Gunn isn't pulling the plug on the projector because *stuff like that doesn't happen to our students.*

Hazel steps back into the shadows. "Make no mistakes. Bullying can kill."

I feel Fire's muscles tighten at the signal—and *boom*, he's lifted me up and thrown me over his head. I fly, fly, stabilize my body to fall stomach-first—

And *boom*, I land on my stomach in a forward fall break—

—and play possum, as Fire instructed me. My heart doesn't beat, it hammers, like my chest was a cage and it needed to escape.

Hazel's voice comes over the PA again. "The outcome cannot be predicted, but everybody needs to be aware what bullying does to the victim. What damage *you,* every single one of you, can cause someone else."

Fire's shoes come nearer as he starts shaking my shoulder.

I don't move.

He's shaking me again.

I don't react this time, either.

I catch a glimpse of him kneeling down next to me, curling down, his face in his hands, as if he were sad. Turning his chin toward me, he whispers, "Get ready. Comeback."

Click—the full lights are back on.

Ben Bullet speaks up. "This match has taken an unexpected direction, Hazel. Look at Spaceman. He's taking MatrixGirl's injury really bad."

Hazel: "I can tell. But I don't get it. I mean, isn't he the one who did this to her?"

Oo-kay, I guess that's it. From my belly-down possum-posture, I draw in my arms. Slooowly. It's all about the show.

A loud whisper goes through the crowd.

Ben Bullet: "Now, be fair. He isn't the only one she ever fought."

Hazel: "True dat, but he was the most vicious opponent."

I pull in my legs.

Somebody claps.

Sit myself up—

Somebody *whoooo*s.

There's Fire, kneeling, face in his hands, still selling his sadness.

After reading all those comments again, after seeing *that* picture of myself, *that* screenshot—it's not exactly difficult to act like I'm angry.

I spring up to standing next to Fire, his face still hidden in his hands. My hands are balled, my body is coiled—

The audience claps and cheers, and I tap Fire on the shoulder.

He looks up—

And I deliver my best stomp kick ever right to his face.

Ben Bullet: "Holy moly! Did you see that stomp kick? That must've nearly blown his brains out!"

Hazel: "Well, you know what they say, Ben. Karma is a bi— bit tough, I mean!"

As if I kicked him for real, Fire throws himself back, both hands holding his head where I supposedly kicked him. I get a huge cheer for that, and sue me, but man, it gives me an endorphin high. Heck, this is *on*! All the anger, all the frustration, all the sadness of the last year and change breaks out at once and enters my blood stream, fueling me.

With two quick steps, I'm next to Fire and kick him in the side once more, making him fly into the ropes next to the ring post.

Ben Bullet: "Matrix Girl has some nice kicks there, I've got to say!"

Fire's eyes are wide as he scrambles up to standing, using the ropes to pull himself up, then leaning against the turnbuckle with his back.

The way he's standing there, his arms wide, backed up by the turnbuckle… An invitation.

And I'm accepting it.

I burst forward and ram my shoulder into his chest. Fire sells it with a little hop, as if my impact had knocked him that much back and up. Fumbling for his arm, I use an arm drag to get him out of the corner, then, just like with Arlo, I give him a good kick in the stomach. Okay, not quite like with Arlo—this one I pull. Pretty nice of me, in the grand scheme of things, right?

Doesn't mean I can't enjoy throwing him around. Boy, does this feel *good* all of a sudden! Grabbing Fire, using his velocity and inertia when he tries to punch me to throw him over my shoulder—*bam!*—on the ground, dropping into an armbar and letting him struggle... It feels fantastic. Terrific. Liberating somehow.

"It's going to be tough for Spaceman to escape from this. She's got him pinned down!" Hazel.

But alas, it's not over yet and yes, I do let Fire escape. He stays on the ground, making a show of gathering his strength to get up. The crowd boos when he makes it to his knees and celebrates when he falls back down on his stomach. For me, it's a good moment to catch my breath and step on the first rope to wave to the audience. And listen to that: I get even more applause!

Ain't that a new sensation.

"And the crowd loves MatrixGirl!" Ben Bullet.

Hazel: "They always did, from the first moment they saw her on TeeVee."

"Besides the bullies, you mean."

"Obviously. But there are always those who can't stop."

"Hey, maybe Spaceman's story is more complicated than I thought. He is acting kinda weird, I've got to say."

Dropping down off the second rope back into the ring, I turn—and stumble, when I see the screenshot up on the screen: a picture of Fire—Fire and… Ronan. Both younger, maybe about two years, both grinning ear to ear, holding up a TeeVee certificate with one hand, the other high-fiving their buddy.

#

Moonsaulting_Spaceman
YESSSSS!!! The first of many more to come, we hope!
#MostSupportersForASingleCause #WeDidIt
#MoonsaultingSpaceman #TeamWork

#

Wait. What—A shared account? They had a shared account, Fire and Ronan?

Hazel: "And it's so confusing with Spaceman. He can be nice, yet he acts like he wants to destroy MatrixGirl."

Ben Bullet: "Agreed. His actions come across as schizophrenic, like two different people. Sometimes—"

For a moment, I'm so distracted that I don't realize Fire is up already and staggering toward me. He makes a show of tentatively reaching for me—

I flinch—

And he pats my shoulder, like I was a puppy.

Uh…

The students laugh, and somebody calls out, "FAKER!"

At this point I'm pretty sure Principal Gunn isn't here, by the way, because Fire looks into the audience and shows them the middle finger, a move that would probably have given Gunn a stroke and more than enough reason to stop this match, especially added to the expletives I'm hearing from some of the students: Their response to Fire's gesture comes back as an immediate, deafening, "BOOOOOO!" And, again, some choice words.

Fire reaches for me again, like before—

And I barely block his wide haymaker punch. Whoa! That's the Big Heat starting, Fire's time to pull out the big stops—

Fire grunts and tries to punch me again, *again*—

Crap! Get with the program, Ever! I block and counter with a punch of my own. *Boom!* He counters and attacks again. Within five seconds, we're exchanging punches after punches, blow for blow—

Hazel: "See? What the heck? Nice one moment, then he's like this!"

Ben Bullet: "And he's not giving up until he has MatrixGirl where he wants her. So much power behind those punches, if they land—"

Out of nowhere, Fire feigns his next punch high—and sinks it straight into my stomach. I mean, pretend-sinks.

The crowd *owws* in outrage, I double over—

"Spaceman is playing dirty!" shouts Ben Bullet. "That punch—"

Hazel: "He hasn't been playing nice for the whole match, Ben! Nothing new!"

Fire shoves me back until I hit the turn buckle, keeps me by the arm—

Hazel: "And now, dunno about you, but I smell a Suplex coming on—"

The smallest acknowledging tug on Fire's lips and one quick glance up to me are all I get to prep, that's it. But in a different life, a life I miss, we practiced this.

Okay, then. They want a Suplex, they can get a Suplex.

Ramming both hands against his shoulders, I push into Fire, who steps back and uses my momentum to lift me up until I'm upside down, my feet pointing to the ceiling—

And lets himself fall over, smacking me backward onto the rings surface in the mother of all big, fat, juicy Suplexes.

The audience explodes into *whoa*s and *oooh*s, and if I'm not mistaken, there are a few *HOLY SHIT! HOLY SHIT!* chants as well. I'm sure it looked pretty spectacular—actually, I hope it did, because, man, I landed hard on that one! It's not helping the mess inside my head at all: Half my brain functions are trying to make sense of what's happening on-screen. I glance over as I'm recovering from the Suplex, catching nothing more than a few buzzwords—

\#

—Puke. Surprised her fat thumbs even hit the right ke—

\#

—I like what you did there, really! Great idea. I wish there was more—

\#

—tygolucky #SkipDinner #EarthquakeCentral #Liposuc—

\#

—Lol! You nailed that! :) :)—

#

Srsly. Go #GetALife, you stup—

The text keeps on scrolling—all of Spaceman's comments and hashtags, even some of the stuff he DM'ed me.

Hazel: "What is wrong with that guy? One moment he's nice to her, the next I'm worried he's gonna break all her bones! But you know what? I trust in MatrixGirl. If anybody can come back from all this, it's her!"

Ben Bullet: "You might be right, but this fight could go on forever. At this moment—"

The crowd boos, alerting me to the fact that Fire is up.

Adrenaline spiking, I whirl around, catch the small wink and nod he's giving me—

And grab him with one hand by the throat, the other under his armpit. That's my Big Comeback, the sprint before the Finish. I squat and push off at the same time as he does so that it looks like I'm lifting him up by his throat before I ram him down with a Choke Slam.

"YES!" shouts Hazel. "I told you MatrixGirl had it in her!"

The audience goes batshit crazy, seriously. They clap, stomp their feet, *whoo* and whistle—

And the moment Fire pops up to standing, they change their chants to a loud chorus of "YOU SUCK! YOU SUCK! YOU SUCK!"

That small tug on the corner of his lips morphs into the hint of a smile. If I didn't know him so well, I wouldn't have seen it. And despite me being mad at him, chapeau: he built up to this moment from the second he walked through that curtain and established himself as the heel, the bad guy, by yelling at the audience, by throwing that boy's cap away. He was the bad guy, and he let them feel it.

And now, the payoff is coming. I can feel it. Out of the corner of my eye, I can see the text scroll faster as well. Fire growls—

Ben Bullet speaks up. "I'd be surprised if the next few minutes didn't decide the fight, Hazel. Look at Spaceman—"

Hazel: "Nuh-uh. Look at MatrixGirl, Ben. That's where the action is."

And here we go: Fire attacks, I clothesline him, he pops up, runs toward me, I duck, hooking one of his legs with my arm and trip him. He lands smack on his stomach but is up fast—

Ben Bullet: "This is sheer craziness! The speed! Incredi—"

I duck under Fire's grasp, reach for his arms from behind, and take him into a Half-Nelson. Fire pretends to fight me—

I pop my hips and lift him up, Fire turns—and I slam him back first into the ground in a Half-Nelson slam. Thank you, judo!

The crowd reacts huge—HUGE—deafening me.

Ben Bullet: "How long can this go? How long can they endure this torture?"

Hazel: "Sooner or later one of them is gonna give, and it ain't going to be pretty!"

Jeez, I hope it ain't me.

Breathing hard, I drop into my fighting stance, and we lock up the second Fire's standing, like it was the most natural thing to do.

Here's a scary thought: with Fire, it somehow is.

Lots of things came natural with Fire.

Being me.

Eating more.

Going out of my comfort zone.

Trusting him.

A pang of loss shoots through my core—

Fire pulls closer. "Stone Cold Stunner, then submission and freeze."

I give the slightest nod. Well, if that's on the menu, I'm happy to oblige. Lightning fast—or as fast as my body still lets me after the adrenaline dump of the last few minutes—I turn, reach back, and grab Fire's head, keeping it over my shoulders when I *BOOM!* drop myself into a seated position.

Smack! Fire plays his role well as I force his head jaw-first onto my shoulder. He bounces off, half-stunned—

Hazel: "Oh my Gawd, Stone Cold Stunner! Did you see that, Ben? That could be it! MatrixGirl could be winning!"

I flip over, grab Fire's leg, lift it up, and pin him with all my body weight on him.

Sergey slides down next to us on his stomach, counting the submission. "One... Two..."

Click!

Like before, all lights besides the spotlight on us are cut. By now, the crowd knows what to expect, and the cheers die down to murmurs, although I do hear more than a few disappointed *aww, maaan*s.

I stay frozen in my position, my side pressed into Fire's chest, his leg firmly in my grasp, my weight on him in a traditional submission hold. Okay, what's next? The fight is basically done—

A chair scratches over the floor to the side of us. Hazel getting up again?

Fire's chest heaves up and down so fast under mine, it's

making me motion sick. Plus, the hammering of his heart bruises my ribs, that's how violently it's pumping. I peek at the screen from the corner of my eye. It's frozen again on

#

#BeverlyBacon
#MatrixGirlBoobs
#GoDieMatrixGirl
#GoDieMatrixGirl
#GoDieMatrixGirl
#GoDieMatrixGirl

#

"This is the story of MatrixGirl and Moonsaulting_Spaceman," Hazel says. "But that's not all of it, and it's far from over."

The text spins and zooms out of the frame, like in a PowerPoint presentation. In its place a picture pops up, a selfie. I feel Fire's breath get stuck in his throat before he exhales long, but with a stutter to it. It's a selfie of Fire, together with Ronan.

In a car.

Ronan in the driver's seat, Fire riding shotgun.

Hazel stays quiet as the image dissolves out of view, and the next picture—

Like a punch to the gut, the next picture pops up. There's no soft introduction, no slow appearance to give us warning, it's just there all of a sudden, hitting us right in the feels: a car—No, that's not a car anymore. It's a heap of metal, bent into irregular, jagged shapes that have nothing to do with a car anymore. What's left of it is all but wrapped around a tree at the passenger side, some rods and a wheel sticking out a yard in front of the tree at odd angles, making it look as if the tree had grown out of this chaotic pile of parts. The hood is gone, the engine block exposed, the roof cut off and discarded to the side. It's nothing but a heap of metal—a smoking heap of metal. Can't even recognize the color; it's burned away, leaving nothing but partially melted metal in its wake.

This is Fire's accident.

Holy cow.

I suck in a harsh breath, and it comes with a confusing skip of my heart.

This is Fire's accident.

Like me, the audience gasps for air.

Knowing about his accident and seeing it are two completely different animals. To imagine he was in there, trapped, while the fire that burned the color off this car, that melted the frame, was about to eat him alive…

My stomach roils with too many emotions to name, but all of them make me hyperaware of the boy in my hold—the boy whose frantic heartbeat is still bruising my ribs.

Whose heart is bruising mine.

I angle my head slowly so I can look down at him—

—and fall right into his eyes, shining with a sad, resigned quality to them that tugs on a heart string. It locks me in place and sucks the air out of my lungs, like he isn't just looking at me, but right into my soul, tying my insides into knots.

Everything about Fire is so confusing. What he did—might've done—to me. How right now I'm becoming more and more aware of how I'm pressed into him, of how good he feels. How good *I* felt when I was with him.

He swallows, the movement of his throat half-hidden by his mask. The hand trapped under my body squeezes my side once as he moves his lips to form four silent words:

I'm so, so sorry.

The emotion carried in his eyes, the regret rolling off of him in palpable waves, the picture, the screenshots—it's all too much. I close my eyes, holding on to Fire's leg for dear life.

The students on the bleachers murmur and whisper, and somebody sobs.

Hazel climbs into the ring and stands next to Fire and me, lifting the mic to her lips again. "We are standing here today to remind you that life is about kindness. About decency. About empathy. About understanding and forgiveness. About not repeating mistakes, but to learn from them." She taps my shoulder and holds out a hand. "Meet MatrixGirl." She helps me up to standing, then lets go of my hand. "And meet Moonsaulting_Spaceman."

Fire stands up and faces the audience next to Hazel on the other side of her. A hushed whisper goes through the crowd.

"So it's *really* Spaceman? Here in our—"

"That's really him?"

"But why the pictures with the Nightmare—"

"Whoa, he's—"

"Celebrity—"

Hazel looks at Fire, who lowers his chin once, curt, her cue to raise the mic once more. "And their story is *still* not over."

A picture of Calan's locker appears on the screen behind us. Since I only see its reflection in the window to the media room behind the audience, I can't read the text, but it's not hard to guess what it might be, most likely some variation of the same Nightmare-Freddy-Krueger crap.

"You're wondering why we're showing you this picture?" Hazel asks. "Because it stands for a million others we could have chosen. It stands for thoughtless comments made in real life, online, or in secret, like on this locker. It stands for lack of empathy and decency. It stands for judging quickly without thinking because *better them than me*. But today," she continues, "today we want you to take a look at yourself and the ones around you and realize what an impact your actions can have, good and bad. Spaceman?" She nods at Fire, who reaches up and around his white Lucha mask for the straps keeping it secured at the back of his head. Within two seconds, he has it undone and pulls the mask off his face.

The gasp of surprise coming from the audience, it's real.

"Calan? That's—"

"He's Spaceman? Are they kidding us?"

"Nightmare?"

"Holy shit, that—"

Hazel gives them a good thirty seconds before she begins to talk again. "Curious, isn't it? Here's his part of the story, and guess what, you're *all* listening to it." She gives me a poignant glance that brings my cheeks to a burn. Not that it was much guesswork after the first TeeVee comments popped up on the screen, but undoubtedly, Hazel planned this well. *You can't not talk and not listen, either.*

I guess I *am* going to listen.

Hazel hands the mic to Fire. He takes it and pulls himself even straighter before he begins to speak.

"I used to be like many of you. A regular guy in high school, not on top of the food chain, but not too far down, either. A bit too geeky for mainstream, since all my life revolved around was wrestling and TeeVee. I had one best friend, and to be honest, he was the reason I didn't get picked on too much. Nobody messes with the cool kid or his friend, right? I was that friend. We did everything together, even shared a TeeVee account; you know us as Moonsaulting_Spaceman. We did pretty well, at least at first. Sometimes my buddy managed the account, sometimes me. Then I came across this girl with crazy good ideas. It was a no-brainer I'd share her campaigns because they were *that* good. She seemed cool and easy to talk to. For me at least. My friend… He had different ideas." He pauses, and from the change in light and from what I can see in the screen's reflection in the windows above the bleachers, another TeeVee screenshot is now displayed.

"That's when I should have stopped him. Should have said what he was doing wasn't cool, but… I didn't. I didn't want him to drop me, didn't want to be unpopular. Instead, I stood by and let him continue bashing this girl every chance he could." He lowers his gaze. "I was an idiot. A coward. I knew it wasn't right what he was doing to her, but I didn't stop him. And then, one day…" Taking one deep breath, he looks straight into the dark pit that is the audience. "We were going to drive to a friend's place when I get a pop up MatrixGirl is streaming live. I open TeeVee and… and there she is, trying to take her own life. In that moment I… I felt like the worst possible human being. The comments kept scrolling by, and they were… disgusting. I didn't know if she read them or not, but she got more and more desperate… And then she made the first cut."

Silence.

Complete and utter silence hovers in the theater, so heavy, it's about to drop me to my knees. I don't think anybody is breathing. I know I'm not. I've got enough to do digesting Fire's words and reliving *that* day in front of the whole school.

Fire's voice breaks. "My friend stopped the car. We looked at the stream, and—I let him take my phone and add a comment: *about time*, he wrote. *About time.* Here was a girl so broken by what we'd done, so desperate she couldn't imagine living anymore, and he wrote, *About time.*"

He pauses and turns his head away from the audience, bringing a fist to his mouth. When he drops it, he makes a conscious effort to stand straight, facing the students again. "It was too little too late by far, but that's when I decided his friendship wasn't worth anything. He continued to drive, but as I was trying to do damage control and typing to MatrixGirl to stop, he reached for the phone to stop me—"

The light changes—

This time, I'm sure which picture pops up. The wreck. I don't need to look. The gasps of horror and mumbled expletives give it away.

"And we crashed. The crash is why I look the way I do. Not because I was high on drugs and my pillow caught fire. Not because I got beaten up. And yes, I heard those comments." He takes a deep breath. "The reason why I look like this is because I was an idiot and coward, and I've been paying for that every single day since the accident. I don't want your pity for that. Not for the accident, not for the way I look. My scars remind me that life is about more than likes. It's about family, friends, decency, and common sense. It's about shutting up when you don't have anything nice to say, it's about figuring out what kind of person you want to be, and to become that person. It's about thinking what problems you yourself might have, if you feel the need to put others down to make yourself feel better. Telling somebody they're fat doesn't make you any skinnier. Telling them they're stupid doesn't make you smarter, either. And guess what? Telling them to go kill themselves doesn't make you any better than them. It makes you worse. It took me one second to decide to not keep my friend from posting these things—and it might take MatrixGirl a lifetime to get over what we did. One second is all it takes to make a difference, good or bad."

Fire lets his gaze drift over the assembled students. It hasn't been this quiet in here since… well, probably never. "At the end of the day, life is about living it so that you can look yourself in the eye. So that you stand up to the bullies because the cost of being a coward is too high." He swallows hard and so loud, the mic pics up on it. "Bullying, being mean to another person, it may give you a short lift and boost, like you're so cool, so much better than them, so strong. But you're not strong. You're weak for not standing up for them and weak for giving in to your own demons. You know what takes real strength? To stand up for the victims. Or, if you didn't, to go up to the person you bullied, face them, and tell them that you're sorry, as hard as it may be."

He lowers the mic, turns—and looks straight at me.

A lightning bolt of… *feelings* shoots through me. Is he—

Fire steps closer and stops about an arm's length in front of me, keeping the mic hanging from his grasp at the side of his body.

His eyes lock with mine, and I've never seen deeper into his soul than in this moment. His chest rises and falls out of rhythm, and his Adam's apple bobs with yet another hard swallow. My heart makes a silly jump, something between a seizure and a jolt, as if it didn't know how to react. Peripherally, I notice it's only him and me in the ring. At some point, Sergey must've stepped out of it, but I surely didn't notice it. Hazel is gone too, leaving me alone with Fire.

"Ever," he whispers. "I've been sorry for what I did every day, since the first time Spaceman turned on you. I thought the accident was fate making me pay for it, and I was all ready to bear that pain as my punishment. But then I met you in person, and… and…" His voice breaks as his eyes shine with moisture. His words together with the last fifteen minutes are swirled together in a cyclone of emotions wreaking havoc inside my chest, none of them easy to name besides the dominant one latching itself to my heart and making it beat stronger and faster than ever.

Fire moves one half step closer. "And you were even cooler in person than online. I fell for you. Hard. But I knew if you knew the truth… So I stayed silent, instead of owning up to what I did, and I ended up hurting you again. I'm sorry what I put you through—twice. I'm sorry I—"

My heart overrules whatever reservations my brain might have had. Taking one figurative and quite literal leap forward, I fling myself at Fire and wrap my arms around his neck. The moment we connect, our sharp inhales are simultaneous. Fire's spine stiffens—

—and then his arms wrap around me, squeezing so tightly, a little squeak escapes me. *Everything* is in this hug. His pain. My pain. His sorrow. My sorrow. But mostly this hug carries *us*, what Fire and Everly are all about.

Somebody *whoo*s in the audience.

Somebody else.

Somebody claps—

And then the whole auditorium breaks out in deafening

applause and cheers, maybe for the performance, maybe for us, maybe for a combination thereof, but it doesn't matter.

All that matters is *us*.

Fire's shoulders are trembling in my embrace. He's crying. "When I said it takes strength to apologize," he whispers, his voice breaking, his breath stirring my hair, "I forgot one thing."

"What?" I whisper back as I hold him tighter.

I feel his lips pull into a smile, that's how tight his face is nuzzled against my neck. "It takes more strength to forgive your bullies, Ever. Much more. Thank you." His arms squeeze tighter around me, so tight, I can barely breathe.

I don't care. Oxygen is overrated. I don't need it. My body is running on Fire these days.

My hand sneaks up into his hair on the back of his head. "Then I guess we should be bowing at this point."

His head tilts the slightest in my embrace. "Huh?"

He doesn't get it, and how could he? My brain jumped a couple of stops here. I gently release my hold on him but keep one hand of his in mine. "We should bow because we're getting applause, and because this is our moment for a new start. To forgive our bullies. Our tormentors." I squeeze his hand as Fire's jaw goes slack.

"A new start," he repeats.

"A new start. For everyone."

I direct him to face the audience, and together, we bow to the deafening applause of the George McMillan High School student body.

CHAPTER TWENTY-FIVE

#Matire

Tension hangs in the air. Like, palpable tension. I don't want to be overly dramatic, but if somebody lit a match, *BOOM*, there'd be a ginormous explosion. That's how charged the atmosphere is.

I'm standing on the top rope, facing outside, wearing my skintight Matrix-outfit. The lights in Ben Bullet's Wrestling Studio are off to highlight the hyper-illuminated ring and me—us—with it. My toes dig into the front of my shoes as I stretch out my arms to the side for balance.

Deep breath in.

Deep breath out.

No pressure, Ever.

I squat down a bit, use my arms to generate power—and push myself off the rope, executing the backflip I've practiced for the last few days on Hazel's trampoline.

Draw in legs, roll up tight, feel gravity take over, don't forget to splay out, look where you're landing—

And—SLAM—I land belly first on Fire, breaking my impact on him with a forward fall break.

"Ugh!" Fire buckles under me, selling the impact—

I grab his leg, pull it up for my submission hold—

And look straight at the phone Hazel is aiming at me from just outside the ring. "Hey, buzzy_bee_05, that was my first official Moonsault just for you. Hope you like it—gotta say, it felt pretty good." I lift Fire's leg higher and shift my weight until he groans. "Fire, say *hi*," I coo down at him.

"Hi there," he croaks into the camera.

I chuckle. "Anyway. Thank you for donating. We really appreciate it, and we're gonna put that money to good use. Stay tuned for more, and remember to use the hashtags at the bottom of the screen." I let one hand go and point to an imaginary area where Hazel will add the hashtags before posting. "See ya next time!" I wave and smile into the camera until Hazel lowers the phone.

"That was a-may-zing, Ever," she says, her eyes still glued to the screen and the most excited grin on her face. "How you pulled off that Moonsault was off the charts. What's next? Double Moonsault? A Diving Crossbody? I mean, that one should be easy after this. Maybe a Frankensteiner?"

I groan. "I have no idea what you just said, and no, thank you. I don't think I'm the type for those aerial maneuvers."

Hazel frowns. "But if they request it—"

Fire wiggles himself out of my hold and sits up next to me. "If they request it and their donation is appropriate, we'll consider it. A gift for a gift."

I'm about to protest, but he cuts me off with a quick peck to my cheek. "Because you're *that* good, and because we're on a run."

I sigh. Right he is.

With a loud squeak, the rolling gate at the far end of the studio lifts, whatever is left of daylight shining in from under it and outlining the shape of two people I'd recognize anywhere ducking under the rising gate.

So do Hazel and Fire. "Look, they made it," he whispers as he gently bumps his shoulder into mine.

I'm not surprised. Ben wanted to come over anyway; it was just a matter of convincing my mom the perfect ending to their dinner date was a short visit to the gym. Apparently, Ben Bullet can be persuasive.

"Guys," he says as they come closer, both in their evening attire. For Mom, that means a nice blouse and a skirt, and for Ben, a pair of tight-fitting jeans and a black dress shirt with the first two buttons open. "Did we miss it? How'd it go?" He nods his chin at me, then at the ring post.

"Ever nailed it." Fire gives Ben a thumbs-up. "We wanted to wait till everybody else was gone to minimize distractions, but man, perfect landing. I'm assuming this post will get us quite a few likes and shares. Should get us up to our threshold, and once we get the senator's time financed, we have one foot in the door." He glides his right foot forward, mimicking blocking said door.

Hazel holds out the phone for Ben and my mom. "Here, look. And that was our first try."

Mom's eyes widen and she covers her mouth with one hand as she watches my Moonsault. "Everly, that... that..."

"Is much better than you thought I'd do?" I supply with a wink.

She huffs. "That for sure, but—not that I'm an expert—but that looked good!"

"Thank you." I bow my head.

"Oh, by the way…" Mom opens up her gigantic purse, pulls out a letter-sized, thick envelope, and hands it to me through the ropes. "This came in the mail this afternoon. Thought you'd want to see it right away."

One glimpse at the sender and my heart skips ahead in excitement. "TeeVee, Fire. Haze. It's from TeeVee."

"Well, open it, come on!" Fire scoots closer on his knees, then sits down behind me, one of his legs on my right side, the other on my left. Both hands wrap around my midsection as he looks over my shoulder, his chin resting on it.

I tear the envelope open and claw through the bubblewrap. Could it be…? Already? This early? A red, blue, and white plaque peeks at me and I all but rip it out of the envelope. "We've got it! We really got it!" A happy laugh breaks from my throat. We're *so* on a roll!

Fire squeezes me and presses a kiss against my neck. "Told ya. With our combined followers and the press we've been having, it was a no-brainer we'd get it."

I glance over my shoulder. "Says you. I was more pessimistic." Since I'm still working on restoring my faith in the good in humanity. Anyway. "Mom. Look." I hold the certificate up for her.

#

SLAMDUNK CERTIFICATE
TO
MATRIXGIRL AND FIRE
AWARDED FOR 250K INTERACTIONS IN RECORD TIME
"LIKE IT OR LEAVE IT"-CAMPAIGN

#

It lists the details under it, the likes, shares, number of comments and interactions, etc. *#lol.* Quite ironic.

Mom takes the certificate back, scanning over it. "So this is for the... for what again? I swear, I'm trying to keep track, but it's confusing me."

"No worries, Mom." I don't need her to keep track. She's showing interest—way more than *before*—and that's all I'm asking. After all, I'm a pro at this. To a degree, at least. "This is for getting a double-whopper petition through for TeeVee to not charge for likes anymore *and* to hide the numbers of likes, shares, etc. under the post." Not charging for likes was the harder sell of this campaign, but the more important one. Campaigns, yes, they still get financed the same, because that's the heart of TeeVee— getting support and feedback to *get stuff done*, thank you very much. What's not at the heart of TeeVee is posting crap like Nevaeh did and making money off the likes.

Ben glances at the certificate in my mom's hands, one of his arms wrapped around her waist. "Still love that idea. Hopefully, there will be less hustling for likes when nobody besides the post's owner sees them."

"And when they're not paid. That's the idea." And while I'm going to miss the feeling that others can see how well my posts are doing, I don't miss it enough to be willing to keep the doors open for the trolls pouring hate. "People are supposed to focus on the content, not how many likes they're getting." And both, trolling and pouring hate over people, is much quote-unquote nicer if you can show off your post's popularity to the world. And it gains velocity from there, because many people just go with the flow: You click like on what's already trending, jumping on the bandwagon of popularity. Psychologically speaking, apparently we like to be part of the cool-club *and* we're still herd animals, falling in line with the perceived majority. Says Doc Shamus, not me, by the way. But still: puke. Sorry, trolls, if you needed that short high of a liked post to make yourselves feel better. Take up knitting or something. I hear it's calming to the nerves.

Hazel slides up on the ring apron, one leg stretched out on it, the other dangling down. "Don't you like that they had to list exactly how many likes we got on that certificate? I mean, given that that was the campaign that took that specific feature from them?"

I grin. My thoughts exactly. "Quite ironic, indeed." It was about time TeeVee brushed up on a few much-needed safety- and decency-issues.

Mom carefully slides the certificate back into the envelope. "So, what was today for then? The Moonsault? Another campaign?"

Fire shakes his head. "No. Today was requested as a reward for a donation. They gave a sizable chunk of money for us to get air time with the senator, which will hopefully lead to new anti-bullying laws for apps. We're calling it *Three Strikes*. Most gaming platforms do it already. You're bullying somebody, it gets reported times three, you're kicked out. And the kicker: we want that rule applied to *all* social media platforms *and* apps sold or downloadable in the US or based in the US. Working on the legal fine print."

That's also what the money was for, funding the digital rights and laws lawyer, since we're expecting quite the backlash from basically everybody, TeeVee included: Once the trolls can't troll anymore, we're expecting a drop in popularity for those platforms or apps, resulting in decreased income for whichever social media platform we're talking about, and that might lead them to move their company out of the States' legal system. But we'll face that problem when—if—we get there.

"You three amaze me," Mom says.

"Thanks," we reply in unison. Because we're cool like that.

"That's why those two need to keep wrestling and working on new moves, hint-hint," Haze adds. "They need to keep their awesomeness up. Since the school performance went viral, interest in them wrestling is, like, through the roof. There's tons of stuff online, like those pages where—"

"She gets it, Haze." My cheeks burn—not because of the praise or the fact that we went mega-viral, but because yes, there is tons of stuff online, including a lot posted under *#Matire*—yes, correct: Fanfic. We're the Brangelina, the Kimye, the Bennifer, only with not-such-a-fun name. And also yes, I did make the mistake once to look at some of it. Never again. I'm not prude, but I still haven't recovered from what I read. To be fair, I appreciated the hashtag OTP. I agree. *#Blush*

Fire jumps up. "Hey, Ben? Could you show me the Flying Neckbreaker again, please?"

Huh? Where's that coming from?

"But of course!" Ben says. "My pleasure." He grabs his shirt with two hands and rips it open, buttons popping off and flying through the air. With one hand, he undoes his belt—and half a second later, he steps out of his jeans... in wrestling shorts and kneepads.

Mom's eyes couldn't get any wider if she tried. "You were

wearing this the whole time…?"

Ben's face lights up in a wide grin. "Honey, you're dating a wrestler." He gives her a fast kiss on her cheek and slides into the ring on his belly, popping up to standing and dropping into a fighting stance. "Warm me up, Fire."

As the two guys lock up, I scoot out of the ring to the apron next to Mom. She has this look on her face I only see when Ben's around, this… I don't know, wondrous expression. I hope I don't look at Fire the same way. *#Embarrassing*

I turn and watch Ben and Fire lock up and do what Ben calls warm-up, but any normal person would call a match. Both their movements are spot on, but they're so different in their styles. Fire is like a black panther in his outfit, smooth and surefooted. Ben, on the other hand, is the steamroller, wide-shouldered and strong.

Mom makes a little surprised *oh*-sound when Ben lifts up Fire for a Suplex. I look over my shoulder at her. "Aww, Mom. Look at you. You're dating a wrestler," I repeat Ben's words from a minute ago.

She blushes. "Everly, I'm dating a teacher who happens to wrestle. There's a difference." Still, the awed expression on her face stays. She's got the hots for Wrestler Ben, that's for sure—which, come to think about it, is probably why Fire asked in such a weird way for Ben to show him that move: Ben *wanted* to wrestle in front of her.

#RomanticAtHeart #ShowOff

I pat her shoulder. "*Dating a teacher who happens to wrestle,*" I mock her. Lovingly, of course. "Sure, tell yourself that. *I'm* dating a *wrestler*, and I'm proud of it." A thought comes to mind and I chuckle. "Dad is probably thinking he's in a parallel universe. You never liked him watching wrestling, now you're dating Ben and

I'm knee-deep involved in wrestling as well."

"Dad can think whatever he wants, as long as he leaves me in peace. And you," she adds with a side glance at me.

"He has." I shrug. "Like he promised." Thank you, Hazel, for sending Dad the whole performance, entrance to curtain fall. I assume it gave him something to think about—at least the boarding school hasn't come up since—and I'd be lying if I said Dad hadn't made an effort to be more considerate and sensitive with me.

Won't make me beg him to call me more often, but it's a start.

Mom jerks when Fire does a ropewalk and tackles Ben with a flying clothesline. "My goodness. It looks so real."

Ben is on the ground, escaping Fire's submission attempt as we speak.

"That's because those guys are good, Mom."

"They are." She hesitates. "Do you and Fire… Do you want to grab dessert with us? Portos, maybe?" Hope makes her voice shake, and I get it. The last few weeks have been a whirlwind: I'm back on TeeVee, the very platform we declared the enemy not too long ago. I'm together with Fire, whose role in my mental state, previously bad, now soul-soothingly good, cannot be underestimated. And to top it all off, I'm not only seeing Doc Shamus more often, I'm actually doing some of the talking. Out of my own free will and without pressure. I think that was the straw that broke the camel's back and made my mom question my sanity, pun intended.

So no, I can't fault her tiptoeing around me, especially when it comes to eating. We're at a truce, a cease fire, and have been for the last few weeks. She doesn't push eating on me, and I'm trying to be more proactive. Her asking me out to get dessert of all things…

It's another step in the right direction for both of us.

I scoot back some more and lay an arm around her shoulders. "Love to."

Mom reaches for my hand over her shoulder, squeezes it once and holds on to it. No words necessary.

Inside the ring, Fire high-fives Ben Bullet, both with shit-eating grins on their faces that speak of the ease they feel with each other and the fun they have in the ring. Right as he's moving into the next technique, Fire glances over to me, catching my eye. One quick wink, one lightning-fast blown kiss—and he's back to preparing Ben for whatever he has planned because *#TheShowMustGoOn.*

Huh. I tilt my head, remembering that moment before I went back to school for the first time after the mobbing campaign and attempted suicide, when I thought about exactly that: how much my life was a show, a *#PopularityContest*… Kind of ironic that my life's much more of a show now, a mere few months later. The only difference is, this is a show I'm in control of: I write the script. I dictate the moves.

I lean into my mom some more.

In fact, right now my life is a real' good show.

And, to stay with that analogy, I'm glad it wasn't cancelled when I ran that blade across my radial artery because when fate wrote her script, she threw in a couple of turns and twists to the storyline that changed it for the better.

In the ring, Ben Bullet throws himself to the ground, using his falling body and outstretched leg to guide Fire over in a forward dive, i.e., well-executed sacrifice throw. Fire hits the ring with a thud, and Mom twitches again.

The whole scene, standing here with my mom, watching two guys wrestle, is somehow completely surreal, yet it carries a feeling of… belonging. Home. Love.

I squeeze Mom's hand, and she squeezes right back.

Yeah. I'm really glad my show wasn't cancelled.

Really glad.

#PlayingWithFire

#Matire

#MatrixGirlRocks

* * *

About the Author

Micky O'Brady is a pediatrician-turned-writer living in beautiful, dry Southern California with her husband and two critters (one son, one dog). Micky loves to write YA thrillers with a romantic twist, mainly because she wishes her life had been such an awesome mix of action and cute guys when she was a teen.

When she isn't up at around 3 a.m. (with a cup of tea, Earl Grey, hot) drafting stories she can't get out of her head, she can be found at a martial arts dojo, though maybe not at 3 a.m. She holds a 2nd degree black belt in Judo and a brown belt in Krav Maga, and is convinced every girl should know how to kick some butt.

Micky also is a firm believer in the healing powers of Nutella eaten straight from the glass and in the magic that can happen on a rainy day, as long as there are fuzzy socks and a cup of hot tea involved.

Her previous publications include a doctoral thesis and several medical articles as well as a medical book about emergency communication. None of them are as fun to read as her YA novels though. Her first YA-novel, THE PRESIDENT'S DAUGHTER, and its sequel TRIAL BY ICE, are published by Curiosity Quills and available through all major retailers, such as Amazon, B&N, Kobo, and Smashwords.

Through Snowy Wings Publishing Micky is the author of YA-sci-fi romance BETWEEN WORLDS and PLAYING WITH #FIRE, and is happy to announce more novels will be coming your way. Stay tuned!

9 781952 667145